# ESCAPE TO THE COUNTRY

ALISON SHERLOCK enjoyed reading and writing stories from an early age and gave up office life to follow her dream. Alison lives in Surrey with her husband and a daft golden retriever.

# ESCAPE TO THE COUNTRY

## Alison Sherlock

www.ariafiction.com

First published in the UK in 2018 by Aria, an imprint of Head of Zeus Ltd



9 7 5 3 1 2 4 6 8

A CIP catalogue record for this book is available from the British Library.

ISBN (E) 9781786694935

**Aria**
c/o Head of Zeus
First Floor East
5–8 Hardwick Street London EC1R 4RG
www.ariafiction.com

## Also by Alison Sherlock

*A House to Mend a Broken Heart*

# About *Escape to the Country*

Everyone is running away from something – but will an escape to the countryside suit everyone?

Journalist Eleanor McCartney leads a glamorous life in London exposing the sordid secrets of famous celebrities in Hot Gossip! magazine. But her perfect life is a sham. So when her world collapses, she escapes to the country to see her best friend Annie at Willow Tree Hall.

Tom Kingsley, global singing sensation has sought refuge in Willow Tree Hall as well. He is completely burnt out after a grueling worldwide tour and is escaping the paparazzi after yet another scandal. Eleanor cannot believe her luck. A story on the world's biggest superstar would be the ticket that gets her job and glamorous life back in London. But soon both Eleanor and Tom begin to fall under the spell of Willow Tree Hall. Eleanor begins to wonder whether she can really betray his trust...

As a heatwave soars, friendships are made, truths are told and, with the help of a stray dog, perhaps love can be found as hearts are healed. By escaping to the country, maybe Eleanor and Tom have found their new beginning.

This book is dedicated to Cara Maidens who loves romantic fiction.
Cara, nobody deserves their own happy ever after more than you. x

# Chapter 1

Eleanor McCartney had dreamt of being a reporter ever since the first time she had seen *The New Adventures of Superman* at the age of ten. The excitement, the glamour and Dean Cain in tights. What more could a girl want?

Of course, Lois Lane would be laughing her glamorous high heels off if she could see Eleanor at that moment in time.

The rain dripped behind her collar and onto her neck as she crouched down behind a large hedge. She shuddered and pulled her denim jacket tightly around her. But nothing would keep out the relentless downpour. She was also freezing cold despite it being the last day in May. So much for the predicted summer heatwave that was apparently on its way. She was drenched from head to toe.

It was typical May bank holiday weather. And yet another public holiday that she was forced to work whilst everyone else was relaxing and enjoying themselves.

She just hoped the story would be worth the possible onset of pneumonia. It had to be worth it. She *needed* that promotion. She had sacrificed too much along the way to fall at this last hurdle now.

She glanced up and down the street, one of the most exclusive addresses in the heart of London, but there was no sign of life. Why would there be at almost midnight on a wet, cold Monday night?

She inhaled deeply and realised she was actually sitting next to a rose bush. She recognised the familiar early-flowering type, the same variety that was in her Mum's garden. The perfume from the pink petals sweetened the air, despite the flowers bowing down from the pressure of the heavy rain.

She made a mental note. When she got that promotion, at the top of her to-do list was to find a flat with a garden. Somewhere to relax and enjoy being outside again. She had spent too many years in the city looking out of windows onto everyone else's plots of greenery.

She sighed and checked the empty street once more. At least the lack of people meant that nobody else had the scoop. Especially Kourtney, her new junior colleague and rival for the best stories. Or rather, Killer Kourtney as their editor, scary Theresa Brown, had dubbed her. Ever since arriving at the magazine six months previously, Kourtney appeared to have a knack for finding the juiciest, most scandalous stories. Her star was on the rise whilst Eleanor was feeling distinctly overlooked.

But Eleanor had been given an anonymous tip-off

earlier that day that she had kept to herself. She was sure that inside that flat on the other side of the wet street, Tuesday Tavistock, the famous high-class escort, was entertaining an A-list celebrity. Maybe even a politician with a squeaky-clean record. Once that person left the flat, Eleanor would see who it was and get the story. It might even make the front cover of *Hot Gossip!* magazine.

*At last*, she told herself with a firm nod. The years of stress, guilt and lies would be worth all the sacrifices she had made over the years.

Eleanor shuffled from foot to foot, trying to bring some kind of feeling back to her freezing-cold toes.

She had been working for *Hot Gossip!* magazine for eight long years. Her first job after finishing her journalism degree at university, it was supposed to have been a brief stepping stone on her way to getting a senior writer's position at one of the daily newspapers. That was where her future lay.

After all, that was what everyone back home expected from her. Her friends and family would never know that she spent her days sharing private details about Z-list celebrities. Never *needed* to know. Because she wouldn't be in the job for very long.

At least, that was what she had thought at the time.

So she had created the lie that she had been quickly promoted and was now a reporter for a magazine within the same media group that covered financial investments. In the fiction that she had crafted for herself, she wrote about stocks, shares and other city financial stuff that she had absolutely no idea about. Something that anyone she knew and loved wouldn't be remotely interested in. And it had worked.

And yet, here she was, all these years later, still writing for *Hot Gossip!* about which co-stars had been caught canoodling, the latest singer who was cancelling his world tour due to 'exhaustion' and some reality star who had just had a facelift.

Worst of all, she was still lying about her job to everyone she loved.

In the beginning it had been exciting working on the magazine, she had to admit. The endless, glamorous parties were a stark contrast to growing up in the tiny, quiet hamlet of Cranley. Mixing with famous people had given her a thrill. The goody bags full of expensive stuff she would never have been able to afford had been treasured and admired.

And yes, there was the joy of exposing some of the more ghastly celebrities for what they really were.

She had convinced herself at the time that it was retribution for her own pain. If she had learnt anything from the whole heart-breaking experience with her father, it was that fame was one of the new deadly sins. After all, he had abandoned his own family to seek out the same glamorous, celebrity-filled lifestyle and had left his wife and daughter far behind many years ago.

But these days the whole show business life just left her numb. The thrill of dazzling wedding ceremonies, sweet new babies and wild parties had gone many years ago and been replaced by the guilt of what harm her job really did to the people she wrote about. As she had begun to know and like various celebrities over the years, it made her feel even worse when she had to reveal personal details of their lives. Especially the ones that didn't court publicity.

She was weary of glamorous parties every night. She wanted a bit of peace in her life. To stop and literally smell the roses, she thought with a smile, glancing over at the flower bush next to her once more.

And yet she kept going. She *had* to until she landed the job of her dreams. The weight of everyone's expectations lay heavy on her shoulders whilst she carried on with the illusion of her perfect life.

But thankfully relief was just around the corner.

Theresa had announced the previous week that a senior position had just become vacant within the media group that Hot Gossip! belonged to. It would involve proper investigative journalism. That would mean no more gossip. She could write articles that actually interested her and could make a difference.

Eleanor knew that she alone was the senior member of staff on the team. She had worked there the longest. All it would take was one more big story and the promotion was hers. Then she could leave the celebrity world far behind in the capable hands of Killer Kourtney.

Finally she could have a job that she could be proud of. A job she didn't have to lie about any more. She could relax and be herself for the first time in a very long time.

Eleanor shivered, her clothes were soaking. Her knees were almost at breaking point in her crouched position. She had been there for two hours and was chilled to the bone. How much longer would she have to wait? She longed for a hot shower.

She grabbed her phone and automatically checked her appearance. With a grimace, she saw that her long dark brown bob was beginning to kink and curl in the rain. Thankfully her mascara and eyeliner hadn't run, but her face looked pale and gaunt in the harsh glare of the street lamp.

Thank god, nobody was around to see her like this. Eleanor prided herself on her immaculate looks. Feeling less than perfect on the outside panicked her. Even her boyfriend Lucas had never seen her without make-up on. She liked to look polished and poised at all times. Soaking wet with messy hair wasn't a good feeling for her and added to her misery.

She gave a start as the mobile suddenly rang out into the quiet of the night. Seeing the name on the screen, she immediately grimaced. It was her editor, the fearsome Theresa. A woman so rude and abrupt in nature that she could make Cersei Lannister look cute and cuddly.

With her phone in one hand, Eleanor reached out with the other to stroke the smooth pink petals of one of the roses. Her floral comfort blanket.

'Hello. You're working late,' said Eleanor, faking a bright tone of voice.

'That's because I got called into the boardroom this evening,' snapped Theresa, straight to the point as always. 'Circulation is down. The owners want to know why.'

'Well, everyone in the industry is struggling at the minute,' began Eleanor. 'It's tough out there in the current climate, what with...'

'Your stories have been a total snooze fest recently,' said Theresa, talking over her.

Eleanor was taken aback. 'Well, it's getting harder and harder to get an exclusive when everyone is so empowered with Twitter and Instagram these days. But I've had a tip-off that...'

'Kourtney manages it.'

Eleanor took a deep and calming breath. 'Kourtney's Dad owns a Formula One team. She has access to all those secret parties.' *The ones that you know I can't possibly get into*, she added silently.

'Quite. The London season is coming up and I need someone young like Kourtney to handle it.'

'Young? I'm only thirty,' blurted out Eleanor, with a shocked laugh.

'Anyway, I've decided to make Kourtney the senior reporter in my team.'

Eleanor quickly stopped laughing. 'What? No!'

'Look, thanks to her contacts, she can bring in exclusives that you can only dream about,' said Theresa.

'But I've earned this promotion!' Eleanor told her, beginning to lose her temper. 'I've spent eight years working on this magazine! She's only been with us for six months!'

'Kourtney assures me that she can bring in a different angle on things, liven up the stories and that will boost circulation.'

Eleanor could feel her pulse racing as her heart hammered away in panic. It was the third time this month that it had happened. She had assured her doctor that her stress levels would be back to normal soon. But that had been when she had thought the promotion was hers.

'Theresa, listen to me,' said Eleanor, rubbing her throbbing chest. 'Please. I can't carry on doing these celebrity stories any more. I just can't. I'm losing the will to live on a daily basis. You've got to give me a break, let me do something different. I beg you.'

'Well, there may be some relief for you there, I suppose,' drawled Theresa. 'I'm afraid that I've got to let you go. The board want us to downsize. Cut our overheads.'

A chill came over Eleanor that had nothing to do

with being soaked to the skin. 'Downsize?' she repeated, in a daze.

'I'm sure you understand.'

'Actually I don't think I do,' said Eleanor, struggling in her shock to form a coherent sentence. 'I'm out of a job? Who's going to get the celebrity stories for you now?'

'Kourtney's going to do both for the time being. It makes more sense.'

'But I need this job.' Eleanor could feel her dream of a garden flat slipping far out of reach. Even a bad job chasing celebrities was better than no job at all.

'Surely working somewhere that makes you lose the will to live on a daily basis can't be good for you?' She could hear that Theresa was almost smiling down the phone as she carried on speaking. 'I'm sure you can find something more suited to your lofty position.'

'I was kidding!' said Eleanor, quickly. 'I mean, aren't there any other vacant jobs in the company that I could take? I don't care which department they would be in.'

'The board are making cuts all over the place,' Theresa told her. 'It's not just you. Now, I've had a look at your contract. Your redundancy package will be in accordance with your time of service, of course. Three months' pay, I think. I'll email you the details first thing. I'm sure you'll find it more than fair. But it's probably for the best that you don't come into the office any more. Internal politics can be so exhausting. Make sure you return your pass to reception at some point.'

Eleanor's head was reeling, trying to take in everything she was being told.

Theresa finally took a beat. 'Look, if you can find me a decent story at some point over the summer, call me and we'll talk.'

Then she hung up.

Eleanor sank onto the ground, barely registering the wet grass soaking through her jeans. She couldn't believe it. She had just lost her job. What was she going to do? What was she going to tell everyone back home in Cranley?

Her Mum and best friends, Annie and Megan, actually believed in the fake lifestyle that she had created for them so many years ago. The fiction she had told them bore no resemblance to her real job. They would all be horrified if they knew that she had been lying over and over to them. And now, at the end of so many wasted years, it turned out that her gut instinct had been right all along. That she wasn't the big success in the city that she had pretended to be. That deep down beneath the expectations of her friends and family, she really was just a big, fat failure after all.

On the opposite side of the street, the front door opened to Tuesday Tavistock's apartment just as a taxi drew up outside. Eleanor watched in a daze as Tuesday kissed an elegant woman on the cheek. They looked so alike it could only have been her mother.

The tip-off had turned out to be nothing. Just like the rest of her career.

Eleanor slowly became aware that she was still holding the rose, clutching the petals so hard that as she let go, they floated down to the sodden ground next to her, along with her dreams.

Whatever the future held, it was unlikely that her very own Superman was going to show up and rescue her. Tights, cape or otherwise.

# Chapter 2

Tommy King smiled and waved to the adoring crowd in the packed O2 arena as he left the stage after his final song.

They continued to cheer and stamp their feet, demanding a second ovation. High on adrenaline, he looked at his manager expectantly, hoping to go back out on stage. But Sam shook his head at him. Time was up. The show was over.

As they walked down the corridor to his dressing room at the rear of the arena, the noise from the crowd reverberated around the walls. 'Tommy, Tommy,' he could hear them chanting over and over again.

But as he moved further away from the stage, Tommy King the musical sensation faded away in his mind and he reverted back to being plain old Tom Kingsley.

Not that Tom Kingsley could ever be described as plain. Both he and Tommy shared the same good looks, with dark brown eyes and a wide jaw. Short dark blonde hair that was always messed up no matter how many times he tried to style it.

But it was only on the outside that they were similar.

Having an alter ego was a ploy used by quite a few popular singers. Beyoncé channelled Sasha Fierce to get a sexier, sassier vibe when she performed. David Bowie had created Ziggy Stardust. Even Paul Hewson had decided that the name Bono sounded more rock god than his real name.

For Tom it was like having a superhero secret identity. Tommy King belonged to the fans, the press and the world but Tom Kingsley was protected. This way, he still could retain some privacy. He could still hang onto his sanity. But only just, it felt like these days.

They reached his dressing room and Tom sank down onto the sofa, exhausted. Normally he was flying high after a great gig, but after six long months on the road, he felt only a sense of relief that it was all over. He needed to relax, but that seemed harder and harder at the minute.

'Well, that was a great end to a brilliant tour,' said Sam Harris, his manager as he sat down next to him. 'Did you see the VIP rows in the front? Everyone I can think of is here tonight.'

Tom yawned as he nodded in agreement. Each venue across Europe had been packed and the shows themselves had received rave reviews, admired for the strength of his song writing as well as his singing.

'London's always such a great crowd to finish a tour,' carried on Sam, smiling. 'So, how's the next album going?'

Tom shot his manager a look. 'Give us a chance,' he replied. 'I haven't been home for months.'

Not that the thought of going back to his brand new apartment filled him with joy. It was a very expensive penthouse in North London which he had bought a year previously but it didn't feel like home. It was just a place with walls where he had locked himself away before the tour, hoping for a peace that had never come.

'Primrose Hill is lovely,' said Sam, nodding his head in approval. 'You should get to know the neighbourhood.'

Tom shook his head. 'Since the fans found out where I live, it's impossible to go out anywhere without getting hassled,' he said, rubbing his forehead and wondering when he could finally sleep.

'Are they still shoving Maltesers through your letter box?' asked Sam, with a chuckle.

But Tom didn't laugh. 'I only mentioned them that one time.'

It had been one interview amongst so many that he had given. He couldn't even recall which magazine it was for. This particular interview had been a quick-fire question and answer. All he had said was that Maltesers were his favourite chocolate fix of choice. From then onwards, he had been sent thousands upon thousands of the damn things. Some days he had been barely able to open his front door due to the sheer number of sweet packets piled up inside. He had tried eating them at first, but now it was highly likely that he would never be able to face a packet of Maltesers ever again.

'Well, at least now that the tour's over you can finish your next album,' said Sam.

Finish it? He hadn't even started writing his next album. Tom inwardly grimaced and stayed silent. The truth was that, for the first time ever, he had a total block. The new words and music just wouldn't come. Three hit albums of songs that had almost written themselves. But now, there was only white noise where the words should have been.

The pressure from his record company and his fans was overwhelming. But if he didn't carry on making music, what else did he have in his life these days?

As he stayed quiet, he could feel his friend studying him.

'You're just tired,' said Sam eventually.

Tom didn't know what he was these days. Everything felt strange and unfamiliar.

The dressing room was suddenly invaded by members of his backing band who had decided that they must have an end of tour party, despite Tom trying to tell them otherwise. But they wouldn't take no for an answer and instead of finally going home, Tom found himself going with the large, noisy group to a nearby bar where they quickly took over the place.

Sam had one beer with them and then told Tom that he had a taxi booked to take him home.

'This late?' said Tom, glancing at his watch. It was nearly midnight and Sam lived far out in the countryside, away from the bright lights of London.

Sam grinned. 'I need to see my girl.'

His manager had fallen head over heels for a woman named Annie and they had been apart for a couple of weeks, thanks to the tour. Tom had picked up on the vibes that it had been a struggle for them both not to see each other during that time.

'Don't party too hard,' warned Sam, as he shrugged on his jacket. 'Remember Paris.'

Tom sighed at the memory before taking a sip of his sparkling water. He had been at his lowest ebb six months ago, having just lost his beloved Gran. She was the only one that had ever cared about him throughout his tumultuous early years when his own parents had been too busy partying to bring up their only son. But even the strongest woman he had ever known couldn't beat the wretched disease and he had delayed his world tour to sit with her through those hard, sad, final days at the hospice.

His first gig after the funeral had been in Paris and the whole night had been a disaster.

'I know I drank too much,' he said, with a shrug. 'You know how upset I was. But it wasn't my fault that the band threw me in the fountain, was it?'

Suddenly he was splashed, literally, all over the front pages, hundreds of column inches filled with how poisonous fame could be, how easy it was to hide away in drink and drugs.

Not wanting to deal with life with the aid of a whisky bottle like his father, Tom had not drunk any alcohol for six months.

'Just watch out for the paparazzi,' said Sam. 'We don't want any more bad publicity.'

Tom rolled his eyes. 'Anyone with a phone these days is basically paparazzi, you know that. But yeah, I'll watch out.'

As Sam left, Tom briefly wished that he had someone to go home to. A pair of warm arms to wrap around him and hold him tight all night long.

He was surprised to find himself thinking that way. Having been rejected by most people when he was growing up, he normally didn't rely on anyone else. But the loss of his gran had knocked his whole steady world off its axis. He missed her so much, he ached inside.

With the wave of grief threatening to overcome him once more, he felt a sudden need to blot out the rest of the world. He reached out and grabbed a shot of tequila from the tray of glasses that one of his backing singers had just brought over.

He would deal with real life when he woke up in the morning.

He briefly thought of Sam's warning before downing his first shot.

What harm could a couple of drinks do?

# Chapter 3

After a sleepless night of tossing and turning, Eleanor had finally fallen asleep at dawn. When she woke up, it was late in the morning. Her boyfriend Lucas had left for his high-flying city job many hours earlier.

She got up out of the huge bed and staggered over to the window. Flinging open the curtains, it took her eyes a moment or two to adjust to the bright sunlight. But when the city view finally came into focus, she sighed. London. That big, beautiful, brash, bonkers capital city. *Her* city, or at least it had been for the past eight years after leaving university.

It had been such a contrast to the tiny village of Cranley where she had grown up. It had taken a while to get used to the busy streets and the constant noise. But she had battled through her fears and had finally conquered the metropolis.

Most of all, it had been a city to escape to, away from the pain of her teenage years and her parent's broken relationship.

And now? She still couldn't believe that she had been made redundant. What on earth was she going to do?

Glancing at her emails gave her some idea. She had

been called into the Human Resources department that afternoon to receive her redundancy package and to hand back her office pass card.

She scratched absent-mindedly at her neck. She could feel yet another eczema patch appearing. She dragged her hand away, not wanting to make it any worse and went to check in the mirror.

She sighed at her reflection. There it was. An even bigger patch of scaly skin than the last time. She glared at herself in the mirror, her green eyes scowling. She hated her eczema. It showed through every make-up and disguise that she had tried. And she had learnt a long time ago that looking anything less than perfect meant an unhappy ending for everyone.

She knew the eczema was a sign of stress. But Lucas's fancy bathroom soap that he insisted on using didn't help either. The stuff her boyfriend used was hideously expensive, which was ridiculous given the number of chemicals it had in it. Although it did smell very nice, she privately thought.

She glanced down to see the red patches forming at the base of her fingers as well. She smeared a layer of E45 cream over the various patches but knew that it would be weeks before they went away again.

If she had the time, she could make up her own cream as she had done many years ago, but there was never any time these days. Every day she was rushing to some book or album launch, a party, some kind of movie premiere. Besides, the eczema always appeared when she was worried and, right now, she was on a high level of anxiety.

The trouble was that she was just so used to being in control of her own destiny. She had wanted good grades and had achieved them at college. She had wanted a career and she had made it happen. Okay, so it hadn't exactly been the high-flying journalism job that she had craved but she had gone along with it for as long as she could.

Except her career had just crashed to a halt. The floor had been taken away from her and she could feel herself tumbling downwards with no safety net.

Feeling her pulse begin to race with the stress once more, she turned away from the window and decided on a plan for the rest of the day. She just had to take control again. That was all. She could handle it. She was strong enough.

She quickly got dressed and paced across the polished floorboards into the lounge, glancing at the designer sofa. Expensive but not exactly comfortable. Not that she wanted to relax anyway. She was too uptight.

She briefly thought with longing about her own studio flat where she had lived for two blissful years. After years of flat-sharing, she had found a tiny place to rent by herself. The rent had been extortionate and had eaten up most of her meagre salary, but it had been worth it to have her own space, without worrying about her flatmates 'borrowing' from her designer wardrobe. Best of all, there was a tiny Juliet balcony where she had been able to plant up some window boxes full of flowers and herbs which she had used for various oils to help her skin.

But then her precious little flat had been declared unsafe due to subsidence so she had temporarily moved in with Lucas whilst deciding where to go next. Her landlord had promised to find her another apartment but it had never happened. So after seeing Lucas for two years she had moved in three months ago. It had been a reluctant joint decision. Neither of them had been quite ready for the next step in their relationship. And it was the longest she had ever lived with anyone apart from her mother. But after a few nervy first days, they seemed to be getting along, even if his choice of bathroom soap was causing her skin problems to flare up.

She stared around the huge space of the lounge, wondering what to do next. As usual, she decided not to hang around the flat on her own. It was too empty. Too cold, despite the sunny day outside. And she didn't like the way every noise echoed around the place.

So she decided to head across the capital to pick up her redundancy package.

Back at the office, Eleanor was grateful not to bump into Theresa or Kourtney in the corridors or the lift. That would have been particularly awkward. Thankfully the meeting with the Human Resources manager was brief and she was able to quickly get out of there. On the way home on the bus, she flicked through the paperwork, at least assured that the magazine had given her the three months' pay-off that she had been promised. That would last her the summer, but then what?

The trouble was, the newspaper and magazine worlds were in sharp decline due to online competition and jobs for experienced journalists were thin on the ground.

Sighing, she glanced out of the window and just caught sight of the Shard, glinting in the afternoon sun. She smiled as she recalled meeting Lucas for the first time up on one of the top floors, the city glittering far beneath them. It had been a fancy party, full of celebrities and high-flying bankers, one of which was her future boyfriend. He had been handsome, witty and, she had quickly realised, a like-minded spirit, somebody who was anxious to move quickly up the corporate ladder. Except his career had headed higher and higher whereas hers had stagnated.

She shook her head and brought her phone out of her handbag. She was a victim of bad timing, but that didn't mean she had to think like one.

She set about working her way through all the contacts she had made in the media. But after spending the rest of the afternoon searching, she felt exhausted by the lack of work out there. Her worst fears were confirmed. Things were tight across the whole industry. There were no spare jobs to be found anywhere.

Feeling overwhelmed, she decided she needed a drink. She took one of Lucas's crystal wine glasses from the display cabinet and poured herself a large chilled Prosecco.

She continued to idly flick down the list of contact names but knew it was a fruitless search. She bit back the tears, feeling more frightened that she had done in a long time. What on earth was she going to do now?

She was halfway through her third glass of wine when Lucas finally returned from work later that evening. She automatically checked her hair, smoothing down a rogue wave that had kinked out of place. She'd just slicked on some more lip gloss so that was already in place. Finally, she switched on a smile. 'Hi.'

'What a day,' said Lucas, by way of greeting. 'Bloody markets had millions wiped off them.'

Eleanor watched her boyfriend as he continued his rant. Some might have said that he was a little too obsessed with money, with an excessive amount of one-upmanship over his colleagues at the stock exchange where he worked. But she found that competition healthy, exciting even. It showed drive and initiative.

Lucas's eyes suddenly frowned as he stared down at the wine glass on the coffee table. 'Is that the Villeroy and Boch?'

'I don't know,' she replied, suddenly on edge. He

could be a bit precious about his belongings, most of which appeared to come with a high price tag.

'Jesus, Eleanor!' He picked up the glass and glared at her. 'You know I only use them on special occasions. You've already broken one. Do you know how much they cost?'

She rolled her eyes. She didn't need another bout of nagging about how accident-prone she was. 'Sorry,' she said. 'But I didn't think it was that important considering I *lost my job*.'

Lucas was holding up the wine glass to the light, checking for damage, when her words appeared to register with him. 'You lost your job?'

She nodded miserably. 'Yup.'

He looked shocked. 'What happened?'

'The magazine's downsizing.' They locked eyes. 'I found out last night but you were asleep when I came home and then you left early. I wanted to tell you face to face.'

'You should have text me.' Lucas ran a hand through his short black hair. 'I don't understand. Why you? I thought that new girl had less experience.'

Eleanor ground her teeth. 'Yes, but Kourtney's Dad owns a grand prix team. She's going to have better access to celebrities than I ever will. These things make a difference apparently. Compared to, I dunno, real actual experience.'

'Wait a minute.' Lucas frowned. 'Does this mean that

those Silverstone tickets are gone as well?'

'Well, yes,' she told him. 'I would think so, seeing as I won't be going there to cover all the parties anymore.'

Eleanor stood up to receive a hug, whilst waiting for words of comfort regarding her own predicament.

But the only thing Lucas said was, 'I'd better call my boss. Damn. I'd promised them to him. There goes my massive bonus. What a godawful day this has turned out to be.'

Eleanor blanched at his brutal words but tried to remain calm as she sank back onto the sofa. They were two peas in a pod, her and Lucas. They lived and died with their careers.

After a short phone conversation, Lucas wandered back into the lounge. 'It appears I'm unscathed, thank goodness.'

'Oh, goody,' said Eleanor sarcastically, her calm posture suddenly snapping. 'Any kind of sympathy would be great, you know, when you get over your own personal loss.'

Lucas looked sheepish. 'Sorry. It really sucks. You know I'm upset for you. It's just things are tight at the bank at the minute as well and I could have done with your connections. Look, I'm sure it'll turn out okay.'

He had just stepped forward as if to take her into his arms when her phone rang.

Eleanor snatched at her mobile eagerly, hope surging inside that it was about a job. But it was only her mother.

'Hi, Mum,' she said, picking up and automatically fixing on her smile. 'How are you?'

Expecting to bluff her way through the rest of the call as normal, she was horrified when her mum began to cry down the line.

'What's the matter?' said Eleanor, feeling frantic with worry. 'Are you okay?'

'Oh, Ellie. I've done the most stupid of things,' she said in a shaky voice. 'I've broken my foot.'

'Oh my god! How?'

'Tripped over one of the kittens,' said her mum.

Eleanor rolled her eyes down the line but didn't say anything. There was no point trying to nag her mum about the number of animals she had in her house at any one time. That battle had been lost many years ago unfortunately.

'Are you okay?' she asked. 'Where are you?'

'I'm back home now,' said her mum. 'I've spent all day in A&E getting X-rays and then having the plaster put on.'

'Poor you. Look, it's late now,' said Eleanor, checking the time. 'I'll come down on the train tomorrow and see you, okay? Maybe I'll stay until the weekend.'

That caused her mum to cry again. 'No, no,' she said. 'I don't want you getting in trouble at work. You're so important to them. You mustn't rock the boat.'

'It'll be fine,' said Eleanor, with a grimace known only to herself. 'It's bank holiday week so it's really quiet at work. Don't worry.'

'Well, it'll be lovely to see you after all these months.'

There was no sarcasm in her mother's voice, but Eleanor still bit her lip in guilt. She had meant to go home at Easter but there had been that VIP party and she had had to stay in London to write up her story. So she hadn't been back to Cranley since Christmas, and even that visit had been cut short because there had been rumours of a reality star checking out of rehab and she had needed to be there to get the scoop.

'I'll see you tomorrow,' Eleanor told her.

'Okay,' said her Mum. 'I love you, Ellie.'

'Me too,' she replied, as always her voice stalling over those particular words. Some hurts could never be overcome.

She hung up and explained to Lucas what had happened.

'So, I guess you'll be needing to take care of your mum for a while then. Look, this is awkward,' he carried on, suddenly not making eye contact. 'My timing is obviously a bit off what with everything that's happened, but I was actually kind of hoping you'd be moving out soon anyway.'

Eleanor took an intake of deep breath. 'Move out?'

'It was only supposed to be temporary, wasn't it? You know, because you couldn't stay in your flat. But it's been, what, thirteen weeks?'

He'd been counting?

Lucas finally looked up at her, giving her a small smile. 'Hey, you know me. I'm just a bit of a neat freak and you're not, are you? You've got all your girly stuff everywhere. And you know I don't do flowers.' He glanced at the vase full of cut roses on the coffee table. 'Besides, I'm just not ready for all that commitment, living-together stuff yet. You feel the same, I know you do. So maybe we'll just take a little break from each other and see how we feel.'

The silence stretched out until she could finally splutter, 'I see.'

Except she didn't. Why hadn't he mentioned this before? Or, she wondered, perhaps she just hadn't picked up on his heavy hints.

'But hey,' said Lucas, frowning at her aghast face. 'No rush. Take your time. There's no need to start packing this very minute, okay?'

Packing? He wanted her out that soon?

'I know! If you're going down to your mum's tomorrow, maybe you can leave your stuff with her for the time being? Look, I'm going out with the lads. It's someone's birthday. We'll talk more later and sort something out, yeah?'

She nodded, putting on her bravest smile. As if she didn't care that he was rejecting her. That everyone in London had rejected her during the past twenty-four hours.

Once he had left, she wandered into the bedroom and sank down onto the thick duvet.

She opened up the drawer of the bedside cabinet that Lucas had generously allowed her to use. She brought out the small keepsake box she had picked up a few years ago. Inside were a few trinkets, nothing special. But there, at the very bottom of the box, was a framed photograph of three teenage girls. She smiled, as she always did at this faded photo of her oldest and best friends.

Yes, Annie was now engaged to a future earl and living in an enormous stately home. And Megan had married her high school sweetheart and had three children. But here they were, captured in time all those years ago, trying to be cool, as all teenagers are desperate to be. Annie's blonde hair was scraped back into a ponytail. Megan's red hair had been cut ferociously short and was incredibly curly. Eleanor's own long dark hair had been braided. But their wide grins all matched.

Their matching khaki cargo pants and black T-shirts made her smile. How many times had they sung that All Saints album into their hairbrushes?

Eleanor put the photo back and closed the lid of the box, sighing heavily at the thought of the little village that she had been so desperate to escape in her teenage years. Instead of hating it as she had done back then, right at that moment she yearned to see the village, have a long gossip with her friends and a huge hug from her mum. Megan was still living there and Annie had returned to Cranley the previous year after a long absence abroad.

She missed her friends terribly. They still phoned and messaged all the time, but she had only managed to see them for a couple of hours at Christmas before she had to head back to London. Once back in the city, there was always so little time to talk and catch up when she was dashing around from party to party in the middle of the night. It was a sacrifice she had thought was worth it. Until yesterday.

She made up her mind to make proper use of her time back in Cranley whilst she was there. She was going to catch up on all of her friends' news. To rediscover each other and get close again. To help her mum whilst she was there and, literally, get her back on her feet.

Then, when she was ready, Eleanor hoped she could head back to the city feeling stronger and more in control than ever before.

She just wasn't sure how on earth any of that was going to happen.

# Chapter 4

Tom woke up, his head throbbing as he moved it. He groaned and opened his eyes to see his manager Sam sitting on the chair next to the bed.

'Good morning,' mumbled Tom, half asleep and still trying to work out where he was.

'Afternoon actually,' replied Sam, putting his mobile down. 'I'm not sure what to ask about first. Your hangover or your foot?'

Gradually, Tom began to focus and took in the sterile room with its strip lighting, single bed and crisp white sheet covering him. Oh yes. It was all coming back to him now. He was in hospital.

He stared down the bed to where his right foot was bandaged and raised up on top of a pillow. 'The hangover's disappearing,' he lied, wincing as even speaking was painful at that moment. 'The foot might take a bit longer to heal.'

He glanced around the large private room in the hospital that he only just about remembered ending up in the previous evening. It was already filled with balloons and flowers wishing him a speedy recovery.

'What the hell happened?' said Sam, looking as if he

were trying to remain calm. 'You had a great gig, finished a fantastic tour on a real high and then, what? You got blind drunk and broke your leg as you passed out in the street!'

Tom shook his head and groaned as even that hurt. 'It wasn't like that.'

'So tell me,' said Sam, his eyes glaring.

'I only had a couple of drinks,' Tom explained. 'You know I haven't drunk anything for months. Honestly. I was exhausted and actually finished the night relatively early on, believe it or not. But I slipped off the pavement on the way to getting a taxi and somehow managed to tear a ligament. No bones broken. No drunken disgrace.'

'Tell that to the media,' said Sam, grabbing his phone and handing it over to show Tom the various screens as he flicked past them.

TOMMY DRUNK AGAIN! screamed the headlines, he managed to catch. PASSED OUT IN THE STREET! IS IT TIME FOR REHAB, TOMMY?

Tom closed his eyes and sighed. 'They're just exaggerating everything, as per usual. Trying to make a story out of nothing.'

'Well, it's working,' Sam told him. 'You're the number one trend on Twitter today. Congratulations.'

Tom glanced through a couple more of the photographs before pushing the iPhone back towards Sam in disgust. No wonder he didn't trust anyone.

People had taken photos of him lying down on the pavement in obvious pain. No-one in the crowd had offered to phone for an ambulance or check that he was actually okay.

He hadn't been comatose. Merely in agony from a misstep. That was all. And now it was everywhere. Everyone was talking about him, thinking that they knew all about him.

*Judging him.*

Like he hadn't been used to that from day one of his life. As usual, he felt his inner defence shields rise in response.

Tom shifted in his bed and immediately felt a twinge of pain from his foot. Apparently it would take up to six weeks to heal the tiny tear in his ankle. Rest and recuperation are your best bet, the doctor had told him. Since when had he last done that?

'You look exhausted,' said Sam.

'I don't know if you remember but I've just finished a massive world tour,' drawled Tom.

Even saying the words still sounded unbelievable to him. The fame itself had been remarkable in its speed.

He was a carpenter by trade, having completed his college apprenticeship on the job. He had left school as quickly as possible, desperate to be independent. The song writing had only been a hobby in his mind. A daydream that could never come true for someone like him. He had however managed to wangle a couple of sessions to play at a local pub in Hampstead after fitting some new cupboard doors in the kitchen. The landlord liked the acoustic nature of his playing, just Tom and his guitar.

Slowly, thanks to the power of social media and a couple of local reviews, the word got out that he was talented and it had become a regular gig, gaining in popularity.

Then, one night after he had finished playing, Sam Harris had introduced himself as he was standing at the bar. He told Tom that he managed a number of bands and singers – the most famous of which was Hazy Memory, a seventies rock band. Tom had been impressed by the portfolio of artists he had on his books. After all, Sam was only the same age as him.

Sam was quietly spoken but firm in his belief that Tom had talent. He promised nothing but said that he could work with him to develop his song writing ability. Tom agreed to his proposition, trusting Sam – itself a rare thing in his life so far. They quickly developed a strong bond and Tom felt able to rely on his new manager's encouragement and advice.

Tom had been halfway into writing his first album of songs when something amazing happened. The American rapper Jazz Goldblatt had been in London on tour and had happened to visit the pub where Tom had been playing.

Jazz tweeted his three million followers about the

'awesome Brit boy' and suddenly Tom had become an overnight sensation. A clip of him playing at the pub went viral on YouTube and had twenty million hits.

Sam began to be inundated with phone calls from his contacts across the music industry and a bidding war for Tom's first album erupted between two record labels, the result being a contract worth millions.

Before they signed, Sam sat down with Tom one day to ask whether he wanted to use his own name. Up until that time, Tom had always wanted to be known as himself. But he had begun to have a few weird phone calls from overeager fans and journalists and had quickly concluded that a pseudonym would be better. Suddenly he was craving anonymity.

Hence Tommy King was born.

That had been over eight years ago. Fame and fortune had arrived quickly. His first album had won the prestigious Mercury Prize and had gone double platinum. His status in the music world increased with the second album, which garnered him a Brit Award and sold over five million copies. His third album finally gave him his much yearned for Grammy and he broke America, holding a position in the Billboard Top Five for over twenty weeks.

With over thirty million album sales in total so far and a couple of sell-out worldwide tours, Tom had been given financial security beyond his wildest dreams. With the help of Sam and a financial advisor, he purchased his flat in an expensive London neighbourhood. Wise investments meant that he would never feel the sharp pang of starvation or a lack of roof over his head ever again.

But suddenly he was tired and desperate to break free of the shackles of fame.

Being a global superstar meant that he had to carry on courting the media, going onto chat shows and talking about himself. His natural instinct was to hide away from the spotlight. All he ever wanted was to just play his music. The lack of privacy was draining.

He didn't have time to think these days.

Didn't have time to rest.

Didn't have time to grieve.

The pain hit him hard over and over. He missed his beloved Gran. She had been the only one who had ever truly cared about him. If she had been around, she would have been fretting about him ending up in hospital. As always, she would have dispensed wise words which would have helped. But now she was gone and he felt horribly alone.

Sam had been studying his friend for a couple of silent minutes.

'Tell you what, why don't you come and stay with us for a week or so?' he said eventually. 'Have a break from everything here in town. It's not like we haven't got the room.'

Out of the blue, Sam had suddenly declared six

months previously that his family belonged to a long line of English earls, with an impressive ancestral home deep in the English countryside. Sam and his fiancée Annie had spent most of the winter and spring bringing the crumbling Willow Tree Hall back into the twenty-first century.

Sam was a good guy, who Tom trusted implicitly, both as a manager and a close friend. And that was rare for someone who didn't trust anyone. With good reason, he knew from bitter experience.

But Tom liked his independence. He had carefully cultivated his self-reliance. The protective shield that helped him cope with the endless rejections over his life.

He glanced at his bandaged foot and almost laughed. Was he really coping that well?

Adding to the strain, he knew that every time he stepped out of line, there was somebody standing nearby to make a headline about it.

'Come on,' urged Sam. 'It'll be good for you.'

Tom wasn't so sure. He cherished his privacy. He didn't like being around too many people. It was easier to keep everyone out than let anyone in. That way he couldn't be let down again.

However, he was surprised to find himself tempted by his friend's proposition. He had never been to Willow Tree Hall but understood the place to be in the middle of nowhere. The peace was tempting for a week or so.

Torn between wanting to keep his privacy and not

wanting to upset Sam, in the end Tom nodded his agreement.

Sam looked delighted. 'That's great. You can recharge your batteries at Willow Tree Hall. And who knows? Maybe you'll get that album of yours finished in record time.'

Tom kept quiet, thinking that at some point he was going to have to tell his manager that he hadn't even started the album yet. And that he had no idea where the next song was going to come from.

Perhaps staying at Willow Tree Hall would help. But it was a family home. And family was something that had never worked out for him. Everyone in his life apart from his Gran had ignored him until the fame had arrived. Now they all just wanted a piece of him without even wanting to get to know him better. They only wanted Tommy King. Would he ever find someone who would be happy to settle for plain old Tom Kingsley instead?

# Chapter 5

Eleanor glanced up from her phone and realised with a jolt that the taxi was nearly in Cranley village.

She had spent the majority of the long journey refreshing her emails and recruitment websites, all to no avail. There were no job offers. Nothing but lots of text messages from her friends on the magazine, asking if she was going to the new Tom Hanks film premiere in Leicester Square that evening. They all loved sneaking in on the back of her press pass to the best of the parties. She had reluctantly replied that she had been made redundant. Now the messages were full of sympathy for her situation.

Eleanor sighed and automatically reached up to touch the sore spot on her neck. The eczema patch was worse than ever. Sometimes she scratched it without even realising she was doing so.

She forced her hand down away from her neck and looked out of the window instead. Everywhere was bright green with the fresh growth of spring. As June had nearly arrived, there was finally some real warmth in the sun and the days were getting longer. Summer was just around the corner. She recognised the hill they were driving up and quickly looked out of the other window towards the view that she adored. There was always a glimpse of Cranley as you headed over the last rolling hill towards the village. Seeing it through the trees, Eleanor couldn't help but feel a little proud of her pretty home.

There it was, nestled in a green valley amongst the hills. A tiny English hamlet. In the centre was the ancient church of St Barnabus, its wobbly spire high above anything else in the village. Along the main street was the infants' school, a couple of shops and The Rose and Crown pub. In the surrounding avenues were rows of cottages of sand-coloured stone, all tiny with chimneys. Most of the houses were built in the same bricks that matched the main property of the estate, Willow Tree Hall, which could just be seen peeping through the trees, surrounded by lush green fields and, out of view, the river. It was all very pretty and completely rural. Lovely, in a Jane Austen adaptation for a television series kind of way. Not so great if you craved catching a convenient Tube into Covent Garden before covering a movie premiere in Leicester Square.

A few minutes later, Eleanor got out of the taxi, pleased to be able to stretch her legs at last after the long journey.

It had been very generous of Lucas to pay for a taxi from London all the way to her home village of Cranley. Maybe it was too generous, she wondered. Perhaps he really had been desperate to get her out of his pristine flat after all this time. But at least it meant she had been able to pack up all her many clothes and possessions and bring them all with her. It would have been a total nightmare on the train and buses, trying to travel with everything.

Her last conversation that morning with Lucas had been to decide that their relationship should be left as 'open-ended' until she returned to London. Eleanor had no idea what that actually meant in reality but was relieved just to leave all her troubles behind her for a while until she had the strength to face them.

As the taxi driver dumped her suitcases and bags on the pavement, she checked her phone once more, but there were no new messages apart from the ones from her friends Annie and Megan, who were delighted that she was coming back to Cranley, even temporarily. She couldn't wait to see them both.

Once alone, she turned to stare up at the tiny detached cottage in front of her. The Forge. She was home. Truly home.

It was the familiarity that touched her deep inside and she was surprised to feel the tears welling up. All she wanted, all she needed right at that moment, was a hug from her mum. Then surely everything would be all right in her world again.

She hadn't been back since Christmas but almost six months on, nothing had changed except the passing of the seasons. Nothing ever changed at The Forge. The gate still needed fixing. The front door still needed a coat of fresh paint. With a pang, she reminded herself that she should make the effort to do a few more things around the house now that she had the time. Her mum had always struggled with keeping the place tidy on her own and it seemed in more need of repair than ever before.

She lifted and pushed the rotten wooden gate open and dragged the heavy suitcases over the bumpy paving stones towards the faded blue front door. Her arms were aching from the effort and she was grateful again for not having carried them all the way from London. The bags were even heavier, bulging full of make-up and beauty lotions.

She drew out her key and slid it into the lock with the slight wiggle that it had always required in order to work. Using her shoulder to push the stuck door wide open, she called out, 'Hi, Mum! I'm home!'

She was immediately enveloped in the familiar aroma of home baking and, she grimaced, animals. As if on cue, a tabby cat rushed out of the kitchen at the end of the hallway, closely followed by a black and white spaniel she had never seen before. They were headed straight for her. Eleanor braced herself for impact.

'Don't let the dog out!' shouted her mum from the kitchen.

The cat rushed out of the front door, leaping over her

suitcases as it went. Eleanor just managed to close the door before the dog could get out too.

'Not so fast,' she told him, leaning against the door. He barked at her in protest and then drooled down her leg.

'Ewww,' she said, trying to wipe off the white foam on her designer black jeans.

In addition to the spaniel, a Great Dane sauntered out of the kitchen to stroll up and sit on her feet. 'Geroff,' she muttered, pushing the huge beast off her squished toes. Somewhere above the barking and panting there was the sound of some kind of exotic bird.

*Ah yes*, she thought with a sigh. *The animals*.

Most wives whose husbands leave them for a woman twenty years their junior either hide themselves in a vat of wine or lose fifty pounds and gain a toy boy. Sadly her mum, June McCartney, had done neither. Instead, June had taken refuge in the animal kingdom and made the ex-marital home a sanctuary for all creatures great and small.

For the last twenty or so years, if you lived near Cranley and found a stray animal, this had always been the place to come. Her grandfather had been a farrier, using the very place where they lived to shoe his horses. Eleanor had always presumed that her mum had inherited his love of animals, as well as The Forge itself.

In addition to the strays, cats and dogs of all sizes would arrive for a short holiday, thanks to her mother's pet-sitting service. This was presumably where the spaniel and Great Dane came in.

'Mum, where are you?' she shouted.

'In the kitchen, love,' came the reply.

Eleanor picked her way over the piles of knocked-over books, newspapers, scratched floorboards, dogs and all-round chaos of the tiny hallway. She walked past the small front room and went through to the large kitchen. At one time, it had been the workshop and was therefore a large, airy room with wooden beams and generous windows.

June was sitting at the wooden table in the middle of the room, her foot in plaster and propped up on a stool. Her face was pale and she was obviously in pain.

'Oh, Mum!' said Eleanor, rushing over to give her a hug.

'I'm okay,' said her mother, holding her tight. 'Just a stupid accident.'

Eleanor leant back to search her mum's face. 'Does it hurt?'

'A little. They've given me some pills to take if it gets too much. Anyway, let me have a look at my beautiful, glamorous daughter.'

Eleanor breathed in her mum's soft perfume and had to bite back the tears as she could see the pain in her eyes.

They shared the same emerald-coloured eyes. Same dark hair, except her bob was always immaculate and her mother's hair was always worn too long and wavy. June had never seen the inside of a professional hairdressers when the kitchen scissors could do the job for free. Eleanor's love of stylish clothes was also in stark contrast to her mother's throw it on and make-do style.

Her mum had never been a money person. Nor a glamorous one. She had always declared that she didn't have time to concentrate on herself. All her time and effort had been taken up raising her daughter single-handedly after Eleanor's philandering father had left them both, to chase after some yet-to-be-discovered actress.

'What happened?' asked Eleanor, sitting down at the table.

'It was on Monday,' said her mum, shifting in her seat as if trying to get comfortable. 'I tripped over a tree root in the garden as I was trying to get one of the chickens back in the coop.'

Eleanor automatically glanced out of the window to the messy corner plot beyond. 'Chickens? You told me it was one of the kittens.'

'Oh. Did I?' Her mum looked sheepish.

Eleanor raised her eyebrows. 'Since when did we have chickens?'

'Ben found me some that needed a good home.'

Ben was her mother's best friend. A gentle giant of a man who ran the veterinary clinic a few miles away.

They had known each other since childhood and he was an honorary uncle as far as Eleanor was concerned.

'And the fresh eggs are lovely,' said her mother quickly. 'Ever so good for you.'

A soft mewling drew Eleanor's attention back indoors and she spotted the metal crate holding five kittens who were curled up in tight furry balls asleep. 'I thought we talked about this at Christmas,' she said, trying to keep her nagging tone soft. 'Where did this lot come from?'

'That awful pet shop,' said her mum, looking stern. 'Horrid man. Thankfully I heard he was going bankrupt and bought the lot before he could do his worst. You know what kind of man he was. They would have ended up in the river.' June shuddered and gave the kittens a soft smile. 'Aren't they cute?'

'Very.' Eleanor sighed. There was no denying that the kittens were gorgeous but she had been here so many times before with her mother who just didn't know when to stop. 'So you're looking after a couple of dogs and the kittens. Is that it? Apart from the chickens, which we'll talk about in a minute.'

'Yes.' Her mum avoided eye contact with her. 'Maybe a cockatoo.'

That explained the cawing bird somewhere in the house.

Something moving extremely slowly across the kitchen counter caught Eleanor's eye. 'And the tortoise?'

she asked.

'Oh, he's no bother,' her mum said, waving a dismissive hand.

'I should think not at that speed,' said Eleanor.

There was a short silence filled only by an unexpected and loud hee-haw from the garden.

Mother and daughter locked green eyes.

'We might have a donkey now,' muttered her mum.

'A donkey!' Eleanor sprang up and looked out into the garden. Yes, there amongst the messy vegetable patch, the overgrown flower borders and the chicken coop was a shaggy brown donkey standing in the middle of the ruined lawn.

'Oh Mum!' Eleanor rolled her eyes in despair. 'This is too much! We don't live on a farm. We live in a tiny cottage next to the high street. What are you going to do with a donkey when winter arrives? What kind of shelter will it get and don't say the garden shed!'

'Oh Ellie! I couldn't say no,' said her mum, with teary eyes. 'Where else would they go?'

'They?'

Eleanor spun back around to look outside once more and, sure enough, a white goat had appeared from somewhere else in the garden.

'Is that it?' she asked, staring in disbelief for a moment before turning away. 'No giraffes in the bathroom? Polar bears in the front room?'

'No. That's it,' said her mum, holding up her hand. 'I

know! I know. I thought I'd get on top of them all this week, but then this!' She gestured at her leg.

Eleanor took a deep breath. She couldn't be mad with her mother for long, no matter how much she despaired. 'Well, I'm here to help now,' she said in a resigned tone. 'How about I make us a nice cup of tea?'

'That would be lovely.'

Eleanor rinsed out the mugs twice on account of the dust and other flecks in the china that she didn't want to think about. She glanced at the tortoise that was making slow progress along the kitchen counter. Lucas had only visited her mother's house just the once in the whole of their two-year relationship and she had seen the horrified look in his eyes, despite his polite manners. He had refused to come back after that.

'Are you even allowed to keep a donkey in your back garden?' she wondered aloud.

'It's only temporary and I'm sure Arthur won't mind.'

Arthur Harris, Earl of Cranley, was the owner of Willow Tree Hall and the estate, which included all the cottages in the village which were rented to local families. The McCartneys had rented The Forge from the Cranley estate since before Eleanor was born.

'How are you going to cope at work with your foot?' she asked, as the tea stewed in the pot.

Her mum shrugged. 'I'll survive. Mr Pennyworth says I can sit down at the till. And he's given me until next week to get used to the crutches.'

Her mother worked at the local farm shop. Yet another worrying source of additional animals to add to their home.

'And that nice Sam, you know Annie's fiancé, has said that I'm not to fret about the rent.'

Sam Harris was Arthur's grandson, heir to the earldom and now living at Willow Tree Hall. With Sam helping out his grandfather Arthur, Lord Cranley, Eleanor realised that her mum would now be one of Annie's tenants in the future when she became the countess. The thought of Annie as a future countess made her smile.

After pouring out the tea and giving her mum a cup, Eleanor brought in her suitcases and bags from the front door and dumped them in the hall.

Her mum craned her neck around the corner. 'What have you got all that with you for?'

Eleanor deliberately made her voice casual. 'I thought I might sort out a few things whilst I'm here. I've got far too much stuff these days.'

'You won't have time for that by the time you've caught up with Annie and Megan. And then they'll be desperate for you back at your job in a few days.'

Eleanor gulped and braced herself. Once her mum had recovered from the devastation caused by her husband walking out, she had channelled all her hopes and dreams onto her daughter. Sacrificing everything for Eleanor, June had encouraged her to go to university and then to follow her dream career in journalism. 'You're so talented,' she repeatedly told Eleanor. 'You mustn't let it go to waste.'

But despite the two of them being so close, Eleanor had never revealed the truth about her job. She had lied and told her mum that she worked for the financial magazine. She never wanted to tell the truth about which particular magazine she worked for. *Used* to work for, she reminded herself. She hadn't wanted to embarrass her mum with her gossip and mindless stories, she had told herself at the beginning. Especially when they had been the subject of all that gossip a very long time ago. Some wounds would never heal.

She opened her mouth to finally tell the truth. But then she saw her mum wince in pain as she flexed her foot and Eleanor quickly decided that there was already had too much to cope with. She would tell her at a later date.

Instead she found herself saying, 'Look, as it happens, I'm actually owed some holiday. How about I stay and help out for a couple of weeks. You can't possibly cope with this zoo whilst you're on crutches.'

'Oh that would be lovely!' said her mum, smiling but teary. 'But I don't want you getting into trouble at work.'

'The markets are very stable and quiet at the minute. I'm sure I can arrange something with my editor whilst you're recuperating over the next few weeks,' said

Eleanor, the lies flowing quite easily now.

In reality, she had no idea what on earth she was going to do once she had finished taking care of her mum.

She sat down and drank her tea, glancing around the messy kitchen. What a stark contrast to her lovely glamorous life back in London. She would normally have been picking out her outfit to wear that evening. A new film premiere. Then she would have gone onto a new nightclub owned by that controversial rapper. Then home to Lucas.

Eleanor frowned as she scratched at her neck. Except there was no West End premiere, no glitzy nightclub, not even Lucas for the time being either.

'How's that nice boyfriend of yours?' asked her mum.

Eleanor gulped. This was one truth that she could actually say out loud. 'We're taking a break,' she said. 'I'm not sure if it's going to end up being a permanent one or not.'

'Oh, love! I'm so sorry,' said her mum, reaching out to squeeze her hand. 'You must be so upset.'

Eleanor made a sad face, even though she knew that deep down she wasn't exactly heartbroken over the break-up. Shouldn't she be swilling vodka and sobbing into a massive bar of chocolate?

But no. All she felt was relief that she wouldn't have to hide the evidence when she broke another one of his expensive but actually quite hideous plates. Lucas was the type that would likely invoice his girlfriend for the breakage.

Perhaps she wasn't meant to have true love in her life. Maybe that was for the best. She had seen the damage that loving her dad had inflicted onto her mum's kind heart.

'So how are things in the romance department around here?' asked Eleanor, her tone deliberately bright. 'Have you got any hunky bachelors wining and dining you on a nightly basis?'

Her mother blushed as she moved her hand back to clasp her cup of tea. 'Don't be silly,' she said, her cheeks bright pink. 'Who's going to want me?'

Her mum had never had any confidence in herself, especially after her husband had left her for a much younger woman. He had destroyed any self-worth that she had had. 'You can only trust animals,' June had frequently reminded her daughter. 'They can't hurt you.'

Eleanor could still remember every moment of that ghastly day because it had been such a huge bolt of shock for both mother and daughter. They had had a lovely family day out. First of all they had gone shopping and then ice-skating at the rink in Aldwych. They had just finished tea when her dad stood up at the kitchen table and announced that he was leaving.

'You're going out?' she remembered her Mum saying. 'I thought we were having a quiet night in?'

'I'm sick of quiet nights in,' he replied, his face

hardening. 'I can't do this anymore. I'm still young. I need to live. To feel free. You've clipped my wings, June. So I'm leaving. For good.'

The shocked silence had stretched out. Eleanor, at twelve years of age, couldn't believe it.

'But you can't go, Dad,' she said, jumping up from the table. 'Please stay. I love you. We both do.'

But her dad had just shaken his head. 'It's not enough, love. Not for me. You'll understand when you're older.'

'But we've had such a nice day,' stammered Eleanor.

Her Dad smiled then. 'I wanted our last one together to be a good one,' he told her.

Then he had gone upstairs to fetch the suitcase that he had already packed and hidden in his wardrobe the night before.

It was only once the front door had clicked shut behind him that mother and daughter burst into tears.

It was the last time she had said 'I love you' to anyone.

It had been the worst of times for both of them, but somehow they had just about managed to hold things together and come out the other side. Although the hurt still lingered on.

'Anyway, there's enough romance up at the hall at the minute,' said her mother. 'Can you believe it? Sweet Annie Rogers becoming a countess when she gets married!'

'At least one of us made it,' said Eleanor with a wry smile.

'The girls are desperate to meet up with you,' her mum carried on. 'Megan popped by for a cuppa this morning. They're so excited to have you back in the village.'

'Me too.' Eleanor cleared her throat. 'But it's not forever, Mum.'

'I know. But let us enjoy having you here whilst we can, eh?'

Eleanor grabbed her phone. 'I'll text Megan and find out when they're both free.'

'You'll have such fun catching up,' said her mum. 'Megan says Sam's lovely. Just right for our Annie.'

Eleanor had tried to remember Sam from when they were younger. Because Sam and his younger brother Will had gone to boarding school, they had only been around in the summer holidays to visit their grandparents. Once they were older, they had both left the village, as she had done. It was only once Sam had returned to take care of Willow Tree Hall the previous winter that she knew more about him. According to Annie, he had been travelling abroad a lot before he had come back after Arthur had suffered an accident and needed help with the estate.

'Oh and Megan said she can't wait for you to meet Hazy Memory!'

Eleanor looked up from her phone. 'Who?'

'You know, that band with the awful Christmas song,' said her mum. 'They've been around for years.'

Eleanor frowned. 'I know who they are, but why would they be coming here of all places?'

'Didn't you know? Sam is some kind of, what did Annie call it, a rock band manager.' Her mum shrugged her shoulders. 'Whatever that is.'

Eleanor abruptly stopped texting and googled Sam Harris instead. She couldn't believe it. How had she managed to forget what Annie's fiancé did for a living? Of course, they hadn't had a proper catch-up for ages which didn't help. But she had only been thinking of his life at Willow Tree Hall and not his actual day job.

She stared down at the Google results in wonder. It turned out that Sam managed a whole load of famous bands, the most popular of all was Tommy King.

She looked up at her mum and broke into her first genuine smile that day.

This was it! This was her chance! She felt a lightning bolt of excitement surge through her. Who would have thought that there could be a story here in sleepy Cranley, after all? With a connection to so many music stars, surely she could dig something up, even here in the middle of the countryside?

The relief inside was immense. Perhaps she would discover such an amazing scoop that she would blaze a trail back to London, arriving in glory. She would even have scary Theresa begging her to come back.

In fact, all of the print press in London would be desperate to hire her if they found about her scoop. But finally it would be on her terms. With this one last story, she could leave the celebrity world far behind her once and for all and become a serious journalist.

Then nobody back home would ever need to know how close she had been to revealing her perfect life was a sham.

# Chapter 6

To his surprise, Tom was enjoying the taxi journey out of London. Having been released from the confines of his hospital bed after two days, it was a pleasure to see the countryside outside the window.

In fact, it was a novelty to be out and about during the day at all. In between stages of the lengthy world tour, he had locked himself away and had stopped going out. Some days he hadn't even spoken to anyone. He had slipped into keeping twilight hours for the past six months, waking late in the afternoon and then either going on stage or song writing. Or rather, frustratingly staring into space trying to think of words before giving up and watching whole box sets on Netflix.

But heading to Willow Tree Hall meant that at least he was out of the apartment and away from the hospital, where he had been all too aware of being Tommy King, with people peeking into his private room. The newspapers were still full of his drunken mishap, apparently. Not that he read them anymore.

So it was good to be in the back of the chauffeured car that Sam had organised. The sun was out and he had the window down as they drove through the beautiful countryside on a sunny day. The birds were singing in the trees above, the breeze was fresh on his face. He felt alive. Free.

It was one of the quirks of becoming famous. He had spent so much time dreaming about having hit records. The thought that a crowd could know every line of a song that he had written was still an incredible feeling. But he had never considered the downside to everyone knowing his face, his name. And how quickly life as he knew it could change.

As the driver pulled up at a red light, he glanced down to check his missed calls. They were all from Melissa. He threw the phone back onto the passenger seat in disgust.

He had met Melissa at some party that his record label had thrown a few months ago whilst he had a rare day home from his world tour. He had quite liked her. He had even thought that there was a connection between them. Until she had sold their story to the press after a couple of dates and had given out intimate details of what he had thought had been a genuine romance.

He shook his head. He had been a fool to trust her. To trust so many people in his life that let him down. Now that he had lost his gran, it was left to Sam to be the only person that he could rely on and speak freely to.

The journey to Willow Tree Hall led him through Cranley village. From what he could see, it was a tiny hamlet with only a handful of cottages and shops. All the buildings were made from a sandy coloured stone, which made the whole place very attractive to look at.

It was all in stark contrast to his early years. Picturesque country scenes and the peace of nature had been in pretty short supply growing up in the inner-city concrete jungle of London's East End. He had always enjoyed an affinity with wood and trees, which is why he had gone into carpentry, but lately he had stopped looking outside so much. There was never any time when there was another interview or concert lined up.

A mile or so on from the high street, the driver turned the car through some rusty iron gates and into the long driveway leading up to the house. Sam had only recently confessed that his grandfather was the 7th Earl of Cranley. But Arthur, Sam's grandfather, had suffered with ill health during the winter and Sam had stepped up to take responsibility for the ancestral home, Willow Tree Hall, albeit reluctantly at first.

Bouncing up the drive, the driver slowed the car down to a crawl. Now Tom understood why Sam had recently purchased a Range Rover and got rid of his beloved Porsche. The potholes were massive.

Despite the huge craters in the narrow lane, Tom couldn't help but appreciate the stunning setting. The driveway was long, bordered on either side by huge fields of grass and sun-bleached picket fences. In the middle of the front lawn stood a huge willow tree, presumably so ancient that the hall had been named after it all those centuries ago. The willow tree's long boughs of newly blossomed green leaves swayed gently in the soft breeze.

Then the house came into view. Tom couldn't help but be amazed. It was a large, wide-fronted building, two stories high and built in the same sandy coloured stone as the rest of the village. Like a miniature Buckingham Palace in shape, it had sixteen large sash windows spread evenly across the front. The centrepiece was a huge front door, framed by large round stone pillars on either side. Tom couldn't believe that Sam lived in such a beautiful place. Nor that he knew someone of English nobility.

It looked stunning in the bright spring sunshine, especially now that the place had begun to be renovated. From what Tom had heard, it had desperately needed serious work only one year previously. All the sash windows appeared new, as did the doors, walls and most of the fixtures and fittings. In fact, Sam had ploughed most of his hard-earned money into making the place habitable. But somehow it had retained its air of aged splendour.

They parked up and the driver was just helping Tom out of the back seat when the huge double red front door opened.

Sam appeared and came outside to greet him.

'How's the foot?' he asked, gesturing at the crutches, which Tom was fiddling with so he could stand up straight.

'Not bad.' It was a lie as it was still extremely painful, but Tom had never shown weakness to anyone. He had a vast supply of painkillers that he would most definitely need until the foot began to heal.

They were just about to head inside the hall when an elderly gentleman appeared at the door and walked towards them.

Arthur Harris, the Earl of Cranley, was an older version of his grandson Sam. They shared the same strong chin and tall build, although Sam was much broader and more muscular than the fragile-looking earl.

Sam had confided in Tom that, after the tragedy of losing both their parents, Arthur and his wife Beatrice had taken over guardianship of their grandsons and had done their very best under difficult circumstances. It had been a time of intense grief and Tom knew that the whole family had taken many years to come to terms with their loss.

'Welcome to Willow Tree Hall,' said Arthur, in his clipped aristocratic tone. He held out his hand, the other grasping onto his walking stick.

Tom fiddled with his crutches to reach out his own hand so they could finally shake.

'Wretched things, aren't they?' said Arthur, gesturing at the crutches. 'Got rid of mine a few months ago. I've only got this stick for the time being. Hoping my new hip will be fully operational soon.'

'You just be careful,' said Sam in a warning tone. 'We don't need any more accidents around here.'

'He's so bossy,' said Arthur, giving Tom a wink. 'And how long before you're able to get rid of your crutches?'

'About a week, the doctor said,' replied Tom.

'So what do you think of the house?' asked Sam.

Tom nodded his approval. 'Pretty amazing.'

'Isn't it?' said Sam, looking back up at his home. 'Took some doing but we finally made it.' He laughed. 'On the outside anyway.'

'I didn't think it would be so big,' said Tom, taking in the whole place.

Having grown up in foster homes, he had been amazed that he even had a friend who could own such a lavish home. Even his expensive flat in London paled into insignificance next to such an elegant mansion.

'Oh, we're just your average stately home in the middle of the countryside,' Arthur told him, smiling. 'Vast overheads and all.'

'We're trying to work on that,' said Sam, in a pointed tone.

'Indeed,' said Arthur, his eyes twinkling. 'In fact, we've even managed to reduce our staff numbers due to the fact that my housekeeper recently left her job.'

Sam and Arthur exchanged a private smile. Tom understood that Annie had actually been the housekeeper but, somewhere along the way, she and Sam had fallen in love and were planning a wedding later in the year.

Feeling awkward at the ease with which the men shared with each other, Tom turned around to look at the quiet grounds surrounding the house. The peace and tranquillity washed over him and he could feel himself beginning to relax. There were definitely worse places in which to spend a few days.

He spotted a couple of builders' vans parked next to what appeared to be a triple garage. 'I thought the house was finished?' he asked.

'I'm not sure it'll ever be finished,' Sam told him with a grimace. 'Anyway, they're here to finish up the new recording studio in the barn.' He pointed to an outbuilding, almost hidden behind some trees in the back of the grounds. 'My new money-spinning project. It's almost done,' Sam carried on. 'You should see it. State-of-the-art equipment. It's all there. You must be desperate to carry on working.'

The last thing Tom wanted to think about right now was his yet-to-be-even-started-on album.

Arthur must have spotted something in Tom's face as he stepped forward to say, 'I should think the only thing Tom is desperate for right now is a cup of tea and to rest his foot.'

'That sounds great,' said Tom, breaking into a grateful smile of thanks.

Following them inside, Tom couldn't help but stop and stare around the entrance hall. Despite the deep red walls, it was still a light and airy room. A wide, dark oak staircase curved up to the first floor. All along the stairwell were portraits of generations of the Harris family. From the double-heighted ceiling hung a chandelier, glittering in the afternoon sunshine. And when winter arrived, a large fireplace was waiting to be lit.

'This is one of the few rooms that has actually been finished,' said Sam, following his friend's admiring gaze.

'According to your fiancée, she would have preferred work to start on the kitchen instead,' said Arthur.

'It's next on the list,' said Sam, grinning. He turned to face Tom. 'We've had to prioritise. It's been an absolute nightmare, to be honest. We're a bit behind, thanks to some dodgy builders at the beginning. But at least the drawing room is finished. As is your guest bedroom, you'll be glad to hear. Actually, it used to be Annie's. I'm afraid, it might be a bit girly for your taste.'

'It'll be fine,' said Tom.

He had run away from so many foster homes that he had lost count of how many nights he had spent on park benches during his teenage years. So anything with a bed and a roof counted as okay with him.

Sam pointed to a large corridor on the opposite side of the hall. 'That's the east wing,' he said. 'The kitchen's down a couple of steps at the end of the corridor if you need it. Just help yourself. But watch out for the uneven tiles with your foot. It's still a real mess.'

'Where's Annie?' asked Arthur, looking around. 'She was very keen to meet Tom.'

'She's gone into the village,' Sam told him before turning to Tom. 'You'll get to meet her later. How about I get you settled in the drawing room and we'll get the kettle on.'

They were just heading into the west wing when they nearly crashed into an elegantly dressed old lady rushing out of a nearby room.

'Darlings, look at this,' she said to Sam, in an aristocratic tone of voice that sounded much like Arthur's. She thrust out a letter she was holding. 'He says he used to work here as an assistant gardener in the late eighties. Wanted to know if I could remember what the white rose was called in the front bed out there!' She rolled her eyes. 'Ye Gods, man. I don't even remember which husband I was married to back then!'

Sam gave her an indulgent smile. 'This is my Great-Aunt Rose. Aunty, this is Tom.'

She held out a bejewelled hand. 'Just Rose will do,' she said, with a naughty wink. 'Lovely to meet you. So nice to have more young blood in the house. Eh, Arthur? We don't want it turning into an old people's home with us elderly folks, do we?'

'Speak for yourself,' replied Arthur in a dry tone.

'Shall we have a little drink to celebrate the arrival of our new house guest?' asked Rose eagerly.

Arthur's grey eyebrows shot up. 'It's only four

o'clock,' he told her.

'Yes, but it's six o'clock in Nairobi and that's plenty late enough,' she replied, turning to head back into the room. 'Come and join us in the drawing room, darling.'

Tom presumed both the 'darling' as well as the invitation was for him, so he followed Rose into the first door on the left. It was another large, elegant room painted in soft green, with oak floorboards, comfy-looking sofas and chairs. The large sash windows overlooked the front grounds. There were framed photographs, antique ornaments and candlesticks everywhere. It felt homely, warm and welcoming.

Tom was interested to spot an old record player in a corner with a stack of vinyl LPs next to it. He wondered whom it belonged to. It reminded him of his gran's little bungalow, where there had always been music playing. He suppressed the pang of hurt that suddenly shot through him.

'So how long are you planning to be with us?' asked Rose, heading over to a globe that was on a stand. She lifted the lid and revealed a small drinks cabinet within. 'Not that there's any hurry for to you leave.'

'I'm not sure,' Tom told her, carefully sitting down on a sofa.

'Well, we've got plenty of room,' she replied, selecting a bottle of gin. 'Do come and go as you like. It's an open-door policy in our home. Especially to my bedroom.'

'Aunty!' Sam rolled his eyes. 'It's hardly surprising that you went through four husbands.'

'I'm still hoping for an uneven five,' she announced, turning to give Tom a wink. 'And I haven't had a toy boy since husband number two. The painter.'

'Yes, and we all remember how well that little adventure turned out,' drawled Arthur, sitting down next to Tom. 'It cost me a small fortune to pay the blighter off.'

'Whatever happened to those nude paintings?' said Sam with a thoughtful frown.

'A necessary bonfire,' said Arthur with a shudder.

They were all so at ease with each other, thought Tom. Despite the generational gap between old and young, they were obviously a really close, loving family. He knew Sam had a younger brother, Will, who was working away in Europe. Sam's parents were the only ones missing from the happy family set-up. Arthur's only son and daughter-in-law had been tragically killed when the boys had been young.

A close family was something Tom had never had, apart from his gran. It had been foster homes all the way for him since the age of four. Perhaps that was why he barely trusted anyone. If your own parents didn't want you, then why would anyone else?

But perhaps he could manage to stay for a few days at Willow Tree Hall. Who knew, maybe the new recording studio might even provide him with some inspiration?

After that, he was certain that he would want to retreat back to his flat in London. He would have had enough of family gatherings by then, no matter how welcoming they were.

They were just a further reminder of everything he had never had in the past and probably never would have.

# Chapter 7

Eleanor woke up with a start. It took her a moment to work out where she was, until the peace and quiet reminded her that she was back home in The Forge.

The tranquillity of Cranley village was always a shock after the noise of central London, where there were loud neighbours, packed pavements and people shouting into their mobiles wherever she turned.

With relief, she sank back against the soft pillow. She closed her eyes, intending to drift back to sleep when she heard the hee-haw of the donkey.

With a groan, she dragged herself out of bed and walked over to the window. Her bedroom overlooked the back garden, where she could see her mum shuffling slowly around the makeshift animal pens.

Eleanor quickly got dressed and headed downstairs, feeling irritated that she hadn't had time to straighten her hair or put on her make-up yet. In any case, her mother was the only person to have ever seen her without make-up on. But she still hated the feeling of not looking her best.

'Mum!' she said, heading straight outside. 'You should leave that to me.'

Her mum had been struggling to undo a large bale of hay that had appeared from goodness knows where.

'Morning, love,' said her mum, sinking down gratefully onto a nearby low wall, which looked as if it could crumble at any moment. 'It's fine. It just takes me a bit longer at the minute.'

'Tell me what to do,' said Eleanor.

'Daisy needs her breakfast,' she answered. 'You just need to scatter some of the hay around for her.'

Eleanor inwardly rolled her eyes. By naming the donkey Daisy, her mother appeared to have bonded with the animal. She sighed. The donkey was quite sweet in a chunky pony kind of way. But the garden was far too tiny for any kind of animal that size.

'She needs her water filling up as well.' Her mum pointed to an old tin bath which appeared to be the new watering hole in the garden.

Whilst her mum went inside and put the kettle on, Eleanor gave the donkey her breakfast.

She stretched her back as she straightened up, watching as the last petals of apple blossom drifted down in the gentle breeze onto the lawn. Or rather, the lack of it. The donkey and the goat had seen off any grass that might have been growing.

'Buttercup will need milking if you can manage it,' shouted her mum from the kitchen.

Eleanor spun around in shock. 'What? I'm not milking a goat!'

'Please, love.'

'Jeez.' Eleanor turned to look at the white goat who was chewing on some hay. 'What do you do with the milk?'

'Drink it, of course.'

Eleanor blanched. 'Shouldn't it be, I don't know, pasteurised or something? Boiled so that it's safe?'

Her mother stood by the back door and shook her head. 'No. It's absolutely fine.'

A little wooden stool was produced, which Eleanor recognised as one of her childhood ones. How times had changed, she thought, sitting down and placing a bucket under the goat's teats.

'Sorry about this,' she muttered, glancing at her newly manicured nails and wondering whether it was too late to put on a pair of gloves. But then again, what was the point when her eczema had become so bad that it was now at the base of nearly every finger on both hands.

Buttercup seemed quite happy to be milked. Which was more than could be said than Eleanor's point of view of the whole situation.

It took until late morning to sort out all the animals, by which time Eleanor was finally able to head back upstairs and put on her make-up and do her hair properly.

She had fed the donkey and goat, picking up a large bale of hay and getting a prickly rash down her arms in thanks. She had milked the goat and didn't really want to repeat that experience too often. She had also fed the kittens and stopped a few escaping or getting trampled under the donkey's hooves. She had chucked some pellets on the floor for the chickens whilst dodging their sharp beaks in order to pick out their freshly laid eggs. The tortoise had had its morning greens. The cockatoo had had its tray cleaned out whilst it had flown around the lounge and nearly out the back door. The battle to get it back in its cage had taken almost an hour. Finally the dogs had needed feeding and walking.

Now she stared at herself in the mirror in dismay, realising she was going to have to get changed into her second outfit of the day already. She was covered in fur, drool and other indistinguishable stains that she didn't want to think about. All in all, she felt a mess and looked it as well, which made her even more irritable. The fact that her mum was so grateful for her help with the animals made Eleanor feel a hundred times worse.

She just wished she didn't have to lie to her, that she could find a real job that would make her mum proud. But there were still no emails regarding any jobs. Instead her phone was full of messages from both Annie and Megan, giddily excited to see her. They had agreed to meet up at Willow Tree Hall that afternoon so that Annie could show Eleanor around her new home before going out to the pub for a much overdue drink to celebrate her friend's engagement.

Eleanor changed out of her dirty clothes and stared around the room as she sank onto the bed. The whole room was unchanged from her teenage years. Apart from the Spice Girls posters that had been ripped down at some point, of course. There were various dust-covered stuffed toys dotted around the bed. A few abandoned novels. And the cup awarded at the annual village summer fete for best collage, which she had made from dried petals. Sitting there, she felt trapped in a time machine. All the hopes and dreams that had led to nothing were now gathering dust around her too.

But she knew she had to force herself to carry on. The hope that any story about pop stars hanging around Willow Tree Hall might just be enough to get her job back. After all, they weren't just her own dreams and aspirations. They belonged to her mum as well.

And Eleanor couldn't let her down after everything they had been through.

# Chapter 8

Eleanor felt a strong sense of déjà vu when she walked down the street later that sunny afternoon. It was a route that she had taken most days in her childhood, picking up Megan first and then Annie as they walked to school, their cheerful chatter filling the air.

She turned to head up the front path to No 2 Cherry Tree Avenue. The garden was a little messier than she remembered. Probably because Megan's dad, who had been a keen gardener, had moved up to Scotland with her mum a few years previously, enabling Megan and her husband Neal to move in and have their own family home.

But at least their garden didn't have a donkey in it, thought Eleanor with a shudder.

She had barely reached the front door when it was flung open and Megan rushed out.

'I couldn't wait any longer!' she almost shouted, pulling Eleanor into an enormous bear hug. 'It's so good to see you!'

'And you too,' said Eleanor, her teary words muffled in her friend's shoulder.

She inhaled the familiar scent of Coco Mademoiselle

as she was clutched tight. She had a sudden memory of picking out the perfume bottle in Selfridges for her friend's birthday a few years ago.

'Let me look at you,' said Megan, stepping back to give her a wide smile. 'As bloody glamorous as always, I see.'

Eleanor glanced down. It was true that she had taken care with her outfit, but it was only a smart-casual look of a pair of white jeans, wedges and cute pale blue top and matching cover-up. Her elegant armour against the real world. Of course, her friend hadn't seen her a couple of hours earlier, milking a goat for goodness' sake!

'I should have worn something smarter,' muttered Megan.

'You look great,' replied Eleanor automatically.

It was almost true. Megan was wearing black leggings and a long pink tunic top which clashed with her red hair but concealed her mummy tummy.

'It's the only thing that isn't covered in some kind of stain,' said Megan, with a shrug.

'It's fine. Anyway, you've cut your hair,' said Eleanor, in approval.

Megan touched the red strands that only just reached her shoulders now. 'Oh, that was months ago, didn't I tell you? It takes less time than when it was long.'

Months? Eleanor bit her lip. It had been too long since she'd caught up with her friends. Especially after such a brief visit at Christmas.

But Megan's round cheerful face looked just as youthful as always, if you didn't look too closely at the dark shadows under her eyes. That was probably due to having three children under the age of six.

'Where are the kids?' Eleanor asked, peering around to peek into the hallway. 'I haven't seen them for ages and need my godmother hugs.'

Megan shook her head. 'Neal's mum has got them for tea as he's working late again. I told her it was an emergency as I haven't seen you for so long.' She jangled a heavy set of keys in her hand. 'Come on,' she said, slamming the front door shut and heading towards a grubby Fiesta parked in the street. 'You can see them another time. Annie's desperate to see you as well. And I need a drink after being on playground duty this afternoon.'

Eleanor slipped into the passenger seat, dismayed to see a host of grubby marks and crumbs. Hopefully her white jeans would survive intact.

'Sorry about the mess,' said Megan, crunching the car into gear before setting off. 'I'd blame the kids, but it's mostly me.'

It was warm in the car, so Eleanor wound down the window. The weather forecasters were promising a hot summer, but they had all heard that too many times before to believe it would come true.

However, the wild rhododendron bushes that grew

along the wide road were full of bright purple and pink flowers. It was a riot of colour and immediately cheered her up after such a dismal few days.

Megan was driving pretty quickly in her haste to get all three of them together, so they were soon going down the long bumpy driveway towards Willow Tree Hall.

'I haven't been up here in years,' said Eleanor, staring out of the window at the overgrown fields, a riot of long grass and wild flowers. Beyond the large willow tree that stood in the front of the house, the elegant stately home came into view. She had forgotten how huge it was. 'It's so beautiful.'

Megan nodded her head as she crunched down a gear. 'Isn't it? Mind you, I come up here at least twice a week to help clean the place so I'm almost used to it.'

Eleanor shook her head in disbelief. 'I still can't believe Annie lives in a place like this. And not as an employee any more but as a member of the family.'

'Talk of the upwardly mobile devil,' said Megan, screeching the car to a halt and pulling up the handbrake. 'There she is.'

As she got out of the car, Eleanor looked across to the huge double front door to where her friend had just appeared. Desperately trying not to run, Annie was speed-walking towards the car, the ponytail holding her long blonde hair waving back and forth.

'Yay! You're here at last!' said Annie, grinning. She stepped forward to envelop Eleanor in a warm hug. It wasn't quite as crushing as Megan's but it was just as genuine.

'Hi there, your majesty,' said Eleanor, breaking into a cheeky grin.

'Shut up,' muttered Annie, a red blush spreading across her cheeks. She looked radiantly pretty as always. Her eyes lit up with happiness at having her friends all together at last.

Although dressed in skinny jeans and pale yellow T-shirt, Annie looked relaxed in her elegant surroundings. After all, she was home now. This countess-to-be was more Primark than Harrods, but maybe that wasn't a bad thing, thought Eleanor. She could bring some humility to such an intimidating place.

'Right,' said Eleanor. 'First things first. Show me your ring!'

Annie automatically held out her hand, the square diamond solitaire engagement ring flashed in the sunlight.

'Wow, that's gorgeous! Very classy,' said Eleanor, nodding in approval.

She also noted Annie's soft, smooth hands which were in marked contrast to her own red, flaky ones. But then again, her friend probably had no stress to deal with. After all, she was the one living in a huge mansion with the man she loved.

'It was very expensive,' added Megan. 'That's where your new kitchen went.'

'Shurrup,' said Annie, grinning. 'So? Do you want to look around?'

'Of course I do,' Eleanor told her, in an eager tone. 'I've never ever been inside, I think.'

'Why would you?' said Megan with a wink, as they headed towards the front door. 'We're only the country peasants after all.'

Annie rolled her eyes. 'If you two are going to carry on like this, I'll shut you in the servants' quarters. And they haven't been renovated yet.'

Eleanor couldn't stop smiling. It was so lovely to be back in their threesome once more. She was always more relaxed when she was with her friends. She had never felt like this at any time during her years in London. But that's because no one knew her as well as Annie and Megan.

They stepped inside and Eleanor stopped to stare around the vast entrance hall in amazement. 'Wow,' she murmured. 'It's so elegant.'

'That's one of my favourite bits too,' said Annie, following her gaze high up to the huge chandelier hanging overhead.

'If this had been a year ago, you wouldn't want to have been standing underneath it,' said Megan with a grimace. 'Unless you wanted a trip to A&E.'

'That's true,' said Annie, nodding. 'The whole place was falling apart.'

Eleanor remembered the frantic texts and calls from

Annie at that time. 'It's hard to believe it never looked as lovely as this.'

'Ugh, honestly, some days she was covered from head to foot in dust,' carried on Megan.

'And you could see the sky through the patches in the roof,' said Annie, with a smile of remembrance. 'Happy days.'

'Seriously?' asked Eleanor.

Annie nodded.

'When the builders arrived so did Sam,' cooed Megan. 'She had a crush on him from the moment they met.'

As she and Annie grinned at each other, for a second, Eleanor felt a little out of the loop. They had obviously gone through quite a bit together. *Without her.*

She felt a jolt of worry about being left behind. But then, whose fault was that?

Annie must have picked up on something in her friend's face. 'You wouldn't have wanted to be here in all that dust and dirt,' she said. 'Not in those lovely clothes of yours. Come on, I'll show you the rest. We'll start with the west wing.'

'You have separate wings?' muttered Eleanor, still looking around in amazement.

'Doesn't mean either of them aren't still a mess,' said Megan, with a knowing smile.

Eleanor's disbelief in her friend's new home continued past the elegant drawing room and into the library. A long wall was covered from floor to ceiling with a vast number of bookcases filled with numerous classics. There was also a full-size snooker table which looked to have been used recently, although one end was propped up with more books.

'All the windows are new,' said Annie. 'And the fireplaces work too, thank goodness. It was so cold in here last winter.'

But the rest of the room was obviously still waiting to be refurbished.

On the opposite side of the corridor was Arthur's study, which was a bit messy, although not as bad as the music room, which Sam was utilising for his work. That was covered in piles of paperwork. Both rooms also had new windows, but the remaining furniture looked ancient and there were still cracks in the plaster across the walls.

They carried on to the end of the corridor.

'This is the ballroom,' announced Annie as they entered the last room.

Eleanor's mouth dropped open. 'You have a ballroom?'

'Doesn't everyone?' said Megan, with a grin.

Eleanor stared around in wonder. Despite the shabbiness and decay of the peeling and cracked ceiling, the double-aspect room was enormous, with new windows at the front and huge French doors at the back leading onto the garden. The walls were patterned with paintings, their frames gilded with what could have been gold many years ago. It was hard to tell under all the dust and grime of the years.

'Isn't it wonderful?' said Annie, walking slowly around the room. 'Apparently even members of the royal family used to come to the parties here. And this is where I'm going to have my wedding reception! Can you imagine? Me!'

Annie was so cheerful despite living in what appeared to be semi-derelict conditions.

'Is it going to be cleaned up before the big day?' asked Eleanor, wondering how quickly that was going to happen.

'Of course,' said Annie, waving a hand as if it were a small matter. 'Phase three of the building work starts this autumn and it's going to be all about the ballroom. And our wedding!' Annie was positively giddy as she spun around to face them both. 'Right. Now that we're *finally* together for the first time since I got engaged, there's something I want to ask you both. Will you be my bridesmaids?'

There was a collective shriek. 'Oh my god! Of course!' they both replied, rushing over for a teary group hug.

'I can't believe you've waited this long to ask us!' moaned Megan.

'I had to wait for Eleanor to be here so I could ask you face to face. I didn't want to do something this important on the phone,' Annie told her, before looking anxiously at Eleanor. 'You will be here, won't you? I mean, not just for the wedding but for some of the other stuff as well.'

'Of course I will,' Eleanor told her. 'You know that.'

But it surprised her that Annie obviously didn't know. That both she and Megan thought that there was even a possibility that she wouldn't be there to support her best friend when she was getting married.

'I always knew you'd ask us,' said Megan. 'After all, you were both my bridesmaids.'

'We know,' drawled Eleanor. 'We still haven't forgiven you for those bright pink meringues you made us wear.'

'Don't worry,' said Annie, with a shudder. 'This time it's understated elegance all the way, I promise. Eleanor can help us out with that.'

'Absolutely,' said Eleanor, nodding.

'And then we can repay the favour for when she gets married,' said Megan.

Eleanor grimaced and quickly turned away. She had seen what marriage did to couples and was determined to hold off for as long as humanly possible if not forever. Besides, she was more worried about finding a job than a husband at the moment.

'Come on,' said Annie. 'I'll grab my handbag and then let's go and get a drink. We've got so much to catch up on.'

They headed back along the corridor to the entrance hall.

'What about upstairs?' asked Eleanor, glancing up the wide stairwell.

'I'll show you up there next time,' said Annie, still walking. 'Besides, Tom's still asleep and I don't want to disturb him.'

'Tom?' said Eleanor, raising her eyebrows. 'Is that Sam's brother?'

'No, that's Will,' said Megan, her eyes gleaming. 'She means Tom as in Tommy King. In which case, I think we should definitely disturb him. Even I haven't met wonder boy yet.'

'Shush,' said Annie, heading towards a corridor on the opposite side of the wide entrance hall.

Eleanor glanced up the stairs as she followed them. So Tommy King was actually staying there at the house with them? This was unbelievably good luck on her part! She had assumed he was in rehab after he passed out in public a few days ago. Instead he was here in Willow Tree Hall!

Would he be as wild and crazy as everyone suggested? Was he out of control? The idea of a story on one of the world's biggest superstars was beginning to become a reality. If she ever got to meet him, of course.

Eleanor was still mulling over her yet-to-be told story as they went past a couple of rooms in the west wing, one of which appeared to be the dining room as it had a large table but it was still in a mess. Then they went down a couple of steps into the kitchen.

She suddenly had a vast appreciation as to how derelict the whole place had been before the house had begun to be renovated. The kitchen cupboards were shabby and rotten, the hinges barely holding onto the doors. The sink was cracked. The tiled floor very uneven. The pine table in the middle was scratched and stained.

'Isn't it awful?' said Annie, looking cheerful as she picked up her handbag. 'But Sam promises me it's next on the list.'

'I would have thought the kitchen would have been the first thing to get done,' said Eleanor, looking around in dismay.

'You're kidding,' said Megan. 'The whole place had no windows or heating for a long time.'

'Come on,' said Annie, heading for the door. 'Time to celebrate!'

Eleanor almost wanted to hang back, desperate to meet Tommy King and begin work on the story that would propel her back to London.

But for the first time in a long while, she actually felt as if she had something to celebrate. Okay so she didn't have a job, didn't have her exclusive story and perhaps she didn't even have a boyfriend or a home to call her own, but she had her friends, the very best friends in the world.

And that, for now, was worth raising a drink to.

*

It was such a nice afternoon that they decided to sit outside in the beer garden of the Rose and Crown pub. Besides, there was really nowhere else to go out in Cranley for a drink. The pub was full of people stopping off after work, rolling up their shirtsleeves and shrugging off their jackets in the warmth of the sun.

Eleanor poured out the drinks and then placed the bottle of Prosecco back in the ice bucket.

'Congratulations,' she said, holding up her drink.

'Cheers,' said Megan, as they chinked their glasses together.

'Here's to being together again,' said Annie, with a wide smile.

'And to your wedding,' added Eleanor before taking a sip of the icy cold drink. 'It's been so long since I came here,' she said, glancing around the other wooden benches and realising that she didn't really recognise anyone.

'We don't really come here much these days either,' said Megan. 'There's never any time – or money – to go out.'

'Well, I don't care where we are just as long as we're together,' said Annie, reaching out to squeeze Eleanor's hand across the table. 'You're finally home. I can't believe it.'

'Yeah,' drawled Megan. 'What gives?'

'What are you talking about?' asked Eleanor.

'I mean you coming home. Now. In June,' said Megan. 'It's not Christmas, Mother's Day or anyone's birthday. What's happened? Is everything okay?'

Eleanor was mortified. Was that how they saw her? And was it true?

'I was just desperate to see you both after so long,' she replied. 'And with Mum breaking her ankle, I need to give her a hand for a while.'

Her pulse drummed with the stress of leaving out the rest of the reason for her unexpected visit. She hated keeping secrets from them both.

Megan took another sip of her Prosecco. 'She is getting a bit accident-prone, bless her. First her wrist and now her foot.'

Eleanor was nonplussed. 'Her wrist? What are you talking about?'

'She slipped on some ice during the winter and hurt her wrist,' said Annie, frowning. 'Didn't she tell you?'

Eleanor shook her head.

'It was only a sprain,' said Annie quickly, exchanging a quick look with Megan. 'I mean, nothing for you to worry about.'

Eleanor shifted in her seat. What else didn't she know?

She tried to recover. 'And look at you now,' she said,

looking across the table at Annie. 'You've made it. You're going to be a, what is it again?'

'A countess,' said Annie, blushing. 'But that's years away. Only when Sam inherits the full title. I'm happy being plain old Mrs Annie Harris in the meantime.'

'She's in luurve,' cooed Megan. 'But he's a pretty nice guy, so he gets my vote.'

'I can't wait to meet him again,' said Eleanor. 'I can barely remember him from when we were younger.'

'He's good enough for our friend,' said Megan in a fake haughty tone, causing them to laugh. 'And he's got more blue blood than my Neal.'

'Yes, but you're lucky too,' said Annie, ever the fair one. 'You're happily married with three beautiful children.'

'Yes,' said Megan with a sigh. 'Remember we used to go to the health club and sit in the Jacuzzi with a glass of wine and think it was luxury? Now it's having a bowel movement without someone shouting at me through the door wanting to come in.'

Annie and Eleanor laughed, even though Megan didn't join in quite so much.

'Wait a minute. So now I'm best friends with a future countess and mother of the year?' said Eleanor. 'God, I've just realised. Am I the only unmarried spinster of the parish now?'

'Probably,' said Megan, nodding before looking at Annie. 'So does that make me your maid of honour?'

'Maid of dishonour, more like,' said Eleanor, with a smile.

'Exactly,' said Megan, laughing. 'Can't wait for the hen party.'

'I don't care what you call yourselves,' said Annie. 'I just want you both with me on the day. And to help with everything before then. There's so much to plan!'

'Count me in,' said Megan. 'I need some romance in my life.'

'Me too,' said Eleanor, nodding.

'What about Lucas?' said Annie, with a gleam. 'I thought you two had moved in together.'

Eleanor sighed and shook her head, deciding to come clean about some of her life. 'We're taking a break. His decision.'

'Oh no! You must be heartbroken,' said Annie.

Eleanor shrugged her shoulders. 'That's the thing. I should be, shouldn't I? We were together for two years. But I'm not upset. Not really.'

'Maybe you both need a break to think about what you really want,' said Annie, giving her hand a squeeze.

Eleanor nodded. 'Maybe.'

'And if he's not the one, then you're bound to meet some other rich banker the next time you go to one of those Bank of England parties, said Megan. 'I mean, you're out every night. I know you have to entertain for your job in the finance sector but even so, I'd kill for your social life.'

Eleanor drained her glass, wondering how to even begin to tell them that she'd lost her job.

'I can just imagine your flash apartment in the city,' carried on Megan. 'I mean, look at what you're wearing. You've got it all. Fashion. Parties. Nightlife. It's all come together for you. I'm so bloody jealous I could cry.'

Eleanor knew that her apartment had been far from flash. It had been damp and cold. It had also had subsidence. But her friends, just like her mum, had always expected so much from her. Too much. A great career. A wonderful life in the city. She didn't want to let them down.

'Yeah, you're this amazing career girl and all I want is a functioning kitchen!' laughed Annie.

Eleanor took a deep breath. It was time to confess about her so-called perfect life. But the conversation had already moved onto the wedding once more. Annie looked so excited and it was such a lovely, happy subject that Eleanor didn't want to bring down their mood. So she decided she would definitely tell them the next time they were together.

Unless she met Tommy King, of course. Because then she could write up her exclusive story on him and she wouldn't have to reveal any of her lies to her friends.

Then she could carry on pretending. Forever, if necessary.

# Chapter 9

Tom drank his coffee on the sunny back patio whilst sitting on a rusty bench, looking across the grounds at the back of Willow Tree Hall.

He had woken up in his guest bedroom and been astonished to find it was late afternoon. The painkillers he was on had completely messed up his head and body clock. But his foot was still too painful not to be able to function without them.

So, despite feeling drowsy most of the previous day, he had then found himself wide awake until almost dawn, watching rubbish on his iPad.

It was also a bit strange sleeping in such a large place. In a way, it reminded him of growing up in the children's homes. Aware of people sleeping all around him in different rooms. And of him being different, as usual. Standing out. A loner.

Except this was a family. Which was also new to him. And that they were kind and affectionate towards each other. And to him too.

But during dinner last night, he had found the questions and chatter almost too much to bear. And the food too.

'How's the mash?' Annie had asked. 'No lumps, are there?'

'It's great,' Tom had replied. 'I haven't had a home-cooked meal like this since…' Then his voice had trailed off as the only lump had then been in his throat as he remembered being at his gran's house.

The silence had stretched out across the table. He had glanced up briefly to see Arthur looking at him. Then the Earl had suddenly said, 'Do you know, I think we have cygnets down by the river?'

'Do we really?' Rose had replied. 'How sweet. I must go and see.'

'Not in your high heels,' Arthur had told her, with a soft smile.

'I do have wellington boots, you know,' she had countered. 'They just happen to be leopard-skin-patterned.'

The conversation had swiftly moved on and Tom had felt himself relax once more. He knew that Arthur had spoken to take away his embarrassment and he was grateful. They were generous with their hearts and spirit towards him.

It was all a stark contrast to his own family experiences.

It was hard growing up knowing that your own parents didn't want you. But he had learnt the lesson so well that the walls he put up around himself kept out everyone else. Including people wanting to foster or adopt him. He rebelled hard against any kind offers, thinking that strangers would only let him down even more so than his own kin. His gran had suffered ill health ever since her husband had died and wasn't able to bring up him by herself much to her dismay. So he battled and raged against everyone else until he was old enough to fend for himself.

And that's how he'd lived his life ever since, which made this new living arrangement even more strange.

Tom was only intending to stay at Willow Tree Hall a few more days, but in the meantime, it was a welcome refuge. The press was still going crazy trying to get hold of him. Even suggesting that he was probably drying out at rehab. He just needed to hide out in the countryside and wait for the hubbub to calm down.

Sam had placed him in the only guest bedroom that had been completed. It was Annie's old room and had thick carpets, a comfortable bed and a sweet fireplace.

'Six months ago, you would have been sleeping in a hurricane of a draught,' Sam had told him. 'The house really was in a shocking state. It's taken us this long to drag it into being weatherproof.'

'Trust me, I've slept in a lot worse,' Tom had said, thinking of the occasional nights' sleep on the streets when he was young and life became too much.

'I know,' replied Sam, softly.

He was the only one that knew. The only one that perhaps understood. But Sam's parents hadn't abandoned him. They had died. But the hole left by a lack of parents in both of their lives had ramifications that had rippled out beyond that time and into the present.

Tom blinked away the memories and took refuge in the view of the grounds. Huge wild rhododendron bushes grew at the far boundary, smothered in pale lilac and bright pink blooms. The whole ground was green and fresh with the new growth of summer A little too much growth, he added to himself, looking at the overgrown hedges and bushes. Nature was running rampant as far as the eye could see. But the birdsong and buzz of insects was a welcome change to the hum of heavy traffic. He glanced back to the huge stately home. So, here he was. On a large country estate belonging to an ancient ancestral family. If only those that had known him when he was younger could see him now.

'You're nothing.' He could hear the taunts now in the playground. 'Nobody wanted you, did they? Your dad walked out. Not even your mum liked you.'

The smug mocking face had soon become bloodied when it came into contact with Tom's fist. He had learnt from a young age that it was fight or flight. And he had never been one to run away.

What had happened to the spoilt, rich boy who had picked on him all those years ago? Tom didn't care. Because Tom was now the one with money. The one with the fame and fortune.

So why did he feel so unhappy? Why did he feel like he had the whole world and yet felt empty?

'I suppose you smashed your own face against a wall, did you?' He could see his gran's concern as she looked at yet another black eye. She had known. Of course she had. 'Or did you fall off your bike again?'

'Got any cherry cake?' he would say, ignoring her question.

Of course she did. There was always cherry cake. His favourite.

He sighed, so soft it disappeared on the breeze as he sat there. He had tried buying a cherry cake recently, but it hadn't tasted the same. The missing ingredient was his gran's love.

He felt Sam stand next to him. 'Not so bad, is it?' he said, his voice full of pride as he looked out across the grounds.

'Definitely not bad,' said Tom, draining his coffee cup.

'Are you up to a tour of the grounds?' Sam nodded at the crutches. 'Unless your foot is too painful.'

It was. And the codeine was making him feel woozy. But he needed to try and wake up.

'Unless you're thinking about jogging round,' said Tom, as he slowly stood up.

'Well, the estate actually stretches for about five miles, but I'll keep it local for today,' said Sam, breaking into a grin.

They walked slowly along the patio which spread across the length of the back of the house.

'Watch your step,' warned Sam. 'You don't want to do the other foot in.'

It was pretty uneven as many of the paving slabs were broken, with weeds growing through them.

'We ran out of money before I could do the garden,' Sam explained, with an apologetic smile.' But we still have Bert.'

'Who?' said Tom.

'Bert is our elderly gardener.' Sam glanced around him and then lowered his voice. 'He's nearly as old as grandad. In fact, I think they even went to school together. But he still wanders up twice a week to keep an eye on the vegetable patch. The rest, well, as you can see, it needs something more drastic. But Annie will kill me if I don't get the kitchen sorted next.'

Tom noted that Sam's eyes were softened with love as he spoke about Annie.

Beyond the triple garage were a couple of outbuildings in the distance. 'That's the old dairy house,' said Sam. 'There's also a large stable block and, somewhere in the far distance, is the gamekeeper's cottage. Just by the river. All in a complete state of disrepair, of course. It's so frustrating. I care so much about trying to preserve the heritage of the place. I want to safeguard it for generations to come.' He sighed. 'If only there wasn't quite so much of it.'

Tom realised that beautiful Willow Tree Hall also came with a heavy burden of responsibility.

He tried to cheer Sam up. 'You've got a river?'

'Just the one mile that goes through our grounds,' said Sam. 'Thankfully that doesn't need any investment. Grandad taught me to fish down there. I'll have to show you one day.'

Tom looked over with interest. Fishing he could certainly handle. On the boundary of the lawn, there was an ancient wood. A faint haze of blue remained from the faded bluebells that must have carpeted the ground in the spring.

'But it's a bit of a trek on crutches and our interest lies the other way,' said Sam.

They turned and slowly went back across the patchy patio.

'If you need anything whilst you're here, just let me or Annie know.' Sam cleared his throat. 'Are you two getting on all right?'

Tom smiled to himself. He knew what Sam was asking.

'I like her,' Tom told him.

He had found Annie warm and friendly. And she was certainly a much better fit for his friend that his previous girlfriend, the famous singer Cassandra. Although her own career had come to an abrupt halt just recently. Tom didn't feel particularly sorry for her. She had, unknown to Sam, made a pass at Tom one evening the previous year. But Tom wasn't about to cheat on his friend, especially for someone as high-maintenance as the famous diva.

Sam beamed. 'Annie's one in a million,' he said, his voice full of love. 'It's like a bloody thunderbolt. You'll know. When it happens to you.'

Tom wasn't so convinced. To let someone love you, you had to trust them completely and open yourself up to let them in. He just couldn't see himself ever giving that much of himself to anyone.

As they reached the east side of the patio, the paving slabs stopped and gave way to a worn stony path.

'There's a walled garden over there,' said Sam, as they carried on. 'That's the vegetable patch, which at least is well tended. But as you can see, the rest of it is run wild.' He sighed. 'Oh well. We'll get there eventually.'

Tom looked out behind him. The lawn was vast and overgrown, already up to almost knee-height. It desperately needed cutting.

The path was pretty uneven and Tom was careful not to catch one of his crutches on a tree root.

'We'll have to get this sorted if we're going to be taking a lot of people down here,' muttered Sam, mainly to himself.

'You're expecting visitors to the vegetable patch?' asked Tom.

Sam grinned. 'To the recording studio,' he said,

pointing at a large barn in the near distance. 'This was my brainwave. We need all the money we can get, so I was hoping to rent it out to my artists instead of the expensive studios in London. Hopefully it'll help keep me down here more often and maybe the grounds and house will provide a bit of inspiration for everyone as well.'

That was the thing about having a good manager, thought Tom. Sam was well organised and that left Tom able to focus on exactly what he wanted. The music.

He felt the jolt of guilt once more that the music, for once, wasn't coming. That it felt more like a burden than a gift. He had been forcing songs out, but they were pretty terrible. They would probably be hits anyway thanks to his name, but he knew deep down that they were awful. The problem was that they weren't coming from the heart. But for now his heart wasn't telling him what it wanted. He was afraid that it might never do so again. That perhaps he had used up all inspiration and that there was nothing left.

To take his mind off his worries, he asked, 'What was this place before you resurrected it?' as they drew near a large barn which still had a full skip of builders' rubbish outside.

'The cowshed,' said Sam with a sheepish grin. 'But I think we've finally got rid of the smell.'

He pushed open the door and they went inside. The large empty space inside the barn had actually been divided into two. The first area was the control room containing the digital equipment required for recording, editing and mixing the music. Through a window Tom could see the second room, the actual studio. This had obviously been soundproofed and set up to maximise the quality of the recording. It was mainly empty, apart from a couple of chairs and extensive microphones.

'I'm impressed,' he said, nodding.

'There was so much hassle in London over recording studios that it's nice to get things simple again. As it happens, we were lucky enough to have Dan Fraser live in the next county. He's one of the best sound engineers I've ever come across. We've got all the latest equipment.'

Tom looked down at the recording deck. To him it looked like some kind of Star Trek control desk, a vast array of switches and levers.

'It's mainly a project studio,' carried on Sam. 'I just wanted some place where you could all come out and chill. There's so much pressure in hiring a studio. Here there's no time limits, no constraints. Get relaxed and the music will be quality stuff.'

Tom blew out a silent sigh. His last album had been a massive, professional affair. Lots of edits and songs fiddled with. Not much quality, in his opinion. This time he wanted to strip the music down to the bare minimum. Just him, his guitar and a piano to start with. The guitar that he hadn't even picked up in weeks.

Sam had privately agreed that his previous album had been overproduced and had agreed that back to basics was the way forward for his artist.

Tom was hoping that the new recording studio would be the start of a different direction. He just hoped he could think up some new songs to use it.

# Chapter 10

Sometime in the afternoon and still struggling with a Prosecco-induced headache from her night out with the girls the previous evening, Eleanor flung open the back door, feeling close to despair.

'How was the walk?' asked her mum.

Eleanor glanced down at herself. 'I can't remember,' she replied, picking a lump of what she hoped was mud off her T-shirt. 'I was too busy hiding behind a tree.' She looked across at the Great Dane as he slurped his way down the water bowl in seconds flat, leaving a trail of water across the floor. 'He's an absolute terror. I'll be thankful when he goes back home this weekend. I will never understand what it is you like about them.'

The dog finished his drink before trotting up to collapse next to her mum, who leant down and stroked his head. 'Unconditional love,' she replied, choosing not to notice the water stain now appearing down her leggings. 'They don't care how scruffy I am.'

Eleanor stared down at her damp, slightly torn, muddy jeans which had been quite expensive. 'Well, that's where we must differ.'

'You've always liked to look nice,' said her mum,

nodding her approval. 'I think you must get that from your father.' She cleared her throat before continuing. 'Have you spoken to him recently?'

Eleanor shook her head. 'No. He doesn't bother much with me these days.'

What was the point? Her mum was the better person. The nice parent. The caring one. The peacemaker, despite the way he had treated her. Her dad only contacted her at Christmas and on her birthday. And then it was just out of guilt.

'I'm going up to get showered and changed,' she announced, heading up the stairs, feeling desperate to look like herself again.

'What are your plans for the rest of the day?' her mum called up.

'I thought I'd see the girls tonight if you don't need me to do anything for a few hours.'

Eleanor was keen to at least make a start with her story about Tommy King. But she was also anxious to catch up with the girls again, just in case she ended up heading back to London in the near future.

She called Megan first after her shower. 'Hey,' she said. 'What are you up to later? I thought we could meet up.'

'Really?' said Megan, sounding surprised. 'That would be great. We only usually get to see you once before you bugger off to the city to be with your more glamorous friends.'

Eleanor felt sheepish at the gentle ribbing, but knew in her heart that it was probably true. She hadn't spent an awful lot of time with Megan or Annie in recent months. Or years, come to think of it. She had to start making amends.

'What about your job?' carried on Megan.

Eleanor gulped. Was it possible that Megan had guessed what had happened? Surely not.

'They've given me some extra time because of Mum's leg. So how about we meet up later for a drink?'

'I'm not sure I can stomach any alcohol again. I haven't recovered from yesterday yet. But sure. We'll do something. Neal can have the kids for once.'

'The only thing is, I don't have a car,' said Eleanor.

'No worries. I'll pick you up.'

The lack of a car was a bit annoying, especially as there was nowhere around to hire one from. Also, Eleanor was reluctant to spend her three months' pay-off from the magazine. Goodness knows how long she would have to make that last. She knew that if she got desperate she could always borrow her Mum's bicycle. But that had a basket on the front and more rust than actual solid metal. But there was no public transport in the middle of the countryside. She longed for the ease of the underground and red double-decker buses.

Dwelling over the ease of her old life, she sent a quick text to Lucas.

Hi. Save me, she wrote. I'm knee deep in the

countryside, surrounded by farmyard animals. Please send an SOS package of caviar and Prosecco immediately.

But she got no reply, although she could see that he had read the message.

With nothing else to do, she repainted her nails and smoothed on some more antiseptic cream in the hope that it might help the eczema on her hands.

The hours dragged by until Megan picked her up.

Her friend raised her eyebrows when she arrived. 'Nice outfit,' she said, a smile playing on her lips. 'I thought we were staying in at the Hall unless we're going to a wine bar or something?'

Eleanor glanced down, feeling slightly overdressed compared to Megan's cut-off jeans and baggy T-shirt. Perhaps her khaki silk jumpsuit and high heels were a bit much in the countryside.

'Shall I get changed?' she asked.

Megan shook her head. 'God, no! We need a bit of glamour around here.'

When they arrived at Willow Tree Hall, they found Annie in the drawing room.

'You always look so pretty,' said Annie, with a sigh when she saw them. She was wearing her usual skinny jeans.

'It's only clothes,' said Eleanor, with a shrug. She had got so used to wearing her designer armour that she had forgotten how to dress down these days. Even Lucas had expected her to maintain a certain glamour, she realised.

'Does anybody fancy a gin and tonic?' asked Annie. 'Sam said he can always drop you both home. Unless you just want a cup of tea?'

'Bring on the gin!' said Megan, her eyes gleaming as her hangover was quickly forgotten. 'Two school nights in a row. How naughty!'

Whilst Annie went to find the glasses, Eleanor settled down on the sofa, trying to take in the size and style of the drawing room. It was stylish but homely. Modern but scattered with antiques. And the sofas were pretty comfortable too, she thought. It was a large room with high ceilings and a vast fireplace. But it felt used and lived in, as if the family had always gathered there.

'Who was your interior decorator?' she asked, when Annie finally returned.

'A friend of Sam's,' Annie told her, placing the tray holding three glasses and a bottle of tonic between them on the coffee table. Then she headed over to a globe, which appeared to house the alcohol. 'He's called Alex. A right character.'

'He's an absolute hoot,' added Megan, reaching out to pour them each a large drink. 'Are you going to invite him to your hen night? It'd be hysterical if he was there.'

'I haven't even got that far.' Annie blew out a sigh. 'There's so much to think about.' She stared at the pile of wedding magazines on a nearby table. 'I've got so many checklists to start on. And it all costs so much money.' Annie's voice trailed off. It seemed that stately homes were astronomical to run and that the lavish wedding that she had dreamed about was under threat.

'Well, at least you've got the venue sorted,' said Eleanor.

'Even if the ballroom isn't renovated yet,' Annie reminded her, biting her lip.

Eleanor wished she could help her friend out. Even staying with Lucas rent-free for the past three months hadn't freed up any more money. All her resources had been spent on the latest fashion, shoes and make-up. She had used every penny to keep up appearances on a life that, unbeknownst to her, was actually falling apart.

'You'll be fine,' said Eleanor. 'We'll help you with organising everything.'

'Even when you're back in London?' asked Annie, looking hopeful. 'I know you're busy, but that would be great.'

Eleanor nodded. 'Of course.'

Here it was. Now was the chance to confess everything to her friends. To tell them that she might not be returning to London for a while, if ever. But before she could speak, they were interrupted by a glamorous older lady sweeping in.

'Hi Rose,' said Megan.

'Hello, darlings,' said Rose, blowing an air kiss at Megan and Annie. 'I'm on my way to the village hall. I must show my face, otherwise they'll have nothing decent to look at.' She grinned as she turned to face Eleanor. 'Hello. Have we met?'

Eleanor shook her head. 'I don't think so.'

'This is Sam's Aunt Rose,' said Annie. 'This is Eleanor.'

'Ah! The famous Eleanor. These girls talk non-stop about you.' Her eyes gleamed at Eleanor's silk jumpsuit. 'Sweetie, that's beautiful. Prada?'

Eleanor was surprised. 'Yes. Although it's a few seasons old now. How did you know?'

'I used to work in the fashion industry and still keep up with all the latest styles. Well, it'll be lovely to have someone else as glamorous as me around here.' She gave Eleanor a cheeky wink.

'You should see Rose's wardrobes,' Annie told her. 'It's like *Vogue* magazine up there.'

Eleanor had already noted the classic Chanel jacket and trendy flared trousers along with many strings of pearls. This was definitely a lady with style.

Rose bent down to kiss Annie's cheek. 'One day I'll get you dressed up as well.'

Annie blushed. 'You know I don't do that very often. Anyway, Eleanor's always been the smart, fashionable one.'

'Well, at least I'm glad to see you girls are having a little drinkie,' said Rose, pointing at the gin bottle. 'We're going to have such fun this summer, especially if we keep the Pimm's flowing.' She placed a hand on

Annie's shoulder. 'By the way, darling, as future countess, you need to come along to the WI meeting I'm hosting here tomorrow evening. They keep asking for you.'

Annie looked horrified. 'I'm not sure I'm up to that.'

'Of course you are,' said Rose. She appeared to be the type of person that would never be flummoxed in any situation. 'Bring your gorgeous girls here for support. You'll be fine. It's deadly dull, of course. They're in desperate need of our style and wit.'

After Rose had swept out, Annie took a large gulp of her drink. 'I'm not sure that the village is ready to see me as the next countess. They're probably all going to look down their nose at the former housekeeper.'

'Just be yourself and they'll love you,' Eleanor told her.

'Exactly,' said Megan with a firm nod.

Annie took another gulp of her drink, still looking nervous. Eleanor understood why. Annie had been badly bullied when she had been growing up and even now had trouble believing in herself.

'Sam loves you,' said Megan, nudging her friend with her shoulder. 'He didn't care about you being a housekeeper, remember? If you feel yourself starting to panic, just glance at that massive diamond on your finger.'

Annie instantly broke into a smile.

'That's better,' said Eleanor. 'So when do I get to

meet your fiancé?'

Annie suddenly looked brighter. 'Come on then. I think he's in the kitchen with Tom.'

'Absolutely,' said Megan, shooting out of her seat. 'And we mustn't keep the gorgeous Tom waiting either,' she added, rushing out the door.

Eleanor and Annie exchanged a smile but, hidden inside, Eleanor's own stomach had a few butterflies as she went to meet the very person who could be a lifeline back to her career and life in London.

*

Tom had spent the afternoon in the recording studio, trying and failing to think up any new lyrics. His foot was aching and he had a splitting headache as well.

He and Sam had had a long chat in the kitchen about the style and direction of the new album. But Tom was still drawing a blank. It wasn't that late, but he was thinking that a large glass of water and an early night might be the best thing for him that evening.

They were just standing up when Annie arrived in the kitchen.

'Hi,' she said, with a warm smile. 'I thought a couple of introductions were long overdue.'

Sam raised his eyebrows. 'I think we've already met,' he murmured, drawing her close for a soft kiss.

Annie gave him a gentle shove. 'You know what I

mean,' she said, blushing. She looked across at Tom. 'Tom, these are my best friends Megan and Eleanor,' she told him.

'Hi Tommy. I'm Megan. I work here part-time,' said the redhead, rushing around the table to give his hand an enthusiastic shake.

'Well, I think working is perhaps pushing it,' murmured Annie with a smile.

'Hi,' he said, shaking Megan's hand. 'And it's just Tom.'

Megan giggled nervously and, blushing, sat back at the table.

His eyes shifted along to study the other friend, who was very attractive and more reserved.

'And this is Eleanor, our best friend who's come down from London for a while,' said Annie.

He gave her a nod by way of greeting.

'Hi,' she said, with a wide smile.

Tom watched as she turned to face Sam.

'Hey,' said Sam, with a nod towards them both. He crossed the kitchen and held his hand out for her to take.

'Hi,' she said, still smiling. 'Long time no see.'

'I seem to recall the last time we met you pushed me into the river,' he told her, grinning.

She joined in Sam's laughter which lit up her pretty face. 'God, I'd forgotten about that! Anyway, everyone else was going in so I thought you didn't want to be left out.'

He joined her laughter. 'Even fully clothed! Yeah, thanks for that! Even fifteen years on, I remember the teasing.'

As they continued to reminisce, Tom was able to appreciate her fine body, highlighted in the silk jumpsuit she was wearing. A strange, glamorous choice for the countryside. He guessed she didn't visit that often. Either that or she was extremely high-maintenance. She seemed in vast contrast to her two friends, who were far less fussed about wearing fancy clothes.

'Belated congratulations on your engagement,' she was saying.

'Thanks. I'm sure Annie will need all the help she can get with the wedding plans. Are you down from London for a few more days?'

'Hopefully a few weeks,' she said.

'The magazine can spare you for that long?' asked Sam.

'Magazine?' Tom suddenly became very alert and on guard. 'You're a journalist?' he said.

'Well, only a financial one,' she said, turning to face him.

'What was the name again of where you work?' asked Sam.

She was nodding quite manically now. '*The Money Chronicle*,' she replied. 'Deadly dull, of course.'

Tom was still frowning. There was something not

right about her.

'We need snacks,' announced Annie, opening a cupboard and bringing out some Pringles.

Eleanor picked up a tube. 'Can I tempt you?' she asked, with a flirty smile as she waggled the crisps at him.

The zip on the front of her jumpsuit was appealing for a brief moment, but then his protective walls closed up once more. 'I'm fine, thanks,' he told her.

'So, what are you working on at the minute?' she asked, changing tack.

What was this, an interview? He didn't like the feeling of being scrutinised.

'This and that,' he replied, glancing up at her as he manoeuvred the crutches under his elbows.

Her green eyes appeared to be challenging him, but he was used to holding his own. Perhaps it was just small talk and she wasn't used to dealing with famous people. He found everyone treated him differently these days. He longed for how they had treated Tom Kingsley the carpenter. As if he were a real person and not a superstar.

'You know, when you've got a minute,' said Sam to Eleanor. 'I wonder if you could advise me as to what kind of investment opportunities there is for the meagre savings we've got left?' asked Sam.

She looked a bit startled for a second. 'Of course,' she said in a bright tone.

Tom had heard enough and left the room with his drink, aware of Eleanor in particular watching him as he shuffled up the stairs.

Up in his bedroom later, he heard a commotion outside at the front of the house. He hobbled over to the window to see Sam trying to manoeuvre a tipsy Megan into his car. Eleanor and Annie were holding onto each other and laughing at the state of their friend. As Eleanor hugged her goodbyes, he realised that she suddenly looked completely different. Because she was being natural, he realised. Herself. Real. And suddenly he was tempted to get to know better.

But she was a journalist. Totally off limits, financial or otherwise. She was definitely hiding something and he'd had enough phony relationships during his life.

Besides, he didn't need anyone. He just needed to concentrate on his music at the minute. That had never let him down so far.

He drew the curtains and shut out the night sky beyond.

# Chapter 11

It had been a slow day for Eleanor, helping out with the animals whilst her mum went back to work at the farm shop. Thankfully the Great Dane and cocker spaniel had returned to their own homes, which at least cut down some of the work. So Eleanor had had some free time to mull over meeting Tommy King the previous evening. Or rather, Tom, to his friends.

Which she most definitely wasn't. She wasn't sure he would allow anyone that close, to be honest. Tom had been an impregnable wall. He had been fairly sullen and unresponsive. She'd had on her sexiest jumpsuit and winning smile and yet he had left the room so quickly he had almost left skid marks on the floorboards. But there was also the nagging feeling that they had made a connection, but that was probably just because he was good-looking.

In fact, having met so many celebrities, she hadn't been prepared for her own reaction to meeting him in the flesh. She had met loads of famous people before. Really attractive ones. But this guy beat them all, even though he had been wearing tracksuit bottoms and a white T-shirt, which, she remembered, had clung to him in all the right places.

Then again, he had been very bleary-eyed. Typical star, thought Eleanor. Sleeping all day and expecting everyone else to rush around taking care of him. Although she had to admit that the crutches did actually look real.

The papers had been full of questions about Tom's problems but nobody seemed to know for sure. She wondered what had really happened. Were there alcohol problems? This was the kind of exclusive that her editor could only dream about.

And yet, he was close to Sam. Who was Annie's fiancé.

Eleanor bit her lip in worry. The last thing she wanted to do was hurt her friend who had already been through so much.

Feeling thoroughly confused, she really wasn't in the mood to attend the local WI meeting with Annie and Megan, but she had promised.

Anyway, the way things were going, it looked like she would be in Cranley for a long time. At least she would be around to help plan her friend's wedding. And having met Sam again for the first time in years, she thought he was really nice. Not at all the stuffy earl in waiting she had perhaps been braced for.

She scratched the eczema patch on her neck, worrying once more about her friends.

At some point she would have to tell them that she

had lost her job. But she was sure that just as soon as she'd confessed, then everything would be all right. Wouldn't it?

*

When Eleanor and Megan arrived at Willow Tree Hall, they found Annie shuffling a big pile of boxes around the cluttered dining room.

'This is all out of the kitchen ready for the cupboards to be torn down on Monday,' she said, peering inside a box before shaking her head.

'What are you looking for?' asked Eleanor.

'Some glasses,' said Annie, with a sigh. 'I thought I'd better dig out some of the best crystal for the WI meeting.'

'Are you all right?' asked Eleanor.

'It's just this meeting,' said Annie. 'I'm feeling really nervous.'

She looked slightly panicked and Eleanor understood for the first time the pressure that Annie faced by agreeing to be a future countess of Cranley.

'I think you're putting way too much on yourself with this whole countess stuff,' said Eleanor.

'I know I am, but it's really important,' said Annie. 'There's been an earl and countess of Cranley for hundreds of years. We have tenants and people relying on us. Of course I want to be the best I can for them.

And for Sam too. And I can't let Arthur down. I just can't!'

'And you won't,' said Megan, squeezing her arm.

'Exactly,' said Eleanor. 'You're fabulous and you're going to be a fabulous countess as well. We're with you every step of the way, okay?'

'Yeah,' Megan told her. 'You jump, we jump. Remember?'

Annie gave her a smile and even Eleanor was touched.

It was the quote from their favourite movie when they had been growing up, *Titanic*. Leonardo DiCaprio had urged the heroine Rose that they could jump off the sinking ship together. The threesome had said the same phrase to each other over and over. *You jump, we jump*. If they needed to, the three of them would join hands and jump into any kind of troubled waters together.

Eleanor hadn't heard the phrase for quite a few years though.

'You'll be a fantastic countess,' Megan carried on, still trying to cheer up Annie. 'Look, distract yourself with this.' She held up the *Hello!* magazine that had been on top of the one of the boxes. 'Lovely engagement photos. Love. Romance. Happy ever after and all that rubbish. You can even get some ideas about your wedding.'

But Annie was digging around in the crates for more glasses, so Megan carried on flicking through the pages on her own. 'Awww,' she cooed, showing Eleanor a double-page spread on a couple of soap stars. 'Aren't they sweet?'

Eleanor was concentrating so hard on her friend's lack of confidence that she found herself accidentally blurting out, 'Apart from the fact that he's gay and she's sleeping with her personal trainer.'

Megan looked aghast. 'No! How do you know that?'

Eleanor blinked back to reality. 'I heard a rumour, that's all. It's all round town about them,' she said quickly.

Megan still appeared shocked. 'But this couple are okay, aren't they?' she carried on, turning the page to show some love-struck movie stars. 'They've just got married.'

'They hate each other,' Eleanor replied, rubbing her forehead as it began to tense up. 'They only got married to resurrect their dying careers. If she gets pregnant, it won't be his. It'll be by her so-called "cousin" Brad.'

Even Annie had stopped pacing now. Taking the magazine from Megan and flicking through a couple more pages to another film actress, she asked, 'What about her?'

'She likes to wander around the house in the nude, according to her bodyguards,' said Eleanor with a sigh. 'She enjoys the look-but-no-touch approach.'

Megan pointed to a photo on the next page. 'What about her?

'Steals everything from the hotels she stays in,' Eleanor told them. 'If it's not nailed down, she takes it. Mirrors, bedlinen. The lot.'

Her friends were goggle-eyed. 'This is amazing,' said Megan, shaking her head in wonder. 'How do you know all this?'

Eleanor thought quickly. 'Our sister magazine is one of those celebrity gossip ones. I flick through it now and then.'

'It's awful,' said Annie, shaking her head miserably. 'It's all a lie.'

'I know,' said Megan. 'I hate fake people. But just think of what I can tell the other mums at the school gates.'

Eleanor gulped. How were they going to react when they found out that she had been lying to them for so long?

Anxious to change the subject, she checked the time on her phone. 'The WI ladies will be arriving soon. We'd better get these glasses ready.'

'Absolutely, my darlings,' said Rose, appearing at the door. 'We're going to need a drink to keep us going. The whole thing can be terribly dull. Unless I'm there, of course.'

'I'm a bit nervous,' said Annie, wringing her hands together.

'You'll be fine,' Rose told her, carefully taking Annie's hands in hers. 'I believe in you, my lovely sweet girl. I truly do. My darling Beatrice, the late Countess of Cranley, played a huge role in the local Women's Institute and it appears they want you to carry on the tradition. You know what, let's have a stiff gin and tonic before they get here to help you relax.'

A while later, the group of women were gathering in the drawing room. It took a gentle shove from Eleanor to get Annie through the doorway to greet everyone.

It was a mixed age group of a dozen or so women. They were all looking at Annie with a combination of interest and disdain. As if she were something to be studied but not really listened to. They were obviously well aware that Annie used to be the housekeeper. Instantly, Eleanor felt protective of her friend.

But she watched in admiration as Annie took a deep breath and walked over to a nearby group who were standing next to the fireplace. 'Hello,' she said, fixing on a wide smile. 'I'm Annie. Welcome to Willow Tree Hall. Isn't it a lovely evening?'

'Not really,' replied one of the women. 'Doris here has just announced that she needs three more radiotherapy sessions.'

'Oh.' Annie's sweet face blushed. 'I'm so sorry.'

'What ghastly luck, darling,' said Rose, coming over to smother Doris with a hug.

'What do you need from us?' asked Annie, still looking concerned. 'I mean, there must be some way we can help?'

'Absolutely,' said Rose, with a firm nod of her head. 'That's what the Harris family are here for, of course. Have been for generations and young Annie here will be no different, I can assure you.'

The women exchanged impressed looks before smiling more warmly at Annie than they had done before.

The chairwoman called the meeting open and they all sat down on the various sofas. Rose had been right, thought Eleanor. It was terribly tedious, at least until the floor was open for additional topics.

'The local cottage hospital has been ever so good,' announced the lady called Doris. 'I thought that we could raise some money for them this summer. The whole place needs updating and desperately needs some funds. When you spend as much time there as I have recently, it can be a bit depressing.'

'What does our future countess think?' said the chairwoman.

All heads turned to Annie who was now blushing furiously as she slowly rose from her seat. 'Well, of course I agree,' she spluttered. 'After all, everyone knows someone who has suffered because of cancer. Be it a partner, friend, family or work colleague.'

There were quite a few heads in the audience nodding in agreement.

'So, of course, I think we should consider ways to raise as much money as possible so that everyone coping with that terrible ordeal can at least be comfortable.'

There was more vigorous nodding as Annie stood and waited expectantly for the women around her to voice their ideas.

'How about a beetle drive?'

'A cake sale!'

'Sponsored knitting!'

Annie was nodding robotically but Eleanor found herself shaking her head. This would never do. Knitting? How was that going to raise enough funds?

'Actually,' she found herself saying in a loud voice, 'I took part in the London Moonwalk a few years ago. Maybe we could follow the same idea here. The Moonwalk highlights and raises money for breast cancer by having everyone walk a marathon route in their bras.'

The nodding in the audience abruptly stopped.

'You want us to walk around the village in just our bras?' said the chairwoman in a shocked tone.

Eleanor broke into a grin. 'Well, you'd be wearing trainers and shorts as well. And the bras can be worn over T-shirts, for modesty's sake. But yes, in principle, I think it could still work.'

A lot of the women were exchanging startled looks. Annie was looking alarmed as she stared down at her friend.

'Of course,' carried on Eleanor, thinking quickly as she stood up next to Annie. 'That's just to highlight breast cancer. Perhaps underwear could be used to highlight other areas that have been affected.'

A heavy silence followed, but Eleanor carried on, ignoring the shocked vibes spilling out in the room. 'I mean, if someone had suffered with prostate cancer, maybe they could walk the route in a pair of underpants over their shorts.'

'Like Superman?' said someone in the audience, to a few stifled giggles.

'Absolutely,' said Eleanor, grinning widely. 'It's the silliness that raises the money, you see? And what's a small embarrassment compared to what they've all gone through? It's about making a difference and trying to change lives for the better. After all, that's what I've been told village life is all about. Being there for one another.'

'Hear! Hear!' said Rose, suddenly. 'What a marvellous idea! And what fun!'

Gradually, the women in the room began to clap and stand up, eventually giving Eleanor a standing ovation.

After a few moments, the chairwoman held up her hand to quieten down the audience. 'Well, I can see Eleanor McCartney has fulfilled all that promise she showed during her years at my school.'

It was then that Eleanor realised that she was looking at her old headmistress.

'So, do I take it that you will be the one to organise all of this to happen?'

All heads turned to Eleanor.

'Well, er, yes, I suppose so,' she told them. What on earth could she say otherwise? 'It's probably best to strike whilst the iron's hot and hold the walk within the next week or so,' said Eleanor. 'Whilst we generate a big buzz about it in the village, I mean.'

That at least would mean she would still be in Cranley to organise everything, just in case some miracle job offer came through from London.

Annie turned and gave her a spontaneous hug. 'You're so brilliant,' she whispered in her ear. 'I would never have thought of that.'

Eleanor smiled at her friend, grateful that she hadn't let Annie down when she needed her.

After the meeting had broken up, she watched the women huddle around Annie, all laughing and gossiping in enthusiasm. Megan too was chatting away with another group. Eleanor stood awkwardly to one side, feeling more out of sync than ever before with her friends. She had always had trouble fitting in at the magazine. Now she seemed to be out of step back home too. Annie and Megan had lives and friends here in the village. What did she have?

Maybe she just didn't fit in anywhere. Perhaps it was for the best that she wrote her exposé on Tommy King, without implicating Annie or the family, of course. Then she could go back to her comfort zone in London.

So she slipped out of the room and went to find someone who could make that happen.

# Chapter 12

Tom had slept in late again.

The codeine was still playing with his body clock and continuing to make him feel sleepy. The foot was still too painful to get any sleep without it, so it was a lose-lose situation at the moment, it felt.

Not that his vampire hours appeared to be affecting anyone else in the big house. Everyone kept telling him not to worry and to just do as he pleased.

He hadn't realised how used to his own company he had become though. He was finding the family dinners around the dining room table incredibly awkward. Small talk wasn't really his thing. But the family had been generous with their time.

And their offer of accommodation had been equally generous, he was quickly realising. Sam had mentioned in passing that he had reduced the number of artists that he now looked after; the running of Willow Tree Hall was taking up a lot of his time. And also his money, Tom understood. There was still so much that needed to be done to the house that it made Tom feel even guiltier that the writing wasn't happening for him. He owed Sam everything. And without his cut of the next Tommy

King album, Sam might not even be able to afford to get the ballroom refurbished for his own wedding.

Determined to try and stay awake, Tom had headed to the recording studio after dinner. He had switched off his phone a day or so previously. If it was business, they could get to him through Sam. Otherwise, he was off the grid for a while.

And it felt good. Nobody hassling him. Nobody needing him. He felt free.

He picked up the guitar he had brought with him. It had been a gift from his gran. It had belonged to her late husband; a man Tom had never met. But he must have been exceptionally lucky to marry such a woman.

He stroked the smooth wood. It was a friend over the years. A mate. Something to trust. A special bond. He closed his eyes and began to feel the whisper of a melody.

'Hello.'

He jumped at the voice, frowning at the intrusion.

The small bar of music had disappeared. Snatched away by the interruption in his thoughts.

He turned his head to find Annie's friend Eleanor standing in the doorway, wearing her usual wide fake smile. He gave an inward groan, not needing another awkward conversation.

'I think everyone's up at the big house,' he told her, hoping that would be the end of their discussion.

'Actually it's you I've come to find.'

She walked into the middle of the room and sat down next to the keyboard. As she crossed her long legs, he realised she was wearing high heels again. Her hair was immaculate, not one strand out of place. Her make-up was natural, but there was quite a lot of it. She looked so perfect that she could have been a mannequin.

'I've just been at the WI meeting and have been tasked to organise a charity walk to help raise some money,' she told him. 'The local hospital is in desperate need of funds.'

'I'm not sure I'm up to any charity walk at the minute,' he replied, nodding at his nearby crutches.

'Oh, no!' she said, laughing. For a second her soft green eyes lit up and then she went back into manic grin once more. 'What we need is a celebrity to start off the proceedings. Maybe cut some kind of ribbon. I don't know all the details yet, but it should be within the next week or two. We're hoping to get the county newspaper involved. We need to raise a lot of funds. It's important.'

He sighed but found himself unable to refuse. His gran had died of cancer. It was a cause close to his heart.

'Sure,' he told her, with a shrug of his shoulders. Would it matter if he had left Willow Tree Hall by then? Possibly not. He was sure Arthur could take his place.

'That's fantastic!' she said, leaping up from the stool. 'How incredibly generous of you.'

She was acting as if he had actually discovered a cure for the disease rather than cutting a ribbon to start a charity walk.

'No worries. Well, if there's nothing else,' he began.

Eleanor picked up the small carrier bag she had brought with her and held it out for him to take. 'I was hoping you might agree to give us a hand,' she told him. 'So I bought you an early thank you present. Or perhaps even a bribe!'

He opened the bag and stared down at the huge box of Maltesers. He just about managed to stop himself grimacing.

'Thanks,' he muttered.

'No, thank you!' she told him, with a wink.

For a second they locked eyes and he found himself staring at the thick long lashes and the dark green of her eyes.

He still felt rattled by the intrusion after she had gone. And yet he found himself scribbling down one line of a lyric about different shades of green.

# Chapter 13

Ten days later, Eleanor found herself standing in the warmth of the late afternoon sun. It was nearly the middle of June and with the summer solstice just around the corner, the air was finally warming up. Which was quite handy given the fact that she was wearing one of her prettiest and most expensive satin bras and nothing else on her top half.

Well, at least it's a different outfit to try out on Tommy King, she thought. Heaven knows, nothing else had worked over the past week. She had accidentally on purpose bumped into him three times up at the Hall during that time but to no avail. She had merely received a grumpy nod of his head in greeting before he had disappeared.

She was beginning to think that the charity walk might be her last time to make any kind of connection with him before he left Cranley, taking the chance of her exclusive story with him.

She glanced down the long driveway towards Willow Tree Hall, but there was still no sign of anyone else appearing, especially famous singers on crutches.

Smothering her irritation, she fixed on her most

positive smile as she looked around the small crowd of people that had gathered at the front gates.

She recognised the WI members who had been at the meeting just over a week before. Female family members and friends had also all been roped in so that there were at least fifty of them ready to walk around the village. With the event being timed after the last lessons of the day, the children were also able to join in.

As per her idea, most people had either their bra or knickers over their normal clothes, apart from the younger participants who, like Eleanor, were wearing just their bras or, in some cases, just a pair of frilly knickers on their bottom halves.

A few enterprising souls had wrapped themselves in bandages to indicate bone cancer and there were a few heads bandaged up as well.

But the air was humming with good humour and anticipation.

'Even in your bra, you still look good,' moaned Megan, glancing down at her own black bra and leggings.

Eleanor checked that her white shorts were not marked. Of course she had made an effort. She didn't want Tom to see her and flinch, although she had no idea why she wanted to impress him. She patted her head to make sure that no loose strands had come away from her French plait. She also had on her best and most waterproof make-up, in case she became hot and sweaty.

'Don't you ever act like a slob?' asked Megan. 'Eat ice cream out of a tub? Lounge around in the oldest sweatshirt you own watching soppy movies? Or is that just me?'

Eleanor shook her head. 'I'm out every night for work and I always have to look good.'

'We'll have to have a girls' night in whilst you're still here,' said Megan.

'Definitely,' said Eleanor, smiling. She had found herself growing ever closer to her friends the longer she stayed in Cranley.

The route of the charity walk that had been agreed upon would take them around the fringes of the hamlet and then along the river until they were in the grounds of Willow Tree Hall. Although it had been classed as a marathon, a distance of about five miles, all in their outfits, had been agreed upon to assist the more mature walkers.

It had only been a short time, but word had spread like wildfire about the walk and there was a huge buzz about the village. Sponsorship was, apparently, very high.

A young male journalist from the local newspaper headed over to Eleanor.

'So?' he asked. 'Who's this rumoured star that's going to start the proceedings?'

Eleanor watched as his eyes flickered down to her bra and remained there until she felt the urge to slap him.

'It's a surprise,' she replied. 'Any minute now!' She quickly turned her back away from his gaze at her chest and walked away. She glanced back down the driveway but there was definitely nobody in sight.

Annie shuffled over to stand next to her. 'I've just called Arthur,' she murmured. 'He says Tom's not in the house.'

'Where the hell is he then?' muttered Eleanor. 'It's not as if he can get lost on the way. He only had to come down the driveway. He said he would do this.'

Worse still, she had believed him. On reflection, she had thought it would take an enormous amount of persuasion to encourage Tom to start the charity walk, but it had been so easy.

Too easy, she thought with a grimace. She should have known someone as famous as Tommy King would let her down.

'What are we going to do?' asked Annie, her eyes wide and anxious. 'Everyone's expecting someone to start them off.'

Rose came over to stand by them. Eleanor was struck by how she was covered up with a dark silk shirt. Perhaps she felt too old to be wearing a bra in public.

'What's going on?' she asked. 'The natives are getting restless.'

'Tom's a no-show,' Eleanor told her. 'We haven't got anyone famous to start them off.'

'Nonsense!' cried Rose, before turning to face the

crowd. 'Is everybody ready?'

A wave of anticipation and nervous giggles sped around the crowd.

'And who are you?' asked the journalist, holding out his phone.

'Me?' Rose straightened her back and lifted her chin. 'I'm Rosemary Genevieve Harris, sister to Arthur, Earl of Cranley. My family is seventh generation and my home, this estate and the whole village have been in our name for nearly two hundred years. Shall we begin?'

With a winning smile, Rose flung off her silk shirt to reveal a pointy-cupped bodice that even Madonna would have been envious off.

There was a gasp of appreciation and shock before a small round of applause broke out.

'Rose!' said Annie, blushing on her behalf. 'What are you wearing?'

'Dolce and Gabbana, darling,' said Rose. 'I've been waiting for an opportunity to wear this for years!'

Thankfully the sight of a seventy-year-old woman in a designer leather bodice was enough to capture the journalist's interest.

'I don't know what Sam's going to say about this,' muttered Annie. 'Thank god he's away until this evening.'

'I think she's bloody brilliant,' Megan told her.

'So do I,' said Eleanor, laughing in amazement.

'Let the inaugural Cranley Charity Walk begin!' cried

Rose, with a flourish of her hands.

And Eleanor, Annie, Megan and the others set off.

As it was late in the afternoon, quite a lot of people were stood out on the paths and in their front gardens cheering all the walkers on.

Eleanor found that she was enjoying the chatter and cheerful atmosphere as the route took them around the village. She was pleased to see her mum clapping them as they went past. June had been quite upset that she couldn't participate because of her broken foot but had set cups of lemonade and water along the front wall for people to help themselves to. Eleanor was pleased that her mum appeared to be in less pain as the days went by. Of course, that meant that her services as a helper were no longer as necessary. Her mum had even begun to subtly ask when she was returning to London. Eleanor had yet to think up a decent excuse and had carried on with the 'holiday owed' line.

She tried to use the rest of the walk to try and work through any solutions to her problems but came up with nothing, as usual.

Due to the advanced age of some of the ladies, they walked at a slow pace and therefore did not arrive at the finishing post at the back of Willow Tree Hall until just after seven o'clock in the evening.

'Well done everybody!' called out Arthur, standing on the patio as they all walked towards him. 'What a marvellous undertaking. Come and have a refreshing drink inside.'

'Gin and tonic for everyone!' called out Rose, ushering everyone indoors.

Eleanor watched as Arthur's grey bushy eyebrows shot upwards at the sight of his sister in her bodice, but he had the good manners not to say anything. In public, at least.

Eleanor made sure that nobody had been left behind and was just about to follow them inside when she noticed a light in the woods to her right. Someone was in the recording studio. Annie had already told her that Sam was away at a meeting until later that evening.

Which left only one person.

Tom was obviously working there, concentrating entirely on himself and not bothered in the slightest at not showing up to help start the marathon.

Okay, so she hadn't been entirely unselfish when she had asked Tom to be involved in the walk. In fact, her main priority had been to find out more about him in the hope of writing her story but now she couldn't help but feel annoyed at him letting everyone down.

All of her frustrations about everything that had happened recently bubbled up inside. Eleanor drew herself up straight and marched towards the barn. Pushing hard against the main door in her increasing fury, it ricocheted off the wall and bounced back towards her again with a loud bang.

As she strode inside, she realised that the noise had

managed to wake Tom, who must have been fast asleep on a couch. Which made her even more angry.

'Oh, I'm sorry!' she snapped, going to stand next to him. 'Did I wake you?'

'Whattsamatter?' he muttered, struggling to sit up.

'Where the hell were you?' she shouted, putting her hands on her hips.

Tom rubbed the sleep out of his eyes. 'What are you talking about?'

'I'm talking about you breaking your promise! You said you were going to open the charity walk for us!'

She had the satisfaction of watching the realisation hit right before the guilt crossed his face. 'That was today?' he asked, still sounding groggy.

'No,' she retorted. 'I always walk around wearing just a bra!'

Tom's eyes snapped open at her words. He quickly looked up and took in the sight of her wearing only her shorts and bra. Suddenly feeling uncomfortable under his intense stare, she crossed her arms in front of her chest. She also felt quite short without her normal heels on, wearing her trainers instead.

'You've let everyone down,' she told him, trying to take control of the situation once more

'I'm sorry. The medication makes me sleepy.'

'Yeah, right,' she drawled, rolling her eyes. 'More like you couldn't be bothered.'

Like every other famous person she had met. He was

only interested in himself.

'I'm telling you the truth,' he told her, sounding more irritated now.

'I don't believe you,' she said. 'And, for the record, it's not just me you let down. It made Annie look bad and that makes me mad, because she's the kindest, sweetest person you'll ever come across.'

'Is that why you only see her, what, once or twice a year?' said Tom, standing up to tower over her. 'Some good friend you are.'

'I'm just busy at work.' Eleanor was beginning to get flustered. She was feeling uncomfortable under his scrutiny. 'But this isn't about me,' she managed to carry on. 'This is about you letting her and everyone else down. Stop acting all diva-ish. It's as if you feel like we're all beneath you. But hey, newsflash! You're flesh and blood just like everyone else in this village.'

He took a couple of hobbled steps to stand in front of her. 'Where you don't even live anymore!'

She frowned. 'What's that got to do with it?'

He glared down at her. 'If this village is so great, why don't you live here?'

'Well, I've got to now that I've lost my job, haven't I?' she shouted without thinking.

Then she stared up at him, her heart hammering in her chest as she realised what she had said.

'You can't tell anyone about that,' she said quickly, scratching at the eczema patch on her neck.

He raised his eyebrows. 'Really?'

Horrified that this man knew the truth about her, Eleanor tried to leave with some dignity. She dropped her hand and straightened her back. 'You're just like every other so-called star,' she told him, heading to the door. 'You're only interested in yourself.'

She flung open the door and marched up the path towards the house whilst grabbing her phone out of her pocket. She quickly typed out the words, I'll have a big story on Tommy King for you by the end of the summer.

And then she sent it to Theresa, her ex-editor, in London.

That would serve him right, she thought, as she re-joined her friends and the other walkers inside the main house. So why did she feel the need to drain her glass of wine so quickly? Why were her hands itching worse than ever? And why was her heart thumping madly when surely she should be happy that she might be able salvage her career after all?

Perhaps because she wasn't quite sure what she had just set in motion.

# Chapter 14

Tom was angry with both himself and Eleanor as he headed towards the main house for dinner.

She had no right to say those things about him. She didn't know him. Didn't need to know him.

He groaned at his own failings. He shouldn't have agreed to cut the ribbon for the wretched walk. The village had nothing to do with him. He didn't know anyone there. It had only been the trigger of the word 'cancer' that had persuaded him to say yes.

The problem was that he was still here at Willow Tree Hall in the first place. One day had led to the next and then the next. It was time to leave before he became too close to everyone.

Still feeling irritated with himself and everything, he sat down at the dinner table in the dining room. He had tried to decline their invitation to eat with them every evening but to no avail. 'You're family,' he was repeatedly told. Except he wasn't.

He had no family. He was better off alone. That was the only way to get through life, wasn't it? The only way to survive.

Everyone chatted about the walk, which appeared to

have been a huge success, despite his lack of appearance.

Tom kept his head down and tried to get through the meal as quickly as possible.

But, as usual, he was swept into the conversation.

'I hope your foot isn't too sore,' said Arthur, looking across the table at him.

'It's fine,' said Tom, realising his sullen tone of voice made him sound like a teenager. 'Thank you.'

'Well, darling, you were most definitely missed,' said Rose, reaching across to help herself to more salad.

'Yeah, where were you?' asked Sam. 'I hear you missed the ribbon cutting.'

'It doesn't matter,' Annie quickly told him.

'I agree,' said Rose. 'Mainly because I totally stole the show in my bodice.'

Sam muttered something under his breath about being glad he wasn't there.

'Anyway, you can come and open next year's walk for us, Tom,' carried on Rose. 'Do your bit for cancer, as it were. Just wait until you hear what I'm planning to wear next time!'

But Tom had heard enough. 'I don't intend living here forever,' he snapped, abruptly standing up. 'So I won't be here in a year's time. In fact, I think it's best I leave as soon as possible.'

Only the sound of a shocked silence filled the room before he quickly walked out of the room. He hobbled across the entrance hall and flung open the French doors to head out onto the patio at the back of the house. There he took gulps of fresh air to calm himself down. And then he groaned at what he had done.

He had been rude to a warm, loving family who had treated him as one of their own. They had opened their home to him and he had snapped and snarled like a surly teenager. What was wrong with him? The last thing he had ever wanted to do was hurt Sam or his family.

He sank down onto the rickety wooden bench with a heavy sigh.

'Thought I'd find you out here.'

Tom looked up to find Sam walking across the patio towards him.

'I'm sorry,' said Tom. 'I'll apologise to the family.'

'Don't worry about that now,' said Sam, sitting down next to him. 'They understand, you know. You should have seen what they put up with from me and Will when we were younger.'

'Yes, but I'm over thirty,' said Tom with a sigh. 'I can't get away with acting like a stroppy teenager anymore.'

Sam shrugged his shoulders. 'We all have pressure valves that need releasing once in a while. Even someone as closed off and private as you.'

'Is that what you think I am?' Tom frowned. 'Closed off?'

Sam was quiet for a moment before he replied. 'I

think you had no one to teach you or show you how to behave when you were growing up. Most people let you down so you had to figure out everything on your own. And you've continued to battle everything on your own throughout your adult life as well. You never ask for help. And it's tough to cope with everything alone. Especially now you haven't got your gran.'

Tom bowed his head and stared down at the crooked paving slabs beneath his feet. 'It was the mention of cancer,' he said. 'It just brought it all back.'

'I'm not sure the grief ever leaves us,' said Sam, staring out across the garden. 'It just hurts a little less with each passing year.'

'I keep trying to hide mine,' said Tom. 'And look where that's got me.'

All alone, he added to himself.

Sam shook his head. 'I think Will's definitely still running from his, if it makes you feel better. Even after all these years. There's no manual for this kind of thing.'

'It doesn't, but thanks.' Tom took a deep breath. 'There's something else. Something I have to tell you.'

Sam frowned. 'Okay. Go on.'

Tom forced himself to speak. 'I've got writers' block and it's bad, I'm afraid. I haven't even started on the new album yet. I can't think up a single lyric at the moment.'

To his amazement, Sam sagged back on the bench in what appeared to be relief. 'Is that all?'

Tom was shocked by the lack of reaction. 'What do you mean?'

Sam laughed. 'I thought you were going to tell me that Aunt Rose had made a pass at you or something.' He looked at his friend. 'For the record, I had realised about the album. That's why I thought you might like coming out here to stay with us. Obviously I was wrong.'

'No, you weren't,' said Tom, surprising both of them with his words.

It was time to admit to himself that he had been enjoyed the majority of his stay at Willow Tree Hall. That despite the minor irritations he had begun to find a certain amount of peace there. 'I'd like to stay for a while longer actually, if that's okay with everyone. It is helping, the quiet here.'

'Good. That's what I thought,' said Sam, before standing up. 'I'll talk to the family.'

But Tom shook his head. 'Nope. I'm old enough to apologise for myself.'

He found Rose and Arthur in the drawing room.

'I'm sorry for my rudeness just now,' he said, standing in front of them both.

'Dear boy, there's really no need to apologise,' said Arthur, waving away any concern with his hand. 'We would hate to see you leave, of course, but nobody from this family will judge you if you do. You'll always be welcome back here.'

'Thank you,' said Tom. 'And I was very much hoping it would be okay for me to stay on a while longer. If you'll have me.'

'Darling, of course we will!' said Rose, leaping up to give him a hug. 'And never apologise for having passion running through those veins.' She leaned forward to whisper, 'It makes the sex much more exciting!'

As he gave her a smile to mask his blushes, he saw Arthur roll his eyes and realised that Rose hadn't whispered quietly enough. Or perhaps that was deliberate.

Next, he went to find Annie, who was washing up in the kitchen.

'I'm sorry for my outburst,' he told her. 'I shouldn't have been so rude.'

'Thank you,' she replied with a soft smile. 'But there's really no need for an apology.' Then she hesitated before carrying on. 'You know, if any family can help you with whatever it is that you're struggling with, then this is the one. They're a warm, loving bunch, who open their hearts and home up to anyone they think needs it. Including me.'

Tom wondered what had happened to Annie to cause her such pain.

'I had no one when I came here,' she carried on softly. 'Apart from Megan and Eleanor, of course, but even Eleanor was in London. I'll bore you with my story another time, but trust them, these are good people.'

He nodded. ‘I will. And I’m hoping to stay on for a while longer, if that’s okay with you.’

Annie broke into a smile. ‘That’s great. And Sam will be really pleased as well. You’re a good friend to him.’

Tom went up to his room, thinking how easily they’d forgiven him. And wondering what on earth he could do for the family to repay their kindness.

# Chapter 15

The following morning, Eleanor woke up feeling sore from the long walk. But also rattled and unsettled. She had accidentally blabbed about losing her job to Tom. What were the chances that he was going to tell everyone? Quite high considering she had lost her temper with him.

On reflection, he had seemed quite dozy when she had marched into the recording studio. She also remembered Annie saying that he was on really strong painkillers.

That was no excuse for not showing up though, she reminded herself. But even so, the seed of doubt remained that he might have been telling her the truth.

To add to her guilt, she had received a short text back from Theresa saying that whenever she had a story, she would be listening.

Eleanor automatically scratched at the patch of eczema on her neck. What was she going to tell her friends? How was she going to even begin to let them know she had lied to them?

She was feeling so muddled about everything and just couldn't think straight.

Thankfully, the long list of chores dealing with the animals helped keep her occupied for the morning. They were running low on food, so Eleanor had offered to head to the local farm shop where animal feed was plentiful and cheap, thanks to her mum's employee discount.

Unfortunately her mum didn't have a car, so Eleanor had no choice but to use the rickety old bicycle.

'It's a nice day to be outside,' her mum had told her.

But the weather had other ideas and the sky was growing very dark, very quickly as Eleanor made her way through the village. She was just struggling up the hill on the other side when the first raindrop splattered down onto the rusty handlebars. She glanced upwards and quickly upped her speed as it grew dark around her. Then it really began to rain. Hard.

She huffed and puffed as she tried to go even faster. The farm was just around the corner when suddenly something pinged around her ankles. Almost immediately, the bike came to an abrupt halt and she was catapulted out of the seat and onto a nearby grass verge.

She was struggling to a sitting position when a car drove past, splashing through a muddy puddle that had quickly formed in a nearby pothole.

'Thank you very much!' she shouted at the car, her anger spilling into the air.

*Great*, she thought staring down at her torn jeans.

*Another pair of ruined trousers.* But at least it didn't feel as if she had broken any bones.

To her horror, the brake lights of the car suddenly lit up and the vehicle was put into reverse. Her anger quickly disappeared and she feared the driver had heard her.

Oh well, she thought. *Take a ticket and join the back of the queue.* She'd reached her limit this month as to the number of people she could upset.

'Come on then,' she shouted as the driver got out. 'Come and have a go if you think you're hard enough!'

To her horror, it was Tom limping around the vehicle instead of some road-rage thug. Through the heavy rain, she could see him looking surprised but amused at her words.

'Well, I'm still a bit crocked, what with my foot and all,' he drawled. 'But I can put up a pretty good fight if you're in the mood for a scrap. What happened?' he asked, giving her the once-over. 'Are you okay?'

Eleanor decided that she was too wet, shocked and cold to be embarrassed. 'I think the chain fell off or something,' she told him, with a shrug. 'I'm fine. I'll live.'

She struggled to stand up and realised that she was coated in mud.

'I'm not sure your bike will survive,' said Tom, glancing over at the crumpled steel mess that was left. 'Come on,' he said. 'I'll give you a lift. Where are you going?'

'I can manage,' she muttered.

'How do you figure on doing that?' he asked.

The silence stretched out between them.

'You think I should just leave you here in the pouring rain?' he added.

She could feel her hair plastered against her head by the heavy rain. 'Okay,' she said before realising how ungracious that sounded. 'I'm going to the farm shop just down the road. Thanks.'

He glanced down at her filthy mud-coated jeans. 'Maybe I'd better put down some kind of cloth over the seat,' said Tom. 'I'm not sure Sam wants his car completely wrecked inside.'

'I'm surprised to see you up and about so early,' she said, her voice heavy with sarcasm. Just because he was being nice to her, didn't mean that she wasn't still cross about his no-show at the charity walk.

'I've taken myself off the codeine,' he told her, lifting the bicycle into the boot of the car before turning to face her. 'It was making me sleep all day. Hence missing the walk yesterday, which I think I did apologise for.'

Had he? She had been so cross, she couldn't remember.

Still feeling a little defensive, she asked, 'Are you all right to drive with your foot?

'I am now that I've stopped taking the heavy painkillers,' he told her, slamming the boot shut. 'Also it's an automatic.'

As the rain continued to pour down around them, there was a rumble of thunder overhead. A second later, a large grey blur dashed across the road and went straight underneath the car.

They looked at each other in shock.

'What the hell was that?' asked Tom.

They both bent down, peering underneath the car to discover a large, hairy, grey and white dog shivering, his big brown eyes wide with terror.

'Poor thing,' said Tom, reaching out his hand.

The rain had plastered his T-shirt to his torso and Eleanor was disgruntled to find herself staring at his toned stomach.

To distract herself, she looked around. 'I wonder where it came from.'

They tried to coax the dog out, but in the end Tom had to lie down on the wet road to reach hold of it by the scruff of its neck.

'Come on, big fella,' said Tom in a soft tone as the dog was slowly pulled out from under the car.

'There's no collar,' said Eleanor. 'I wonder if he slipped his lead whilst on a walk.'

But on closer inspection, the dog looked filthy, unbrushed, and possibly underfed as well. Definitely unloved.

'It looks more likely to be a stray,' she said.

'I agree,' said Tom.

He crouched down and held the trembling dog against him as the rain continued to splatter down.

Eleanor thought that was quite brave considering he didn't know if the dog would snap or bark at him. But the stray did neither, just dug in even deeper into Tom's arms.

Tom looked up at Eleanor. 'What do you think we should do with it?'

'We'd better take him to my mum,' said Eleanor. 'She deals with all the waifs and strays around here.'

She was reluctant to add any more animals to the growing menagerie at home, but the dog was clearly in trouble and so there wasn't really any other choice.

'Okay. Well, let's do that then,' Tom agreed.

It was only when he reopened the boot that they remembered the mangled bicycle.

The dog was still shaking as it leaned up against him. 'He's obviously pretty freaked out,' said Tom. 'Do you think you should sit on the back seat next to him?'

Eleanor grimaced. 'Sure,' she said. 'It's not like my jeans can get any worse at this stage.'

'And I'm sure Sam can always get the car valet cleaned tomorrow,' said Tom.

She got in the back seat of the car and the dog leapt in beside her. At another rumble of thunder, it snuggled in close to her. The dog smelt pretty bad and was soaking wet, but she still put her arm around it and gave it a reassuring stroke.

'You poor thing,' she told him softly. 'You're safe with us now, okay?'

'So what's the deal with your mum?' asked Tom, after she had given him directions. 'Is she a vet?'

Eleanor shook her head. 'No. Just an animal lover.'

He looked at her in the mirror for a second before concentrating on the road.

She wondered what he was thinking. And how she could possibly bring up the subject of her lack of job before he spilled her secret to her mum.

Because once that secret was revealed, chances were all the others would come rushing out to follow it as well.

# Chapter 16

Unfortunately for Eleanor, the journey went by too quickly and they arrived with the stray dog at The Forge before she had a chance to say anything to Tom about her job.

'Look, you don't have to come in,' she said quickly. 'I mean, we can handle the dog from here.'

More than anything, she was desperate for him not to see what kind of house she lived in.

But Tom was already shaking his head. 'No, that's fine,' he told her. 'I feel a kind of responsibility, seeing as he dashed under my car.'

He clearly wasn't going to take no for an answer. He picked up the dog and struggled to carry it down the path. She noticed that he was still hobbling despite the fact that he didn't have his crutches with him.

As they reached the front door, Eleanor tried once more to put him off. 'It's a bit of a mess in there,' she warned him.

That was an understatement, she thought, as she pushed against the front door and Tom followed.

A couple of cats watched warily as they went inside, which caused the dog in Tom's arms to shake even more.

'Mum!' she called out. 'I've got another stray for you.'

'In here!' came the shout from the kitchen.

As they went into the back of the house, Eleanor's heart sank. The kitchen was a total muddle. Washing-up was piled in the sink. There was animal feed and water bowls everywhere. Papers and books scattered all around the place. And, to top it all, there was a donkey peering in through the window from the overgrown garden outside.

*What must he think of me?* thought Eleanor in despair. *Of us?*

She glanced at Tom, who, to her surprise, appeared to be taking the world's messiest house in his stride. At least he had the decent manners not to look down his nose at the place. But he was probably used to a fancy penthouse and would be horrified by it all, she thought. To be honest, she was pretty horrified most days.

Her mum smiled at Tom as he was introduced, completely oblivious that he was one of the most famous singers in the world. She was more focussed on the dog as she placed it on the kitchen table to check it over.

Another goal for food hygiene, thought Eleanor in despair, as she looked at the dog's muddy paws.

But her mum was in her animal zone. 'Hello,' she said, stroking his fur gently. 'So, who do you belong to?'

The dog licked her hand in tentative response.

'There was no collar,' said Eleanor.

Her mum nodded. 'Right. Let's give you a once-over and see what we find,' she said, beginning to feel the dog over for any injuries.

'What kind of dog is it, do you think?' asked Tom.

'It's an English setter,' said her mum. 'And in a pretty bad way, I'm afraid. Matted fur. Underfed. I can feel his ribs. Poor thing.'

Watching her mother's soft face and adoring gaze as she looked on the poor dog, Eleanor braced herself for yet another addition to the home. She glanced over at Tom, but thankfully he appeared to be relaxed about the state of the place.

*

In fact, Tom was actually pretty shocked at how Eleanor's mother lived.

He'd imagined that she'd been brought up in some kind of footballer's wives mansion or something. What with her fancy clothes and slightly snooty air. But this rundown cottage filled with all sorts of animals was a surprise. A massive understatement of a surprise.

Appearances could most definitely be deceiving, he reminded himself.

Eleanor had disappeared to change out of her muddy trousers. When she came back downstairs, he noticed that she had fixed the mascara that had run underneath one eye and that her hair was smoothed back into a ponytail. He wondered why she felt the need to look so immaculate all the time.

She was in stark contrast to her mother whose clothes had seen better days. She seemed slightly scatty but was kind and gentle as she felt around the dog's body. 'I can't feel any breaks or ticks,' she said. 'You should take him to see Ben to find out if he's got a microchip.' She looked up and smiled at Tom and he realised she didn't have a clue who he was. He was thankful for the anonymity, which was a rarity these days.

'The vet's only down the road,' said Eleanor, looking at Tom. 'I can deal with it, if you need to be somewhere. We can always call a taxi.'

'No worries. I have the car,' he told her. 'I can take you.'

He found himself reluctant to leave this scene quite yet.

'That's good,' said her mum, nodding. 'We still need that pet food from the farm shop, if you wouldn't mind.'

Her mum opted to stay behind so once more it was Eleanor and the dog sat in the back seat. She quickly purchased some pet food at the farm shop before they headed onto the vet's.

As he drove, he asked, 'So your mum takes in strays?'

'Yes.' He heard the strain in her voice. There was a short silence before she added, 'Ever since my dad left us.'

She didn't elaborate and he didn't push. It wasn't any of his business, but still, he was surprised she had briefly opened up to him.

Going into the vet's surgery, he braced himself for the inevitable response to his superstardom. But thankfully Ben the vet was in his late fifties and didn't recognise Tom either.

But he obviously knew Eleanor's mother very well.

'How's her foot?' asked Ben, checking the dog over.

'The plaster's driving her crazy,' said Eleanor.

Ben nodded. 'I'll take her to the pub on Sunday. That should cheer her up.'

Eleanor smiled. 'Thanks. She always enjoys going out with you.'

There was an ease to their conversation which made Tom presume that Ben was an old friend of the family.

Ben finished his check-up. 'No microchip unfortunately,' he confirmed. 'But the dog appears healthy, although underweight. His fur's severely matted as well. Do you think your mother's up to giving him a bath?'

'I can do it,' said Eleanor, with a shrug of her shoulders. 'We'll just have to keep it with us until the owner comes along to claim him.'

Ben smiled. 'Of course. Where else would a stray animal go in Cranley?'

Only Tom caught her soft sigh. So the animal thing was definitely a problem.

Once they were back in the reception, Eleanor asked if Tom wouldn't mind holding the dog. 'I'd better pick him up a collar from the pet shop next door.'

'You sound like you've done this before,' said Tom.

She smiled, but it was without humour. 'Oh yes,' she replied. 'Just a few times.'

Once the dog had been fitted with a brand new green collar, they headed back to her mum's house. As Tom parked the car outside, Eleanor paused.

'Look, I'm sorry about shouting at you last night,' she said, scratching at her neck which he had noticed she did frequently. 'I think I might have overreacted a bit.'

He turned in his seat to look at her. 'I really was intending to come along and honour my commitment to you,' he said. 'I'm not in the habit of breaking my promises. I went into the recording studio and drifted off to sleep. The painkillers are too heavy for me. I didn't wake up until you came in. I should have set the alarm or something.'

'Okay.' She nodded before clearing her throat. 'Look, I think I may have told you last night about losing my job at the magazine.'

A blush was spreading across her creamy white cheeks.

He nodded. 'In between shouting at me, you mean.'

'Yes. Well, quite.' She shuffled in her seat, obviously uncomfortable. 'Anyway, I'd be grateful if you didn't mention anything about it to my mum. Or Annie. Or anyone else, come to think of it. I haven't got round to telling anyone yet.'

He was surprised that she would keep such a thing secret but merely replied, 'No problem.'

She seemed taken aback that he would be so amenable. But also grateful. 'Thanks,' she said, before getting out of the car.

Back in the messy cottage, he expected to drop off the dog and leave them to it. But as soon as the stray setter walked into the kitchen, one of the cats began to hiss and take a swipe at it. In panic, the setter ran to hide behind Tom's legs.

'I'm not sure this is going to end well.' said Eleanor's mum, looking worriedly at the cat. 'Trouble is, Samson's owners aren't due back from holiday for another week and he's something of a terror.'

When the cat went for the dog again and began to chase him around the kitchen table, they were all almost knocked off their feet in the mayhem.

So Tom made his decision. 'Look, you're obviously not quite up to homing another stray at the minute,' he said. 'How about I keep the dog up at the house whilst we wait for someone to claim him.'

Eleanor's mum looked surprised but pleased. 'How lovely of you to suggest that. Where are you staying?'

'At Willow Tree Hall,' Eleanor told her.

Her mum looked surprised. 'Oh. Are you a friend of Sam's?'

Tom nodded, still grateful for the anonymity. 'Yes.'

'Well, hopefully it'll be all right with Arthur.'

'I'll text Annie and check with her,' said Eleanor.

Tom knelt down and stroked the dog's head whilst Eleanor sent a text to Annie.

'How about you come home with me, mate,' said Tom, softly. 'I know what it's like to be unwanted.'

He felt Eleanor glance back at him, but she didn't say anything.

He carried on stroking the soft fur, as the pair of big brown eyes stared up at him. The dog was obviously wondering whether he could trust yet another human or if he would be let down again. Tom suddenly felt a connection between them. Both unwanted strays, desperate to trust the next person they met but not believing anything too good to be true.

Eleanor's mum handed him a small bag of treats and some dog food. 'That should keep you going for a couple of days. Just in case.'

'Annie says it's fine to bring the dog home,' said Eleanor, looking up from her phone.

'Wonderful,' said her mum, smiling. 'Now then, he'll need a name in the meantime, of course.'

'No, he doesn't, Mum,' said Eleanor, in an exasperated tone.

'Nonsense.' Eleanor's mum turned to face Tom. 'You found him, Tom. What do you think?'

He glanced down into the dog's big brown eyes. 'I

don't know. I've never named a dog before.'

'Well, there's always Snoopy or Scooby Doo,' said her mum.

Tom grimaced. 'I'm not sure about that.'

He glanced over at Eleanor who was trying and failing to smother a smile. 'How about your favourite singer?' she prompted.

She was obviously enjoying the fact that her mum didn't have a clue who he was.

'I've got so many,' he told her. 'I dunno. The Stones. Eminem. Bob Dylan...'

'How about Dylan?' said Eleanor, nodding her approval.

Tom leant down to the dog again. 'What do you think, boy? Do you like the name Dylan?'

The dog wagged its tail.

'Dylan it is then,' he said, breaking into a grin.

'Oh! You are a true doggy person!' said her mum, smiling tearily at him. 'That's lovely. I'm sure he'll be fine with you. Now, I've written down the food instructions. Just light meals to start off with until we know how he gets on. Who knows what he's been living on. Plenty of accessible water. Let me know if you have any questions.'

Eleanor helped carry all the extra doggy paraphernalia out to the car. 'Will you be okay with him?' she asked.

Tom nodded. 'It'll be fine, I'm sure. How hard can it

be, compared to, say, a donkey?'

Her shoulders slumped. 'Yeah. Well, it's good of you to take care of the dog. As you can see, the Ark is pretty full at the minute.'

She was shuffling awkwardly from foot to foot.

'I think it's great that your mum loves animals so much,' he told her.

She rolled her eyes. 'It's not so great if you have to take care of them every day.'

He looked down at her. 'Trust me, there's not too many people that would make such an effort.'

She glanced at the dog on the back seat. 'Right back at you.'

He smiled. 'So, is this a temporary truce whilst we take care of Dylan?'

'We?' Her eyebrows shot up in surprise.

'If you think I'm bathing him all by myself, you've got another thing coming,' he told her, as he sat behind the wheel.

Her laughter surprised them both and made her face seem far more alive and animated. 'Okay,' she said. 'It's a deal. I'll see you in the morning up at the hall.'

As he drove off, he glanced in his rear-view mirror and saw that Eleanor was still smiling as she turned away to head indoors.

It was the first time he had seen her smile properly and be natural, he realised. And he liked it.

# Chapter 17

As Megan worked part-time cleaning at Willow Tree Hall on Monday and Friday, Eleanor was able to hitch a lift to the house with her the following morning.

After her accident the previous day, the bicycle was now completely unusable, which she was secretly quite grateful for. However, she was still a bit battered and bruised from her pole vault over the handlebars.

'I never heard from Annie yesterday,' she told Megan as she got into the car. 'What with stray dogs and mangled bicycles. Any idea how much the walk raised?'

'No idea yet,' said Megan. 'It's probably good that Tom took the dog off your hands anyway. Especially with Mrs Briggs nosing over the back fence.'

Eleanor was confused. 'What are you talking about?'

'Didn't your mum tell you?' Megan sighed. 'You know what old Mrs Briggs next door to The Forge is like. Such a nosy parker. Anyway, apparently she's complained to Arthur about the number of animals your mum's keeping these days.'

Eleanor felt a flush of embarrassment. 'Oh God. I'll have to have a word with Mum. It's getting out of hand. But you know how much she loves having them all.'

'But it is a lot of work for her,' said Megan. 'Especially since she hurt her ankle.'

'Well, I've been helping out for the past fortnight.'

'Yes but you'll be gone again soon and then she'll be trying to deal with it on her own, as usual.'

As usual. Eleanor tried but she couldn't ignore those last two words, even though there had been no malice behind them. There was so much she had left behind trying to pursue her career. So much that her mum had had to carry for herself, she knew.

They pulled up outside the house. Megan knocked on the huge red front door and then let herself in.

'You have a key?' asked Eleanor.

'No, but it's always open during the day,' said Megan. 'Everyone just lets themselves in. Anyway, this time next week it'll be full of builders once again.'

They went into the huge entrance hall and Megan hollered out a 'hello!'. There came a replied shout from Annie that she was on the patio at the back of the house. They found her sitting at a dilapidated table and chairs, with a large pot of coffee and some cups.

'Come and have some caffeine,' said Annie, in between yawns and gesturing lazily for them to sit down.

'I hope that's Sam keeping you awake all night,' said Megan, giving her a nudge.

'Another male, unfortunately,' said Annie, blushing. 'Dylan howled for most of the night until Tom smuggled him up to his bedroom.'

'Oh no, those lovely new carpets,' said Megan, shaking her head. 'Oh well. So where is this famous, filthy pooch?'

'Yeah, where's Dylan? And Tom?' asked Eleanor, looking around.

'Keen, aren't you?' said Megan.

'To give a dog a bath? Not particularly,' said Eleanor quickly. 'I was just asking.'

'Yeah, yeah.'

Actually, she was a little disappointed that Tom wasn't there, a thought which wasn't making her feel any less awkward. Mainly because she suspected that her disappointment was nothing to do with the story she was supposed to be writing on him.

'Sam's taken Tom to his doctor's appointment,' said Annie. 'Dylan went along for the ride as well. Not that anyone had much choice about that. I think he and Tom are going to be inseparable.'

'You don't mind him staying here until the owner comes forward?' asked Eleanor. 'Or rather if someone comes forward.'

'No,' said Annie, before taking a sip of coffee. 'He's such a cutie. He's won us all over already, despite his desperate need for a bath. And at least it takes my mind off the walk.'

Eleanor was confused. 'I thought it was a huge success?' she asked.

Annie shrugged her shoulders. 'No idea, unfortunately. But Mrs Havers, our old headmistress, is popping in to tell me the grand total later on.' She gulped. 'What if not much money has been raised?'

'Have a biscuit,' said Megan, pushing the plate towards her anxious looking friend.

But thankfully there was no need for them to panic. The WI chairwoman and her committee were beaming from ear to ear when they arrived later that morning. The walk was declared to have raised the biggest total ever in their history of fundraising.

'Well, I must confess that we were all a little nervous when we first heard about our future countess,' Mrs Havers began, as they stood in the entrance hall. 'Especially as more and more of the big houses in the area are being bought up by people who aren't interested in the village at all. But I think we can all agree that our new WI members are a breath of fresh country air.'

Eleanor glanced at Annie who was smiling, flattered by the praise. Even Megan was standing up a little bit straighter.

'Perhaps we can even make the village Moonwalk an annual event?' asked one lady.

'Absolutely,' said Annie loudly, giving Eleanor a small nudge with her elbow.

Eleanor was just pleased that Annie was looking so relieved.

Mrs. Havers smiled broadly. 'And I, for one, can't

wait to see Annie's ideas for the summer fete, which I'm guessing she can't wait to resurrect. It'll be quite a show in the hands of our capable future countess!'

The excited babble of conversation carried on around them as Annie stared at her friends in horror. She managed to hide her shock though, merely continuing to carry her rictus smile until everyone else had left and it was just Rose and her friends standing in the entrance hall.

'Darling, I'm so sorry,' said Rose, looking aghast. 'I completely forgot about the summer fete.'

'It's fine,' said Annie, looking as if it really wasn't. 'So do Sam and I have to attend in our Lord and Lady mode?'

Rose smiled gently. 'Of course you do, sweetie. Especially as it's held here.'

Annie's eyebrows shot up. 'Here? Inside our home?'

Rose shook her head. 'No, in the front grounds. On August bank holiday weekend.'

'I remember now!' said Eleanor, having a flashback to her childhood of the summer fete. 'It was huge!'

'We haven't had one for a good few years though,' said Megan, frowning.

'Oh my god,' said Annie. 'I remember too. How many people are we talking about?'

Megan bit her lip as Rose answered, 'Well, a lot of people come in from the other villages too so maybe two or three thousand.'

Annie was shocked. 'Three thousand people!'

'I seem to remember there were a few stalls and things,' said Megan, frowning in thought.

'Of course, it hasn't taken place since we lost dear Beatrice,' Rose added. 'She organised it all. Perhaps Arthur couldn't face it. But I think the village would love to come out to our little home again and congregate for the afternoon.'

Annie looked hopeful. 'Maybe we can keep it small and simple?'

Rose laughed. 'Darling, they'll expect a big show. So that's what we'll give them, naturally.'

As she headed off upstairs, Annie sank down onto the bottom step. 'Everyone's going to expect the fete to be amazing,' she whispered, clutching her head.

'It'll be fine,' said Megan, rushing forward. 'We'll help you, won't we?'

'Of course,' said Eleanor, trying to convince herself more than her friends. 'You can do this. You really can, you know.'

Annie shook her head. 'I really can't.'

'I used to come here for the summer fetes,' said Eleanor. 'My dad used to play in the cricket match they held on the front lawn.'

Megan raised her eyebrows. 'That must have been a long time ago.'

Eleanor blew out a sigh. 'Yeah.'

They'd been happy then. A little family unit. Idyllic

summers. Laughter at Christmas. It all felt like ancient history.

'Anyway,' she carried on, brushing the painful memories out of reach once more. 'From what I remember, the fete was actually pretty small. A couple of cake stalls which, thanks to the *Great British Bake Off*, we'll be able to fill. A few drinks. Some lame tombola. That's it.'

Annie shook her head. 'I don't want it to be lame!' she wailed. 'I want it to be the best one ever, because it's our first one. I don't want people thinking Sam and I can't do this.'

Megan exchanged frantic looks with Eleanor. 'Okay, calm down,' she said, putting her arm around Annie's shoulder. 'We'll put some thought into it, okay?'

'Not lame?' asked Annie, sounding more hopeful.

'Definitely the most un-lame fete ever to be held,' said Eleanor. 'We promise.'

'I can't do this on my own. There's too much going on. The kitchen's about to be done up. There's so much to do for the wedding. And now I've got some fete to organise?' She grabbed their hands. 'We've got to stick together, okay? I jump, you jump, remember. You girls are my squad, okay?'

'Yeah,' said Megan. 'Just like Taylor Swift's but quite a bit shorter and maybe rounder too, in my case.'

They all burst out laughing.

'Well, that's a welcome sound,' said Arthur, stepping

out of the west wing and heading across the entrance hall. 'Good morning, ladies.'

'Hello Arthur,' said Megan, obviously used to conversing with an earl of the realm.

Eleanor, surprisingly, felt a little more shy. After all, Arthur was her mother's landlord. A lord. A real-life Earl of Cranley. He had always been a forbidding figure when she had been growing up. But on reflection, he had kind eyes and a gentle smile as he nodded his greeting at her. Of course, he was far more frail than he had been when she was growing up, but there was still that air of aristocracy about him. Albeit slightly shabby.

'It's Eleanor McCartney, isn't it?' asked Arthur, holding out a hand. 'I don't think I was able to introduce myself to you the other evening.'

'Yes,' she replied, briefly taking the hand gently in hers. 'Hello.'

'How is your mother's foot? I hope she's not in too much pain.'

'It's easing a bit, thanks,' Eleanor told him.

'And, how are you? I understand you were in a bicycle accident yesterday?' asked Arthur.

'I'm fine, thank you,' said Eleanor.

'I'm glad to hear it. Tom was quite concerned about you when he was telling me.'

Eleanor found herself blushing at the thought of Tom talking about her. 'Unfortunately, the bike is a right-off,' she said, trying to move the subject on.

'Well, you can always borrow mine,' said Arthur. 'I think my Tour de France days are over.'

'Oh, that's a good idea,' said Annie, coming to stand next to them. 'And now I don't need to worry about you getting any crazy ideas about cycling around the village.'

His eyes twinkled as he smiled down at Annie. 'You worry too much about me,' he said. 'Now, where do you think we left it?'

'I think it was outside near the patio,' said Annie.

They had just stepped through the French doors at the back of the entrance hall when the front door opened. There was a sudden scrabbling of paws as Dylan charged across the floor towards them, followed by Tom and Sam.

'Don't jump up!' said Annie, stepping in front of Arthur to protect him.

Dylan merely ran around and around them in a mad dash before veering off across the lawn.

'He's a bit mental,' said Megan, staring after the dog as it jumped around the long grass.

'He's certainly got a lot of energy,' said Arthur, nodding in agreement.

'Morning,' said Tom, as he and Sam joined them on the patio.

Eleanor felt inordinately pleased to see him, for some reason. 'How's the foot?' she asked. 'What did the doctor say?'

'Sore but definitely on the mend,' said Tom, smiling

in his obvious relief. 'The crutches are finally gone. Gentle exercise has been prescribed, so I'm going to take this fella for a stroll around the grounds after his bath.'

'Well, we've plenty of grounds for you to use here,' said Arthur, looking across to where Dylan was digging a large hole in the lawn. 'I must say, it's nice to have a dog around the place again. Regardless of what our gardener will say about it. Has the chap got a name?'

'He's called Dylan,' said Eleanor.

'After Bob Dylan,' added Megan. 'He's an American singer.'

'The answer is blowing in the wind,' quoted Arthur. 'Thank you, my dear, but I was young too once, you know. Although it may be hard for you to believe it.' He gave Eleanor a wink and then walked slowly away, saying, 'I'm sure we must have some old tennis balls somewhere in my study for the young pup to play with.'

As Sam took a call on his mobile, Tom excused himself to get changed.

Left alone once more with her friends, Eleanor drew her face up to the sun, enjoying the warmth that it now held in its rays.

'Isn't it lovely?' said Annie, also relishing the sun. 'I thought it'd be a nice lazy summer this time round, but I can't see me having any time to sunbathe out here.'

Eleanor tried to remember the last time she had been able to enjoy a day like that. She couldn't recall any at all. Most of her time had been spent indoors and mainly at night. On the plus side, that did mean no freckles. But it also meant no tan either, except what St Tropez would give her occasionally.

She tried to throw a couple of the balls for Dylan that Arthur managed to find. But the grass was still wet from the previous day's rain. Her white Converse were soon sopping wet and dyed green. And Dylan looked more shaggy and in need of a bath than before. She felt pleased when she saw Tom join them on the patio a while later. Perhaps Dylan would help her get the story she so badly needed. Who would have thought a stray animal of all things would finally bring her some good luck?

# Chapter 18

Tom walked carefully back downstairs, having changed into his cargo shorts in preparation for what was likely to be a wet bath for him, as well as Dylan.

His foot was a bit sore having been pulled and prodded, but he definitely felt far more clear-headed for taking himself off the painkillers.

He still felt guilty about the moonwalk and had apologised again to Annie earlier that morning.

'It doesn't matter,' she had told him. 'Honestly. I think we still raised a ton of money.'

He asked for the details of the hospital from her, intending to add his own personal contribution later to the other donations.

'Hey,' said Sam, heading across the hall to see him as he reached the bottom of the stairs. 'We've just had the most amazing news. It turns out that Chris Martin has contracted some kind of virus, unfortunately.'

Tom raised his eyebrows. 'I'm not sure that's amazing news, especially for Chris.'

But he could sense the excitement bubbling away at Sam. 'Yeah, I know. But that was Emily Eavis and they'd like you to do the Sunday night gig instead of

Coldplay.'

Tom hadn't had much sleep, thanks to Dylan howling the house down until he had brought him upstairs to sleep next to his bed. 'What are you talking about?' he said, dragging a hand through his hair.

'Glastonbury, mate. I'm talking about you headlining a week on Sunday at Glastonbury!'

Tom was shocked. 'Me?' He immediately began to shake his head. 'I don't know if I'm up to that. What about my foot?'

'Nobody's asking you to dance.'

Tom's gut reaction was that he really didn't want to play Glastonbury. Which was ridiculous, he told himself. It was the ultimate festival. The most famous one in the world. It was likely to be a once-in-a-lifetime offer. But he had just taken himself away from all the pressure and crowds. His massive world tour had just finished. He really just wanted some peace. However, he could sense Sam's excitement. And after all the recent bad publicity, it would probably help smooth things over with the record company.

'Come on,' urged Sam. 'You know you want to. And you'll be my first ever artist to headline at Glastonbury!'

The reviews would probably be awful, thought Tom. The press were likely to have the knives out for him. And he'd end up doing his foot more harm than good.

But after looking once more at Sam's excited face, he finally nodded his agreement. He owed his friend so much that he should do this one big favour for Sam.

'Fantastic!' said Sam, whooping with delight. 'I'll get back to them.'

Tom took a deep breath, still somewhat in shock. He was therefore pleased to see Eleanor playing with Dylan on the back lawn and went out to them, thankful of the distraction.

Dylan leapt up to greet him.

'Hey, boy,' he said, crouching down on one knee to stroke the dog's head. Dylan wagged his tail in response.

'Is he ready for his bath?' asked Eleanor.

'*He* might not be,' said Tom. 'But it was pretty smelly in my bedroom this morning so, yes, definitely.'

Dylan was less than impressed about his bath but he stood relatively still whilst Tom hosed him down with water near the outside tap on the patio. The dog almost seemed to enjoy the rub-down when Eleanor used the mild dog wash that her mum had given her.

'He's going to need at least another bath before he's fully clean,' she said, rubbing his back into a frothy, foamy cloud. 'And a clip. Mum knows someone who could give him a decent haircut.'

Tom began to rinse Dylan down with the hose. At least he was beginning to look and smell better. 'He might have to wait for the next bath,' he said. 'I won't be around at the weekend.' He paused. 'I've been asked to step in to replace Coldplay at Glastonbury at Sunday.'

Eleanor looked up at him. 'That's amazing,' she told

him. 'You must be thrilled.'

He nodded. Was he thrilled? He wasn't sure.

Tom had just finished giving Dylan his final rinse down when the dog gave himself a good shake, causing water to shower over them both.

'Eewww!' cried Eleanor, now dripping with water.

'Here,' said Tom, lobbing a tennis ball across the lawn for Dylan to chase. 'That should dry him out.'

He glanced over at Eleanor who was wringing out her wet top. He noted that it was expensive-looking material, probably designer. However, he had a feeling that the real Eleanor had been the one he had seen at The Forge.

He could understand why she was quite defensive about the messy house. Perhaps that was why she always liked to look so smart. Maybe she was trying to be the complete opposite of her mum. She had seemed fake and unreal when he had first met her and yet he was certain there was real pain there.

'I was going to stretch my legs and take a short walk around the grounds,' he said. 'Hopefully Dylan will dry out at the same time. Want to join us?'

She looked pleased. 'Of course. Maybe I'll dry out too.'

They both watched the dog rush ahead of them across the overgrown back lawn, trying to chase the butterflies which were fluttering over the weeds that were flowering everywhere.

'I checked with the vets,' she told him as they walked. 'Nobody's claimed him yet.'

Tom felt secretly glad. He had never had a pet growing up. He had had enough trouble trying to feed himself, let alone anyone else. But Dylan came with no pressure. He had spent the last part of the night curled up on a huge mound of old duvets that Annie had produced. No barking, no whining. Just happy to be there with him. Tom wasn't sure how many people had ever felt like that about him personally.

Dylan came bounding up to them, covered in grass and flower seeds.

'I don't believe it. Eleanor's just taken an extra splashing to get you clean,' he told the dog before turning to smile at her.

They locked eyes for a moment before Tom closed his eyes and held his face up to the sun. The warmth was flooding his body, helping the aches and pains fade somewhat. At least he was sleeping well. In fact, even though he hadn't taken any painkillers for a couple of days, he was sleeping more soundly than he could remember. It must have been all the country air.

They followed Dylan towards the west side of the grounds. Tom glanced over at the recording studio and then quickly turned away. He'd pretended to spend the previous afternoon there for Sam's sake, but nothing was happening. The words were still far out of reach. But at least he had finally come clean with Sam. Maybe together they could face his writer's block.

They continued walking in silence towards the side of the house and onwards so that they were facing the front lawn. Rose and Arthur were getting into the car with Annie. They all waved before they headed off down the driveway.

After his minor meltdown the previous evening, Tom had to admit that he was starting to enjoy being around the family. He liked watching them interact. The love, warmth and humour they shared was in stark contrast to the scattered pieces of his own family. Not that he counted any of them as family.

Apart from his beloved gran, of course. Nothing had been the same since she had passed away during the winter. That was when the writing block had begun, because he felt as if he had nobody else to write for. Nobody to impress. Nobody to listen who knew the real him. He still couldn't shift the feeling of loneliness that surrounded him all the time.

Eleanor had found a stick and had thrown it across the front lawn for Dylan to retrieve. However, he picked it up and rushed off towards the willow tree.

'You're supposed to retrieve it, you fool,' said Eleanor, chasing after the dog.

He watched her rush through the knee-length grass, anxious that Dylan shouldn't get into any more trouble. It gave him a brief moment to enjoy her lithe figure, especially as he himself wasn't up to running at the moment. She was soon at the boughs of the great willow tree and disappeared through the leaves.

However, she was gone for such a long time that Tom started to worry and made his cautious way through the tangle of grass. He couldn't wait until his foot was fully mended and he felt fit and healthy once more.

Once he had reached the tree, he pulled the curtain of greenery to one side and found Eleanor having a tug of war on the ground with Dylan. Her jeans were now grass-stained and wet. Her top was crumpled and splattered with mud.

Eleanor looked up and blushed when she found him watching her. 'Sorry,' she said, with a rueful smile. 'I was trying to get back to you but Dylan here had other ideas.'

'No worries,' he replied.

In fact, he was enjoying watching her play with the dog. Her dark hair was flying around her face and she looked relaxed for the first time since he had met her. As if this was the true Eleanor.

Suddenly, a line of a song came to him from nowhere. 'Suddenly I see the real you,' it whispered into his head. 'As if the stars have come out at night.'

He continued to watch her play with the dog, her green eyes flashing as she laughed and tried to wrestle the stick from the dog.

And he realised he was definitely not in a hurry to

leave Willow Tree Hall any more.

# Chapter 19

The following day, an excited-looking Rose rushed into the kitchen. 'Have you all seen the local newspaper?'

Eleanor looked up. She had been helping Annie pack up some of the bigger items from the kitchen before the builders moved in to start the renovation after the weekend.

'Is it the charity walk?' asked Megan, straightening up from a box she had been packing.

'Well, yes, but it's mostly all about me, darlings!' said Rose, flourishing the paper.

They all rushed forward to look at the photo which was, indeed, Rose wearing her bodice as she strode through the high street.

'They've caught me in a very flattering light, I must say,' cooed Rose. 'This is going to do my husband-hunting the power of good!'

'What does it say?' asked Annie, looking hopeful as she peered over Rose's shoulder.

'It says some lovely things about the local WI. And how it was all Eleanor's idea, of course,' carried on Rose.

Eleanor noticed that Annie's smile had dropped a

little as she turned away.

'Well, it was Annie that brought everyone together,' she said quickly. 'She's the countess around here!'

'And I've been thinking,' carried on Rose, powering her megawatt smile towards Eleanor. 'We must compare wardrobes. You must come and see my little fashion show upstairs. Nobody else appreciates my designer clothes around here.'

'Well, that's nice, I must say! What about me?' asked Annie, half-joking as she started to pack up another box.

'Darling girl,' said Rose, giving her a squeeze. 'You're many things, but you're no lover of fashion. Whereas Eleanor here, well, look at you today!'

Eleanor checked what she was wearing. Victoria Beckham trousers. Wedge heels. Funky logo top. She had been particularly pleased with her outfit. Not that she had anything else to concentrate her mind on at the moment.

They were interrupted by the arrival of Arthur and Tom coming into the kitchen through the back door.

Rose waved the newspaper at him. 'We're back in the news. Isn't it marvellous?'

'I read it this morning. Jolly good show. And I understand it was all your idea, my dear,' said Arthur, beaming at Eleanor.

Eleanor blushed and shrugged her shoulders. 'It was nothing.'

'I disagree,' Arthur told her. 'I understand that it is

the largest amount ever raised by the WI for one of their charities. And that, in conjunction with Tom's kind donation, will make a vast difference to those struggling with cancer.'

Eleanor looked across at Tom. 'You gave the hospital some money?'

Now it was his turn to look uncomfortable. 'Just a small amount,' he muttered. 'To make up for me not opening the walk as I promised.'

Eleanor couldn't believe it. Was he actually blushing? 'Thank you,' she said.

He gave a shrug in reply.

'I think that I can safely say that it was a most generous amount of money,' said Arthur, before he frowned. 'And I've just remembered that you also wanted it to be anonymous. My apologies, dear boy.'

'That's fine,' said Tom, heading across the kitchen.

'Oh and I've dug out my old bicycle for you,' carried on Arthur, looking at Eleanor. 'Tom has just checked the brakes and chain.'

'Thank you so much,' said Eleanor, still looking at Tom, who seemed anxious to leave.

There was a short silence before Tom said, 'Well, I'd better get back to the recording studio, otherwise I'll be in trouble with Sam.'

Eleanor was still mulling over the huge donation that he had made to the hospital.

'Of course,' said Arthur, following him. 'And I really

must see to my paperwork.'

Eleanor squeezed in front of Arthur and dashed into the entrance hall after Tom, who was already at the French doors leading onto the patio.

'Why didn't you tell me?' she asked him, rushing up to stop him going any further. 'About the donation, I mean.'

He looked down at her. 'It was a personal decision and nobody else needed to know.'

He turned away, leaving her feeling mortified that she had ranted at him a week ago.

She sighed. He was a nice guy. Too nice, she told herself. It was no use pretending to herself any longer. She was never going to write an expose on him. It just wasn't fair.

Because she really was beginning to like Tom and enjoy his company. She inwardly groaned.

Besides, he was too close to Annie and the family. She couldn't let any scandal touch them. She wouldn't betray any of them.

So what did that mean for her future now?

She headed back to the kitchen deep in thought, nearly bumping into Rose as she went down the stairs.

'Just remember,' said Rose, as they went in opposite directions. 'My wardrobe is always open, darling! But I'll only show you mine if you show me yours.' She gave a gurgle of laughter.

'Thanks,' said Eleanor, smiling. 'I will.'

But she was still so deep in thought about Tom that she didn't register how quiet it was in the kitchen until she reached the table. Then she looked up and realised that Annie was looking upset.

'What's the matter?' she asked.

'I'm being silly,' said Annie, with a shrug.

'What do you mean?' said Eleanor.

Annie blew out a long sigh. 'This whole pressure to be a good countess is so hard. You're the one that thought up the charity walk. But I'm not sure the fete will be any good when you're not around to help.'

'Gee, thanks a bunch,' muttered Megan.

Annie looked at her friend. 'You know what I mean. You're so busy with the kids. I've got the wedding to organise and the family to take care of. And Eleanor will go back to London. And then it's all on me to make this fete be the best it can be.'

Suddenly Eleanor was sharply reminded how low Annie's self-esteem was. Her teenage years had been particularly bad and had wrecked what little confidence she had ever had.

'But I can help,' she said, stepping forward to give Annie a hug of reassurance when she realised that Megan was shaking her head at her.

'Sometimes you don't answer our texts until the next day,' Annie said gently.

'Well, that's going to change from now on,' Eleanor replied, in a firm tone.

And she realised that she meant it.

Now that she had decided that she couldn't possibly write the story on Tom, she had some changes to make in her life. She was so sick of lying. So tired of her make-believe world. It was time to be honest. It was time for the truth. She owed that to her friends, regardless of how it would affect her burgeoning friendship with Tom.

She took a deep breath. This was it. The moment she had been dreading. 'Actually, I'm not sure I will be going back to London after all,' she began.

Annie frowned. 'What are you talking about?'

Eleanor took a beat. 'I lost my job.'

'Oh no!' They both rushed forward to give her a hug. She let herself be smothered by their support before forcing herself to step backwards. She looked at her friends.

'It's okay. They're downsizing and all that. It's rubbish, but I'll live. But there's something else I need to tell you. The job that I just lost. I lied about what I really did for a living. And to Mum too. Nobody knew the truth.'

Megan and Annie looked at each other before staring back at her.

'What are you talking about?' said Megan. 'You weren't a call girl or something like that, were you?'

'What? No!' said Eleanor. 'I still worked in the media but instead of working at the *Money Chronicle*, I was a journalist on a celebrity magazine.' She picked up a piece of bubble wrap that they had been using and played with it, avoiding eye contact with them both.

The silence stretched out between them all. Eleanor automatically scratched her neck as she waited for them to respond.

'But you were always going on about all that financial stuff,' said Megan, looking confused.

'It started off as some silly lie and then I just didn't know how to stop it,' said Eleanor. 'I should have told you before now.'

'How many years have you been lying to us?' asked Megan.

'Eight,' muttered Eleanor.

'Eight!' Annie was boggle-eyed. 'The whole time you were in London? Why didn't you say something?'

Finally, Eleanor looked up at them. 'Because I didn't want to let you down. You thought I had this amazing career, but I didn't. You two are the ones that have made it. Not me. I'm a failure.' She bit her lip, trying to hold back the tears.

'You're not a failure if you managed to keep a job in London for that long,' said Annie, shaking her head.

'So which magazine was it?' asked Megan.

'*Hot Gossip!*' Eleanor told her with a heavy sigh.

Megan's eyebrows shot up. 'Blimey. I thought you were going to say *Elle* or something fancy like that, especially with your designer outfits. And you used to do what for them?'

Eleanor took a deep breath. 'I used to get the latest scoop on whichever celebrity was behaving badly. Not very nice work, I admit, snooping around. You see...'

'Wait a minute,' said Annie, suddenly springing back into life. 'Is this why you've been coming up to the hall all the time? To get a, what was it, a scoop on Tom?'

Megan turned to look at Eleanor, equally aghast. 'Oh my god! Is it?'

Eleanor shook her head. 'No! I didn't even know he was staying here, did I?'

Annie's eyes filled with tears. 'I thought you came back here to see us!'

'I did!'

But Annie was too upset and carried on. 'I thought it was so nice that you wanted to make up for all that time you've missed with us. But we were just a story, weren't we?'

'No! It's not like that!' said Eleanor. 'Look, I messed up. I know that.'

'Are you going to write a story about Tom?' asked Annie, glaring at her. 'Because let me tell you something, he's a good guy. He doesn't need any more of those paparazzi lies.'

Eleanor was shaking her head so hard she thought it might fall off her shoulders. 'No. There's no story. I wouldn't do that now.'

'What do you mean *now*?' said Megan, frowning.

'Does that mean you had thought about writing a story about him?'

'No, of course not,' said Eleanor, gulping.

'I don't know if I can believe you any more,' said Annie.

They both looked so horrified at her that, with a sob, Eleanor grabbed her handbag and ran out of the back door. She saw the bicycle but ignored it. She couldn't take it now. Not after the way her friends had looked at her. So she walked down the long driveway, the tears streaming down her face.

She had been struggling by herself for so long that she had forgotten to look after her friends as well. Her lies had become more and more tangled and now the truth was just one big mess. There had been the possibility that she could still write a story about Tom. But she knew now that she could never do that. Regardless of the fact that it would get her back to London, she knew it was wrong. And her friends would hate her even more.

In that moment she knew that losing her job was nothing compared to the pain she felt that she had lost her dearest friends forever.

# Chapter 20

Eleanor finally staggered through the front door of The Forge an hour later after the long walk home.

'Hi.' Her mum turned around from the kitchen table and was aghast to see her daughter's upset face. 'What is it? What's happened?'

'Oh Mum! I've made a mess of everything!' Eleanor burst into tears again. Would she ever be able to stop crying?

'Come and sit down,' said her mum, leading her over to the table. 'What's the matter? Is this to do with your ex-boyfriend?'

'It's all of it, Mum.' She took a deep breath. 'I lost my job. Restructuring or something.'

'Oh.' Her mum looked concerned. 'Well, I'm sure there are plenty of other positions out there for a wonderful journalist like yourself. You'll see, they'll be chomping at the bit to have you work for their newspapers.'

Eleanor shook her head. 'But I'm not a wonderful journalist, Mum. I never told you the truth.'

Now her mum was looking shocked. 'So what is the truth?' she asked slowly.

Eleanor took a deep breath. 'I work, I mean I used to work, for this awful gossip magazine. You know, one of those cheap, tacky ones that are just filled with rubbish about celebrities. I took the job to further my career but that was eight years ago and now I've ended up with nothing.'

Her mum took a deep breath. 'Eight years?'

Eleanor nodded. 'I know. I was too embarrassed to tell you. You were so proud of me and I knew you wouldn't be if you knew the truth. And then time went on and on and it just became too big a lie.'

Her Mum frowned. 'So it was a gossip magazine? Like the ones…' Her voice trailed off.

Eleanor gulped away more tears 'The ones that wrote about dad all those years ago. I'm so sorry. It was the only job I could get at the time. But the last thing I ever wanted to do was upset you. So I kept on lying.'

Her mum reached out to stroke her face. 'Darling, I love you. I'll always be proud of you, regardless of what job you have.' She took a beat. 'I suppose the gardening leave was all a lie as well?'

'Yes.'

Her mum gave her a soft smile. 'I did wonder, what with you having the last month off and all.'

Eleanor was shocked. It turned out she hadn't really fooled her mum after all. And that her mother's reaction to her job hadn't been as bad as she had feared all those years.

She shook her head. 'It wasn't wonderful at all though. My fabulous, glamorous life in London? I didn't really know anyone. I just bought lots of clothes to make me feel better, but even they didn't really make a difference. I actually felt alone quite a bit of the time. Do you know what I mean?'

Her mum nodded. 'I think I do. Of course, I've been lucky enough to have friends like Ben here in the village and I've got the animals.'

'I don't think I really had any real friends in London,' said Eleanor, with a sigh. 'I did go out all the time but it was always for work. I was lonely, even with Lucas. I don't even know how I ended up with him. He liked the exclusive tickets I had access to. But there were no feelings there.' She stared across the kitchen as if realising the truth for the very first time. 'We never laughed.'

'Well, that is sad,' said her mum, reaching out to squeeze her hand.

'But the worst of it is that I told Annie and Megan the truth,' said Eleanor.

'Well, that's a good thing,' said her mum, looking pleased. 'They're your true friends so it's important to be honest with them.'

The tears began to fall once more. 'No, it's not. They think I'm here to do a story on Tommy King and that I've betrayed them.'

'Tommy who?'

‘You know Tom who brought the stray dog? Well, he’s actually a famous singer. Really famous.’

‘Is he really?’ Her mum looked surprised. ‘Well, I’d have never known. He was ever so nice.’

‘Yes, I think he truly is,’ groaned Eleanor. ‘And that makes it all the worse.’

‘Look, they’re your best friends. They’ll understand once they’ve calmed down.’

But Eleanor wasn’t sure. ‘I don’t know,’ she whispered. ‘You should have seen their faces, Mum. They were really cross.’

‘They’ll come round,’ said her mum gently. ‘You might just need to give them a little time.’

Eleanor nodded, thinking privately that it might take a very long time indeed for her friends to forgive her.

*

Tom found himself looking forward to walking Dylan around Willow Tree Hall each day. It was beginning to feel like home to him.

Except he didn’t have a village to call home. Or anywhere really. He’d run away more times than he could count from every foster home.

Now he felt free and rudderless, drifting towards who knew what. It was both unsettling and exciting at the same time.

Determined to just focus on the present for now, he

needed to finalise his set for Glastonbury. So he went in search of Sam and found him in his study.

On the desk was an iPad, blaring out music.

'What do you think?' asked Sam, nodding at the speakers. 'It's Hazy Memory's latest album.'

'It sounds great,' lied Tom. It was a symphony of loud guitar riffs and general wailing, none of which were any good.

Sam's eyebrows shot up in surprise. 'Honestly?'

Tom cleared his throat. 'It's not really my style.'

'I'm not sure it's anyone's style of music these days,' said Sam with a sigh. 'I don't know where the band goes from here, to be honest.'

Dylan, who had followed Tom into the study, began to howl in time to the music. Tom and Sam both burst into laughter.

'Nice to see Dylan agreeing with us,' said Tom, sitting down on a box nearby. 'Are the band coming to Glastonbury with us?'

Sam shook his head. 'No. Been there, done that many decades ago. I'm not sure they're cool enough these days. But they're talking about coming here next month for a while. God help us all. I must remember to warn Annie.' He looked up at Tom. 'Will you still be here?'

'I'm not sure yet,' he replied.

The truth was that he really wanted to stay but how peaceful would it be once a rock band descended on them all? Maybe then he would move back to his flat.

After all, Cranley wasn't his home any more than Willow Tree Hall was.

'Well, the more the merrier,' said Sam with a shrug. 'You know the room is yours as long as you want.'

'Thanks.' Tom hadn't had a room in anyone's home since he stayed with his gran many years ago. 'Have you got a spare minute to go over my set?'

'Sure,' said Sam. 'Let's head on over to the studio and run through everything. I'll grab a Diet Coke for us both on the way.'

Tom wandered outside on his own and found Annie curled up on the wooden seat. The sun was beating down, despite the horizon being dotted with heavy rain clouds. To his surprise, she was reading *Hot Gossip!* Magazine.

'What are you reading that trash for?' he asked, somewhat bemused.

But he blanched as Annie looked up at him. Her eyes were red and she had obviously been crying.

'Is everything okay?' he asked her.

She nodded. 'It's fine,' she told him. 'Just having a bad day. This really is a load of rubbish, isn't it?'

He took the magazine from her and flicked through the pages. 'Yeah. But a lot of people like to read about this kind of stuff. I guess they want to know that anybody famous can live a more exciting life than they can. For some people it's an escape from their own struggles.'

Annie nodded thoughtfully. 'What do you think of the people that write these articles?'

Tom was a bit surprised at her question. 'Well, I guess everyone's gotta make a living somehow,' he told her, with a shrug.

'I guess,' muttered Annie, her forehead creasing into a frown.

Sam came outside, holding two cans of Diet Coke. 'Hey,' he said, also realising that Annie looked upset. 'You okay?'

She nodded.

'Is this to do with that silly row with Eleanor which you won't tell me about?' He crouched down in front of her. 'Go and see her. Thrash out whatever it is that you've argued about and move on. She's one of your oldest friends. I'm sure you can work through it.'

He gave her a gentle kiss on the lips and Tom decided to wander away, leaving them in their embrace.

As he walked, he was still trying to work out what Eleanor and her friends could have possibly disagreed about.

# Chapter 21

Eleanor was trying very hard to keep busy to stop her from worrying about her friends. She had spent the previous afternoon tidying up the kitchen in The Forge. In the evening, she and her mum had watched television.

She was still reeling from her mum's lack of reaction regarding her job at Hot Gossip! Maybe she should have told her years ago. Maybe she should have told her friends as well then things wouldn't have got so out of hand.

She hadn't slept well. Tossing and turning, she spent hours dwelling over the possibility of having lost her best friends through her own stupidity. In the end, she fell into such a heavy sleep after dawn that she woke up late. With no texts or calls on her mobile from either Annie or Megan, Eleanor was feeling so depressed that she couldn't even be bothered to get dressed before going downstairs to start sorting out the animals.

Then it had been so busy that she was still in her pyjamas collecting the chicken eggs at nearly midday.

As she came out of the coop carrying the freshly laid eggs, the donkey gave her a gentle nudge with its nose.

'Get off,' she told her. 'You'll make me drop them.'

She gently put down the eggs by the back door and went to carry the large bundle of hay from the back of the garden to where the goat and donkey needed it.

As she dropped it onto the ground, she scratched at her neck. What with the animals and the hay, the eczema was worse than ever. She felt such a mess.

But for once she didn't care. She didn't care that she hadn't bothered with her hair. That she had no make-up on. That she was in her old T-shirt and pyjama bottoms. Nothing mattered any more. She just felt numb.

As she bent down to undo the string holding the bale together, the donkey gave her such a nudge with its nose that she went straight over, face first, into the hay.

She swore under her breath and struggled to get up. It was only then that she felt she was being watched.

She quickly spun around and saw Tom and Arthur standing at the back gate.

'Good morning,' said Arthur, undoing the latch on the gate. 'I do hope we haven't come at a bad time.'

'Good morning,' she managed to mumble, shocked that Arthur and, perhaps worse, Tom would find her in such a state.

'It seems you forgot to take the bicycle with you,' said Arthur, coming into the garden. 'I thought perhaps you might need it if you wished to visit your friends. It's been so nice to hear you all laughing and chatting away together each day.'

She tried to take in what Arthur was saying as she

watched Tom wheel the bicycle into the garden and close the gate behind him.

'Anyway, we were just passing and thought it might be an opportune time to visit your mother,' carried on Arthur. 'Is she in?'

Eleanor nodded, still feeling absolutely mortified that they had found her in such a mess.

Arthur, on the other hand, appeared completely oblivious to her appearance. Class and good breeding probably did that, she thought.

'Mum!' she called out, her voice a little shaky. 'Arthur's here.'

'Is he really?' Her mum came hobbling out of the kitchen. 'Hello, Arthur. What a lovely surprise. I'll put the kettle on.'

Arthur followed her mother into the kitchen, chatting away about the weather.

As they went inside, Eleanor hid her flaming red cheeks by trying to undo the string on the bale once more. She almost jumped out of her skin when a pair of large male hands quickly appeared and wrenched the knot open almost immediately.

'Thank you,' she muttered, straightening up but still not making eye contact with Tom. Instead, she scratched her neck as she fretted. After all, this man had been the main reason that her friends were so angry with her. Her main downfall. None of which was his fault which made her guilt even worse.

He reached over and gently stroked the donkey's mane. 'Just to warn you, I think Arthur's going to talk to your mum about perhaps decreasing the number of animals she has.'

Eleanor was surprised that Arthur had mentioned such a thing to Tom. Perhaps they were closer than she realised. In shock, she made eye contact with him and saw him glance at her neck. She immediately dropped her hand and covered up the eczema patch with her hair.

'Well, thanks for the heads-up,' said Eleanor, trying to appear casual and confident despite her pyjamas and lack of make-up. 'Have the neighbours been complaining?'

'Not all of them,' he replied, with a soft smile.

Eleanor sighed. 'I don't blame them. I mean, look at it.' She waved her arm around at the mess.

He glanced around the garden. 'Has she always been like this?'

Eleanor shook her head. 'Only since Dad walked out on us. Now it's like living in London Zoo. I think we've lost the tortoise at least five times so far this week.'

'Well, it's not like it can get very far, is it?' His blue eyes crinkled up at the edges.

She tried not to match his smile. 'Very funny.'

She almost started to relax about him finding her like this. It wasn't important what she looked like, she realised. Nothing mattered any more. She just felt so sad that she didn't really care.

However, she did get changed before joining the visitors in the kitchen for a cup of tea. But she only threw on a T-shirt and shorts. She tied her messy hair back in a ponytail and checked her face but, in the end, she figured it would have been too obvious to suddenly appear fully made up, so she slicked on some lip balm and went back downstairs.

'Perhaps Ben can help you find a home for some of them,' Arthur was saying.

Eleanor glanced at her mum, who was trying to hide how upset she was. 'I think that's a good idea,' she said. 'Aren't you seeing him tomorrow night? You could mention it then.'

Her mother nodded sadly.

Eleanor looked at Tom in despair.

Thankfully he picked up on her signal. 'The bicycle's all fixed up for you,' he said in a bright tone of voice.

Eleanor was grateful for him to change the subject so easily, especially as she could feel her mum relax as the conversation moved on.

They went outside and showed her mum the bicycle and then headed on their way.

'Thank you,' murmured Eleanor, as they left. 'For being so gentle with her.'

Arthur gave her a soft smile. 'Everything will work out, my dear. You just wait and see.' He gave her arm a squeeze and then walked away.

Tom stopped and looked down at her. 'Annie's been

pretty upset,' he said. 'It's not my place to intrude, but whatever it is you've had a row about, it can be fixed.'

Eleanor gulped back the pain that reappeared deep inside. 'I'm not so sure,' she told him. 'But thanks anyway.'

As she looked up and gave him a small smile, she found herself thinking that he had kind eyes. At that moment, she was extremely grateful that she hadn't exposed his private life to the world. He didn't deserve that. He was too nice. Then she closed the back gate and went back indoors.

Her mum was still mulling over the idea of not keeping so many animals. Eleanor knew nothing she could say would sway her decision, so she went back upstairs. She curled up on her bed, staring at the photograph of her, Annie and Megan when they were younger. It had all gone so wrong and she had no idea how to fix it.

# Chapter 22

At some point in the afternoon, Eleanor had drifted off to sleep on her bed, still clutching the photograph of her friends.

She woke up to a knock on the door and realised it was nearly teatime. 'I don't want any food, Mum,' she called out. 'Just sort out dinner for yourself. I'm really not hungry.'

It was true. She still felt sick to her stomach with loss and worry.

'Good job we brought some chocolate with us then,' said Megan, stalking into the room and throwing a box of Maltesers on the bed. 'Tom had a stash of these, so I promised I'd give them to the kids. I'm saving their milk teeth and sharing them with you instead.'

Eleanor struggled to sit up, feeling shocked as she watched Annie follow Megan into the small bedroom and look around.

Megan stared up the walls. 'Wow. Your mum hasn't changed anything here in decades, has she?'

Eleanor shook her head. 'Well, you know what Mum's like,' she said.

The bed jumped as Megan threw herself onto the

end. Annie remained standing, avoiding eye contact.

The only sound for a few moments was Megan ripping open the box and grabbing a handful of Maltesers. 'Anyone?' she offered, holding out the box with her other hand.

The response was a deafening silence.

Megan sighed. 'Well, this isn't at all awkward,' she said, rolling her eyes. 'What's that?' She pointed at the photograph which Eleanor was holding.

Still in shock, Eleanor handed it over to her. She did notice that Annie couldn't resist peeking over Megan's shoulder to see what it was and was thankful to see a small smile of recognition pass Annie's lips.

'I've got this same photo on my bookshelf,' said Megan before handing it over to Annie. 'You?'

'On my bedside cabinet,' muttered Annie.

Megan took the photo from her and peered at it. 'God, we look so young. I think this was one of the last photos we had of us together before you both abandoned me.'

'Abandoned *you*?' said Annie.

Megan looked up the bed at Eleanor. 'You went to London and Annie sailed around the world. And don't think I've forgiven either of you for that yet.'

'Doesn't mean that I was happy,' said Annie, looking utterly miserable.

Megan looked at her. 'I always imagined you like Kate Winslet in *Titanic*,' she said. 'You know, arms stretched wide at the front of the boat.'

'With Leonardo DiCaprio right behind me,' added Annie with a sad smile.

They all sighed in unison. 'How many times did we watch that DVD?' asked Eleanor softly.

'Too many,' said Annie, sitting down on the bed. 'It was nothing like that, of course. It was horrible and lonely.' For a second, Annie looked bleak. She had had a rough time after her father had died and part of the reason for working on the cruise ships was to get away from her wretched home life.

Eleanor would have done the same, but she could never leave her mum. Except she had, she realised. She'd moved away as quickly as she could and her mum was stuck here with the animals. Yet another regret to add to the growing list.

'So are you going to move back to London?' Annie suddenly asked, looking straight at Eleanor.

Eleanor shook her head. 'No. I'm not. No job and it turns out that I was pretty lonely there as well.'

Annie frowned but didn't reply.

'What about all the celebrity parties you went to?' asked Megan, in between mouthfuls of chocolate. 'They must have been fun.'

'Not really,' said Eleanor. 'If you're a celebrity then you get the VIP treatment. But they all know that you're a journalist so treat you like a leper and you're left alone in case they say anything they shouldn't. Most of the time, I ended up near the bar, grabbing a free drink.'

'So why did you carry on if you hated it so much?' asked Annie.

Eleanor shrugged her shoulders. 'I didn't know what else to do. And I didn't want to let Mum down. She'd given up so much for me to go to university and live out my dreams. I didn't want her to know they hadn't come true, so I kept on lying.' A tear rolled down her cheek. 'I'm sorry I lied to you both for so long,' she said. 'I was an idiot.'

'Well, that we already knew,' quipped Megan before looking serious. 'Are you going to write a story about Tom?'

Eleanor shook her head fiercely. 'No. He's too nice to deceive. Besides, I don't want to go back to that way of life.' As she said the words, she knew it was true. That part of her life was truly over. 'I don't want to be that person any more,' she said aloud.

'So don't,' said Megan, with a shrug.

'It's not that simple,' Eleanor told her. 'What do I do instead?'

Megan grabbed some more chocolates. 'Anything that makes you happy.'

Eleanor shrugged her shoulders. 'I don't know what that is any more. I just feel a bit lost.'

'Then stay here,' said Annie, reaching out to squeeze her hand. 'You're home. The village, your mum and us, what else do you need?'

'Apart from a steady pay check? Nothing but you two,' Eleanor told her, another tear rolling down her cheek.

There was a muttered oath and then the three of them were hugging and crying and promising never to fall out again.

'We probably put too much pressure on you,' said Annie.

'No, you didn't. It was all me. But you know how I feel about you guys, don't you?' said Eleanor, looking from friend to friend. 'How I really feel about you?'

Megan smiled. 'We love you too,' she said.

'I just wanted everything to be perfect,' said Eleanor, scratching at a flaky patch of eczema between her fingers. 'I needed to be perfect.'

'But you aren't,' said Megan in a soft tone.

'Nobody is,' added Annie.

It turned out that the only person who had expected 100% perfection was Eleanor herself. And look where that had left her these past few weeks.

'But I thought that if I wasn't then maybe you wouldn't like me anymore.'

Megan rolled her eyes. 'You idiot! We're not your dad. We don't feel like that about you. We don't care about that scar on your knee where you tried to jump over the wall on the way to school and failed spectacularly.'

'Or the hundreds of freckles on your nose,' said

Annie.

'Or your split ends, if you had any,' added Megan.

'Oh, I've got loads now,' sighed Eleanor. 'I need a decent haircut.' She frowned. 'Maybe I should take mum with me as a treat.'

'So I can trust you around Tom?' asked Annie.

Eleanor nodded. 'Absolutely. I'm definitely not writing a story about him. But I don't want him to know about my past. He knows that I lost my job.'

'Does he?' said Annie, looking surprised. 'How?'

'It's a long story,' Eleanor told her. 'But please just let him think that I was a financial journalist. I know that means more lies, but I think...'

'Oh my god! It's because you like him!' said Megan, her eyes gleaming.

'Of course I don't,' said Eleanor quickly.

'You're blushing,' Annie told her, grinning.

'I'm not,' said Eleanor, even though she could feel the heat spreading across her cheeks.

'This is so exciting,' said Annie. 'You and Tommy King! Can you imagine?'

The trouble was, Eleanor could and was desperately trying not to.

'Oh, great,' drawled Megan, making a face. 'So you both get this amazing love life and I'm stuck at home with Neal.'

'Neal's lovely and you know it,' said Annie, before beaming at Eleanor. 'I can just see you two together.'

Eleanor was frantically shaking her head. 'No,' she told them. 'It's never going to happen. He's never going to look at someone like me.'

'Rubbish,' said Annie. 'Look at me and Sam! If I can be a countess, you can be a famous singer's girlfriend.'

Megan sighed. 'Your lives are so exciting.'

'I don't want exciting,' Eleanor told them both. 'I want dull. I'd be really happy with boring and dull right now.'

But she let Annie rattle on and Megan pretend to be jealous because she was so happy that they were friends again. She knew how close she had been to losing them and was determined to make sure that would never happen again.

# Chapter 23

Now that Eleanor had made up with her friends, she was desperate to see them as often as possible. So the following morning, she quickly finished her animal chores and cycled to Willow Tree Hall.

On the journey, she mulled over how quiet her mum had been that morning. But she still hadn't mentioned the conversation with Arthur over relinquishing ownership of some of the animals. Eleanor made a mental note to pop in and see Ben to ask his advice. After all, he was her mum's oldest friend.

She arrived at Willow Tree Hall just in time to see Tom loading up Sam's car with his weekend bag and guitar. She wandered over, still feeling slightly sweaty from her bicycle ride. But the last time he'd seen her, she had been in her pyjamas and a complete mess. Did it really matter anymore? He would never be interested in her anyway, so what was the point in bothering?

That morning she had just pulled on her cut-off jeans and a T-shirt. No fancy silk jumpsuit. No pristine white clothes. No heavy make-up. Just some mascara and tinted moisturiser.

'Hey. You're heading up to Glastonbury now?' she

asked, as Tom lifted in the final bag into the boot.

'Yeah,' he told her. 'I need to meet up with my band to rehearse and do some interviews for the TV companies.'

She smiled. 'Sounds very glamorous.'

'It really isn't.'

She found it easier to relax with him. She supposed that now that he had seen her in her pyjamas, soaking wet and generally in a mess for various days running, she could stop putting on her air of refined style.

'What, no tent?' she quipped, glancing in the boot.

He smiled. 'Five-star Winnebago all the way, thank god.' He glanced around, as if to ensure they weren't overheard. 'You've made it up with your friends, I hear.'

She nodded. 'It's all okay now, thanks,' she told him.

They were interrupted by a furry grey blur as Dylan hurtled out of the front door and rushed straight towards them.

'He doesn't seem to understand that I've got to go away for a few days,' said Tom, looking worried.

'He's going to miss you,' said Eleanor as the dog sat down and gazed up adoringly at Tom.

He reached down to stroke the soft fur on Dylan's head. 'Do you think I should sing him a song on stage just to cheer him up?'

'As your number one fan, he would expect nothing less,' Eleanor told him.

'I was thinking about doing a Coldplay number as it

was their slot that I'm taking over,' said Tom. 'Which is his favourite do you think?'

Eleanor felt a thrill at his question. 'I reckon Dylan has always liked "The Scientist" the best out of all of Coldplay's songs.'

He broke into a grin and her heart caught in her throat for a second.

'Will I see you when I come back?' he asked, his voice low.

'You're not heading back to London afterwards?' she asked, her throat still constricted. She was suddenly upset that he was leaving. Suddenly aware how much she was going to miss him for even that short a time. But they had known each other for such a brief time. How was it possible that she had begun to care about him?

'I thought I might stay on here for a while longer,' he said, in a casual tone. 'What about you?'

She nodded. 'I was thinking the same.'

He was staring at her, his blue eyes boring into hers as if he could read what was in her very soul. But then he stood up as the rest of the family joined them and the moment was lost.

Eleanor watched as Annie and Sam also said their goodbyes.

'Maybe you'll fall in love with some glamorous hippie there,' Annie was teasing Sam.

Sam shook his head. 'Nope,' he murmured. 'I've got everything I'll ever need right here.'

As they kissed, Eleanor looked away, trying to remember when she had ever been kissed with such passion.

After they had left, Eleanor stayed at the hall.

'So what shall we do today?' she asked. 'How are the plans for the fete coming along?'

'I don't even know where to begin,' said Annie, staring down at a blank piece of paper.

'Okay,' said Eleanor. 'Well, we'll have to put our thinking caps on.' She turned to look at Megan. 'Oh and I was thinking about offering to babysit for you one evening if you and Neal fancied going out.'

But Megan didn't look excited at the offer. 'Thanks, but we never go out anyway,' said Megan, looking miserable. 'Neal keeps saying that we're saving up, although I don't know what for.'

There was a short silence whilst they all reached for a biscuit, lost in their thoughts.

'Well, at least we know Alex will cheer us all up when he arrives later on,' said Annie.

'Who?' asked Eleanor.

'He's Sam's friend from school. Alessandro... Our interior designer.' Annie looked very excited.

'You've got to meet him. He's amazing,' said Megan. 'I can't believe I'll miss him because I've got to pick the kids up from school.'

'And I can't believe I'm finally going to get my brand new kitchen,' said Annie, beaming.

Eleanor had envisaged someone tall, discreet and very Italian in the way the designer had been described. Only one of those things was right.

'Ciao!' yelled the dark-haired man in jeans rushing across the entrance hall to give Annie a bear hug. He was even shorter than Annie. 'Let me look at you,' he said, stepping backwards. 'Jeez, am I ever going to get you out of those bloody skinny jeans?'

Annie gave him a kiss on the cheek before exchanging a knowing smile with Eleanor. 'Nope.'

'Well, we're going to need a friggin' meringue to put over them if you insist on wearing them at your wedding. You look tired. Has Sam been keeping you awake all night?' he winked.

'Shut up,' muttered Annie, blushing furiously. 'Anyway, he's in Glastonbury.'

But Alex just laughed and hugged her. 'Darling, I've missed you and your shy ways. And you must have missed me terribly!'

Eleanor was agog. He was a real character.

'Of course we have,' Annie told him. 'But it's not our fault you've been in your love nest with Mario every hour of every day. By the way, where is he? I thought he was coming with you?'

'Dumped, sweetie.'

'No! Why?'

'That china doll collection of his I told you about? I couldn't deal with it any more,' said Alex with a shudder. 'The damn things stared at me all night with those glass eyes. Felt like they were giving my performance marks out of ten. Then I accidentally knocked "Josephine" off the dressing table when I was dusting and he went completely psycho. I was outta there.'

'Poor you,' said Annie, laying a hand on his arm. 'I've got some lemon drizzle cake just for you. Shop-bought at the minute because of the lack of kitchen, I'm afraid.'

'I can't eat my way through heartache, darling.'

'There's coffee cake as well.'

'Excellent. Lead the way.' They headed across the hall and Alex locked eyes with Eleanor. 'You're new,' he said, giving her a once-over. 'But at least you've got some style, much like myself. I'd recognise those Primarni loafers anywhere. Thought they'd sold out. Who are you?'

'Alex!' muttered Annie, shaking her head. 'You're so rude.'

'Italian,' he snapped back. 'There's a difference.'

'This is Eleanor,' said Annie, sounding proud.

'Blimey, I thought she was your imaginary friend after all this time,' said Alex. 'Where have you been hiding, lovely?'

'London,' Eleanor told him, feeling nervous under his scrutiny.

'Civilisation indeed,' said Alex, nodding. 'This must all be a bit rural for you.' Without waiting for an answer, he swept past and headed towards the kitchen.

Annie and Eleanor exchanged a smile and then followed him.

In the kitchen, the electrics, lighting and plumbing had now been completed. Brand new appliances were starting to arrive in enormous packaging and the whole room was slowly taking shape.

'A dishwasher! A tumble dryer!' said Annie, with a smile. 'And no mice. Well, maybe not so many.'

Alex shuddered. 'I should think not. So have the plasterers finished upstairs as well?' he asked.

'Last week,' said Annie. 'All the guest bedrooms are just waiting for your magic touch.'

'You wait until I tell you my ideas for these,' said Alex, his eyes gleaming. 'It'll be like the best hotel in the area. Very upmarket but beautiful too. And free, natch. But, heaven help us, only housing crusty musicians. Oh, not gorgeous Tom, of course. I can't believe my first weekend visit and he's at bloody Glastonbury.'

'Try and focus,' said Annie, in a firm tone. 'Now what about my kitchen? You haven't told me what it's going to look like.'

'It's going to be fabulous and that's all you need to know,' said Alex, his eyes gleaming. 'Your fiancé has made you wait long enough, so we can go over budget by a teensy tiny bit.'

Annie shook her head. 'I daren't. We're so broke.'

Alex made a face. 'How dull. Leave it to me. I know

how to get a bargain or two.'

Annie led them outside onto the sunny patio where she planned to serve them tea.

Alex glanced down to a pile of cuttings that had been hidden underneath her notepad on the table. 'What's all this?'

'I was sorting out a few newspaper reports from the last couple of years,' said Annie, with a grimace. 'We've got to host the annual summer fete. It's our duty as future earl and countess of Cranley.'

Alex clapped his hands together in fake enthusiasm. 'A summer fete! How very twee!'

Eleanor looked at the photographs and was dismayed by what she saw. The Queen's garden party, it certainly wasn't. A few stalls, mostly bric-a-brac and other rubbish. Some flowers in pots for sale. A few balloons. 'Where's the bunting?' she asked. 'If it's going to be a proper fete, it should at least be pretty.'

'Everything should be pretty to look at otherwise it's too depressing to contemplate,' said Alex.

Annie shrugged her shoulders. 'I think people came because their parents did and it's sort of carried onto the next generation.' She brought out a large notebook and stared down at the blank pages once more, as if seeking inspiration.

'You'd better put Portaloos at the top of that list,' Alex told her, tapping the blank page. 'I'm not having all and sundry traipsing through this beautiful home that

I've made for you.'

Annie grimaced. 'God, I hadn't thought of that.'

'What had you thought of?' asked Eleanor.

Annie sighed as she handed over the photographs of the previous fetes. 'Just that it had to look better than that.'

Alex grimaced as he looked over Eleanor's shoulder at the pictures. 'It couldn't look much worse. Where the hell's that cake? We need sugar for the shock.'

Annie served the tea and cakes on the rickety patio furniture. To make it a bit more pretty, she had arranged some pink sweet peas which had been plonked into a jam jar.

'Bert grows them. Don't they smell wonderful?' said Annie, sniffing the air. 'They're my favourite.'

'It's like we're in a frigging time machine,' said Alex, shaking his head. 'Albeit a cute, countryside one.'

'We're not that bad,' Annie told him, cutting a slice of cake. 'We're just in the country, that's all.'

'That's it!' exclaimed Alex with a start.

'What are you talking about?' said Annie.

'The fete, dumbass!' said Alex. 'I'm thinking old-fashioned but pretty. Classic. Very English.'

Eleanor stared at him as he grabbed the notebook and started writing down his ideas as he said them out loud. 'Stalls, yes. Lots more than in previous years. But mainly cakes, vegetables, flowers and that type of thing. Home-made cakes. Definitely bunting. Did I mention cakes? People can't get enough of the things. Mary Berry eat your heart out. It's got to be old-fashioned. Pin the tail on the donkey type of thing.' He broke into a wicked grin. 'I'm very good at that.'

'What about a merry-go-round?' said Annie, grabbing the pen from him. 'For the children?'

Alex shook his head. 'Absolutely no way. You don't want the smell and mess of fairground rides. And definitely not a cheap burger van either. It's got to be classy. Croquet. Cocktails. Nice old-fashioned games. Gentrified. A proper country village fete.'

Annie's eyes widened. 'Crikey,' she said, looking at Eleanor for guidance.

But Eleanor was nodding her approval. 'He's right,' she said. 'Bunting everywhere. Pretty rugs and cushions. Tea light holders in jars. Old bottles. Lots of floral cloth.'

'It's got to look like a Cath Kidston advert,' said Alex. 'It's gonna be flippin' gorgeous.'

Eleanor nodded enthusiastically. She knew exactly what he was talking about. It was going to look beautiful on the front lawn, especially with Willow Tree Hall as a backdrop. But he was right about that too. The house would definitely stay closed.

Portaloos, she wrote, grabbing the pen from Annie and underlining the word three times.

'What's the entertainment?' said Alex.

Annie frowned. 'What are you talking about?'

'You need stars, sweetie,' said Alex, rolling his eyes. 'That draws the punters in. Presumably you want to make money for your charity, don't you?'

Annie broke into a smile. 'Well, stars we can probably get hold of, thanks to my fiancé.'

# Chapter 24

Hanging around the hall with Annie and Alex for the rest of the day, Eleanor found that she was still expecting Tom to appear at any moment. But if she was unsettled at that particular thought, it was nothing to the abandonment that Dylan felt. He kept sitting by the front door, refusing to budge until Tom came back. Nobody could distract him or make him move.

'I'm sure he'll be okay later on,' Eleanor told Annie as she got onto her bicycle to head home. 'He'll definitely perk up when it's time for his dinner.'

But that evening, she received a call from Annie. 'You've got to come here and do something with Dylan. He's howling and howling. He won't settle with any of us.'

So Eleanor cycled back to Willow Tree Hall in the late evening sun, thinking that at least she was going to get fitter with all the exercise she was getting.

She could hear Dylan barking inside the house as soon as she drew up on her bike.

Annie opened up the front door before she could even reach it. Dylan rushed out and hurtled round her.

'You silly thing,' said Eleanor, reaching down to rub

his head when he finally collapsed at her feet. 'He's not with me.' She looked up at Annie. 'Have you tried calling Tom? Maybe the sound of his voice will make Dylan settle a bit.'

Annie shook her head. 'We tried that. It made him even worse,' she said, turning to head back into the house. 'What are we going to do?'

'Well, at least he's not howling any more,' said Eleanor, realising that the dog was now walking alongside her as they went into the entrance hall. In fact, Dylan was so close that he was almost tripping her up.

'Thank god,' drawled Alex, heading across from the drawing room. 'He obviously likes you. You'll have to stay here. I need my beauty sleep.'

Eleanor was startled at the suggestion. 'But I haven't brought anything with me,' she said.

'You can borrow my stuff,' said Annie. 'Even if it isn't very designer.'

Eleanor looked at Annie and caught her soft smile. 'That doesn't matter to me,' she told her friend.

'He does seem calmer now that you're here,' said Annie, nodding at the dog. 'Come on. It'll be like one of our old pyjama parties.'

'But with a large amount of gin, hopefully,' added Alex, grinning. 'Anyone for strip poker?'

Eleanor rang her mum who was more concerned about Dylan's unhappiness than sleeping on her own back at home. So Eleanor relaxed and found herself enjoying an evening at Willow Tree Hall, as they sat on the patio, drinking their gin and tonics.

'It's such a lovely setting,' said Eleanor, looking out across the long grass to where the sun was slowly sinking behind the woods. With Dylan sitting on her feet, and a cold drink in her hand, she felt more relaxed than she had done in ages. She had had few moments of relaxation recently, she realised. Far too busy worrying about her job. She also knew from her mum's experience with animals that if she felt calm, then Dylan would be as well. So she forced herself to not worry. Consequently, Dylan curled up and took an evening nap right next to her chair.

'It would be even better if we were sitting on something more comfortable,' said Alex, grimacing as he shuffled his bottom on the hard wooden seat.

'We do need to get some cushions,' agreed Rose, who had joined them, along with Arthur, after dinner. 'And a large umbrella for any hot summer days. There's no shade up here.'

'What about a swimming pool?' said Alex, his eyes gleaming.

'I believe my grandson said something about a limited budget,' said Arthur with a smile.

'Spoilsport,' said Alex, giving him a wink. 'I was hoping to see Tom in his swimming shorts.'

Eleanor gulped as she wondered what that would be like as well.

They stayed outside in the warm air until the sun had set and the stars had begun to come out.

'Time for bed,' declared Rose, with a shiver as the cooler air began to drift over the grounds.

'I hear you,' said Alex, with a yawn. 'I always sleep like a log here.'

'It's the peace and quiet,' said Arthur, nodding in agreement. 'And all this fresh air.'

'And the lack of scary doll eyes staring at me all night,' added Alex.

As Eleanor headed up the huge sweeping staircase, she realised she had never been up to the first floor.

'I love these stairs,' she told Annie, as they went past all the paintings of the previous earls and their families.

'It's very Scarlett O'Hara, isn't it?' said Annie, smiling. 'I can't wait to come down here in my wedding dress.'

'You're going to look so glamorous,' agreed Eleanor. 'It'll make a great photo.'

'Just as soon as I find a dress to wear,' Annie told her, biting her lip in concern. 'We must go shopping soon.'

'Absolutely.'

At the top of the stairs, there was a beamed gallery which overlooked the entrance hall below. 'That's the east wing bedrooms,' said Annie, pointing down the corridor. 'Rose and Arthur's bedroom suites are down there. As well as a couple more, soon to be finished, guest bedrooms.' They turned in the opposite direction. 'I thought you two would be happier in the west wing,' said Annie, glancing down at Dylan who still wouldn't leave Eleanor's side.

As they went along the corridor, Eleanor glanced into room after room but they were all empty.

'We've managed to clear out most of the rubbish and at least they've all been plastered now,' Annie told her. 'And the whole place is watertight. But the only spare guest room that's actually got a bed you can use is...' Annie finished the sentence as she opened up a door. 'My old bedroom.'

It was a beautiful room, light and airy. Three of the walls were painted a pale cream. The fourth wall, behind the bed, had been covered with the most beautiful cream wallpaper, decorated with tiny turquoise butterflies. The furniture was also pale, but the whole room felt modern and warm, thanks to the turquoise and gold accents dotted about.

'Didn't Alex do a lovely job?' said Annie, smiling. 'I love this room.'

'It's beautiful,' agreed Eleanor, nodding her approval. 'So pretty.'

Then she noticed that amongst the new lamps and candlesticks were some sheets of music. The odd book. Some aftershave.

She turned around to face Annie and raised her eyebrows.

'Yeah, sorry,' said Annie, looking abashed. 'Tom's been using this room. But it's the only one with a bed in it. He seems quite clean and tidy, you know, for a bloke. And Dylan sleeps up here with him, so I figured he might be more settled here with you.'

They both watched as Dylan went over to what looked like a brand new, soft leather dog bed and curled up inside it.

Eleanor could see that Annie was waiting for her reply. 'It's fine,' she told her friend. 'Better than fine. I haven't slept in anywhere this gorgeous for ages.'

'Since your own flat, I suppose,' said Annie.

'That wasn't mine, it was Lucas's,' Eleanor told her, making a face. 'And it wasn't pretty like this. It was all a bit cold and sterile. Not warm and welcoming.'

'Poor you,' said Annie, touching her arm.

Eleanor smiled and shrugged. 'I just needed somewhere to stay. My own flat got condemned so I had to move in with him for a while. Turns out that was the beginning of the end for our relationship, I think. I haven't had a single text from him since I came here. So much for our so-called break.' She turned to her friend. 'Whereas you moving in here was the absolute right thing, especially when Sam moved back in too.'

Annie blushed. 'It was,' she said, nodding happily at the memory.

They hugged each other goodnight before Eleanor settled into the bed. A soft breeze was wafting the curtains at the front, but other than that it was very peaceful and still in the house. As she snuggled deeper into the very comfortable bedding, Eleanor realised that she could smell the traces of Tom's woody aftershave on the pillow. With one last check that Dylan was happily curled up in his bed, she closed her eyes and fell asleep.

# Chapter 25

Eleanor took Dylan for a walk the following day but he would only head out into the grounds when he had exhausted his search in every single room for Tom.

Having decided to stay for the weekend to stop the dog from howling, she quickly cycled home to pick up some clothes and help her mum with the animals.

Finally, in the middle of the afternoon, she staggered back into the drawing room and slumped on a chair. 'Well, that was fun.'

'It doesn't look like fun,' Alex told her, peering over his coffee cup. 'It looks hot and sweaty and not in my favourite kind of way.'

'Although that skirt is so pretty,' said Rose, giving her a once-over. 'Chanel?'

Eleanor shook her head. 'Topshop.'

'They're so clever,' said Rose, nodding her head in approval. 'It's only the quality and the workmanship of the seams that tells the difference.'

'It looks okay to me,' said Annie.

Rose stood up. 'Darling, let this be your first lesson in fashion. Follow me.'

So Eleanor, Annie and Alex followed Rose up to her

bedroom. It was a proper lady's boudoir with luxurious carpets and decadent trimmings such as silver candlesticks and ornate mirrors. Alex had done a tremendous job designing the whole room, which suited Rose perfectly. Eleanor marvelled at the three huge wardrobes all bulging with designer clothes.

'This is amazing,' she said, running her hand along the rail.

'When you work in the fashion industry, there are so many freebies,' said Rose. 'And I never could bear to throw anything away. Now, where's that Chanel?'

Eleanor sat down on the end of the bed with Alex and Annie.

Rose closed one set of wardrobe doors and opened the next one along. 'Ah, here we are,' she announced. 'This is the 1960s and 70s closet. Here's some Chanel, of course.' She brought out a black and white checked suit.

'Lovely,' said Alex, nodding his head in approval. 'But the skirt's a bit long, don't you think? We need something younger. More edgy.'

'I agree,' said Rose, putting the suit back again and bringing out a silver dress that shone in the afternoon sun coming through the window.

'Wowsa,' said Alex. 'That's hot.'

'It's got lots of material missing,' said Annie, making a face as she reached out to feel the edge of the large round holes cut across the material.

'Darling girl,' said Rose, with a sigh. 'It's a classic

cut-out dress. Very funky, as they said in those days. And perfect in your size.'

'No way,' said Annie, shaking her head. 'I can't wear that. Half of it's missing.'

'Rubbish,' said Alex. 'Put it on.'

In the end, realising that they weren't going to take no for an answer, Annie took the dress into the en-suite bathroom and changed.

Meanwhile, Alex got up from the bed and headed over to an ornate dressing table. 'Shall we?' he asked, smiling at Rose.

'Why not,' replied Rose. 'It's never too early.'

In reply, Alex opened up the cupboard of the dressing table, which was actually a drinks fridge stocked with mini bottles of champagne.

'This was my little house-warming gift to Rose,' said Alex, bringing out four mini bottles and matching chilled champagne glasses.

'Which is why I love him so dearly,' said Rose, blowing a kiss across the room.

At that moment, Annie came out of the bathroom in the cut-out dress.

Alex wolf-whistled. 'Looking hot there, skinny jeans girl!'

'It's more draughty than hot,' said Annie, looking at her reflection. 'You can see my bra and knickers!'

'There's a simple solution to that,' said Alex, with a wicked laugh.

Rose too gurgled with laughter as she handed a glass of champagne to Annie. 'Here, darling. Drink this.'

'Where did this come from?' asked Annie, looking around in surprise.

'Never you mind,' Rose told her. 'It's our little secret. And one must have champagne when one is in fashion heaven. Don't you agree, Eleanor?'

'Absolutely,' said Eleanor, taking a sip of the drink that Alex had just given her. 'By the way, Annie, I'd kill for your legs.'

'I know,' said Rose, nodding sadly. 'Isn't she beautiful? God gave me many talents and gifts, but, alas, stunning legs wasn't among them.'

'Take off your underwear,' said Alex, holding up his phone. 'Then I can send your photo to Sam.'

'Don't you dare!' said Annie, laughing.

However, after she'd finished her champagne, Annie did as she had been told and almost immediately received a phone call from Sam.

Eleanor smiled as she watched Annie blush at Sam's hushed words down the line.

'She'd better keep that dress,' said Alex, also noting Annie's soft expression. 'Especially if we want to expand the family line in a few years.'

They enjoyed a raucous afternoon with Eleanor, Annie and even Alex trying on various clothes from the 60s and 70s. Finally, they all slumped downstairs in the drawing room to watch the first night's television coverage of Glastonbury with Arthur. Eleanor looked at the TV screen. The mud had increased hour by hour, thanks to the constant rain that week. The sun came out briefly but mostly it rained. A lot.

'So Rose, did you ever go to Glastonbury?' asked Eleanor, reaching for the bowl of peanuts that Annie had laid out for them.

'Of course, sweetie,' said Rose, with a wave of her manicured hand. 'Naturally, I can't remember most of it.'

'Anyone for a drink?' asked Arthur, obviously hoping to stop his sister's story. But it was in vain.

'The whole place was as high as a kite back in the early seventies,' Rose carried on.

'Gin? Anyone? Rose?' said Arthur.

'Everyone was naked,' said Rose. 'Hippies. God love them. It was marvellous. A total orgy.' She beamed in memory.

'Well, I definitely need something stronger after enjoying that mental image,' drawled Arthur, heading across the room to the drinks globe.

As they watched the programme, there was an interview with Tom who was headlining Sunday night on the Pyramid Stage. Eleanor found that she had to stop herself leaning forward to take him in. He was charming with the interviewer but reserved. Funny, but there was still a sense that he was holding back. That he wasn't comfortable with the intrusion. She wondered how he would feel about her sleeping in his room whilst he was away. But it was only for Dylan, she was able to tell herself.

*

After the fashion catwalk in Rose's bedroom, the following afternoon Eleanor and Megan took Annie into the nearest large town to try on some wedding dresses.

They found some bridesmaid dresses almost immediately. Annie had decided on silver, to fit in with her wintry colour theme as the wedding was to be in December.

'I thought silver would go with the red flowers I want,' said Annie.

Eleanor nodded her approval. 'That will be lovely with touches of greenery everywhere.'

'And hundreds of fairy lights,' said Megan, spinning round in front of a mirror. 'What do you think?'

The long dresses were a subtle sheen of silver which suited both Eleanor's dark colouring and Megan's red hair.

'I love them,' said Annie, smiling.

So did Eleanor. She just needed to sort out the patches of eczema on her neck and hands which would look horrible on the official photographs.

So the bridesmaids' dresses were sorted. But despite trying on quite a few wedding dresses, none were declared good enough to be 'the one'.

'I was hoping for something unique,' said Annie, looking downcast. 'I don't know. Different perhaps.'

'Don't despair,' Eleanor told her. 'There's plenty more time for dress shopping. You've got six months yet.'

Afterwards, they went to Megan's house to watch the second night of Glastonbury. Eleanor was surprised to find Megan snapping at Neal, especially as they'd had such a fun-filled day, but she didn't say anything. Having three kids was stressful enough without being judged as well.

Whilst they were there, Annie received a call from Sam. 'I'm with the girls,' she said. There was a pause and she smiled. 'I miss you too.'

Megan rolled her eyes and reached for the bottle of wine to top up their glasses.

'What?' shrieked Annie suddenly.

'Shhh!' said Megan, running to the door to listen out to see if the children had woken up.

But Annie was looking wild-eyed at them. 'Sam's got us tickets!' she said, breathlessly.

'For what?' Eleanor was confused.

Annie pointed at the television. 'Glastonbury!'

Sam had got them passes for the whole of the last day, with VIP passes to gain backstage entry for Tom's set, which was closing the whole festival. Then they all screamed so loudly that this time the children definitely woke up.

'What will we do with Dylan?' asked Eleanor, once everyone had settled down again.

Annie frowned in thought. 'We'll be home late tomorrow night. I'm sure he'll be okay until then with the family.'

'Whee! We're going to Glastonbury!' shouted Megan.

Eleanor was so excited. Even more so when she realised that she would be seeing Tom again the following day.

# Chapter 26

Late on Sunday morning, the chauffeured car which Sam had arranged dropped them off at the gates to Worthy Farm. Eleanor couldn't believe the scene in front of them. There was lots of mud, of course. And it was raining. But there was also talk of the sun coming out later. There were people everywhere, wearing a variety of mud-strewn rain macs and ponchos. A lot of people didn't seem to care and weren't bothered about being soaked to the skin. But everyone was happy. And the music was very loud.

Thank god they had decided to wear their wellington boots, thought Eleanor, spying quite a few abandoned flip-flops that were stuck in the mud.

She couldn't remember laughing as much as she did that afternoon with Annie and Megan. Their wellies were caked with mud. They each had a braid in their hair. They had sung along loudly and, quite possibly, very out of key. They had basically reverted back to being teenagers again or so it felt. No responsibilities. No careers or boyfriends to worry about. Just her and her girls, having a laugh. She felt free for the first time in a very long time.

'I've missed this,' she said, as Annie applied glitter to her cheeks.

'You should come to my house when we're doing a craft day,' said Megan. But then she smiled. 'It's so nice to be silly and feel like a grown-up.'

'I love my girls,' said Annie, giving them both a hug.

'Me too,' said Eleanor.

Things were definitely beginning to feel a little bit fuzzy as they'd had a few cocktails and very little to eat. She and her friends trudged through the mud towards the Pyramid Stage, giggling as they held on to each other.

Feeling a tiny bit unsteady, Eleanor's wellies slipped in the mud as she wandered backstage and she slammed straight into Tom who had just appeared nearby.

'Hello!' she said, feeling brave.

He broke into a wide grin. 'Hi,' he said. 'I see you've been enjoying the hospitality of Glastonbury.'

'Just a little bit,' she said, giggling.

God but he was handsome, she thought.

'How's my dog?' he asked.

'Pining for you,' she told him.

He glanced over her shoulder to where the audience was stretched out. Eleanor turned and gasped. She had never seen so many people in once place.

She looked back at Tom. 'Aren't you nervous?' she asked him, wondering how it felt to go out and sing in front of that many people. It would frighten her to death.

He nodded. 'I am a little, I guess.'

A small frown appeared on his brow and she had the urge to smooth it away with her fingers. Wanting him to stop fretting, she leaned forward and whispered, 'I know what will help. Just imagine the audience is naked.'

He briefly ran his eyes up and down her before they settled back on her face. 'Well, it's Glastonbury, so chances are some of them definitely will be.'

She giggled again.

He reached out and caught the braid in her hair with his fingers. 'That's new.'

'Not exactly Mayfair,' she told him, making a face. 'But I don't care. It doesn't have any hay in it. Or goat hair, come to think of it.'

'I like it. It's more you,' he said, nodding. 'Anyway, thanks for the advice.'

'You're welcome. Knock 'em dead,' she replied.

She watched him head off to talk to his band.

Knock 'em dead? She rolled her eyes so hard at herself, she nearly fell backwards. She was an idiot. It was as if she had never met a famous person before in her life. What the hell was the matter with her? She needed to sober up fast otherwise god knows what she would say or do next.

*

Despite his nerves at performing, Tom was enjoying Glastonbury. Sam had even arranged for him to stay in his own private yurt so he could hide out from the crowds.

He had been to the festival once before, a few years previously when he was first starting out. The stage had been miniscule then. He smiled at the memory. The small audience must have thought one of the crew had wandered on stage by mistake.

And yet, here he now was. Tommy King. A multi-platinum Grammy-award-winning artist.

He had never expected anyone to buy his first album. And then everyone bought it and the awards and acclaim followed.

But so had the fame and hassle.

Only the previous evening, he had been approached by another manager.

'Look,' the agent had said, placing a chubby hand on Tom's shoulder. 'That Sam Harris is okay, but I can take you cosmic, yeah? I'm talking product placement. It's all about the ker-ching, isn't it, baby?'

Tom had shrugged the hand off his shoulder and pulled on his leather jacket. 'No, it's not,' he'd replied, before walking away.

Why did everyone think he was in it for the money? He just wanted to write and play his music.

The previous evening, he had crept backstage and looked out to the audience beyond. There were flags waving everywhere. Lights. Mobiles held up. And people. So many people. More people than he had ever seen in one place in his life.

He gulped now, trying to keep confident about what kind of reception he would receive. Chances were that most of the audience would think he was some kind of washed-out addict, just arrived out of rehab. Luckily, his foot had finally stopped hurting which was something less to worry about when he finally made it onto the stage.

In the far distance, as the day faded and night began, he could just make out the fields of tents. Everyone would probably be a bit jaded by now. But they needed one more party. One more singalong session. And he was going to make them forget about the mud and give them the rousing finish the great festival deserved.

He was trying to keep his nerves in check. Trying to remember his set.

And trying to ignore the feelings that Eleanor was stirring up inside. He glanced over to where she was chatting with Annie and Megan. Her short denim skirt showed off her fabulous legs, even though they were splattered with mud and she had wellies on. She wore a leather jacket with a Rolling Stones T-shirt underneath. She looked like every pop artist's dream girl. He liked the braid and the lack of heavy make-up. It made her look less polished. More real.

He shook his head. He needed to focus now. He took

a deep breath and began to get into his zone. He looked out at the people jammed in front of the Pyramid tent. A sea of one hundred thousand people. An ocean of faces. There was mud everywhere. But now the rain had finally left the shire. A shaft of sunset peeped through the heavy clouds as they began to clear away, leaving clear skies above.

The voice came over the tannoy announcing his name. His heart thumped. This was it.

He took a deep breath and walked on, clutching onto his guitar.

The crowd screamed and yelled as he appeared on stage. He managed to make it to the middle without falling over, which he figured was a good start.

'Hi,' he said, giving them a small wave. 'You've been wet and cold, but are you miserable, Glastonbury?'

'Noooo!' shouted one thousand people in response.

He grinned. 'Let's go then,' he said, launching into the opening bars of one of his hit records. It was an up-tempo number and everyone was now jumping up and down to the beat.

As he played and sang, he could feel himself relaxing. He could do this and do it well, he knew.

He stared out, seeing the different colour anoraks and hats in the dusk. Everyone appeared to be caked in mud. There were pretty girls sitting on their boyfriend's shoulders. And so many flags waving in front of him.

He felt instantly at home.

*

Eleanor watched, amazed that this was the same person that she had met only a month ago. *This* was quiet 'just call me Tom' who had been playing with the dog and drinking tea on the patio at Willow Tree Hall?

She had heard his songs on the radio so many times, of course. But here, on stage, he was a rock god. He played superbly, his voice strong and pure.

He didn't banter too much with the crowd. He just wanted to play his music for them. But during one of his many hits, he let them sing the main lyrics. Their voices soared as one and made him grin in response.

'You sound great,' he told them after the song had finished. 'Better than I could have done. Ready for another?'

She realised that he was giving the people what they wanted. The audience wanted to sing along. They wanted to jump up and down to the beat. They wanted to have a good time.

And he just wanted to entertain them.

An hour into Tom's set and darkness had begun to fall. Now the lights were twinkling all around the stage. Pyrotechnics and multi-coloured strobe lights spun across the crowd, adding to the party atmosphere.

But then it quietened down as Tom sat at the piano. He was sweaty, hot, slightly out of breath. Eleanor felt a stab of pure lust. He was absolutely gorgeous. She tried to breathe normally. He had a natural chemistry with the audience. That was what she was reacting to. She had a temporary crush that was all. Once they were all back in Cranley, that would quickly fade again.

But as he sat at the piano, Eleanor could feel the hairs stand up on her arms as he sang. There was no band, just him and the piano. The crowd went still, merely lighting up their phones and holding them aloft. It was magical.

At the end, she shouted and screamed her response as well as everyone else in the field.

She never wanted this evening to end.

Tom stood up and grabbed his guitar once more. As he reached the microphone in the centre of the stage, he said, 'I thought I'd sing a song in tribute to an amazing band who should have been here tonight instead of me. Coldplay.'

He began to strum 'The Scientist' on his guitar. Eleanor was dumbstruck. She couldn't believe that their brief conversation had ended up with him playing her nominated song at Glastonbury.

It was just him, the guitar and the huge audience singing along. She quickly joined in, reminding herself to tell Dylan all about it when she got home later that night.

Tom glanced up briefly at her at the end of the song and grinned. She found herself smiling straight back at him, lost in their own personal secret.

*

Tom was pleased to see Eleanor looking so pleased that her choice of song had made it into his set. He realised that now that the nerves had dissipated, he was having an amazing time. He loved playing his music to a crowd. Any crowd. They were singing along to *his* lyrics. Singing *his* melodies. Would that thrill ever fade? Probably not. He just wished his gran could have seen him. But he knew she was with him somewhere, cheering him along.

There were only two more songs to go. Two more numbers, but he never wanted it to end.

The crowd swayed and sang along in time to his final song and he left the last line of his favourite hit for the audience to sing. As the closing bars faded, he held one hand aloft and punched the air. The crowd roared.

'Thank you, Glastonbury,' he told them. 'You've been incredible.'

Their next roar was drowned out by a plethora of fireworks shooting out from behind the stage and lighting up the sky. The fireworks boomed and crackled but he could still hear the crowd shouting his name.

He waved as he came off stage, feeling high on adrenaline. He was elated, flying as high as the fireworks in the sky overhead.

Sam and various other people hugged him and were talking to him. But he couldn't make out anything they were saying. He was buzzing. It was most incredible feeling in the world. It had taken his senses and made them zing. His whole body hummed. It was as if the whole world was on mute and he could barely comprehend anything.

He barely registered Annie giving him a shy kiss on the cheek, the roar in his ears overpowering the words she was saying. Megan also gave him a kiss before attempting to give him a high five, but she missed his hand completely and just fell about laughing at herself.

Suddenly Eleanor was in front of him. She was mouthing some words at him, but he still couldn't hear anything though he was able to take in every inch of her. Her green eyes were shining as she leant up to kiss him on the cheek. But at the last minute, in the crowd and confusion, she turned her head and he found himself kissing her on the mouth. His body continued to tingle with the feeling of her soft mouth on his, her lips touching his.

A flash went off somewhere, probably from the fireworks. But it woke him up enough to step away from Eleanor in a daze and then he was surrounded by people once more.

# Chapter 27

Eleanor woke up mid-morning in Tom's empty bed at Willow Tree Hall.

At some point, she had wearily let Dylan out to head downstairs but had staggered back to bed after arriving at some late hour in the middle of the night.

She lay there, still feeling in a dreamlike state. The hangover didn't help, of course. But most of all, it was the fact that Tom had kissed her.

Tom had kissed her! In front of everyone! Well, in front of her friends anyway. It had only been an accidental meeting of lips and had lasted a second or three. But at the time it had felt like hours.

And she hadn't wanted it to end.

That, to her, was the most shocking realisation of all. But she was desperately brushing it off. It was a crush. He was a talented, good-looking superstar. That was all.

She felt embarrassed about what had happened. And suddenly uncomfortable about sleeping in Tom's bed. She quickly got up and dressed, meeting Annie as she reached the bottom of the stairs.

'Morning,' she said, wincing slightly as she spoke.

'Morning,' muttered Annie, looking as rough as

Eleanor felt. 'Coffee? Tea? New head?'

'No, thanks,' said Eleanor. 'I'd better head back to Mum. She's been on her own for a few days.'

'Of course,' said Annie, rubbing her temple. 'Megan text to tell me that she's never drinking ever again.'

Eleanor grinned. 'She says that every time.'

'I know.' Annie gave her a hug. 'I had such a great weekend with you. It was so lovely to have you stay with us.'

'I really enjoyed it,' said Eleanor, giving her friend a squeeze.

'Dylan's going to miss you,' said Annie.

'And I'm going to miss him too,' said Eleanor. And she meant it, having spent so much time with the dog over the weekend. 'Just don't tell anyone I said so.'

'I won't. I think Tom's back later so he'll settle down again.'

Eleanor gulped and immediately made her exit. She headed back to The Forge shortly after, desperate to get away before Tom arrived back.

How could they have ended up kissing? And how could something so brief feel so good?

But the chances were that he wouldn't stay long at the hall anyway and would be gone soon. Then things would settle down in Cranley again, she told herself.

Her mum was sitting at the kitchen table with the newspaper when she finally made it home.

'Did you have a good time?' asked her mum. 'I

looked out for you on the TV, but I couldn't see any of you. Apart from that nice Tom, of course. Wasn't he amazing?'

Eleanor nodded, still thinking of their kiss. That had been pretty amazing too. She stroked the braid that she still had in her hair as she replayed it over and over in her mind.

'I bet it was incredible to be there,' carried on her mum, putting down the newspaper with a heavy sigh.

'It was,' said Eleanor, staring down at the huge photo of Tom on the page. She wondered whether she could cut out the photo and then realised that her crush was perhaps worse than she'd thought. 'You've never seen so many people. It was like...'

But she stopped as her mum's face crumpled into tears.

'What is it?' she asked, rushing over to crouch next to her. 'Is it your foot?'

Her mum shook her head. 'I'm just being silly,' she replied. 'Tell me about your fun evening.'

Eleanor shook her head. 'Not until you tell me what's made you cry.'

Her mum brushed away a tear from her cheek and gave a small giggle as Daisy the donkey peered through the back door.

'You see?' said her mum, smiling. 'Animals understand.'

Eleanor held her mum's hand and tried to ignore the

donkey staring at them. 'You know I can't bear to see you upset, Mum. What is it?'

'Oh, it's everything!' she answered, sounding more upset than Eleanor had heard her in a long time. 'I mean, it's lovely having you around. But I envy you. You had this fabulous life in London and now you're down here with your friends and going to rock festivals.' She gave her daughter a teary sad smile. 'I just keep wondering when mine will begin.'

Eleanor sank down onto the chair next to her mum in shock. 'I've never heard you talk like this before.'

'Maybe I didn't want to admit it to myself,' her mum told her with a shrug. 'I'd love to see other countries and a bit of the world. Even have a small holiday. If only I didn't have so many responsibilities.'

They both glanced to the door where Daisy had wandered away and was gently hee-hawing at Buttercup the goat.

It suddenly struck Eleanor that her mum had trapped herself in taking care of her daughter and now all of the animals.

'Maybe Arthur is right. Perhaps it's time to rehome the zoo,' said Eleanor gently. 'Maybe it's time to let yourself be a bit selfish, like I've been.'

'You're not selfish,' her mum told her.

But Eleanor knew that wasn't true. 'You gave up so much to raise me by yourself,' she said, taking her mum's hand and giving it a squeeze. 'If I haven't ever said thank you then it's because I'm an ungrateful cow. I'm sorry. I should have been around more these past few years.'

'You're just fine, my beautiful girl.' Her mum suddenly looked serious. 'You really think I should let the animals go? I don't know if I can.'

'I honestly do think it's for the best,' Eleanor told her. 'I know you've been trying to help, but maybe there's other places where they can be. Better places more suitable for them.'

Her mum nodded, deep in thought.

Eleanor pressed on. 'I was googling how to take care of Daisy and donkeys like a mate. And it's not just Daisy. Buttercup needs other goats too. They need other animals. They get lonely.'

'They're not the only ones,' muttered her mum.

Eleanor looked at her mum. 'Maybe it's time to be brave and get out there into the dating world again.'

Her mum grimaced. 'I don't think so. Not after last time.'

'Mum, that's ancient history.'

Her mum gave her a soft smile. 'I'll think about it,' she told her daughter.

'Which bit?' asked Eleanor.

'All of it,' said her mum. 'I promise.' She visibly brightened up. 'So what are your plans today?'

Eleanor shrugged her shoulders. 'I have no idea.' She realised with a shock that it was true. 'For the first time in my life, I don't have a plan or any idea where I'm going.'

'Well, that's not a bad thing,' said her mum. 'Stay here with me for a while. You'll find your path soon enough. In the meantime, you've got your friends here. I love you, you know.'

Eleanor wrapped her arms around her mum, grateful for the warmth and strength that she was feeling. 'And you as well,' she murmured back.

Afterwards, as Eleanor headed into the hallway, she gave a start at herself in the mirror. Her hair was a mess and was that yesterday's mascara under her eyes?

If Tom saw her now he would think the absolute worst about her.

She scratched at her neck. The eczema was worse than ever. She wasn't sure if it was the hay, the stress or the donkey, but whatever the reason, she had to get it sorted. Surely she could control that small part of her life?

She could just about remember the ingredients she had used in the past to treat her inflamed skin. She was hoping she had enough to at least soothe the itching. Once in her bedroom, she ripped open one of the boxes she had brought with her and started to assemble everything. She had the remains of some shea butter in a tub, which would just be enough. She didn't have nearly the right amount of beeswax but had a tin or two of lip balm which she thought might help. In fact, she didn't have many of the ingredients required, but desperate times and all that, so she would have to improvise.

She carried her box downstairs and used an old teacup to measure everything out. Half a cup of sunflower oil from the kitchen cupboard went into an old glass bowl. She added the two beeswax oil lip balms as well. Then she tipped in the remainder of the shea butter. Finally she put in a few drops of vitamin E oil that she had found right at the bottom of the box.

She was just about to start melting the whole lot when she spotted a small bottle of lavender oil in the corner of the box. She tipped in the last few drops from the bottle as well. Then she placed the glass bowl over a pot of simmering hot water and let it all gently melt. Once it was liquefied, she stirred it with an old wooden spoon and left it out to cool.

She was exhausted by the weekend and had already decided to have an early night. Just before she went to bed, she remembered the cream and slathered it all over her neck and hands.

The following morning, she stared in the mirror. Her neck was far less inflamed. In fact, it was almost normal skin colour. No redness or soreness remained there or between her fingers. For the first time in a very long time, Eleanor felt a small sense of accomplishment.

# Chapter 28

Eleanor was still admiring her less inflamed neck when Annie sent her a text late that morning, asking her up to the hall for a coffee.

She put on her favourite casual outfit and some light make-up, feeling ridiculously excited to be seeing Tom again. Not that she was only interested in seeing Tom, of course. She would be seeing Annie and the family as well.

Now that July had begun, summer was in full swing. The sky was blue and the trees were alive with the sound of birds singing as she cycled her way down the long driveway at Willow Tree Hall. Butterflies floated from one wild flower to the next. It was a great day to be outside.

'Hi,' she said, as Annie opened up the front door. 'Isn't it a lovely day?'

'Not really,' said Annie, with a grin. 'You should see the state of Megan.'

'She's not hung-over again, is she?'

'No, this is worse than that.'

Eleanor followed her into the kitchen where the first of the brand new units were beginning to be unveiled.

Gradually the room was coming back to life. But the most interesting feature that morning was Megan whose nose was bright red.

'Look at me!' she wailed, staring at her reflection in her phone.

'It's only sunburn,' said Eleanor, trying and failing not to smile as she sat down at the table. 'What happened?'

'Kids sports day yesterday. I lathered up the kids with suntan lotion but I was so hung-over after Glastonbury that I totally forgot about me. I look like Ronald McDonald,' she carried on. 'What am I going to do? It's going to peel and then it's going to look even worse.'

'What's all the fuss about?' said Rose, appearing at the kitchen door. She did a double take at Megan. 'Darling! No, no! One must use sunscreen, otherwise the wrinkles will be ghastly later on.'

Megan hooked out an ice cube from the cold drink that Annie had just given her and rubbed it across her nose.

They all nearly jumped out of their skin when a bunch of carrots landed on the new work surface. Eleanor looked up to see Bert the gardener standing next to them, looking very unhappy.

'You're working early today,' said Rose, putting a hand on his arm. 'All work and no play makes a man very dull.'

'That dog's dug up my carrots,' said Bert, in a surly

tone.

'Oh,' said Annie, looking upset. 'Sorry.'

'Nonsense,' said Rose. 'He was just saving you from having to do all that digging with your bad back.'

She smiled brilliantly at Bert before he finally shuffled away again.

'One has to look on the bright side at my age,' said Rose, reaching out to stroke the frothy fronds growing out the top of one of the carrots. 'You know, when I was in Marrakesh, there was a beautiful redhead. Somebody's girlfriend. I can't remember now. Anyway, she got terribly sunburnt, poor thing. But one of the locals recommended carrot cream. The next day, it had completely disappeared.'

'What were you doing in Marrakesh?' asked Annie, looking up from where she was wiping off the dirt from her precious new granite worktop.

Rose broke into a wicked grin. 'Trying not to get arrested,' she replied with a wink.

But Eleanor was looking at the carrots and wondering about her eczema. 'Do you remember when I used to make those creams for my skin?' she said aloud. 'Anyway, I made one yesterday and it's really helped my eczema.'

'Darling, you should try my Crème de la Mer,' said Rose.

'It's so expensive.' Annie raised her eyebrows. 'Besides, I thought Sam said that we're all supposed to be cutting back these days?'

Rose looked horrified. 'Sweetheart, this is essential! I can't go round looking like some old bag lady. How else am I going to take my next lover?' She looked at Eleanor. 'Now what's all this about face creams?'

'I have bad eczema,' said Eleanor, showing her the patch on her neck, which was still visible although not as bad. 'I've tried all of the fancy stuff but I end up making my own as it's the only thing that sorts it out.'

'Sounds impressive,' said Rose, nodding her approval.

'She's being modest,' said Annie. 'Those creams you made me for Christmas all those years ago were beautiful. Why did you stop?'

'I never had any spare time,' said Eleanor, truthfully.

Megan touched her sore nose. 'Well, if Rose is right about carrots, do you mind trying to whip up something with these? I'm desperate here.'

'And you'll be able to see in the dark as well,' said Annie, with a giggle.

'Darling, with her nose being that red, we'll all be able to see her in the dark,' drawled Rose.

'I'll give it a go later,' promised Eleanor. It was the least she could do for her friends. 'I found one of Dylan's balls in my handbag,' she told them. 'I thought he would want it when Tom comes back later.'

'I think Tom's going to be in London for a few days before he comes back here,' said Annie, checking her phone.

Eleanor tried to ignore how disappointed she was that she wouldn't see Tom that day. On the other hand, she was still trying to work out how she really felt about him, so perhaps it was for the best after all. And they had recently kissed so at least it put off that embarrassment for the time being.

'Did Dylan sleep okay last night without me?' asked Eleanor.

'He slept in Arthur's room,' called out Rose, as she left the kitchen. 'I think they both liked the company, to be honest.'

Annie was still checking her phone when she suddenly took in a deep breath. 'Oh my god!' she said, sitting bolt upright. 'You've been papped.'

'Who?' said Megan.

'Eleanor!' said Annie, holding out her phone. 'You and Tom are on Twitter.'

Eleanor took the mobile and stared at the photo. Somebody had taken a photo just as they had accidentally kissed.

'Wow!' said Megan, looking over her shoulder. 'It says that you're Tommy King's new girlfriend.'

'But I'm not,' said Eleanor frantically. 'Besides, you can't even see my face, only my hair.'

'That's because Tom was all over you,' said Megan, making smoochy sounds.

Eleanor lobbed a tea towel at her before she studied the photo once more. 'You can't tell it's me, can you?'

Megan and Annie peered at the photo before shaking their heads.

'No,' said Annie.

'Definitely not,' added Megan.

Eleanor sighed with relief. That was the last thing she needed. If anyone in London recognised her, then the magazines might get wind of the fact that she used to work for Hot Gossip! and then Tom would know about her old job. And how she had been lying to him about being a financial journalist.

But she was safe. For now.

To create a distraction from her embarrassment, she grabbed the carrots and headed home to make up some cream for Megan.

She cut up the carrots and put them in a saucepan to boil. Once the carrots were cooked and mashed, she added them to the glass bowl as well as the same ingredients she had used for her eczema potion.

Her mum came into the kitchen halfway through the procedure and smiled. 'Well, this takes me back.' She sat down heavily at the kitchen table. 'I don't remember you doing this since…' her voice trailed off.

Eleanor glanced over her shoulder as she stood at the oven. 'We're allowed to say his name.'

'I know,' said her mum, with a small gulp. 'Since your father left.'

'I can't remember that far back.'

It was a lie. Eleanor could remember every part of

week after he had walked out on them. The local newspaper arriving through the letterbox. The photos of her dad and that actress that lived up the road. The tears. The many tears.

Most of all, she remembered cooking dinner that night and many evenings afterwards. Taking care of her mum until she was strong enough to take care of herself once more. Running from school to the supermarket and back again each day, trying to keep the household afloat. She hadn't had much time for dabbling with her lotions and potions from that time onwards. Nor once she had moved to London either, apart from when she needed to whip up a batch for her eczema.

'So what's brought you back in time to do this?' asked her mum.

Eleanor filled up some empty jam jars with the potion. 'Megan's burnt her nose.'

'Oh dear,' said her mum. 'The joy of being a redhead. Well, I'm sure it'll calm down overnight.'

'It never has done before. Hopefully this will speed it on its way,' said Eleanor, putting the jars in the fridge.

After dinner, she dropped a jam jar around to Megan, who was grateful for any help.

When Eleanor got home, she scooped out a large dollop of her own cream and smeared it across her neck.

The following morning, Eleanor received an ecstatic early phone call from Megan, telling her that her nose was now a wonderful golden brown colour instead of bright red. The carrot cream had worked its magic. Who'd have thought carrots could have such healing properties, thought Eleanor. She peered at her neck in the mirror. Between the carrot and her own plain cream, the eczema on her neck was almost non-existent. She was surprised because the stress and worry that someone would recognise her from the photo at Glastonbury still nagged at her. But the sense of satisfaction outweighed the worries, for once.

# Chapter 29

After spending the last night in his yurt at Glastonbury, Tom had headed back to his flat in London. He had a doctor's appointment booked so it coincided nicely with his plans.

He had lived alone for so long that he would have thought he would have been grateful to get back to his normal solitude. Except he found he didn't like being in the peace and quiet of the flat. It was too quiet. And he couldn't seem to settle, as if the peace was more of a burden to him. He even missed the communal dinners with the Harris family.

With not enough people around, he could feel his mood sinking lower and lower. He began to realise that perhaps the isolation of the flat had stopped him writing. Some days he hadn't spoken to anyone. Was that why he hadn't been able to overcome his writer's block? Was that why he had felt so low?

In the end, he was grateful to attend the doctor's appointment and then head back to Willow Tree Hall after only one night in the flat. He had missed the family and their happy shared spirit.

The doctor had been very positive about his injury.

The foot was healing nicely, although he had been advised that he needed a couple more weeks rest yet.

So that was the excuse for heading back to the countryside, if only temporarily. But despite that, he grabbed a couple of boxes that he might need. His carpentry tools. More clothes. And other items that he might need if time continued to drift by and he still found himself at Willow Tree Hall.

So he was feeling quite relaxed as Sam drove them back from London. His friend had told him that it wasn't a problem for him to stay as long as he liked and even seemed pleased that Tom enjoyed the family's company so much.

Although he hadn't intended to stay on, the thought of summer in the country was tempting. The setting was relaxing and after the madness of Glastonbury, the peace appealed to him as well. He could even feel the stirrings of new lyrics and melodies beginning in his head.

As they drew nearer to Cranley, he tried and failed to stop himself looking out of the window for Eleanor.

That kiss. That unexpected kiss. It had just been one of those things, but whereas their lips bumping into each other was an accident, the chemistry had been palpable. He hadn't been expecting the heat between them. He had kissed many women before, but this was different. He had spent most of the night in the yurt wide awake, wanting to kiss her again.

But, as usual, somebody somewhere had been

watching them and now the photo was everywhere, according to Sam.

He just wanted to hide away again until the clamour broke down.

He could try out a few songs. Hopefully he could begin to write again.

And see Eleanor.

All he needed was peace and quiet. But as they began to drive through the village, Sam's phone rang out in the car. Using his hands-free, Sam picked up the call.

'Hi,' said Annie, sounding a little breathless. 'I thought you might need a bit of a warning. Apparently there's lots of teenage girls at the beginning of the driveway looking for Tom.'

'You're kidding,' said Sam, glancing across at Tom and grimacing. 'How did they know he was staying with us?'

'No idea,' said Annie. 'But I thought I'd better give you a heads-up.'

'We'll be home in five minutes,' said Sam. 'See you soon.' He hung up and looked at Tom. 'Sounds like the word's got out, I'm afraid. What do you want to do?'

Tom made a face. He wasn't in the mood to face anyone yet so they pulled up just outside the village and, once they'd piled all of his luggage onto the back seats, he crawled into the boot for the last few miles.

Even in the darkness of the boot, he could hear the gaggle of teenage girls hovering around the entrance.

'Here we go,' said Sam, loud enough for Tom to hear him.

Tom felt the car pull to a stop.

'Is it true?' asked a girlish voice, breathless in excitement. 'Is Tommy King really here? In our village?'

'I'm afraid not,' he heard Sam say. 'Sorry to disappoint you all. It's just us boring normal people. No superstars here.'

The car then slowly began to move once more. Tom had to cling onto his bag as they bounced over the potholes in the driveway. Finally, he was grateful for the car to stop and the engine to be switched off. The boot lid automatically rose and he found Sam grinning down at him.

'Oh, to be rich and famous, eh?' said Sam, helping Tom out of the boot.

'Yeah,' drawled Tom, allowing himself a full body stretch. 'It's all about the glamour.'

Annie headed out across the driveway and round to the side of the house where they had parked. 'You two okay?'

'We're fine,' Sam told her, drawing her close for a kiss. 'I don't think we'll be in danger from any marauding fans any time soon.'

But Sam's certainty was short-lived when they headed into the drawing room. Arthur was at the window, peering out at the grounds through a pair of binoculars.

'Got time for a bit of twitching, have you, Grandad?'

asked Sam, with a grin.

Arthur turned around and smiled at them. 'Hello again, Tom. Welcome home. Yes, my boy. I've seen quite a rare species of bird. The lesser-spotted Girl Guide.'

Tom went to the window and could just about see a few faces peering out of the bushes and trees at the far end of the vast lawn. With the sash window wide open in the warmth of the day, they could hear the clamour from inside the house.

'Tommy! I love you!' screamed one girl.

'Marry me!' shouted another.

'Kiss me!'

Annie turned to Sam in horror. 'What shall we do?'

'I'll go and have a word with them,' said Sam, putting on a determined face.

As he soon as he had left, Rose arrived. 'What's new, pussycats?' she asked.

Annie turned to face her. 'Rose, you didn't tell anyone about Tom staying here, did you?'

Rose thought hard and then comprehension dawned. 'Well, that ghastly Muriel was going on about how her niece is in *Big Brother* or something like that. Made a big thing of it. So I might have name-dropped. Tom doesn't mind, do you, darling?' She gave him a cheeky wink.

'Of course not,' lied Tom, not wanting to upset her.

Annie rolled her eyes. 'Rose, we've got fans

everywhere in the grounds.'

'Have we really?' Her eyes gleamed. 'What fun!'

Sam came back a short time later.

'So?' asked Annie, raising her eyebrows at him in question.

'I told them they were trespassing and they'd better hop it,' said Sam. 'They're probably only as far as the main gates, but at least they won't be a nuisance.'

'How lovely to be young and in love,' cooed Rose. 'I remember flinging my knickers when Tom Jones was onstage one time. He gave them back to me later on that evening,' she added with a gurgle of wicked laughter.

Tom found himself smiling. You really couldn't be mad at Rose for very long.

At that moment, a grey blur rushed into the drawing room and leapt at him. Dylan ecstatically licked his face over and over until, finally, Tom had to push him away.

'Calm down, you mad dog,' he said, looking down at his earth covered feet. 'So that's where you've been? Digging up the vegetable patch again? You're going to be in so much trouble with Bert.'

But he couldn't resist hugging the dog tight against his chest briefly.

'I found a new toy for you at Glastonbury,' he told Dylan, who wagged his tail as soon as he saw the giraffe dog toy.

'We can add it to the collection that Grandad has started,' said Sam in a pointed tone.

Arthur waved away any concerns with his hand. 'The poor doggy was pining for Tom. I had to do something.'

With a ghost of a wink at Tom, Arthur left the room.

'He's really missed you,' said Annie, coming across to stroke Dylan's head. 'In fact, we had to bring Eleanor over to stay because he kept howling the place down every night. He stayed upstairs with her every night apart from the last one when he slept in Arthur's room.'

'Did he?' Tom ruffled Dylan's fur. 'You silly thing. I'll always come back. But I hope you behaved yourself with Eleanor and didn't keep her awake.'

'I think she secretly enjoyed having him with her,' said Annie softly. 'Not that she would admit to such a thing.'

'Well, she's probably a bit overrun with all the other animals, to be honest,' said Sam.

Tom gave Dylan another hug, wondering how long before he would see Eleanor again. And whether he would be able to stop himself wanting to kiss her once more.

# Chapter 30

Eleanor found that by the end of the week, she hadn't managed to bump into Tom. Mainly because she had been deliberately avoiding going to Willow Tree Hall in case she actually had to speak to him.

Then she received a call from Annie. 'We thought you'd gone back up to London as we've barely seen you since Glastonbury,' she said, pretending to be cross.

Eleanor blushed. 'No, I'm still here. I'm just a bit embarrassed about the photo with Tom, to be honest.'

'I thought so,' said Annie. 'I was only kidding. Look, how about we come over to your place later. It'd be good to get away from the house anyway as we can't move for rabid fans hiding in the undergrowth.'

Eleanor frowned. 'What are you talking about?'

'Rose has blabbed to someone about Tom staying with us and now we're overrun with fans.'

Eleanor could feel the panic beginning to swell inside her. Someone was bound to recognise her at some point.

She was still pacing up and down when Annie and Megan arrived.

'Don't fret. Look at me instead,' said Megan, pointing at her pale nose. 'Your cream is amazing. I didn't even peel.'

Eleanor smiled, feeling proud of herself before realising that she hadn't felt that way about any aspect of her working life for a long time.

'It's lovely that you've been able to spend a bit of time making your cream again,' said Annie, sitting down. 'Did you enjoy making it?'

Eleanor found herself nodding. 'It was really good fun.'

'Glad somebody's happy,' muttered Megan.

'Is everything okay?' asked Annie gently.

'It is now I've got wine,' said Megan, before taking another gulp. 'I've just got a really big Glastonbury hangover. It was such fun to do something different. How about a movie or something? Have you got *Magic Mike* for us to lust over?'

Eleanor flicked through her Mum's DVD collection. 'No but we've got *Mamma Mia*.'

'Oh, I love that,' said Annie.

As Eleanor set up the movie, her mum came in to join them. 'Megan, you look so much better than when I saw you the other day.'

'All thanks to your daughter's magic carrot cream,' Megan told her. 'Have you got any more? I used it all up, but I'm bound to get burnt again this summer.'

'It's right here,' said Eleanor, handing her a jam jar full of the newly made up cream.

'Oh! That feels so nice and cool,' said Megan as she

smeared it a little bit on her hand before sniffing it. 'Have you got any other flavours?'

Eleanor shook her head. 'Only plain and carrot cream, I'm afraid.'

'You should experiment a little,' said her mum. 'There's so many wild flowers out at the minute.'

'You know what you should do,' said Megan, warming to the idea. 'You should make up some different types and we'll try them out for you. Like a spa evening!'

'Oh yes!' said Annie, nodding. 'You should come too, June.'

Eleanor's Mum smiled. 'You don't want an old fogey like me being there.'

'Of course we do,' said Annie.

'And you're not old,' added Megan.

'A spa evening,' said Eleanor, deep in thought. She supposed that she could make up a few creams for them all. Plus she had loads of leftover luxury items from various VIP goody bags that she had managed to get hold of. The contents of which she had virtually never touched.

'Sounds great,' said Annie, nodding her approval. 'I'm having trouble sleeping, stressing about all the fete and lack of wedding dress.'

'Haven't you seen anything online or in all those wedding magazines that you keep buying?' asked Megan.

Annie shook her head. 'Nope. I mean, there's lots of lovely dresses but they just don't seem right. I don't know. Maybe I'm being too choosy.'

'Nonsense,' said Eleanor. 'It's your wedding dress. You need to be choosy. Next time we go shopping, I'm sure we'll find one.'

She made a silent note to find something to soothe Annie's nerves.

'We'll invite Rose as well,' said Megan. 'Then we can have a girly evening.'

'I'd better get tidying this place if Rose is coming to visit,' said her mum with a grimace.

Eleanor was staring down at her hands. The cream had helped her neck, but the eczema on her hands was still not fully cleared up. 'I was thinking about trying to make up a bar of carrot soap to see if it would help my fingers as well,' she said.

'Why don't you then, love?' said her mum. 'The kitchen's messy enough so it doesn't matter what you do in there.'

Eleanor frowned. 'You can't make proper soap without caustic soda. And I can't use that here. Not with all the animals.'

'You can do it at my place,' said Megan, with a shrug. 'Neal keeps promising to redo our garden but he never does. It looks like a nuclear war zone anyway.'

Eleanor shook her head. 'Thanks, but I daren't. Not with the kids. It's pretty scary stuff and can really burn your skin if you're not careful. It needs to be away from people, just in case.'

'I know,' said Annie. 'What about the old stable block in the grounds of the hall? I think there's even running water over there. Nobody will disturb you.'

'You can have your very own beauty factory,' said Megan.

Annie suddenly looked excited. 'That's it! Then you can make lots of stuff for the fete! Oh, it'll be wonderful. You'll probably make some money and that's another stall that I can add to the list. Local girl and all that.'

Eleanor wasn't so sure. She looked up at her mum, who was nodding her approval. 'I think that's a lovely idea,' said June.

Annie wasn't taking no for an answer. 'What else are you going to do with yourself this summer? Oh, say yes! Please! For me! I'm desperate.'

They were all looking at her, Annie with such pleading eyes, that Eleanor found herself nodding her head in agreement.

'Okay,' she said. If only to keep the peace with her friends. 'Just as a temporary thing.'

Her mum was smiling as she left the room.

'Have you thought about what you're going to do next for work?' asked Annie.

Eleanor shook her head. 'No idea. I still feel like such a failure.'

'Why would you feel like that?' said Megan, rolling

her eyes. 'You lived in London, for god's sake. I've never even got out of this village. At least you've seen stuff. Life!' She was waving her hand around furiously as she spoke. 'You've been to glamorous parties and all of that.'

'Megan,' said Annie softly. 'You're happily married with three kids. Do you not think that's a life too?'

'I dunno,' said Megan with a sigh. 'I think I'm just mourning my twenties because I had kids and didn't have any fun.'

Annie made a face. 'You know why I had to leave home. My twenties weren't a barrel of laughs.'

'And I ran away from all that awful stuff with my dad to spend my twenties running from party to party, not enjoying any of them,' said Eleanor. 'Oh, and missing my friends.'

'We missed you too,' said Annie, with a soft smile.

But Eleanor was still worried about Megan. 'Maybe you could work from home or something? Then you can manage it around the kids and the school run.'

Megan waved away her concerns with her hand. 'Don't worry about it,' she said with a casual shrug. 'I just get fed up and bored sometimes. But you know what has perked me up? Gareth Blunt got in contact on Facebook.'

'Gareth Blunt from school?' said Annie, frowning. 'That guy you had a huge crush on?'

'Yeah!' said Megan, her eyes gleaming. 'We had one

glorious fumble and kiss at the prom.'

'And then you met Neal a few months later at college,' said Annie, ever the romantic.

Megan smiled but it didn't reach her eyes, Eleanor noticed.

'What's Gareth up to now?' she asked.

'Some kind of TV director or something,' said Megan. 'All very glamorous.'

'Oooh!' said Annie. 'Let's google him.'

Eleanor refilled their wine glasses as the movie played on.

A few hours later, Eleanor stared at the two empty jugs of Pimm's. How had they got through all of that between the three of them? Her mum hadn't even had a drink. But it turned out the Megan had actually finished off most of the Pimm's. Annie and Eleanor had to help her stagger down the street after she insisted she didn't need a lift.

'Man, she was pretty drunk tonight,' said Eleanor frowning. 'Do you think she's okay?'

'Probably just blowing off some steam,' said Annie, with a shrug. 'I think she gets pretty bored at home.'

After Sam had picked her up, Eleanor went back indoors, deep in thought and wondering what she could do to help her friend. But her mind was blank. Especially as her own life left a lot to be desired right now.

# Chapter 31

Tom was trying to control his temper as he went along the east wing corridor to find Sam. The letter he was holding was becoming crumpled in his hard grip. He needed someone to talk to.

But Sam was on his mobile when Tom found him in the music room. From his gestures, he was likely to be some time. So Tom waved at him that it didn't matter and left him to it.

He went back along the corridor and spotted Arthur in his study. Before he could move on, Arthur had smiled and gestured for him to come in. Reluctantly, but not wanting to cause offence, Tom did so.

It was one of the rooms yet to be plastered or decorated, but it looked settled in its careworn way, with the dark wood shelves and desk. Many dusty books were piled up, most of them referring to agriculture and managing estates.

'I found this by my desk this morning,' said Arthur, picking up an old tennis ball. 'I'd hate for young Dylan to lose one of his most prized possessions.'

'And for you to trip over it,' said Tom, with a grimace at the thought. 'I think he's outside so I'll make sure he gets it.'

Tom could see the whole vista of the grounds bathed in sunshine through the window behind the desk.

'I've always thought this one of the best views out of any window,' said Arthur, following his gaze. 'From my seat here, you can see across most of the grounds at the back all the way down to the river. Almost the whole estate.'

'That's a lot for one man to be responsible for,' said Tom.

Arthur nodded. 'Indeed. But it's all I've known, so I guess you could say that it's what you're used to.'

Tom wondered if Sam felt the same. He appreciated the responsibility that his friend was taking on by becoming Earl of Cranley.

'Of course, I'm number seven in the line,' carried on Arthur. 'My father and grandfather were also well aware of their responsibilities. But my great-grandfather almost lost the whole stately pile in a cards match. Of course, gambling has always run amok in the whole family. The first Earl of Cranley won the estate in a poker game, after all.'

'So, in a way, it's a miracle that this place is even here.'

'Oh yes,' said Arthur, smiling. 'But some people make their own destinies, of course.'

Tom glanced down at the letter he was holding and hesitated. Perhaps Arthur could help him, but he didn't want to burden the elderly gentleman with yet more problems.

He started at the sound of laughter as Rose entertained one of her friends in the drawing room and frowned. Looking back, he found Arthur studying him.

'Do you know, a place like this does have some advantages,' said Arthur. 'Would you like to have a bit of fresh air and see one of them?'

Tom knew that Arthur was being kind and getting them out of the house meant they could talk privately. So he let Arthur lead him out the back door in the ballroom where they found Dylan dozing in the shade of the house.

He automatically glanced at the woods to see if he could see anyone hiding amongst the trees but thankfully the fans seemed to have decided that remaining at the front gates seemed to be their best hope of spotting him. So at least the grounds were private once more.

Once Tom had thrown the tennis ball, Dylan soon perked up and they both followed Arthur across the patio and down the dirt track towards the dilapidated dairy house and stable block.

'Long since abandoned unfortunately,' said Arthur, as they reached the buildings. He sounded wistful but not too upset. 'I remember when I was growing up, the place was full of stable lads and people dashing back and forth to the dairy. I think that's what I miss most of all. The people. But times, of course, change.'

They carried on past the buildings. Tom counted at least ten empty stable pens.

As they went further into the woods, the path narrowed.

'Would you like me to go first?' said Tom.

'Lead the way, son,' said Arthur, nodding. 'I daren't risk another broken hip. Annie hasn't got over the first one yet.'

'What happened?'

'Slipped over at the bottom of the stairs,' said Arthur. 'It was my own fault. Mind you, it did have one good outcome. Sam came home and met Annie.'

They carried on through the trees, taking care to step over the roots that were sticking out of the dusty ground. Dylan ran around them, chasing squirrels until they ran up the trees out of harm's way.

Finally, Tom could see water ahead through the large trunks of the trees.

They made their way to the bank and Tom was surprised to find himself standing at the side of a wide stream.

'The River Ley,' said Arthur. 'We get a whole mile of it, thanks to the estate.'

Tom gazed out across the water. 'Is it quite deep?'

'Perhaps not so much during the summer months but still deep enough for some carp. Perhaps the odd barbel. Do you fish?'

'Not for years,' said Tom, smiling. 'And certainly not

in any setting as beautiful as this.'

'Well, you're welcome to have a go whilst you're with us. I've got some old fishing stuff somewhere in the garages. I'll get Sam to hunt it down.'

'That's very kind of you.'

Arthur shrugged his shoulders. 'You're a friend of Sam's so that makes you family. By the way, are your own family from around here?'

Tom shook his head. 'No.' He paused before deciding to go on. 'My parents didn't want me so I grew up in foster homes. Nowhere near as pretty as this place unfortunately.' He looked across the glittering water, soothed by its beauty.

'I'm sorry to hear that,' said Arthur, softly. 'That must have been difficult for you.'

'Yeah,' said Tom. Difficult was an understatement. 'I'm afraid I wasn't very well behaved.'

'Hardly surprising.'

'But in a way, it made me who I am as well,' said Tom.

Arthur nodded. 'I agree, my boy.'

'Have I shocked you?' asked Tom.

'You know,' said Arthur. 'Nothing shocks you if you'd lived in Cranley all your life like I've done. It's a small village and yet it's as if it's the whole world encompassed in a few avenues and lanes. We've had it all. Affairs, divorces, heartbreak and even the odd murder.'

Tom was amazed.

'Not, I might hasten to add, in my lifetime,' said Arthur, with a soft smile before checking his watch. 'Mind you, that record may yet be broken if we don't head back in time for lunch. My future granddaughter-in-law is liable to worry about me these days.'

They slowly made their way back to the house.

'Was there something you wanted to ask me about?' asked Arthur.

Tom drew out the letter from his pocket. 'I just wanted some advice really about my gran. She is, was, my only true relative. She passed away six months ago.'

'I'm sorry to hear that.'

Tom gulped away the pain. 'It's been, well, it's been pretty tough. Anyway, she left everything to me in the will. Not that there's much to be had, just her flat. Probate is being granted at the minute, but I just wanted to ask what happens when someone challenges a will. My dad wants his share now. He hasn't been around for years, didn't want to know or see either of us and yet he expects the full estate to pass to him.'

Arthur stopped and nodded, deep in thought. 'I take it that the will was done properly?'

'Yes. Gran had a local solicitor draw it up.'

'Then I can't foresee any problems. There may be a short delay whilst your father's claim is being dealt with, but I would hope that the full weight of the law would fall onto your side.'

'Right. Well, thanks.' Tom looked down at the letter once more.

'You know, I've used Bill Fullwright for years,' said Arthur. 'He's a local solicitor. Trust him implicitly. When we get back to the house, I'll pass you the details and give him a call. He'll see you right.'

'Thank you,' said Tom. 'That's been a real help.'

Arthur smiled but Tom was horrified to see him trip over a stick that Dylan had dropped and lose his footing. He just about managed to grab Arthur's arm and keep him upright.

'No, no, I'm fine,' said Arthur, as he stood and regained his balance. 'Many thanks. You see? No blue blood and yet you have better manners than many of my ancestors.'

They had reached the stable blocks when they saw Annie coming across to meet them.

'Hello,' she said, smiling at them both. 'What have you been up to?'

'No need for the search party,' Arthur told her. 'I'm in safe hands.'

'Glad to hear it,' she replied, with a knowing smile at Tom before she turned to face Arthur. 'I wanted to ask you something. Eleanor needs to make some soap and it's all a bit tricky apparently. She needs somewhere quiet to work away from people as the stuff she uses is a bit toxic. Is it okay with you if she uses one of the old stables for a little while?'

Arthur smiled warmly at her. 'You know, they're your stables too,' he told her gently.

Annie blushed. 'I'm still getting used to all that.'

'It's absolutely fine,' said Arthur. 'Tell her to come over anytime.'

The three of them followed Dylan back up to the main house for lunch.

Tom felt ridiculously pleased that Eleanor would continue to visit the hall. Presumably, with whatever concoctions she would be creating, he would be seeing a lot more of her.

He even found he was humming a new tune as he made his way towards the recording studio later that day.

# Chapter 32

Eleanor had been at home at The Forge for the past couple of days, waiting for the delivery of the caustic soda with which to make her soap.

Well, that was the excuse she was telling herself and her friends.

In reality, she was still embarrassed about the kiss. Especially now it was all over social media. Thankfully, nobody had recognised the back of her head. And she was hoping to keep it that way.

So she used the delivery, the animals, helping her mum, any pretext she could think of, so that she didn't have to face him again.

But her hands were driving her crazy with the itching. And once the caustic soda had been delivered she knew she couldn't put off making her soap any longer.

So in deference to the full heat of summer, she put on her best cut-off shorts, her favourite flip-flops and her smartest T-shirt. She was oozing confidence. At least, that was what she hoped it looked like on the outside.

But her cheeks betrayed her at the first sight of Tom when she almost bumped into him in the huge entrance hall and she could feel them turning bright red.

'Hi,' he said, smiling.

Hello,' she replied, keeping her tone neutral. Cool but friendly.

'How are you?' he asked.

'Great,' she replied, her voice catching as she looked up at him. 'You?'

'Never better.'

'Great,' she repeated before walking away. She knew she must have sounded like an idiot but she was still smiling when she came across an excited Annie.

'Do you want to see the kitchen?' she said, pulling Eleanor down the corridor before she had a chance to refuse. 'It's finally finished.'

Grateful for the distraction, Eleanor had to concede it really was quite a transformation. Soft baby-blue walls matched the brand new Aga. Cream cupboards filled all the walls.

'It's lovely,' said Eleanor.

'There's so much storage,' sighed Annie, smiling.

Away from the food preparation areas, there was a brand new huge oak table that could comfortably seat ten people. In addition, a couple of comfy arm chairs had been placed either side of the new wood-burning stove.

It was a welcoming space. A room to be cherished. It would be the heart of the home. A place to congregate, chat and relax. No doubt, full of love and laughter.

Eleanor found herself yearning to belong to such a

place.

'I've still got all those old trays and saucepans if you need them for your soaps and stuff,' Annie told her.

'That would be great, thanks,' said Eleanor. She made a pile of the pans, as well as some old wooden spoons, oven gloves. 'Don't you need any of this?'

Annie shook her head. 'Alex insisted that everything should be new.' She glanced over her shoulder before whispering, 'Just don't tell Sam.'

Eleanor grinned. 'Mum's the word.'

'Do you want to see the guest bedrooms as well?'

Eleanor nodded and followed Annie upstairs. The spare bedrooms were now painted and furnished with beds, wardrobes and other cupboards.

'What kind of look are you going for?' asked Eleanor. Apart from the new furniture, the bedrooms were a blank canvas.

'I have this grand idea that they should each be individual,' said Annie. 'You know, the blue room, the green room et cetera. Otherwise there's too many to refer to. And I didn't want to say bedroom one, two and so on. But beyond that I've no idea. I haven't even chosen the colour of the curtains yet. The ones Alex keeps picking up are way too expensive.'

'You know,' began Eleanor, 'my mum is great at stuff like that. If you like, she could make you some curtains.'

'Oh yes please!' said Annie, looking pleased. 'That would be great. Country chic. You know the kind of thing.'

'But without the heavy price tag,' said Eleanor.

'But we'll pay her,' said Annie in earnest. 'Do you really think she'll do it?'

Eleanor nodded. 'I'll ask her, but I think she'd be glad to help. Besides, I think it will give her something to focus on. Especially as a couple of the animals are leaving this week.'

'Awww, the donkey's going?' asked Annie, looking sad.

Eleanor rolled her eyes. 'Not yet. But the local school is having the tortoise and goldfish.' She sighed. 'We're starting off with the small animals. Baby steps and all that.'

She followed Annie back down the wide sweeping staircase, deep in thought. Perhaps this was just what her mum needed. She had always been so good at needlework.

The plan had been for Annie to show Eleanor the stable block, but she suddenly she received a call from somebody regarding marquees for the fete and wandered away to make some notes whilst still chatting on the phone.

'You okay?' asked Sam, as she loitered in the hall.

Eleanor was dismayed to see Tom right behind him, her face immediately glowing red once more. 'I'm just waiting for Annie to finish her call so she can point out where the stables are,' she replied.

Eleanor was still feeling bashful around Tom, so hid her burning cheeks by playing with Dylan who had rushed up to see her.

'I've missed you these past few days,' she said, crouching down to stroke the dog's soft ears. 'Do you want to help me find the stables?'

'I can take you,' she heard Tom say.

'Oh. Thanks,' said Eleanor, trying and failing not to carry on blushing. 'That would be great.'

Feeling a bit nervous, she reluctantly went with him.

'So,' he said, 'what are you needing it for?'

Eleanor felt uncomfortable. This was about her. She didn't open up to many people, but maybe he understood that as well. 'I just need a bit of space to make some soap and few face creams for the fete,' she told him. 'Nothing fancy.'

The stables were only a few minutes' walk from the house. They went out the back door and along the narrow path. Once it had been a wide track, but now it was so overgrown that only one person could squeeze through at a time.

She glanced over at the huge back lawn which had become a wild flower meadow, thanks to the complete lack of care and mix of sunshine and rain. Swathes of bright blue cornflowers were marbled with red poppies and tall grasses. There were certainly worse places to be in the summertime.

But the stable block seemed a bit large when she saw

it through the trees. It all seemed to be a lot of fuss over nothing. Maybe the carrot oil would help her fingers but she was highly doubtful. But as she went to scratch the eczema patch between her fingers, she figured she might as well give it a shot.

As they rounded a large tree, the group of buildings came properly into view. One was what Annie had described as a coaching lodge. There was another barn there as well.

And then there was the old stable block.

Eleanor stopped abruptly, rooted to the path in shock.

'It's falling apart,' she said, staring aghast at the long brick building in front of her.

It was an L-shape block, holding about ten individual stables. Or, it once had. These days, the brick looked to be crumbling apart.

'At least the roof looks intact,' said Tom, staring up at the dark slates.

'It's the only bit that is,' she told him, going across to the stable nearest to her at the end of the block. She went to pull the wooden door open and found only the top half opened. The bottom half of the split stable door was firmly wedged shut.

Tom moved in front of her and yanked it hard until the whole thing fell apart in his hands. He looked sheepish. 'Well, at least it's open now.'

'I don't suppose Annie and Sam will worry about one

more building rotting away,' said Eleanor.

She poked her head inside and looked around. It was actually quite a large room with a window next to the door making it seem bright and surprisingly airy. And it didn't smell of horses, thankfully. Just musty, unused, with lots of cobwebs.

'You know,' said Tom, also venturing inside. 'It's in better condition than you think.' He flicked the light switch by the door and they were both surprised to see the light bulb in the middle of the ceiling come on. 'So the electricity is still working,' he said, nodding in thought. 'A new door would be quite easy to fit.'

'I don't think Sam and Annie want any more costs at the minute,' said Eleanor. Besides, it all seemed a bit unnecessary. 'Maybe I can manage back at home,' she said, beginning to turn away. This had been a silly idea. It had been kind of Annie to offer, but it was too much.

'Look,' said Tom, still gazing around at the space inside. 'I can knock up a new door in next to no time. Maybe a workbench as well.'

Eleanor was shocked. 'You?'

'I trained to be a carpenter,' he told her, smiling at her surprised look. 'I'm actually quite good. If you buy me a beer, we'll call it even.'

A frown creased her forehead. 'I didn't think you drank.'

His smile grew wider. 'Don't believe everything you read in the gossip columns.'

She found that the room suddenly felt a lot smaller with him filling the doorway. They locked eyes for a minute before he turned to study the room.

'You probably need some shelves too,' he said.

'Look, are you sure you've got time for all this?' asked Eleanor.

'No problem,' he said.

She got the feeling that he wasn't going to take no for an answer.

He wandered back outside. 'Did you know there's an outside tap here as well?' he said through the window.

Eleanor turned around and tried to focus on the positives. The place needed a good sweep and maybe a bit of weatherproofing. But there was possibility there.

Perhaps Sam and Annie could rent out the space afterwards if they made it clean and tidy, she told herself.

She found that she was smiling. For the first time in a long time, she felt a tiny ping of excitement in her stomach. Maybe this really could work.

After she and Tom had headed back to the house, there was a few more minutes of small talk before he thankfully left.

With relief, she sagged against the back wall. So neither of them had mentioned the kiss. That was good. They could both move on. Forget the whole thing had ever happened.

Except Eleanor wasn't sure she would ever be able to

forget kissing Tom.

# Chapter 33

Tom was surprised that Eleanor wanted to dabble in making creams and other cosmetics

He was having trouble deciding which version of her was real. The classy clothes horse with the defensive shield? Or the glittery, wellie-wearing Glastonbury one he had kissed?

He still didn't know.

But he found himself more and more intrigued by the third version of this stranger. The one that wanted to create something for her friends.

Figuring the best way to find out more would be to help renovate the stable, he hunted around for some raw materials. There was a pile of leftover timbers from when the first team of builders had almost ripped Willow Tree Hall to shreds.

'Help yourself,' said Arthur, nodding at the huge stack when he was asked about it. 'It's all oak. Do you need some tools?'

Tom shook his head. 'Thankfully I brought my own.'

'Very wise.'

Tom carried the wood to the stable block and placed it on the ground. He rubbed his slightly sore back. He wasn't used to physical work. *You've grown lazy*, he found himself thinking. A bit of actual exercise and hard work would do him some good.

He made a mental note of the jobs he needed to get done and began work. The door was completely rotten so he ripped it off and measured up for a new one. He kept the lock but Eleanor would need a padlock or something else. Not that anyone ever seemed to come here. Not even his fans, thankfully, who were still congregating outside the gates most days.

He also made some measurements for a workbench and shelves. The wooden shutters needed replacing outside of the window too, which, by some miracle, had remained intact.

Before he began to cut the oak planks down to size, he ran his fingers along the wood where it was smooth, the knots formed from many decades. He had missed working with wood and had forgotten the pleasure it brought him.

It also meant that he had a way to pay back the generosity of the family over the past month or so.

Meanwhile, the ever-present Dylan dozed on the warm stone until he became too hot and shuffled over to the cool ground in the shade of the trees.

By the time Eleanor appeared later with a broom, he had almost finished the new door and was ready to hang it.

'You work fast,' she told him before she went inside

to sweep out the cobwebs and years of dust and dirt. 'We could do with you at The Forge.'

He remembered the state of the place, thanks to the animals. But then he recalled the back door sticking. Perhaps he could give Eleanor's Mum a bit of hand there, as well.

He briefly wondered why he was prepared to add yet more carpentry to his to-do list.

By the end of the day, most of the furniture had been made.

'Tomorrow, the painting begins,' he told Eleanor.

'This is great,' she told him, looking at her new table. 'I suppose if the singing career doesn't work out, you could always go back to being a carpenter.'

He laughed at her joke. 'It certainly kept me fed and watered during all those years when I wasn't famous.'

She left a short time later, citing donkey- and goat-feeding duties.

Alone at the stables, Tom took a moment to appreciate the peace. He had really enjoyed his afternoon and felt relaxed, despite his aching muscles.

Now that Eleanor had swept out the inside of the stables, he decided to quickly paint the walls with the old pot of white paint that he had found. Then at least it could dry overnight and prevent any further dust wafting up from the bricks.

It was a small space and didn't take long, so he was able to finish the day by placing the worktables inside, leaving just the shelves to be screwed into place once the paint was dry the following day.

Closing the door, he felt a rare sense of satisfaction. But he was also a tiny bit frustrated. As if he hadn't wanted to finish working. He had found himself humming and writing lyrics as he had worked. But now the job was over.

'If I'd known you were as talented a carpenter as a singer, I'd have saved a fortune getting the main house done up,' said Sam, looking amazed when he joined him at the stable block later on. 'Dinner's ready soon, by the way.'

'Thanks,' said Tom. 'Though I'm not sure you can afford my carpentry skills.'

'I don't think we can afford anyone at the minute,' said Sam with a sigh.

Tom smiled. 'You know, I really enjoyed myself. I think in a bizarre way it actually helped me unlock some lyrics.'

Sam looked surprised but pleased. 'Really? Well, there's always the rest of the stable block to do, if you think it helps.' He waved his hand around the other nine rooms which were crying out for more attention. They looked even worse now that Eleanor's workroom was complete, ready for her to move in. 'You know, this is the most relaxed I've seen you in a long time,' said Sam. 'You've been somewhat out of it since your gran died.'

Tom shrugged his shoulders. 'Grief is pretty awful to

get through.'

'I agree,' said Sam. 'I'm not sure Will has ever got past his.'

'How is your brother?'

'Too wild,' said Sam, shaking his head. 'He's yet to find his way back into the family like I did. And it took me long enough.' He sighed. 'He was talking about doing up the gamekeeper's lodge at some point, so we'll see what happens with that.'

'Nobody can take away someone else's pain,' said Tom. 'But you can help ease it a little.'

'Is that what Eleanor's doing?' asked Sam, breaking into a grin.

Tom smiled. 'Maybe.'

Or was it more? Much more?

He was anxious to change the subject. 'So you think it's okay if I carry on repairing the rest of the stables?'

'Sure.' Sam shrugged his shoulders. 'Everything needs repairing. There's so much to do here, so the more hands to the pump, the better. But don't forget the reason you're here, right?'

Tom quoted some new lyrics at him and Sam seemed pleased.

'That's great,' he said, grinning. 'Well, go ahead. You'll have a hit album if you keep renovating dilapidated old places like this every week. And we've got piles of derelict buildings just waiting for you!'

As he walked back to the main house with his friend,

Tom realised he felt happier and more relaxed than he had done for ages. The work had helped. But also because he was around people again.

Had he closed himself off for too long? Stayed inside when he should have been outside? Was that what had blocked his thoughts and music?

He was coming to realise that it probably was. And that it needed to change.

He also knew that he was enjoying Eleanor's company as well. And that he still wanted to kiss her again.

# Chapter 34

Eleanor arrived at Willow Tree Hall the following day, armed with bottles and old pots and pans, ready to start moving her stuff in.

Almost immediately, she came across Tom in the entrance hall.

'Do you need a hand carrying all that?' he asked, picking up two boxes at once.

Eleanor tried and failed to stop herself glancing at his toned biceps as he picked up the heavy boxes with ease. When had he become all outdoorsy and muscly all of a sudden? The fresh air and carpentry was certainly helping him relax.

She followed him to the stable block and let him unlock the door, amazed by the difference she saw inside.

'You painted it,' she said, turning to him in surprise. 'Thank you so much.'

He held his palms up. 'Dylan told me to,' he replied.

She couldn't believe it. The room looked so much larger now that it was painted white. But it was nice to still see the pattern of the bricks underneath. He had placed two worktables in the room at a right angle and a stool had also appeared from somewhere.

'Wow,' she told him. 'Dylan really worked you hard.'

'He's a slave driver,' he told her, looking a little bit sheepish.

She decided to let him off the hook and began to look through her boxes whilst he put up a couple of shelves for her to use. Then the room was ready for her to unpack whilst Tom worked on the shutters outside.

'We'll have to ask the family what colour they think the shutters should be painted,' said Tom.

'Green would be nice,' she told him.

'I agree but we'd better get their opinion, just in case there's some historical colour or something they'd prefer me to use.'

As they carried on, Eleanor found it was relaxing, working together. She was filling the shelves and tables with all her stuff. He was now working on the door to the next stable along. They felt like a team.

Looking along the bench, she realised she was going to need some kind of stove to warm the ingredients up and wondered if Arthur had an old one knocking about somewhere. Thankfully he came along later in the morning, so she had a chance to ask him.

'I'm pretty certain we kept a few in the garage in case of power cuts,' he told her. Nodding thoughtfully, he added, 'I'll have a look later for you.'

He went over to sit down on an old bench in the courtyard of the stables.

'Wait!' said Eleanor, rushing over. The bench looked extremely rickety.

Tom also hurtled over, but it was too late. Arthur had already sat down and was smiling up at them both.

'Thank you both for your concern,' he said. 'The seat has no doubt weathered, but it's still sturdy. Much like myself.'

Eleanor and Tom exchanged a soft laugh of relief.

'Well, this is all looking quite splendid,' said Arthur, nodding his approval.

'What colour do you think the shutters should be painted?' asked Tom. 'They need something to keep them weatherproof.'

Arthur studied them for a moment before declaring, 'I think some shade of green would be perfect, don't you?'

Eleanor and Tom exchanged a smile as Arthur leant forward to give Dylan a stroke. Tom wandered away to carry on working whilst Eleanor chatted.

'Isn't it lovely to have a bit of sun,' carried on Arthur, with a contented sigh. 'I really do think sometimes we all need a little solar power to get our energy levels back up again.'

'Absolutely,' said Eleanor, rolling her shoulders. 'I've spent more time outside since I came back to Cranley than I've ever done before.'

'And are you reaping the benefits?' asked Arthur.

She knew that her handmade creams were the main difference in the improvement of her skin but she had no doubt that the fresh air had helped as well.

'Apart from my freckles,' she whispered

He smiled. 'They're a sign of beauty, my dear. And you get that from your mother. How is she getting along without some of her animal friends?'

'Better than I thought she would,' Eleanor told him.

'Glad to hear of it,' said Arthur. 'I would hate to see a lovely woman such as June hide herself away when there's so much to be enjoyed in the world.'

With a nod of goodbye, Arthur got up from the bench and went back to the house.

Eleanor watched him for a while, thinking that Annie was blessed to have such a grandfather-type figure in her life. Her own dad was particularly lacking in any kind of parental guidance or even interest.

Enjoying the sun, Eleanor stood still and realised that her pulse no longer raced along in stress. Her whole life and attitude had slowed down. Nothing was a rush now. There was no race to the next story. To the next Tube. Running and running in the sweaty concrete heat of the city. Here in the country she could stop.

However, she did want and need to keep her brain busy so had begun to read up on skincare and how certain flowers could help against various ailments. Roses were wonderful for older skin, helping to soothe and hydrate sensitive skins. Lavender had also real flower power to relax both skin and mind.

She was just googling how to make flower oils when

Tom arrived back from the main house with a picnic basket. 'Annie thought you might be keeling over from starvation. Have you eaten lunch?'

Eleanor shook her head. 'Not yet. You want to share?'

But as they peered inside the basket, she realised that there was plenty of food and drink for both of them.

'Looks like a picnic for two,' said Tom, grabbing a sandwich.

*Not very subtle, Annie*, thought Eleanor. But the cold drink was welcome, as was the food.

As they sat outside on Arthur's bench in the warmth of the sun, she watched Tom lob an apple core at Dylan. He caught it and settled down to have his own lunch.

'Shouldn't you be writing songs instead of working out here?' she asked.

He grinned and tapped his temple. 'It's all still working up here, you know. Let me think now.' He paused before singing softly, '*She fades in and out. Does she know? Does she care? She's a sweet enigma. The girl with the wavy hair.*'

She was impressed until she thought about the lyrics. 'Wavy?' Her hand automatically flew up to her head. She hadn't bothered to straighten it properly for a few days.

'I like it,' he said, still watching her. 'When I first knew you, you were more, what's the word, rigid.'

Rigid? She was horrified.

'Too London, I mean,' he carried on, seeing her upset look. 'Now you're all countrified.'

She made a face at him. 'You mean with the wellies and the bad smell?'

'I mean with the relaxed look, genuine smile and freckles.'

'Aren't they awful?' she said, covering her nose. 'Every damn summer.'

He reached out and removed her hand.

She flinched for a second, worried about the eczema patches in between her fingers. Then she remembered that they had disappeared and relaxed a little.

'I think your freckles are cute,' he told her.

There was a moment when he held her hand and she couldn't look away from his eyes no matter how hard she tried. The world stopped as she held her breath, remembering the moment when their lips had touched at Glastonbury.

Finally, he stood up. 'Well, those doors aren't going to make themselves,' he said softly.

He left her sitting on the bench, realising that she could finally breathe out.

But she was smiling to herself as she sat there, feeling ridiculously pleased that he had called her cute.

Later on, as they walked slowly back to the house, Eleanor watched Dylan leap and bound his way through the long wild flower meadow that should really have been the back lawn. The red poppies and blue cornflowers were vivid amongst the long grasses and got her thinking as to which flowers she could use to add to her creams.

Nearly at the patio, she noticed that a flower bed full of roses was in full bloom. However, some petals had already dropped onto the ground. She picked them up and inhaled the sweet scent that they had retained.

'Aren't they lovely?' she asked.

Deep in thought, it took her a few moments to realise that her mobile was ringing. Feeling relaxed, she drew it out of her pocket expecting it to be her mum. But when she read the name, she immediately felt as if someone had drenched her in cold water. It was Theresa, her ex-editor.

'Excuse me,' she murmured to Tom.

Once she was far enough away from the house, she picked up the call.

'Eleanor?' said Theresa, by way of greeting. 'That Tommy King is all over the press still. What was that story you had for me?'

She stood rigid in shock. This was it. Here was her chance.

Eleanor glanced up at the patio where Tom was playing with Dylan. The rest of the family were nearby and were starting their pre-dinner drinks. Arthur was smiling at something Rose was telling them all. Probably yet another outrageous story. Sam had his arm around Annie as he tried not to listen. Annie was laughing and looking out to see where Eleanor had got to.

And then there was Tom. He had a tear in his T-shirt from where it had caught on a nail. But he looked so much happier and relaxed than when she had first met him. She thought of his kindness with Arthur and how much work he had done in the stable for her.

And she knew she couldn't do this to any of them.

'I was wrong,' Eleanor said down the phone. 'Sorry but it was a non-story, after all.'

'Have you any idea who the girl was in the photo at Glastonbury?'

Eleanor gulped. 'Not the slightest idea, sorry.'

'Pity,' said Theresa before hanging up.

But Eleanor found that she wasn't upset at all as she re-joined the family on the patio. Her life at Hot Gossip! magazine was all behind her now.

# Chapter 35

The following morning, Eleanor realised how much lighter she felt. She didn't need to lie any more. She'd hated that job. And for now, she wanted a clean break from London and all the bad memories. She wanted to stay with her family and friends and enjoy their company, be herself again.

The only slight problem was if anyone back in London worked out that she was the girl in the photograph. Because she was beginning to realise that she didn't want anything to jeopardise her friendship with Tom.

She tried to concentrate on the idea of infused oils instead. She had been wanting to experiment with different oils for a while. So she decided to try out a couple to mix into her basic cream mixture. Perhaps she could try them on her friends at the spa evening they had planned.

The previous evening she had been drawn to the rose petals that had fallen onto the ground, and that had given her an idea. So when she was back at Willow Tree Hall, she gathered up some more loose rose petals on her way to the stable block.

She felt someone watching her and turned around to find Bert the gardener looking on with much amusement.

Deciding that he might be in rare good humour, Eleanor decided to chance her luck. 'Is it okay for me to pick a small bit of lavender as well?' she asked, giving him her most hopeful, sweetest smile.

'As long as you leave some for the bees,' he grunted at her before turning away.

Back in her workshop, she chopped up the rose petals into fine pieces and filled an empty jam jar until it was almost full. Then she covered the petals with some cheap sunflower oil that she had swiped from her mum's larder and filled it to the brim. Finally she screwed on the lid and left it on the windowsill in the sunshine.

She repeated the same process with the lavender as well. Except she ran out of sunflower oil for the last two jars. Deciding to modify her own recipe, and thinking what the hell, she covered the lavender with water instead.

For the next couple of days, she would pick up each jam jar and shake it vigorously before placing it back in the warm sunshine.

The day before the spa evening, she took a couple of the oil infusions with her to her new workshop. Using one of Annie's old colanders, she strained the petals from the oil and then used the leftover oil to mix into her face cream recipe. She made a couple of pots with the rose oil and another few with the lavender.

She looked at the leftover oil. She didn't think that would be good for anything but the lavender water smelled lovely so she poured that into a container to ponder over what to do with it.

Feeling smug with her efforts, she wandered out of the stable to tell someone but Tom wasn't working nearby. In fact, they hadn't seen each other for the past few days. Apparently, he had been holed up in the recording studio and their paths had never seemed to cross, despite her looking out for him at every opportunity. She found she missed having him working nearby. Missed his calming presence and their easy conversations.

With a sigh, she decided to let Annie know what she had been up to instead.

It was a glorious afternoon. The birds were tweeting all around her in the trees high above. White cotton balls of clouds were drifting lazily around in an otherwise cobalt blue sky. In a leafy glade on her way back to the main house, she stopped walking and turned her face up to the sun, warming her cheeks in its rays. Although her hair was scraped back into a ponytail, a loose strand gently battered her cheek. For a moment all she felt was blissful peace. Then she heard her name called out from nearby.

In shock, she turned to see if the face matched the voice. Surely she must be imagining things? It couldn't be him. Not here. Not now.

But the voice was true. It was her dad.

'Hello,' he said, walking through the woods with a wide grin, as if they had seen each other only yesterday. When, in fact, it had been at least a year.

'What are you doing here?' she asked, automatically scratching at her neck even though it wasn't itchy

He looked ridiculous. Who wore a leather jacket in this heat? And those jeans were way too tight for a man of his age. He had dyed his hair, but the black was much too harsh against his skin. It was slicked back, but she still noticed that it had thinned a little more since last she had seen him.

'Well, that's a fine welcome,' he told her, stepping forward to put his arms around her for a hug.

For a second, she let herself relax against him. The smell of his aftershave so familiar even after all of these years. Then she remembered all the pain and stepped away from him.

'How are you?' he asked.

She was about to tell him when Dylan charged up to them. Looking around, she saw Tom appearing through the trees. She tried to tell him telepathically to turn around, but it was too late. Her dad had seen him. She closed her eyes briefly in despair.

Not at all surprised, she watched as her dad immediately turned his back on her and headed over to hold out his hand to Tom.

'Hi there, Tommy,' he said. 'I'm Ken McCartney. Eleanor's father.'

Tom took his hand and shook it, glancing at Eleanor as he did so. She felt almost certain that he could sense her discomfort.

'I've gotta say, I'm a huge fan,' her dad continued. 'And you were brilliant at Glastonbury. I was there, of course. I go every year.'

Eleanor rolled her eyes.

'Thanks,' said Tom, looking as if he was going to step around him.

But her dad blocked Tom's way. 'I couldn't get a selfie, could I?' he asked. 'My mates are never going to believe me when I tell them that you're dating my daughter.'

'What?' said Eleanor, aghast.

Her dad turned to look at her. 'Well, when I saw your mum just now, she told me that you were spending a lot of time up here. And obviously the papers are full of the news that Tom's staying at the hall. It doesn't take an idiot to put two and two together.'

'Well, your answer is five because you're completely wrong,' said Eleanor, putting her hands on her hips.

'Come off it, Ellie,' said her dad. 'That photo from Glastonbury? Well, it looks just like you.'

Eleanor groaned and looked at Tom. 'I'm sorry but could you just give me and my dad a minute?'

'Of course,' he told her.

He walked away with Dylan at his heels, leaving Eleanor alone with her dad.

She waited until Tom was out of view before spinning around to face her father, snatching her hair out of its ponytail and letting it loose in the hope that it might help the stress headache that had suddenly appeared.

'Why did you go and see Mum?' she snapped. 'I don't want you upsetting her.'

'I wanted to find out the latest gossip,' he said, smiling. 'Who'd have thought little old Cranley would get into the newspapers, eh?'

She scowled at him. 'You weren't that interested in it when you left in such a hurry all those years ago.'

He studied her. 'My little Ellie, all grown up,' he said, seemingly oblivious to her remark.

'Don't call me Ellie,' she told him. 'You don't get to call me that anymore.'

'You've changed your hair,' he said. 'It's not straight.'

'No, this is its natural state,' she replied, running her hand through it. 'You would know that if you knew anything about me.'

'Its natural state?' His eyebrows shot up. 'So what, you're letting yourself go now? Becoming a hippy like your mother?'

She rolled her eyes. 'I'm not letting myself go, Dad. I'm being me. I can't do the whole perfect appearance thing anymore. It's too exhausting. Anyway, I kept myself perfect because that's what I believed would bring you back to us. Because you're all about the looks, aren't you?'

'I like to look nice,' he said, becoming defensive. 'There's nothing wrong with that.'

'But you didn't come back, Dad. It turned out you were never that bothered about me in the first place.' Her voice broke.

He didn't reply, just looked confused.

'You're dressed thirty years too young and you look ridiculous,' she told him, becoming irritated at his lack of reply. 'People get older. They mature. But not you. You want to know something? I have freckles. My hair is wavy. I'm not perfect and nor are you!' She grew weary suddenly. 'Why are you here, Dad? I mean, it's not my birthday so you don't need to send me a two-line text. It's not Christmas so you don't have to sit through an excruciatingly painful lunch with me, which, by the way, I always make up an excuse so I can leave early. So what gives?'

He tried to look self-important. 'I just wanted to show my support for my daughter. I read the papers. I know what it's like to be hounded by the press.'

'No, you don't!' She found she was shouting now. 'You loved it! Giving all those interviews. Talking about the wonderful Susanna and how she was the love of your life. Was that the third or fourth love of your life, by the way. I lose count when you get through so many

Z-list celebrities.'

'Now listen, young lady,' he started.

'No, Dad,' she told him, shaking her head. 'You don't get to give me advice or tell me anything! Not anymore.'

He drew up his chin. 'It's my duty as your father to protect you.'

'That's rubbish and you know it,' she told him. 'What did you care all those years ago when you left us for her. Did you even remember us back then when you were busy trying to get famous off the back of that actress?'

'Well, aren't you doing just the same with Tommy King?' he said, sneering.

She took a deep breath. 'No, Dad. I'm not. Funnily enough, that was a real kiss. Just one moment which somebody took advantage of. I'm not using him for publicity. You know why? Because I've never wanted to be famous like you. I don't know what type of person you think I am, but never think for even one second that I'm anything like you.'

The silence stretched out as she continued to glare at him. Then the fight went out of her as quickly as it had arrived.

'Tom and I are friends. Just friends,' she told him, with a heavy sigh. 'That's all. So just leave, Dad. Please. Just go away…'

She stared at him for a long time until he finally

turned away.

'And don't you dare go near the Harris family either,' she called after him. 'Get in your mid-life-crisis sports car and get away from here, okay? You don't belong here anymore.'

Eleanor waited until he was out of earshot and out of view. And then she turned and ran through the woods, finally letting the tears stream down her face.

*

Tom had overheard the argument between Eleanor and her father. He hadn't wanted to eavesdrop but she was shouting so loudly that it was hard for him not to hear her what she was saying.

Once the woods fell silent, he waited and wondered what to do. He had seen her rush by towards the river and through a gap in the trees he could see her sitting on a rock, her knees hugged to her chest.

He wanted to leave her alone, to let her grieve for her relationship with her father, but Dylan had other ideas. He had spotted Eleanor and bounced up to see her.

Tom watched as she gave a start and then smiled before glancing around. He noted the cheeks shiny with tears and that her smile faded when she saw him.

'Sorry,' he told her. 'The idea wasn't to intrude, but Dylan was too happy to see you.'

'Glad someone is,' she muttered, keeping her head

down while she stroked Dylan's face.

Tom went and sat next to her on the rock while Dylan headed into the shallow clear water for a paddle and a nose around.

It was a beautiful setting which he would have enjoyed if only he could take Eleanor's sadness away.

'Did you clear the air with your dad?' he asked.

She sighed. 'Well, I threw him out, so I guess so.' She stared at the water glistening under the sun. 'I can't believe he thought I was like him. That I could ever be like him.'

'You're not, you know.'

'Thanks.'

He wondered whether he could trust her and knew deep down that he could. 'If it makes you feel better, my own dad is spectacularly rubbish as well.'

She brushed away a tear. 'Is he?'

'He never wanted me. And my mum was too busy partying as well to bother with a child. So I was given away at the age of four and went through various foster homes growing up.'

She looked horrified. 'That's terrible. I'm so sorry.'

He looked out to where Dylan was grappling with a stick he had found in the water. 'My gran was the only one in the family who cared. The only normal one.'

'At least you had somebody,' she said, sounding pleased. 'Does she live near here?'

The pain of grief struck him hard again. But he had

to get the words out. 'She died last November.'

To his surprise, Eleanor put her arm around him. 'I'm so sorry,' she told him, hesitating before leaning her head on his shoulder in support.

'You know, I'm the one who was supposed to be giving you support,' he said, gently.

She turned her head and smiled up at him. 'It could be a joint thing, I suppose.'

He stared into her green eyes, her face so close to his. 'Yeah. It could.'

'So do you think we should start the Bad Dads club?' she said.

He shook his head. 'I'm going to break that mould,' he told her. 'When I have kids, they're going to be supported. Loved. Cherished.'

She looked surprised at his words but nodded thoughtfully. 'You're right. And my dad's not going to change me either.' Then she frowned. 'Maybe he did for a while. He's all about the perfect looks, you see.'

He began to understand where the fancy clothes and thick make-up had their beginnings. She took a deep breath. 'About Glastonbury...' she began.

He shook his head. 'It was just one of those things. An accident. But with our lips.' He grinned at her. 'Honestly, it's no big deal. The papers will soon die down about it.'

'Okay.'

For a moment longer, they stared into each other's

eyes. She was so close that he could feel her breath on his neck.

Then she nodded, before leaping off the rock to go and see Dylan.

He wondered to himself whether she believed him. And why on earth he had lied to her when all he wanted to do was kiss her over and over again?

# Chapter 36

It was a subdued Eleanor that headed home to see her mum that evening. She knew that she couldn't avoid the conversation that they needed to have. Or put off causing her mum pain when that was the last thing that she wanted.

'I've just seen Dad,' she announced, as soon as she found her mum in the front lounge watching the television.

Her mum straightened her back as if bracing herself for an incoming assault. 'Well, that's a pleasure that we've both had today then,' she replied.

'Are you okay?' asked Eleanor, sitting down next to her.

'Are you?' asked her mum.

Eleanor burst into tears. 'He thought I was like him. With the publicity about Tom, you know.'

Her mum pressed her lips together as if not wanting to speak out of turn and just held her arms out. Eleanor went straight in for the hug.

'What happened?' prompted her mum, still holding her tight.

'I sent him away,' said Eleanor, snuggling in closer.

'It's awful,' she carried on. 'It's as if he forgets that he wasn't at the end of a phone or here when I needed him for help or any kind of advice. Unlike you.' She drew back to look at her mum. 'You were always there for me.'

'And I always will be,' said her mum softly. 'Do you know what? I fancy a cup of tea and a biscuit.'

They went into the kitchen and after getting the biscuit tin out, Eleanor straightened up and searched her mum's face. 'What about you? How are you doing after seeing Dad?'

Her mum tried to smile. 'I felt bad for looking a mess. He always made me feel like that. And, of course, I've got this stupid plaster on my leg which doesn't help. But I thought he looked older. Not so great, actually. I mean, not ill. Just...'

'Mutton dressed as chicken,' said Eleanor, nodding in agreement.

'It's not a good look, is it?' said her mum, making a face.

Eleanor shook her head. 'No. It's not.'

'I've been thinking about a lot of things this afternoon,' said her mum. 'When I get this plaster off tomorrow, I thought that perhaps things could start to change around here.' She stared out of the window. 'I've been thinking about what you said. I think you're right, the animals deserve better than this.'

Eleanor went over to give her a hug. 'They were so

lucky to have you. As am I.' She gave her mum a squeeze. 'But I think Buttercup and Daisy would probably prefer some kind of field.'

Her mum turned to face her. 'Actually, I think they should all go. Big and small.'

Eleanor was amazed. '*All* of the animals? Even the kittens? What will you do?'

Her mum smiled. 'Have a life. And give them a better one. I think that it's time for me to start living again.'

'Oh Mum!' said Eleanor, reaching forward to give her another squeeze. 'I'm so proud of you. Look, we can start off small. The tortoise and the fish didn't leave much of a dent when they went, did they? But let's start with the little animals, if you like. How about the kittens? Everybody loves kittens, don't they?'

'I'm sure there are some families that would love a kitten,' said her mum, nodding. 'But they'll all need vetting. We can't just give them up to anyone.'

'I know. They have to be the right families.' Eleanor wondered if Megan could help them out with that. 'Why don't we have a chat with Annie, Megan and Rose tomorrow night? And Ben, too. Between us all, we must be able to think of someone.'

Her mum smiled. 'Okay. I must say, it'll be lovely to have a spa evening and try out some of your creams.'

Eleanor nodded, still feeling nervous. 'I think I've got enough for everyone. I've made a rose cream as well as a lavender one. And also the infamous carrot cream. I thought Rose might like to try out the rose cream. It's supposed to be good for mature skins.'

'God, don't say that to her!' said her mum. 'I think Rose is only thirty-two in her mind.'

As it happened, the spa evening was a huge success. Everyone approved of the creams, oohing and aahing at the feel and smell of them on their skins. Even Eleanor was happy with the results. She had already begun to use sweet almond oil instead of sunflower oil. It was a little pricey but worth it for a more luxurious feel and smell.

'You must make some more for the fete,' said Annie, smoothing some cream onto her hands.

'Yes, yes,' snapped Megan, before taking another swig of her Pimm's. 'We know the fete has got to be the highlight of our year.'

Annie looked chagrined. 'Sorry,' she said, giving them a sheepish look. 'Have I been going on about it?'

'Just a bit,' conceded Eleanor eventually.

Annie blew out a sigh. 'I just don't know how we're ever going to have enough stalls to keep everyone happy.'

'Does it matter?' prompted Eleanor gently.

'Of course it matters!' Annie told her. 'This is going to be my heritage. If it starts off rubbish then I'll get a reputation as a rubbish countess, won't I?'

'It'll be fine,' said Megan, removing the cucumber from her Pimm's. 'Can I put these on my eyes?'

Eleanor grimaced. 'I'll get you a fresh pair that aren't

covered in alcohol, shall I?'

'The good thing is that all of your stuff is sustainable. And sustainable is the word of the moment,' said Megan as she picked up another tub. 'As in natural. Everything should be "free from".'

'That's two words,' said Annie.

'Very funny,' said Megan. 'You know what I mean. Plants are in, big time. I really think you've stumbled across something here. Go natural and go big.'

'Exactly how much have you had to drink?' asked Eleanor, grinning.

She left her friends rummaging through what was left of the goody bags that she had picked up from the parties that she had frequented in her former life and headed into the kitchen where she found Rose and her mum in deep conversation.

'Sorry to interrupt,' said Eleanor. 'I just need some more cucumber.'

'Your creams are divine,' said Rose, nodding her approval. 'What a talented family you are. I was just asking your mother about her sewing skills that I've heard so much about.'

'I don't know about that,' said her mum blushing.

'Well, I do,' said Rose in a firm tone of voice.

'But you are going to help make some new curtains for Willow Tree Hall, aren't you?' asked Eleanor.

'I guess it will keep me busy when all the animals start to leave.' Her mum bit her lip, looking nervous.

'I think you're being terribly brave about it all,' said Rose, reaching out to take her hand. 'It takes a huge amount of courage to think that there might be another path to follow in life.'

'Like my daughter here,' said her mum, smiling at Eleanor. 'Mind you, I don't think I've ever used anything like her creams.'

'Well, your skin is fabulous, so you probably didn't need to,' said Rose.

'You didn't used to mess around with make-up when you were young?' asked Eleanor. 'You weren't that old when you had me.'

Her Mum smiled. 'I know I let myself go after your father left. Probably even before he left.'

'It wasn't your fault,' said Eleanor in a stern voice. 'So you didn't put on a full face of make-up every day. So what? That was no excuse for him to leave like that.'

'Well said, sweetie,' said Rose, nodding in approval. 'A real man would see through all that and love the person inside. Someone like our lovely vet perhaps.'

'Ben?' said her Mum, hurriedly getting up from the table. 'I don't think he would ever think of me like that. Besides, we're just friends.' She quickly left the room with the excuse of filling up Annie and Megan's glasses.

Rose looked at Eleanor and shook her head sadly. 'She was so badly hurt by your father. I don't think I've ever seen anyone more devastated. But perhaps a little encouragement might help.'

'Ben and Mum?' wondered Eleanor out loud.

'He's been in love with your mother ever since they went to school,' said Rose, with a sad smile.

'No!' said Eleanor, shocked.

'Oh yes,' said Rose. 'Such a kind, patient man. Why do you think he never married? I'll leave it to you to see what you can do. She must have been so lonely all these years. She deserves a little happiness, don't you think?'

Eleanor was reeling from all the new information. But perhaps now that her mother's plaster was off and she was more mobile again, there was a chance. And she was giving up the animals as well.

When her mum came back into the kitchen, Rose changed the subject to some local gossip, so Eleanor wandered back into the front room to chat with her friends.

But on the way her phone rang. She was amazed to see Lucas's name come up on the screen.

'Hello,' she said, hesitating before picking up. 'How are you?'

'I was wondering if you felt like opening the front door actually.'

In a daze, Eleanor went to the front door and opened it. And there, to her amazement, stood Lucas.

# Chapter 37

Eleanor stared in shock at her boyfriend.

'What are you doing here?' she spluttered.

'I was in the neighbourhood and thought I'd see how you are,' said Lucas, laughing at how ridiculous that sounded. He was dressed in his best jeans and leather jacket, despite the warmth of the evening. In the street was a fancy convertible sports car which she presumed was his.

'Do you want to come in?' she asked, opening the door wide. The sound of girly laughter filled the hallway and front garden.

Lucas shook his head. 'No,' he replied. 'I think we'll be able to talk more privately out here, don't you?'

That was no surprise given his normal reaction to her mother's house. So Eleanor closed the front door and wandered down the path with him.

'How are you?' she asked.

'Great,' he replied. 'Got a promotion. Excellent timing on my part. I should be VP by next summer.'

'Wow,' she told him. 'That really is good news.'

'There's no chance of any more VIP tickets, are there?' he asked. 'It would help me out greatly with the directors.'

Eleanor sighed. Was that the only reason he had come to see her? She shook her head. 'Sorry. I gave all that up when I left London.'

'Shame. I really can't believe you stayed in this place for so long,' said Lucas, glancing up at The Forge with disdain.

'Why not? My mum lives here.'

'I just thought you'd head back to London as soon as possible,' he replied, with a shrug. 'What is there for you to do in a dump like this?'

'Plenty, and it's not a dump,' she said, frowning. 'It's a charming village where people care about me.'

Lucas' eyebrows shot up. 'Well, you have changed.'

She looked up at his sneering face and suddenly felt very defensive. What did he know? How would he understand about the warmth and community of a place like this?

'What's wrong with your hair?' he asked. 'And your face looks different too.'

Eleanor knew that was Lucas speak for 'you look a bit of a mess'. He was just like her Dad, she realised. He wanted her to look perfect all the time too.

She suddenly remembered Tom telling her how much he preferred her to look natural. And that she felt the same way.

'I'm having a spa evening,' she told Lucas. 'I've been making hand and face creams actually.'

He scoffed. 'Seriously?'

'Yes. Why not?' she snapped. 'I like helping people with their skin problems. What did you ever do to help people?'

'Make them rich,' he replied with a wide smile.

Eleanor had had enough. 'You know what, I think we both needed this break from each other. I for one was really glad of it.'

He frowned. 'You mean, absence makes the heart grow fonder?'

She shook her head. 'No. I mean, absence has made me realise that I think our break should be a permanent one.'

'Wait!' Lucas looked panicked. 'Are you sure there really is no way you can get hold of any more VIP tickets?'

She stared up at him coldly. 'Quite sure.'

He looked at her for a moment before he broke into an unexpected smile. 'You know those pictures of Tommy King kissing some mystery girl at Glastonbury? Well, I thought she looked a lot like you.'

Eleanor felt as if she had been drenched with cold water. 'It was the back of someone's head,' she told him, trying not to look panicked. 'It could have been anyone.'

He nodded. 'I agree. Only I came home to an answerphone message a week or so ago from your old editor. Theresa whatsername. Asking about a story on Tommy King. Seems a bit coincidental, don't you think?'

She forced herself to shrug her shoulders in a nonchalant manner. 'That was a different story that I was going to write before I lost my job. Not the same thing at all.' She began to turn away. 'Well, if there's nothing else…'

'So this really is it?' he asked.

'I'm afraid so. As you said back in London, it was only ever supposed to be a bit of fun.

Goodbye, Lucas. Take care of yourself.'

As she turned to head back up the garden path, she noticed the curtain in the front room twitching. Knowing that her friends were waiting for her gave her the strength to carry on and close the door behind her.

She was still standing, sagged against the front door, when Annie and Megan came out into the hallway.

'That was Lucas,' she told them, with a sigh.

'Are you okay?' asked Annie.

'I'm fine,' said Eleanor 'Just annoyed with myself more than anything.'

She followed her friends back into the front room and slumped onto the sofa.

'I just wish I could take back the last couple of years. What on earth was I thinking of?'

Megan shrugged her shoulders. 'Maybe you were just getting by, like everyone else.'

'I think he only wanted me for my press pass into all those parties. Something to impress his colleagues at the bank with.'

'That's awful,' said Annie. 'But you did care for him, didn't you?'

'I don't know. I think I just settled for him because I was lonely in London,' Eleanor told them, before giving a short laugh. 'Of course, now I haven't got a clue what I'm doing with my life.'

'Well, I think you're amazing,' said Annie, gesturing at the pots of cream on the table. 'Maybe you can make some money whilst you come up with an alternative career plan. I'd buy any of your creams.'

'Yeah, you might just have a career after all,' said Megan, reaching for the jug of Pimm's that was on the coffee table. 'Now, what does this do?' She pointed at a box.

'I think it's coloured mascara,' Eleanor told her, handing it over.

'Excellent,' said Megan. 'About time I look my best.'

Annie smiled. 'Whatever for?'

Megan sighed. 'Because I want to be a yummy mummy from now on. Actually, scrap that. I want to be a MILF.'

Eleanor had laid out some of the freebie expensive creams that she had picked up from the many VIP events she had attended. Her own skin was too sensitive for her to use them. She handed a pot of some kind of oil to Annie.

'Looks a bit posh for me,' said Annie, putting it down as if it were made out of diamonds. 'I think my skin is more simple than that.'

But Megan snorted a laugh. 'Mine is crying out for posh, to be honest.' She smeared on an anti-wrinkle mask and lay back on the sofa.

'This doesn't smell as nice as yours,' said Annie, sniffing a tube of hand cream.

'Oh, by the way,' said Megan, still lying down. 'One of the other mums saw how red I was and I told her about your cream helping my sunburn. She asked if she could have some carrot cream for her summer holiday. Actually, I think a couple of people want some.'

'Oh. Okay.' Eleanor beamed with the satisfaction that perhaps she did have something to contribute after all.

'Maybe Tommy King can give you a celebrity endorsement,' said Megan, grinning. 'After all, he is your boyfriend now.'

'Only on Twitter and only with the back of my head,' said Eleanor, rolling her eyes. 'It's so embarrassing.'

'I think it's romantic,' said Annie in a dreamy tone.

Eleanor bit her lip. 'But what if he finds out what I used to do...' Her voice trailed off as she thought about Lucas and what he had guessed.

'Maybe you should tell Tom the truth,' said Annie.

Eleanor shook her head. 'He would hate me. And, I, er, really enjoy his company.'

Annie grinned. 'I know you do. I've been watching the two of you together. Just be careful.'

Eleanor nodded but knew she could never tell Tom the whole truth. He would hate her and she didn't want him to think of her that badly. She realised she really did want him to like her.

# Chapter 38

The following day, Eleanor knew that, there were no more excuses. She needed to be brave and attempt to make some soap.

Thankfully, Tom had told her that he was going to be working in the studio that day and therefore any disasters wouldn't be made with an audience.

She stared down at the ingredients and the pots and pans. Soap was just an alkali mixed with fats. But she also needed the scary-sounding lye, otherwise it would just be a saucepan full of fatty oils floating in hot water. Yuck.

It was just water, natural oil, butters or wax and caustic soda. What could possibly go wrong?

But by mid-afternoon, the pile of ruined saucepans was growing. Thankfully, the basic mixture was beginning to take shape after many disastrous attempts. There was probably time for one more attempt before she had to head home and give the animals their tea. So she started again.

Eleanor changed the measurements for the carrot oil and the last of the shea butter that she had brought with her. She wondered if she could add in the other essential oils that she had made. After all, it wasn't as if she didn't have the time on her hands these days. Then she shook her head. That would come later if she could ever get her soap to set properly. A big if.

Thanks to Arthur's generosity, she now had a small camping stove. So in a saucepan, she slowly melted the fat and oil. Once that was done, she measured out the water to make the lye solution and weighed the sodium hydroxide. Then came the tricky bit. She put on the big thick gloves and plastic apron that she had borrowed from her mum. The goggles she had had to order over the internet. They were uncomfortable but necessary. Outside of her workroom, she tipped the sodium hydroxide into a big pan of water and stirred it with an old wooden spoon until she couldn't feel any more grit at the bottom. Then she went back inside to bring out the melted carrot oil and butter mixture. Coming back out, she came face to face with Tom, who laughed in surprise as he wandered into the courtyard.

'Hello,' he said. 'Is this a science lab or a beauty parlour?' he said, throwing down an old tool bag.

'Neither,' she told him, placing the mixture onto the ground and pushing back her goggles as she straightened up. 'It's a dream factory.'

'Good name,' he said. 'Maybe you should be the one writing lyrics.'

Despite the fact that Eleanor had become a lot less concerned about her appearance since she'd been back in

Cranley, she felt hot and bothered that Tom had found her looking like this. Her hair scraped back. Her goggles. Her old clothes. She felt a right mess.

'I thought you were supposed to be in the recording studio,' she told him, nodding at the tool bag.

'I got side-tracked,' he told her. 'One of Sam's tenants in the village needed a new front gate so I said I'd make one for them.'

'I bet they were impressed that their carpenter is an international singing star.'

He grinned at her. 'I think the young mum was more grateful that the kids could run round in the garden safely.'

'I might have to think about paying you to fix my mum's gates,' said Eleanor. 'The thought of Buttercup and Daisy getting out gives me nightmares.'

'Of course,' he told her. 'And I won't need paying.'

'Oh. Well, thanks.' She hid her blushes by pushing down her goggles and picking up the melted carrot mixture.

'So what's happening?' he asked. 'Why the nuclear fallout fashion today?'

'It's for the lye solution over there.'

He glanced over. 'Okay. Is it that bad?'

'It's just a chemical reaction that makes the fats,' she told him. 'You know, the oil and butter into soap.'

He smiled. 'Fascinating. Were there witches in your family tree?'

She made a face. 'Almost definitely on my father's side, I should think.'

She went over to stand next to the lye mixture, working up the nerve to pour it in again.

'Can I help?' he asked.

'No,' she quickly told him. 'And stand back! Sorry, but it's really dangerous. This stuff is highly corrosive. So be careful, unless you want to lose the top layer of your skin.'

'Well, I'm feeling rather attached to it at the minute, so I'll stay over here.' Tom leaned against the door.

Under his watchful eye, Eleanor picked up the lye solution and carefully poured a very small amount into the melted mixture. She stared down, watching it closely. But it didn't fizz, so she very slowly poured the rest in. Putting down the pan, she stirred the mixture until it was blended but still runny. Then she straightened up and gave him a smile. 'I think we're about there.'

'Is it safe?' he asked.

'Only if you trust me,' she told him.

'Good thing I do,' he replied, walking over to peer into the pan. 'It looks like pancake batter.'

'Well, here's hoping it's fifth time lucky,' she told him and took the mixture back into her workshop to pour it into the mould.

'Now what?' he asked, leaning on the door frame.

'We wait until tomorrow. And pray.' She glanced

around the messy workshop. 'And wash up,' she said, grimacing. What a mess.

'Do you want a hand?' he asked.

She shook her head. 'It should be fine. Hopefully it won't take too long.' So after he had left, she tidied up everything and waited to see what would happen.

In fact, she was so long waiting that Annie wandered up later on as the sun began to sink lower in the sky.

'We've already had dinner. Even Tom's back at the house,' she said. 'Are you okay?'

Eleanor was sitting outside in the courtyard on the bench. 'I was waiting for my soap to set.' She rolled her eyes. 'How sad does that sound?'

'I think it sounds exciting,' said Annie, giving her a nudge with her elbow. 'Come on. Give us a look.'

But before they could head into the workshop, Annie's phone rang. She picked up. 'Hi Neal,' she said, frowning. 'Is everything okay?'

Eleanor's heart lurched as her mind ran through the possible scenarios for Megan's husband calling Annie.

'With us?' Annie looked around wildly. 'Yes, I think she's up by the bar. The signal's terrible in there. I was just outside calling Sam. Do you want me to give her a message?'

Eleanor watched Annie's face grow pink as she began to look flustered.

'Okay!' she said into the phone, faking a cheerful grin. 'I'll let her know.' But once she had hung up, her face immediately dropped. 'Neal thinks we're out with Megan at The Club,' she said.

Eleanor was astonished. 'That fancy new bar in Aldwych? But if she's not out with us and she's not with Neal, who's she with?'

Annie bit her lip and looked concerned.

Eleanor thought quickly. 'Did you talk to her today?'

Annie shook her head. 'No. What about you?'

'Yeah, but it was just a normal conversation. I thought she sounded okay. She said she can give me some unused cupcake trays to use for the soaps. Said she never bothered to make cakes anyway.'

'Maybe she was a bit low?' said Annie.

'Actually I thought she sounded excited, you know?' said Eleanor, recalling how her friend had been on the phone.

'Well, whatever she's up to, I think we should find out,' said Annie.

'Let's go,' agreed Eleanor.

They quickly walked away and back up to the house, the soap long forgotten.

# Chapter 39

Eleanor hadn't been in anywhere like The Club since she had left London.

She realised she had come out wearing her old clothes, no make-up and her hair a mess. But she didn't care. She was too worried about Megan to think about what she looked like.

She tried to think positively as they weaved their way through the hordes of good-looking people. It was Friday night so the place was packed.

'There she is!' hissed Annie, nudging her in the side.

Eleanor followed her gaze to the VIP area. There, under an unforgiving strobe light, was Megan, sitting with a man.

As they edged through the crowd, Annie said, 'Who's the guy?'

'I know who that is,' said Eleanor. 'That's Gareth from school. The one she's been messaging on Facebook.'

Annie was shocked. 'What shall we do?'

'Let's get a bit nearer,' said Eleanor.

They managed to manoeuvre themselves near to the next table along, which had just become vacant and hid behind a large pot plant. Thankfully, the couple were needing to shout to hear each other above the hubbub around them.

Eleanor peered through the leaves of the fake fern at his profile. Gareth hadn't aged well. His eyes were smaller than she remembered, the face bloated.

She could just about see Megan taking a large swig of champagne and looking very nervous.

'God, you're still so sexy,' shouted Gareth, casually putting one arm along the back of where she sat.

'Me?' giggled Megan, taking another large swig from her glass. She was wearing a strappy top with a low V-neck which Eleanor had never seen before.

'I can't believe it,' he carried on. 'Three rug rats and you've still got a hot body.'

Rugrats? Eleanor exchanged a cross look with Annie, who was now glaring at Gareth.

'What about you?' they heard Megan ask.

'Not married and definitely no kids. I'm too busy having fun.' Eleanor could see him run a finger down Megan's bare arm. 'Fun with hot women like you.'

Megan was shuffling in her seat. She was obviously uncomfortable.

'So what kind of work do you do?' she asked, sipping from her glass.

'I'm a love doctor, baby,' he said, leaning forward and suddenly kissing her on the lips.

Megan sprang away. 'What are you doing?'

'Come on,' drawled Gareth. 'Don't go all coy on me now. You know you want it. Why else were you flirting with me on Facebook?'

'Look, I'm sorry,' stammered Megan, standing up. 'I made a mistake. I'm happily married.'

'Come on. You bored housewives are all the same. Gagging for it,' said Gareth.

That was it. Eleanor and Annie sprang up at the same time and rushed around the pot plant.

Annie grabbed Megan's arm and snapped, 'Let's get out of here.'

'What are you doing here?' said Megan, staring wide-eyed at her friends.

'This is an inter-friend-ion,' said Eleanor, reaching for the bucket of champagne and tipping the ice into Gareth's lap. 'Time for you to cool down, you sleazebag,' she told him.

Then they rushed Megan towards the back of the club and into the Ladies' toilet.

'We've come to stop you doing something you're going to regret,' said Annie, finally letting go of her arm.

Megan burst into tears almost immediately. 'It's too late,' she sobbed.

'You've slept with him already?' said Annie, aghast.

'No!' said Megan. 'I should never have come here. It seemed like a bit of fun on Facebook. But as soon as I got here it just felt horribly wrong.'

'Do you know how lucky you are?' Eleanor told her,

grabbing her by the arms. 'Have you any idea how great Neal is? How much he loves you?'

Megan nodded, still crying. 'Gareth's right though,' she said, between sniffs. 'I led him on.'

'Forget about him,' said Annie. 'He's a creep.'

'I've got to get out of here,' said Megan, suddenly looking panicked. 'What if someone's seen me? What if it gets back to Neal?'

'Listen,' said Eleanor, leaning across the sink to open a latch on the window. 'There's never any shame in going out of the bathroom window. Trust me, if I had followed my gut instinct and done the same thing, I'd have never ended up with Lucas two years ago.'

Megan's brief laughter turned to tears once more. So they had a group hug before Eleanor and Annie each took one arm and helped Megan over the sink and out of the window.

Out in the car park, they ran across to Sam's Range Rover that Annie had borrowed and went back to Eleanor's house, where she made them hot chocolate, despite the warm night, and the three of them curled up on the cushions in the lounge, surrounded by various animals.

'You're going to stay here tonight,' said Eleanor, stroking the kitten on her lap. 'You can't go home in this state. Mum's out having a drink with Rose so it's just us, okay? Nobody else needs to know.'

Megan nodded gratefully before taking a sip from her

steaming mug. Her face was tear-stained and pale.

'Talk to us,' said Annie, in a soft tone. 'What's going on?'

Megan shrugged her shoulders. 'I just got so bored. I mean, I love my children, but I miss my life before them. I know I was only in marketing, but at least I had grown-up conversations back then.'

'Have you talked to Neal about this?' asked Eleanor.

Megan shook her head. 'No. I mean, he wouldn't understand. Why would he? He gets to go out every day to work whilst I'm stuck at home.'

'You don't think he would be supportive?' asked Annie.

'I don't know anymore,' sighed Megan. 'He's always working so hard and so late. Does it make me a bad mother to feel like this? I shouldn't be bored, should I? What's wrong with me?'

Annie shook her head. 'You have three children who are all healthy and happy. You deserve a bloody medal.'

'She's right,' said Eleanor. 'Besides, you can do something else as well as being a mum.'

'We just need something that fits in with your family,' said Annie.

'We'll think of something,' Eleanor told her.

Megan nodded before her face suddenly distorted into panic. 'What if he finds out about me meeting up with Gareth? What if he leaves me?'

'Neal loves you,' said Annie. 'And he won't find out.'

'Not from us,' said Eleanor, nodding in agreement. 'You jump, we jump, remember?'

'Thank god for you guys,' said Megan, drawing them into a hug. 'I love you both so much.'

'We love you too,' said Annie.

Eleanor nodded her agreement but, as always, those particular three words would never come.

# Chapter 40

As the end of July approached, the temperature shot up into the late eighties and the whole country sweltered in the heat.

Tom was grateful for being outside, even though his work on the stables was nearly complete. He had written a couple of songs for his new album but found that having the radio on when he was working benefitted both him and Eleanor.

One afternoon, one of his own songs came on. Eleanor appeared out of her workshop and smiled. 'They'll play any old music these days,' she told him, with a cheeky grin.

He smiled at her before singing along with his own voice coming through the speaker.

When he had finished, Eleanor applauded. 'Very good,' she told him. 'It's like having my very own private Glastonbury.'

Her face suddenly dropped and she rushed back into her workshop. He knew she was still embarrassed about the kiss. He, on the other hand, found himself cherishing the memory of it. He only wished that he had an opportunity to repeat it.

Later that day, Annie announced that she would be having dinner outside.

'We really should make the most of eating outside whilst the warm weather's still here,' she said. 'Plus Hazy Memory are on their way next week and we'll never be able to fit everyone around the table inside.'

So Tom helped Sam carry an enormous wooden table further along the patio so that it was in the sunshine.

'Is it safe to use?' asked Annie, giving it a push, which made the table wobble alarmingly.

'I'll put some extra nails in it to make sure,' said Tom.

'There's still no shade though,' said Annie. 'What about that large garden umbrella?'

Sam shook his head. 'Broken.'

'What will we do? Arthur and Rose will need some kind of cover.'

'I can build them one,' said Tom, surprising himself by volunteering. 'There's some old beams down by the stables.'

Annie and Sam exchanged a look.

'It helps him write,' said Sam, palms up.

'That's fine by me,' said Annie, nodding her approval.

Using Arthur's old tape measure, Tom worked out what kind of cover was needed. It would probably be best to be some kind of pergola, he thought. That was a simple enough structure. Just six, or perhaps, eight vertical beams connected by more horizontal ones across the top.

It only took a day to build but he was relaxed, working in the sunshine of the courtyard.

When he had finished, Eleanor came along to view his work.

'Very nice,' she said, gazing up at the structure. 'But it still doesn't give any shade.'

'In the middle east, they drape material across to keep the area cool,' he told her.

But when they suggested it to Annie, she grimaced. 'I'm not sure these are quite good enough,' she said, holding up a couple of old sheets that were dotted with moth holes.

'Mum's got tons of material,' Eleanor told her. 'She'll sort something out for you, I'm sure.'

As they walked back to the courtyard to tidy up, Tom asked, 'How's your mum doing now that the animals are finding new homes.'

'She's okay,' said Eleanor. 'Well, a bit lost, I think, but thankfully Annie has commissioned her to make the new curtains for the guest bedrooms. They're nearly done so that's why I thought she'd be happy to help out with the new pergola. She's always been good at sewing.'

'Are you?'

'Can't stitch or knit to save my life,' she told him, with a wide grin.

'Then it's a good job you're so good at your lotions and potions instead.'

'Isn't it?'

Annie went to The Forge to pick up Eleanor's mum and the swathes of striped material that she had available. Tom helped pin them up across the beams and then they both stood back to admire their work.

'That's great,' said Annie, clapping her hands. 'We'll be lovely and shaded under there.'

'How pretty,' said Rose, coming out to see it.

'I had loads of spare material so I thought you might want a few matching seat cushions as well,' said Eleanor's mum, pointing at the pile of cushions nearby.

'How thoughtful,' said Rose. 'All our current chairs are terribly hard and uncomfortable. Let me go and get Arthur and show him how busy you've been.'

Arthur agreed that it was a remarkable job and invited both Eleanor and her mum to dine with them by way of thank you.

It was a lovely evening. Weighed down by jam jars and small terracotta pots full of herbs and sweat peas, the table was piled high with food and expensive china. It looked like they were using antique plates, thought Tom, staring down at the dainty bone china with pretty rose patterns. It was probably worth a great deal. But Arthur and his family used them as if they had been bought from Argos.

Tom sipped on his beer and found himself relaxing at

the chatter of conversation all around him.

Annie had also covered the new pergola in fairy lights so that as dusk fell, the ceiling above them twinkled. It felt magical.

'Your cushions are so comfortable,' said Rose, raising a glass to Eleanor's mum, who blushed furiously.

Tom had an idea. 'Why don't you make some and sell them at the fete?' he suggested.

A crease appeared in June's forehead. 'Do you think anyone will want to buy them?'

'Of course,' said Rose. 'They're lovely and retro. Very in, sweetie.'

'You're a local seller, reusing second-hand material,' said Sam. 'What could be better than that?'

In the end, June nodded her agreement. Eleanor looked across at Tom and smiled, causing his pulse to pick up speed a little.

'I know it's only temporary for this summer, but I do love it under here,' said Annie, leaning back in her chair.

'We won't have any of this temporary chatter,' said Arthur, in a firm tone. 'This is staying because it was made by Tom.'

Tom shifted in his seat, suddenly feeling awkward at being included as part of the family. He hadn't felt that for a very long time. But he knew that staying at Willow Tree Hall had given him a sense of belonging that he had only ever had with his gran.

'Much more attractive than any old umbrella,' said

Rose. 'I shall have to have my friends over for drinkies.'

Tom felt a nudge by his knee and knew that Dylan was waiting patiently under the table to see if any food was dropped, accidental or otherwise.

'What a good boy you are,' said Arthur, rubbing Dylan's head as he gave him a tiny piece of cheese.

'Definitely the dog with the waggiest tail,' said Sam, glancing down.

'That's it!' shouted Annie, making everyone jump. 'We should have a dog show at the fete!'

Eleanor frowned. 'You mean like one of those agility things?'

Annie shook her head. 'No, more daft than that. We should have awards for the dog with the waggiest tail. Saddest eyes. Things like that.'

'Sounds good,' said Tom, nodding.

'How about best sausage catcher?' Sam threw a small piece of sausage at Dylan who leapt up and caught it in his mouth. 'He's going to be a winner,' he said grinning.

Dylan chomped on his titbit whilst Tom reflected that he would most likely be staying on for the fete now as well.

He tested his heart to see how upset it was about committing to yet another month at Willow Tree Hall, but, to his surprise, he was really pleased about it.

He looked across the table to where Eleanor was chatting with Arthur. She seemed to gleam in the soft fairy lights above.

Yes, he was definitely glad to be staying that bit longer.

# Chapter 41

The following morning, Eleanor was back in the stables to check once more on her soaps. After many failed attempts, she was hoping that this batch might actually work.

Annie brought her up a flask of coffee once she had arrived.

'I'll have to bring you our old kettle,' said Annie. 'I haven't thrown it away yet. It's a bit ancient, but it works.' Her smile faded. 'I still worry that we should have noticed something was up with Megan before it all got out of hand the other night.'

'It's been a bit busy,' said Eleanor. 'You've been rushing around being a future countess, trying to find the perfect bridal dress as well and I've had all this going on.' She waved her hand around the stable. With each passing day, it looked more like a workshop than the derelict room she had first stepped into. She could hear the sawing of wood outside as Tom worked on the other stables. She found his presence quite comforting.

'Even so,' said Annie. 'We'll have to think of something, some way of getting her involved in the fete.'

'Definitely,' replied Eleanor, even though she couldn't

think of anything at that moment.

'And don't mention the dress,' said Annie, with a heavy sigh. 'If I can't find the right one soon, I'll end up wearing the curtains that your mum's making.'

Annie headed back to the house. Eleanor, for once, was grateful to be alone. She was about to test her next batch of soaps and didn't want to show herself to be a failure in front of Annie. Having failed at her job in London, it would be too much to bear if she was to fail in Cranley as well.

Bracing herself, she slowly turned over the plastic and gently pressed on the first soap. With a soft thud, it landed on the counter. Eleanor picked up the cream-coloured bar and turned it over in her hands, peering closely at it. In shock, she carried it outside where Tom had just stopped to stretch his back.

'Look,' she said, quickly heading over to show him. 'I think I've made soap.'

He looked down at her hands briefly. 'It is definitely soap,' he said, his eyes crinkling up at the edges as he smiled at her.

She suddenly felt stupid. She hadn't cured cancer, for god's sake. It was only soap.

'Anyway, I just needed to share with someone,' she said, turning to hide away back in her workshop.

But he grabbed her arm. 'Hey, don't rush off. I was just about to take Dylan down to the river to cool off. Come with us.'

Eleanor wasn't sure but she did feel hot and sweaty, so in the end agreed to go with them.

As they walked along the path through the woods, Tom said, 'I need to ask your advice about Dylan.'

'Has he been chewing your favourite Nikes again?' she said, with a grin.

'Well, yes,' he said. 'But I can forgive him for that. We're well past the limit on anyone claiming the dog, so I was thinking about getting him microchipped. And adopting him.'

'Wow,' said Eleanor, stopping briefly in amazement. 'That's amazing. What are you going to do with him back in London? I mean, you're going to need a garden, aren't you? What about when you're on tour?' She made a face. 'Sorry. Lots of questions. I must get that from my mother.'

'That's okay,' he told her. 'I appreciate that I need to think it all through properly. But by law he ought to be microchipped.'

She nodded. 'I think that's a great first step.'

'Do you have the details of that vet we went to? I can't remember his name.'

'It's Ben. And as it happens, I need to talk to him about something anyway. How about I get us an appointment and we'll go there together?'

'That would be great.'

As they headed into a clearing, they found Dylan leaping about in the long grass, disturbing the insects as he sprang about. Butterflies flew up in the air in his wake. The meadow was certainly looking very pretty. The blue of the cornflowers matched the many poppies. She picked a bunch for her mum to take home with her later.

Dylan came charging out of the long grass as soon as Tom called him.

Eleanor began to laugh as she realised that the dog was almost completely covered in grass balls. 'You look like some kind of alien,' she told him, reaching down to remove the sticky buds from his fur.

'Do you need a hand?' asked Tom.

Dylan collapsed onto the ground, rolled over and showed them both his tummy.

'He seems pretty relaxed about the whole grooming thing,' said Eleanor.

'Perhaps it's just your gentle touch,' said Tom.

They both locked eyes for a second before Dylan leapt up and carried on towards the river.

Seeing the glistening water through the trees, Eleanor was seriously tempted to follow Dylan into the water to cool down. She was just considering kicking off her flip-flops when she saw a movement on the other side of the river. Expecting perhaps to see a deer, instead she saw a couple of teenage girls trying unsuccessfully to hide behind some trees.

'Tom,' she murmured. 'We've got company.'

She could feel him immediately become alert, his

whole body tense. 'Who is it?' he asked, glancing around as he came to stand next to her.

'Behind the other riverbank. A couple of your fans, I think.'

He looked across and made eye contact. They could both just about hear a gasp as the girls realised that they had been spotted. The snapping of many twigs and blur of school uniform confirmed that they were moving away, anxious not to be seen.

'What is it that they want?' he asked, shaking his head in disbelief.

Eleanor laughed. 'They want to see our amazing romance, of course.'

He looked across at her and raised his eyebrows. 'Really? Well, if they want to see romance,' he said, stepping forward to stand right in front of her. 'Let's show them some, shall we?'

Before she could register what was happening, his lips were coming down onto hers.

'It's all for show,' he murmured against her lips as they met.

But somehow, it turned into something else altogether. Time stopped still. It built into a passionate kiss that assaulted her senses until she couldn't think of anything but him. She couldn't stop herself from reaching for Tom to bring him closer to her.

Eventually they broke apart. Eleanor and Tom stared at each other, both breathless and wide-eyed, trying to comprehend what had just happened.

Eleanor stared up at him, still trying to steady her breath. 'Well, that showed them,' she said, her voice sounding husky.

'Exactly,' he told her, looking equally stunned.

And then he broke into a warm smile and she couldn't help but smile back at him.

At the sound of nearby splashing, Tom turned away to play with Dylan, leaving Eleanor standing beside the river on her own, feeling more confused than ever.

This was bad, she told herself. She shouldn't have kissed him back. But it had felt so good. And he had kissed her first, after all.

She tried to tell herself that it was just a crush. It had begun before Glastonbury and their accidental kiss had just made it worse. That was all.

And yet, she knew it wasn't that at all. She looked out for him every day. She enjoyed his company. She had told him things about her dad that only her best friends knew about.

He was just a friend, she decided.

A gorgeous, handsome, good-looking friend.

But she knew deep down that it wasn't a crush. That she had to stop lying to herself.

Because she was pretty certain that she was falling in love with Tom.

# Chapter 42

Eleanor awoke with a start.

With the sun having moved around to shine through the front window, it had to be mid-afternoon. She suppressed a yawn. She must have fallen asleep whilst researching wild flowers and their healing properties on her phone. The heat of the day didn't help. It was slowing everyone down.

She stretched out on the sofa and enjoyed her sleepiness. But gradually she slowly came to the leisurely conclusion that she wasn't alone in the room.

Expecting it to be her mum, and hoping she was bearing a cup of tea, Eleanor turned her face.

'Hello,' she mumbled.

And was startled to find herself face to face with Buttercup the goat.

Shrieking, she leapt up from the sofa. 'Get out!' she shouted. 'Out!'

Buttercup bleated at her in protest before casually wandering out into the hallway towards the back of the kitchen.

Once her heart had stopped hammering in her chest, Eleanor ushered the goat outside and followed it into the sunshine.

Where she came face to face with the next surprise. Tom was fiddling with the latch on the back gate.

'Hi,' he said, smiling at her stunned face.

'Hello,' she replied, nonplussed. 'What are you doing?'

'You mentioned your mum needed a new gate,' he said, as she realised he had his tool bag with him. 'I thought it might be best if, er, well, these fellas didn't get out.'

He gestured behind him to where his captive audience of the donkey, chickens and goat were watching.

'Oh, well, thanks,' she replied. 'I didn't know you were here.'

'Your mum said you were asleep on the sofa.'

*Great*, she thought. 'Yes, well, it's been a bit busy since…' Her voice trailed off.

'Since three days ago,' he said, finishing off the sentence.

Across the garden, his eyes bore into hers.

When you kissed me, she silently added. That kiss by the river. The feel of him against her. The realization that she was falling in love with him. She had thought of nothing else since then which was why she had found every reason under the sun not to go back to the hall since then

She desperately wanted to check what she looked like. Had she been drooling in her sleep? Was her hair sticking up in all directions? How much mascara gunk did she have in the corner of her eyes? But it would have been too obvious, so she just stood there, not knowing what to do next.

Thankfully her mum arrived at that moment.

'All done,' said Tom, picking up his screwdriver and tool bag.

'Oh, you are wonderful, isn't he, Ellie?' Her mum beamed at her.

Eleanor nodded. 'Yes, he is,' she croaked.

'Can I get you a drink?' asked her mum.

'Thanks, but I'd better get back to the hall,' Tom told her. 'Otherwise Dylan will have chewed up the place. Talking of which, you seem to have a few less animals these days.'

Her mum nodded. 'Just these ones to go,' she said, looking around the back garden.

Eleanor was pleased that she didn't seem too sad when she told him. Perhaps she really was moving on.

'Are you coming up to the hall today?' asked Tom.

'Tomorrow,' she told him, avoiding eye contact. 'I've got the girls coming over later. But I've managed to arrange the vet's appointment for tomorrow.'

'Okay,' she heard him say. 'It's a date. I'll see you in the morning.'

She started at the word 'date' and looked back to find him giving her a smile before walking away.

This was bad. She was like some kind of awkward

schoolgirl around him.

She was grateful for the distraction of her friends coming over that evening.

*

'So what's the big news?' she asked Megan, who had teased them both with a text earlier that morning.

'Yeah, what gives?' asked Annie. 'Is it another baby?'

'No!' said Megan, laughing. 'I think three really is enough for the time being.'

'Well, you are positively glowing,' said Eleanor, noting her friend's smiling, relaxed face.

Megan leaned back on the chair with a wide smile. 'That's because my gorgeous, wonderful husband announced last night the reason he's been working so many extra hours. He's booked us a surprise holiday to Majorca!'

'Wow!' said Annie, leaping up to give her a hug. 'That's amazing!'

'Isn't it?' said Megan, laughing.

'When?' asked Eleanor.

'We go in a ten days' time. And we're going for two weeks! To a hotel! With a kids' club! Bliss!' Megan's face dropped a little. 'Which makes me feel even more guilty for what happened the other night.'

'*Nothing* happened the other night,' said Eleanor in a firm tone.

'Exactly,' said Annie, nodding fiercely.

'Okay,' said Megan, looking relieved. 'The thing is, I don't really have any clothes to take.'

'Well, that's not a problem,' said Eleanor. 'Come upstairs. I've got loads of stuff that you can borrow.'

'Really?' said Megan, looking amazed.

Eleanor smiled. 'What else are friends for?'

So they spent a happy few hours bringing out all of Eleanor's designer clothes and having a trying on session. Megan found quite a few tops and skirts that suited her colouring and fitted her.

'What if the kids spill tomato ketchup on any of it?' she asked, looking worried.

'Then it'll either wash off or we'll throw it away,' Eleanor told her. 'It honestly doesn't matter. Look at it all,' she said, waving her arm around at the piles of clothes all over the bedroom. 'I've wasted so much money and I hardly wear any of it. I'd rather you went out and enjoyed yourself, feeling good and confident about how you look. That's better than having all of this stuck away in some suitcase.'

'Don't you want to keep some of it just in case Tom asks you out on a date?' asked Annie in a sly tone, holding up a slithery piece of satin.

Eleanor blushed and shook her head, suddenly tongue-tied.

'This is so lovely of you to lend me all of this,' said Megan, stepping forward to give her a hug. 'I'm so grateful. But I will make it up to you, I promise.'

'Just have a fantastic holiday,' said Eleanor. 'That's enough thanks for me.'

But the conversation obviously played on Megan's mind because the following day she rang Eleanor.

'I've been looking up all the rules and regulations of selling beauty products at the fete,' she said. 'Because people are going to be paying you money, hopefully, and then putting your stuff onto their skin, we need to be able to comply with the law.'

Eleanor sighed as she looked around the workshop. 'That all sounds very complicated and I'm rubbish with stuff like that.'

'I know you are, but luckily I'm not,' said Megan. 'Leave it with me. I just need the full list of ingredients from you to upload it onto the assessment site. It all sounds very straightforward. I'll get it done before I go on holiday.'

Eleanor was astonished. 'Wow, really?'

'Of course. That's what friends are for, stupid.'

Eleanor was still smiling when she came off the phone. It was lovely to hear her friend sounding much more relaxed and happy. And perhaps between the holiday and the paperwork, maybe Megan would become more confident as well.

Which just left her mum needing a gentle nudge in the right direction.

Later on, as agreed, she took Tom along to the vet's

to have Dylan microchipped.

She felt herself tongue-tied sitting in the car as he drove and was actually quite relieved by the time they arrived at the vets. But at least it gave her time to think up a plan to talk to Ben about moving on his relationship with her mum. In the surgery, Ben checked the dog over.

'Well, it's great to see Dylan looking so well,' said Ben, smiling as he stroked his head. 'And getting him microchipped is vital, of course. We've not had anyone contact us regarding lost dogs. So it looks as though if you want him, you're likely to be able to adopt him.'

Tom nodded. 'I just need to sort through a few things first to make sure it's the best thing for him.'

Eleanor felt a flutter in her stomach. Maybe he might even settle out in the countryside now that he was hoping to keep the dog. But she shook her head to herself, knowing that she was galloping ahead of herself.

'Mum's moving around much better without her plaster cast on,' she said.

'Glad to hear it,' said Ben, as he washed his hands in the nearby sink.

'In fact, she was beginning to go a bit stir crazy in the house,' she carried on. 'You know, having been stuck inside all of these weeks.'

Ben wiped his hands dry and looked across at her. 'If you're suggesting that I take her out for dinner one night, you can come right out and tell me, you know.'

He smiled. 'She and I are old friends.'

'Yes, I know you are,' she said, giving him a rueful grin. 'Sorry. I was trying to be subtle. Did she tell you that my dad graced us with a visit last week?'

He looked shocked. 'No. I had no idea. Is she okay?'

Eleanor nodded and took a deep breath. 'Actually, I think it did her the power of good. It made her realise that she has definitely moved on from him and all that pain.'

'Good,' said Ben. 'She deserves to be happy.'

Eleanor remembered the conversation with Rose about how much Ben cared for her mother and decided to chance her luck. 'In fact, she's decided she's ready for a new chapter in her life. You know, she's decided to give up all her animals as well.'

He nodded. 'I do. I've already told her how impressed I am by her courage.'

'Well, that's not all,' carried on Eleanor. 'She told me that she'd like to go out on a date some time.'

Ben's eyebrows nearly shot up to the ceiling. 'Really?' he said, looking concerned. 'She didn't happen to tell you who with, did she?'

'I'd only trust her to go out with someone who really cared about her and who would never hurt her. Obviously it would have to be someone that she really cared for as well,' carried on Eleanor in a casual tone.

Ben stared at her for a beat before laughing with relief. 'You're many good things, Eleanor McCartney, but subtle isn't one of them.' He drew himself up. 'Perhaps I'll give her a call after my next appointment.'

She leant forward to give him a kiss on his cheek. 'I think you should,' she told him softly. 'Maybe it's a new start for both of you.'

'What was that all about?' asked Tom as they left the veterinary surgery.

'Mum's decided that it's time for all the animals to leave the zoo,' she told him.

'Seriously?' said Tom.

Eleanor nodded at him as they got into Sam's Range Rover. 'Absolutely. She's ready to move on and I'm so proud of her.'

She was glad she had had the conversation with Ben and just hoped her mum would be brave enough to go through with the change from friend to romantic partner with Ben.

It seemed as if everyone was getting paired up but her, she realised before shooting a look across to Tom.

He still had the key in ignition but had yet to turn it. In fact, he was looking quite bleak.

'Are you okay?' she asked. 'What's wrong?'

He cleared his throat. 'It was you talking about moving on. I think I need to do the same.'

She frowned. 'What are you talking about?'

He turned in his seat to face her. 'There's something I've been putting off doing. Something I've been dreading. I couldn't face doing it by myself. I was wondering whether…'

His voice trailed off and her heart lurched at the sadness in his face.

'Of course I'll help you,' she told him, reaching out to touch put her hand over his on the steering wheel. 'What is it that you need to do?'

He sighed. 'I need to face my past.'

# Chapter 43

Tom took a deep breath before stepping inside the hallway of the tiny one-bedroom flat. He could do this. He had to do this. His gran's flat would be sold soon but first he needed to see whether there was anything of sentimental value that he wanted to take before it was cleared of everything.

He felt Eleanor come into the hall behind him and forced himself to go on into the lounge at the back of the flat. The two front rooms were the bedroom and bathroom. The tiny kitchenette was in middle and the lounge overlooked the garden.

He was grateful for Eleanor's company, although he hadn't felt much like chatting on the car journey into south London. But, after they had dropped Dylan off at Willow Tree Hall, she had put on the radio and let the music fill the quiet air in the car instead.

'This is very sweet,' said Eleanor, standing next to him and looking around the flat.

Tom smiled. 'Nothing's changed in here for years and years.'

It was true. The armchairs and sofa were the same. The wooden furniture was years out of date. The same plates and paintings filled the same places on the walls as they had always done. Even when he had made his fortune from singing, his gran hadn't wanted anything new or different. So he had bought the flat for her from the landlord, ensuring that the home she had known for so many years would remain hers for the rest of her life.

'What will you do with all of this?' asked Eleanor, gesturing at the furniture.

'I thought I'd get in a house-clearing company,' said Tom.

She nodded. 'But you'd like to take some sentimental pieces, I'm sure.'

'Yeah. That was the idea.' But his voice cracked under the weight of sadness as he spoke.

He felt her hand slip into his. 'How about we take it one room at a time, okay?'

He squeezed her hand in response.

'You don't have to make any huge decisions now,' she told him. 'Just keep anything that you can't decide about. Then, if you change your mind later on, at least you'll have it with you.'

He nodded. 'Okay. I can handle that.'

He found the kitchen easier to go through than he had imagined. Until he discovered his gran's writing in a tatty notebook. Flicking through the pages, he realised that it was her recipe book. His hand faltered when he got to the page titled 'Cherry Cake'.

He didn't know how long he stood staring down at

the book until Eleanor gently removed it from his hands and placed it carefully into a nearby box that she had brought into the kitchen to pack with anything to be kept.

There was nothing in the bedroom that he wanted to keep, apart from all the photograph albums that were stored on a bookshelf. Only the bobbly, brown winter coat hanging up on the back of the door caused him a sharp pang of grief. He reached out to stroke the arm before managing to hold himself together enough to head into the lounge.

He had already decided to take the record player and albums with him. But in addition, there were a couple of paintings that he couldn't decide on, and a precious framed photograph of them both, taken when he was a boy.

'What about the ornaments?' asked Eleanor.

But Tom shook his head. 'I don't think so.'

He watched as Eleanor checked one last cupboard, bringing out his gran's sewing box. She opened the lid and ran her hand across the many spools of ribbon and thread.

'She loved to sew and make things before the arthritis affected her fingers,' said Tom, thinking back.

Eleanor smiled down at the box. 'Such pretty colours.'

'You're welcome to take it, if you'd like,' he found himself saying.

She looked pleased. 'Really? I'm sure I can find a use for some of this. And Mum certainly would.'

Tom nodded. 'I think Gran would like it to be used.'

So they packed up the sewing box as well.

Once everything was loaded into the boot of the car, Eleanor left Tom alone so that he could take one last walk around the flat. It was so quiet, that was the strangest part. He realised it was the music and laughter that was missing. But he could take that with him wherever he went in life.

'Thanks, Gran,' he whispered into the still air. 'For everything.'

And then he turned to close the front door behind him.

He was grateful once more for Eleanor's company on the way back to Cranley. He chatted a little about his gran but mostly he was feeling wiped out from the emotion of the day.

'Dylan will be glad to see you,' she said, when they were on the outskirts of the village at last.

He smiled. 'There's nothing friendlier than a welcome from a dog.'

He and Dylan were so alike. Two mongrels who hadn't been shown much love in the past but were getting used to being part of a warm, loving family now.

It was a massive step for him to adopt a dog. He had been mulling over the idea for a while when he voiced his innermost thoughts to Eleanor. The trouble was, all of the queries that she had raised were true. What would happen to Dylan when he was away on tour? The best thing would be to have a dog sitter, but Dylan was pretty untrusting of most people – apart from Eleanor and the Harris family. And no, his new flat didn't have a garden or anything like the grounds of Willow Tree Hall. If he even went for a walk in one of the many London parks, no doubt he would get his photo taken or hassled on a daily basis. He didn't miss the city at all, he had found. The lack of smog and noise meant that he felt calmer in the countryside.

He glanced over at Eleanor as she looked out of the window. He couldn't have faced his gran's flat on his own that day. And Eleanor was one more thing that would be missing when he went back to London. She didn't appear to have any plans for heading back any time soon.

He had a sudden image of having dinner with her in some country cottage, Dylan snoring nearby. The two of them laughing and sharing a bottle of wine.

These were not his normal thoughts, he knew. He was independent. He didn't rely on anyone else. He didn't need anyone else in his life.

But whichever way he looked at it, staying in Cranley with Eleanor and the Harris family appeared to be the best thing for both him and Dylan.

A few months ago, he knew that thought would have scared him. But now the future felt warm and bright.

Especially if that future occurred with Eleanor alongside him.

# Chapter 44

As the heatwave ratcheted up another couple of degrees, the air became still and sticky. Life slowed down at Willow Tree Hall as August arrived.

Most afternoons, Arthur was to be found dozing in his deckchair under the new pergola that Tom had built. Dylan had also slowed down in the heat and would normally stay next to Arthur, sleeping in the cool of the shade.

Thankfully the house stayed relatively cool. Annie would open all the windows at night to let what fresh air there was inside. The thick walls would keep the temperature low so it was always nice to walk through the house, especially with masses of jam jars and vases filled with the sweet peas from the garden. The beautiful scent filled the air, as did the sound of happy birdsong.

Before she had left for Majorca, Megan had often been found sitting in the paddling pool in her back garden cooling down with the children. Fans were on in every room. Ice cream became a daily treat. Iced drinks were a necessity.

The fresh, albeit muggy air, was having an effect on Eleanor's skin. It was clearer than it had looked for a long time. No dirty London air clogging it up. Early nights and country living, she realised. And perhaps being happy. The biggest side effect was that her pulse had stopped racing every day or so. Her stress levels were low and she was relaxed most of the time.

Now that she had managed to book herself a haircut to get rid of her split ends, she felt even better about how she looked.

Despite persuading her mum to go with her to the hairdressers, June still wasn't feeling quite so relaxed.

That evening, she came downstairs in a complete panic.

'I'm going to ring Ben,' said June, picking up her mobile. 'Tell him I'm ill or something.'

'What? Why?' said Eleanor, taking the phone off her.

'Because I'll probably embarrass him,' said her mum in despair. 'He's taking me to some fancy pub restaurant. We've never gone anywhere like that before. I don't know what he was thinking of.'

'He was probably thinking that you might enjoy it,' said Eleanor. 'And that perhaps it might be more romantic for the both of you.'

'But look at me!' said her mum. 'I can't go looking like this.'

Eleanor stepped back and looked at her mum. Despite her hair looking in better shape that it had done for years, June was wearing her normal baggy top and tatty, cut-off jeans.

'Come upstairs with me,' said Eleanor, grabbing her Mum's hand. 'I must have something you can borrow.'

In her old bedroom, she flung open her wardrobe doors.

'I can't wear any of your stuff,' said her mum. 'It's too posh for me.'

Eleanor dismissed a few items until her hands touched a skirt. 'Not sure why I even bought this,' she said, scrutinising the garment.

It was an A-line skirt, with pale yellow flowers on a white background. Not really her style or colour but she had always felt it was too pretty to get rid of.

She brought it out and looked at it properly. 'It would really suit you,' she said.

'Me?' Her mum looked shocked and quickly put it down. 'I don't think so.'

'I do,' said Eleanor, warming to the idea. 'Right. I've decided. I'm staging a fashion intervention here.'

Her mum was still shaking her head, but Eleanor wasn't to be put off. 'Go on. Try it on. You have shaved your legs, haven't you?'

'Of course.'

'Hang on,' said Eleanor, grabbing a white peasant top with some sparkly sequins dotted across the front. 'Put this on as well.'

Eleanor could see her blushing, but her mum duly did as she was told and left the room.

After a while, she heard her mum softly clear her

throat and turned around.

Eleanor's eyes clicked wide. 'Wow. Look at you.'

Without the familiar baggy jeans, it was like looking at a different person.

'You've got such great legs,' she said. 'And that top's so pretty on you.'

Her mum looked a bit bewildered, as if she couldn't believe she was wearing this beautiful skirt and couldn't stop glancing at her reflection in the mirror as the flowers glittered in the light.

'Right,' said Eleanor, checking the clock. 'There's just time to paint your toenails. Come on. He'll be here soon. You can borrow a pair of my sandals. I've got loads and we're the same size.'

Her mum gulped so loudly that even Eleanor heard it.

'Be brave,' she told her mum, giving her a hug. 'He's not going to hurt you. It's just Ben, remember? Lovely Ben who you've known for years.'

June nodded. 'You're right.'

Ben was completely stunned when he came into the house half an hour later and saw June.

'Well,' he said, clearing his voice as he stood in the hallway. 'You look very beautiful.' He frowned. 'I'm not sure I'm smart enough now.' He glanced down at his short-sleeved shirt and a tailored pair of shorts and made a face.

'Nonsense,' said her mum briskly, putting a hand on his arm. 'You're smart enough for me and that's all that matters.'

Eleanor noticed that her mum wasn't stooping. She was standing straight with the confidence of being with someone she totally trusted.

'Have a lovely evening,' she called out as they headed out of the front door.

And then she closed the door behind them, smiling.

# Chapter 45

It was the waiting around that Eleanor wasn't used to. Once she had mastered her soap recipe, and how to get it out of its mould, she was left with a few spare hours. She was already ahead with making her creams, so she decided that it was such a lovely day that she would take the rest of the day off.

Sitting on Arthur's bench in the courtyard, she allowed herself a bit of downtime. When had she last just sat with a cup of tea and listened to the birdsong? Watched a plane cross the blue sky? Heard the wind rustle the leaves in the trees? When was the last time she had just stopped? She couldn't remember.

But she could feel her shoulders beginning to drop down and unhunch. Her neck was getting longer and she was finally beginning to sleep through the night.

She glanced down at her fingers which were now completely free of eczema. Even her friends had noticed.

'It's thanks to the carrot soap,' she told them.

Of course, she was going to end up with far too much now she had various pans of the stuff in her workshop. So she had handed Annie a couple of bars that lunchtime in the kitchen.

'What's this?' asked Rose, taking one out of Annie's hands and sniffing it.

'It's the soap Eleanor made,' said Annie, sounding proud.

'How marvellous!' said Rose. 'You'll be the next Estée Lauder.'

'Hardly,' grunted Eleanor, feeling shy at the attention.

'Nonsense,' carried on Rose. 'Sweetie, Estée Lauder started making her beauty creams in her kitchen. So why not you? By the way, darling, my friends keep telling me how wonderful and young I look. Everyone's jealous of little old moi. I've told them it's all thanks to your marvellous cream and now they all want some. How much shall I tell them you're charging?'

Eleanor was a bit nonplussed. She hadn't even considered prices for any of her products yet. 'I don't know,' she said, thinking aloud. 'What do you think? A couple of pounds?'

Rose shook her head. 'Darling! No. That's way too low for all your hard work. How about five pounds per pot?'

Eleanor grimaced. 'Don't you think that's a bit steep? It's only a bit of lavender and cream, after all.'

Rose put her hand up. 'Do you know how much I've spent over the years on ridiculously priced creams and none have had the effect that your cream has had. Trust me, I'm a walking billboard for your age-defying lotion.'

She broke into a winning smile. 'Besides, you need to make as much as you can to save up. Have you seen the Chanel line for this fall?'

Rose left Eleanor deep in thought. A bit of money would be nice, she'd thought. Then she wondered what on earth she would spend it on? A few months ago, it would have been new designer clothes to keep up with all the rich celebrities she had been mixing with. But that all felt like a lifetime ago, and why did she need designer clothes anyway? She was mucking out the donkey and messing about all day with an apron on.

She wondered if she should feel sadder than she did about the lack of parties and champagne lifestyle. But as she headed back into her workshop, she realised that the overriding sensation was one of relief. That she was finally being true to herself.

Glancing at her soaps, though, she couldn't help but think that although they were pretty good, they were also very plain.

A nearby sprig of lavender that had somehow escaped when she had been cutting them up caught her eye. She picked it up and pressed it into the top of the soap.

Not bad, she thought. Quite pretty, in fact.

But it still needed some kind of wrapping. A label telling the customer what the ingredients were. She tried and failed to think up any kind of cover. Then she struck on an idea.

She picked up her phone and sent a text. Hey Megan, she typed. When you're back from your holiday, I'm going to be in dire need of your fabulous marketing skills.

In fact, during the time Megan was away, further changes were happening. Her Mum was now officially dating Ben and Eleanor couldn't remember seeing her looking so happy.

Ben had also been a huge help with redistributing the last of the animals. He had found a donkey sanctuary in the next county and arranged for Daisy to join them. Any tears on her mum's part had faded when she saw how happy the donkey was to be with her new friends.

Arthur had new tenants in one of the larger cottages that were next to a field as part of the estate. He had a word with them and it turned out that they wanted to become as self-sufficient as they could. So the chickens and the goat went to them.

'Goodbye Buttercup,' Eleanor had said as she was loaded onto a trailer.

'She's going to a really good home,' said Arthur, who had come to ensure that all went smoothly. 'And your mother can visit any time she wants.'

'That's very kind,' said Eleanor.

She realised how considerate everyone was being towards her mum, including Arthur and Rose. This wasn't about a tenant and her landlord. This wasn't even about the troublesome animals. This was about community. Helping each other.

And as the house cleared of animals, they had begun to sort through her mum's stuff. Most of it was destined for the recycling bin. Other boxes went to charity. But gradually the house felt lighter. Free. Happier. Just like them.

'I might even paint in here,' said her mum that morning, looking around the now quite spacious hallway.

Eleanor smiled at the memory. Everything felt so much better these days. So when the phone rang from her editor later that afternoon, she found herself letting it go to voicemail.

She replayed the message later on. Theresa was pressurising her about a story on Tommy King. She wished, for the umpteenth time, that she had never sent that text all those weeks ago after the charity walk. But Theresa would give up eventually. There wasn't any story to tell. Besides, she didn't want to be part of that world any more.

She wanted to stay in Cranley.

It was time for a new beginning. For all of them.

# Chapter 46

The peace and quiet of the countryside in summertime was somewhat overshadowed by the arrival of Hazy Memory later that week.

Tom knew that they were the first band that Sam had ever managed and had been apparently named after a wild weekend in the early seventies which none of them could remember.

Annie told him that they had all met the band at Christmas. 'They're lovely,' she said. 'Not at all what you would think.'

But when Tom watched them clamber out of a silver Bentley, he realised that the band looked exactly as he had thought. Five leather-clad rockers with long hair and wrinkles that showed a wild social life.

The driver was Mick, the infamous womaniser and scratchy-voiced lead singer.

'What happened to your old jag?' asked Sam, walking across the driveway to shake his hand.

'Broke down on the Kings Road,' said Mick. 'Now gone to the big scrapheap in the sky. But this is the replacement.'

'Nice,' said Sam. 'But couldn't you get anything more

reliable? You know, perhaps something built in this century?'

Mick scoffed. 'Leave off. It's a classic. Besides, are you kidding? I could barely afford this with our royalties.'

*Hazy Memory* had the dubious honour of recording the most annoying Christmas single of all time. They all hated their one big hit song but knew it was the only way to make a living.

As they were enthusiastically shaking each other's hands, Tom glanced over to see Eleanor making her way across to greet them. She was wearing a vest top and denim shorts. Nothing special but his insides still lurched as the lust unexpectedly slammed into him. He had thought of little else since their so-called fake kiss by the river. For him it had been anything but. And then there was the gentle, kind Eleanor who had come with him to his gran's flat. He was falling for her in a big way.

So he watched in irritation as Mick turned his gleaming eyes towards her.

'Hello, gorgeous,' he said. 'And what might your name be?' He was a well-known ladies' man and Tom desperately didn't need him turning his attention towards Eleanor.

'This is my friend Eleanor,' Annie told him.

'Gotta love that song,' said Mick, breaking into a tune. 'Elenore, gee I think you're swell,' he sang.

The rest of the band joined in for the chorus and

Tom was surprised that they actually had decent singing voices, although that didn't make him feel any easier about how he was leering at Eleanor

When they stopped singing, Annie asked, 'So how are you Mick?'

'Wondering how you ended up with my manager as always, beautiful,' he told her.

Tom found himself relaxing somewhat. It appeared that Mick flirted with absolutely everybody.

'Leave off,' said Annie, blushing.

'I agree,' said Sam, putting an arm around his fiancée's shoulders. 'Definitely leave well alone.'

'Anyway, I thought your new girlfriend was joining us this weekend,' said Annie, looking around.

'Oh. Yeah,' said Mick, apparently having temporarily forgotten her. 'Raquel's coming here tomorrow if that's okay?'

'Sure,' said Annie, with a shrug. 'All the guest bedrooms are more or less finished.'

'Are you sure you can't put this lot up in the barn instead? With all the other animals?' drawled Sam.

'That's no way to talk about our guests,' said Arthur, heading across to join them.

'Hello, Your Lordship,' said Mick, shaking Arthur's hand. 'Good to see you back on your feet.'

'Thank you, Mick. Lovely to have the pleasure of your company once more.'

'Hello, gorgeous!' said Mick, the lead singer, heading

across the gravel. 'Oh, and you too, Alex!'

'Thank you!' called Alex who had also just arrived.

Mick embraced Alex. Sam had confided in Tom that they had built up a friendship based on mutual respect, with a side-line in insults.

Alex stepped away and scrutinised Mick. 'Whoever said you could pull off matching leather trousers and a jacket was obviously blind.'

'It works well with the ladies,' said Mick, with a twinkle in his eye.

That was an understatement, thought Tom, who knew of Mick's reputation. He might have been tall and gangly, but his youthful blue eyes held a permanent glint, that he used to the best effect with the many ladies that he had wooed over the years, including his three ex-wives. With his long, dark hair, he had all the hallmarks of a classic rock star, albeit one now enjoying middle age.

'Mind you,' carried on Alex. 'I suppose all that squeaking disguises the sound of your arthritic hips. You know, one day I will get you lot out of that leather.'

Mick laughed. 'Ha! You wish, darling. I'm way out of your league.'

Alex hung back with Tom as they all began to head indoors.

'It's nice the way people still admire ancient relics,' said Alex, shooting a grin and wink at Tom.

Sam gave him a nudge. 'It's so good to have you all

here.'

Tom enjoyed the rowdy but fun evening spent wining and dining on the patio in the late sunshine.

'Any advice for a newcomer like Tom here,' said Sam.

'Don't get divorced, mate,' said Mick with a sigh. 'My ex-wives have cleaned me out.'

'I was thinking more in the career stakes,' said Sam, rolling his eyes.

'What career?' said Howard the drummer, helping himself to another piece of cake.

Sam frowned. 'What's up with you all? You've all been miserable since you arrived. Isn't all this enough for you?' He waved his hand around as they sat on the patio under the pergola.

'It's lovely but we're just a bit fed up,' said Mick. 'Feeling the need to shake things up before we get too old, you know?'

'What did you have in mind?' asked Sam, looking interested.

'You know, I got that message to ask if I wanted to go into the jungle,' said Mick. 'That *I'm a Celebrity, Get Me Out of Here* thing.'

'What happened?' asked Annie.

'I realised that I couldn't do without the three biggest things in my life. Coffee, curry and sex.' He shot Eleanor a cheeky grin.

Tom gripped his glass a little harder. Which was

ridiculous, he told himself. Mick had almost thirty years on him. Eleanor wouldn't be interested in someone as old as that.

'Why are you wearing leather trousers in this heat?' asked Alex. 'You must be all sweaty.'

'Weight loss?' said Ron, with a grin.

'It's what our fans expect,' said Mick, leering at Eleanor's legs in her shorts.

'You should do a cover of "Suit and Tie",' said Alex.

'Justin Timberlake?' Mike rolled his eyes. 'We could own his skinny arse.'

Alex grinned. 'Can you sing like him?'

'Better, love. And we're more handsome too.' He grinned before stretching out on his chair. 'This is the life, eh? Nice digs in the summer to retreat to.'

'Are you coming to our summer fete?' asked Rose.

'Wouldn't miss it for the world, sweetheart,' replied Mick before looking at Annie. 'What fete are we talking about?'

'Willow Tree Hall has one every year,' she told him. 'On bank holiday Monday. We're hosting the whole thing here.'

'Excellent. Can't wait.'

Annie smiled, but Tom could see that she was inwardly grimacing. She wasn't sure Hazy Memory, with their leather outfits and long hair, were quite going to fit in with her dream of bunting and home-made cakes.

He, on the other hand, was finding himself enjoying their company.

As long as they kept their hands to themselves and well away from Eleanor, of course.

# Chapter 47

Megan had come back from her holiday glowing both with a suntan and happiness. As they sat on the patio at Willow Tree Hall in the shade, Eleanor thought that her friend hadn't looked so relaxed for years.

'We're going to save up every year for a holiday,' said Megan. 'It's done us both the power of good.'

She was also hugely enthusiastic about helping Eleanor out with the business.

'You need to think about pricing,' said Megan, running down the list of notes she had made. 'You also need to conjure up some other stuff to make. Creams with something other than carrot or lavender. You've got to speculate to accumulate and all that.'

'Okay,' said Eleanor.

'Is it okay with you if I create a website?' carried on Megan.

'Sure,' said Eleanor, laughing. 'I haven't got a clue about that kind of stuff. But only if you've got the time.' She looked over at Annie but she was busy stressing about the fete. The worry now included the potential weather forecast.

'Do you think it will be too hot on the day?' she

asked, looking across the garden. 'Will we need to put up some shade?'

'Of course, it might actually rain instead,' drawled Megan.

Annie spun round looking horrified. 'Oh God! What if it does? What will we do?'

Rose, who had just arrived home, smiled down. 'Darling, we will soldier on and survive,' she said, putting her arm around Annie's shoulders. 'Just like Willow Tree Hall has all these years.'

Knowing how stressed Annie was, Eleanor decided that the best thing she could give her friend was some lavender water, which was left over from when she made her infusions. She made a note to bring some up with her from the workshop after lunch. Later that afternoon, Eleanor helped Annie put up the last pairs of curtains in the vacant guest bedrooms.

Alex also came with them. 'The curtains are fabulous,' he announced. 'Where are they from?'

'My mum,' said Eleanor, feeling proud.

June had done a lovely job in keeping Annie's ideas of separate colours for each of the guest bedrooms.

'Style really does run in that family,' said Alex, nodding his approval. But then he stopped short when they reached the blue bedroom. 'What the hell's that smell?' he snapped.

Annie grimaced. 'Do you mean the dog?'

'No!' scoffed Alex. 'It's gorgeous and it ain't no

doggy aroma.'

'Then it must be Eleanor's lavender spray that she's just given me,' said Annie with a proud smile as she looked at her friend. 'It's so relaxing. It's really helped me sleep.'

Alex sniffed once more. 'I'll need six bottles to take home with me. This stuff's going all round my apartment. Unless you've got something more earthy? I've got a hot date on Friday night.'

Eleanor thought quickly. 'I'm not sure.'

But Alex had already moved into the guest bathroom. 'Now, what have you put in here? No, no, no! I don't need all that supermarket rubbish cluttering up the place. Hey, London girl. Do you do anything other than room sprays?'

Eleanor thought quickly. 'I've got some hand-made creams and soaps.'

'Perfect. You're hired.'

So Eleanor found herself leading Alex down to the stables so that he could decide which ingredients he wanted.

'Well, you have been busy,' he said, staring around at the bottles of creams and soaps hardening on the benches.

She had hung bunches of lavender upside down to dry them off and used a sprig on top of the soap. She had then experimented by tying a sprig of lavender around each plastic pot to make them prettier as well.

'It's a brilliant space to work in,' she told him.

'Of course, the view's pretty great as well,' Alex drawled, looking out of the window to where Tom was sawing some wood.

'I haven't noticed,' said Eleanor, trying to turn away.

But Alex jumped in front of her. 'What, are you blind? I mean...'

As his voice trailed off, Eleanor glanced behind and saw Tom removing his T-shirt. She stared at the hard muscles of his chest. The smattering of dark hair that went down below his belt.

'Christ, I need a cold shower,' said Alex, gulping.

Eleanor tried to pull herself together. 'Annie's right,' she croaked. 'You're very naughty.'

'Given half a chance,' he quickly replied. 'Right. I'm going to talk to our future countess about bunting. And perhaps stand next to the open fridge for a while.'

After he had gone, Eleanor allowed herself the odd glance at the shirtless Tom before she too had to go and cool down.

# Chapter 48

Mick and the band stayed for longer than anyone expected, especially Annie. She seemed to be run off her feet with all the additional work. But told Eleanor she didn't mind.

Eleanor had to agree that they were all quite nice people, once you got past the flirting and the double entendres.

The lawn was so huge that the band were able to set up a large area for football and enjoyed a kick-around most days. Finally, having ditched their leather for shorts and T-shirts, they were able to relax and enjoy themselves.

The only slight blip in the happiness was Mick's latest girlfriend, a peroxide blonde called Raquel.

'Actually, it's spelt R-A-C-K-E-L-L-E,' she announced within five minutes of arriving. 'Is this Pimm's made with zero-calorie lemonade?'

Rackelle's demands were far greater than anyone else, from what Eleanor could see. Wasps and flies in their bedroom needed to be eradicated immediately. Her nail polish required frequent upkeep. Her stilettoes kept getting stuck in the lawn.

'Can't you have it tarmacked over?' she asked, picking at the grass on her spindly heels. 'These are Louboutins.'

As soon as she was out of earshot, Annie grabbed Mick by the elbow. 'How long is she going to be with us?' she hissed.

'Not long, love. She's nearly past her best before date already.'

Annie's main complaint was that Rackelle slept in until gone lunchtime each day.

'It's very hard to make beds when they're full of people,' she moaned to Eleanor.

'Then don't worry about it,' said Eleanor. 'It's a home not a hotel.'

At least Rackelle seemed to like her creams and soaps.

'This is sick,' she announced, holding up one of Eleanor's soaps one afternoon. 'Where did it come from?'

Eleanor then had to produce various different ingredients for Rackelle to choose from.

'At least she's placed a large order,' said Megan later. 'Make sure you get payment in cash though.'

But Eleanor's worst complaint about Rackelle was her endless flirting with Tom. She obviously felt that her time with Mick was nearly at an end and had decided to move onto the next, far bigger celebrity. She was always pawing at Tom with her long fingernails and thrusting her considerable chest at him.

Thankfully Annie had created a secret hideaway for Eleanor and Tom to sneak away for some privacy. She had dug out some old rugs and striped towels to lounge on in the shade of a large oak tree near the river. Hidden from the house, it was a place where they could both relax.

'And it's just a little bit romantic,' Annie had told her with a wink.

Eleanor groaned. She was having enough troubles dealing with her own feelings for Tom under normal circumstances. Let alone a place with extra romance added.

*

Tom was well aware that he had become the focus of Rackelle's clamber up the fame list. And he wanted nothing to do with it. So he was polite but kept her at arm's length.

Thankfully, she was beginning to drive everyone mad and was rumoured, by Mick, to be leaving shortly.

However, even Rose's easy temperament was being tested.

'Do you have gluten-free bread?' Tom heard Rackelle ask one morning.

'No, we don't,' said Rose, in a firm tone. 'This is Willow Tree Hall, dear. Not Soho.'

So once Annie had shown him the private space that she had set up in the woods, Tom found that he was looking forward to spending each evening alone. Or, preferably, with Eleanor.

The setting sun could be seen through the leafy branches of the trees all around, birdsong filling the air. Butterflies fluttered along the riverbanks. A kingfisher looking for minnows darted across the water. A soft breeze tried to cool the temperature.

Once Dylan had completed his search of the river for sticks, he would collapse to sleep at the bottom of his favourite tree nearby. And Eleanor would be scribbling down notes about a new ingredient or bringing out some ribbons that she used to decorate her soaps to try out various bows. Tom was touched that she was using the ones from his gran's sewing box.

Tom would spend the evening writing his songs, scribbling lyrics on a notepad. The words were coming thick and fast now. He could barely keep up with them.

And when they weren't working, they were talking. In the relaxed privacy of their special place, Eleanor finally began to open up about her dad. How he had left her mum for some twenty-one-year-old actress. And then a model.

'He's had a revolving door of relationships ever since,' she told him one evening. 'You know how fickle celebrities can be.'

As the silence stretched out, she glanced up at Tom

who was smiling at her.

'Not you, I didn't mean you,' she blustered.

His smile grew wider.

'I was just talking about my dad,' she said, beginning to look frantic.

'You're okay,' he told her. 'I was just having you on.'

She lobbed a ribbon at him before she relaxed and giggled.

In turn, he told her about growing up in foster homes. About sleeping rough and about his gran. He thought how much she would have liked Eleanor. Hopefully approved of her.

As the evening dusk came and the owls hooted in the trees, it became even more magical in their private idyll.

One night, Eleanor had brought a couple of cold bottles of lager with her for them to enjoy.

After watching her struggle to undo the screw top, Tom took the bottle from her and easily opened it.

'Thanks,' she said, as he handed it back to her. 'You're my hero.'

He shook his head. 'I think we have to be our own heroes in this life.' He stared into her soft green eyes. 'But it helps to have friends too.'

'Is that what we are?' she asked, her voice suddenly soft. 'Just friends?'

He couldn't stop himself from leaning forward. 'Good friends,' he told her.

And then he reached out to stroke her cheek. Her

skin was so smooth and her lips were so tempting that he couldn't stop himself. So he leaned all the way in and kissed her. It was as good as it had been the first time.

When they finally drew apart, she smiled and told him, 'I don't normally kiss my friends like that.'

'That's because you've never had a friend like me before,' he replied, leaning in once more.

But the sound of someone approaching made them both draw apart. Arthur and Mick appeared along the path.

'I was just showing Mick here our favourite fishing spot,' said Arthur.

'Great,' said Tom, taking a step away from her.

'Super,' said Eleanor, trying to look as casual as possible.

Mick flashed them a wicked grin as if he had correctly guessed what had just been interrupted.

As Arthur and Mick walked to the water's edge, with Dylan suddenly waking up to show them the way, Tom grabbed Eleanor's hand.

He pulled her close to whisper in her ear, 'One of these days, there won't be an audience or any interruption when I kiss you.'

She turned her head to look at him. 'And then what?' she asked, with a soft smile.

He didn't need to reply but merely squeezed her hand before joining the others by the river.

# Chapter 49

With her mum spending nearly every evening with Ben as a cosy twosome, and with no more animals to look after at The Forge, Eleanor ended up having dinner most evenings with the family at Willow Tree Hall.

Now that Rackelle had left, Tom found that he could relax once more.

And the conversation was always interesting, he found.

Especially when Tom told Sam in front of everyone that he wanted to give up touring for a few years. 'I'm tired,' he said, when asked for a reason. 'I got swept up in it all at the beginning but now I just want to write.' He glanced across at Eleanor. 'And to have a bit of peace.'

'Okay,' said Sam, slowly. 'So what will you do instead?'

'I thought I might try out country living for a while,' said Tom, locking eyes with Eleanor from the other end of the table.

It had recently occurred to him that he didn't need to leave. Didn't want to leave. That he had enough money to buy somewhere local and perhaps make Cranley his home. It was good for Dylan, good for his song writing. But most of all, it meant that he wouldn't have to say goodbye to Eleanor.

She finally looked away, blushing but seeming pleased at what he had said.

Mick leant back in his chair. 'I hear you,' he said, nodding in agreement. 'Do you know what's the worst part of being me?'

'I should imagine it's your liver,' drawled Alex who had also invited himself to stay on for a few more weeks.

'Very funny, mate,' said Mick. 'Nah, it's the weight of expectation. You know, the same old records. We created the band because we wanted girls to like us. Then we wrote our music to get laid to.'

'Well, that worked,' drawled Alex.

Howard nodded. 'There are many children that are only in this world because of us.'

'So what happened?' asked Tom.

'We grew up,' said Mick.

'Grew old, more like,' added Howard.

Mick shrugged his shoulders. 'So I don't want to miss a decent night's sleep these days. What's wrong with that at my age? I'm no longer so stressed and bothered by stuff but it would be nice to have one last great album to look back on and think, yeah, that was good.'

'So are you getting a good feeling about the next one?' asked Sam.

Mick shook his head as he reached for another beer.

'What do you think?'

Sam had the good manners not to reply.

Mick shook his head. 'I dunno. It's the same old thing, year in, year out. Cut a record, which, to be honest, are the same old rock songs. Then we hit Christmas with that stupid tune.'

'You mean the same stupid tune that helps pay the mortgage on your large house and lets you keep a Bentley,' said Sam.

Mick shrugged his shoulders. 'It's nothing new. Everything's the same, over and over.'

Sam looked at him. 'You're really upset, aren't you?'

'I dunno.' He broke into a grin. 'Maybe I just need a shag.'

Everyone around the table knew that he was only half-joking.

To break up the gloom of the band, someone had the idea to bring out Arthur's beloved record player. It turned out to be a good idea and they all began reminiscing about the first records they had ever bought.

'What's next?' asked Mick who had carried out a pile of the vinyl LPs outside.

So far they had listened, sometimes briefly, to both jazz and classical music. Tom had thought that the band would throw the music out as soon as they heard it, but they turned out to have quite eclectic tastes and all seemed to be actually enjoying the different tunes.

Sam lined up the next album and placed the needle

onto the vinyl. After the initial crackle, the horns blasted out the first bars of a song. Then 'You Make Me Feel So Young' came on.

'Ah,' came the collective sigh of pleasure.

'Class act, Frank Sinatra,' said Ron, the guitarist.

They all hummed along. Tom found it slightly surreal that this long-haired band of old rockers would enjoy the *Songs for Swinging Lovers* album. But they let Sam play it all the way through, happy to relax and listen to Frank's smooth voice.

There was a long silence when the first side had finished playing, the final bars of 'Our Love Is Here To Stay' fading out to be replaced with the late evening birdsong of a blackbird.

'Now that's proper music,' said Mick eventually, as the sun set and the last remaining light began to dwindle.

'Been years since I listened to that album,' said Howard, lighting a cigarette on the citronella candle that Annie had placed on the table. 'The arrangements were so sweet. Absolutely spot on.'

For a while they all sat in quiet contemplation until Sam spoke. 'Anyone up for a trip to the studio? We can see what today's songs sound like.'

'I can tell you what they sound like, if you really want to know,' said Ron, with a grimace. 'But we've got company, so I'll keep it polite.'

'Come on,' urged Sam. 'Maybe you'll feel better after

a break.'

Eleanor said goodnight at that point to head home so Tom went along with the band. However, he could feel their brief good mood disappearing as they sauntered along to the studio. Nobody's heart was really in it.

'I don't want to listen to our stuff,' said Mick, opening the main door. 'It'll break my good vibe.'

'Me neither,' said Howard, putting out his cigarette before heading indoors.

Whilst Sam ignored them and set up the day's recording on the computer system, Mick wandered into the main studio.

Jeff the keyboard player was still humming one of the Frank Sinatra songs to himself. He sat down at the piano in the studio and plucked out the song on the keys.

Mick began to softly sing along. Away from the shouting bawl of his usual songs, his voice was quite lyrical.

Howard wandered in, sat down and began to tap out the beat on the drums.

Ron followed him, picked up his guitar which had been abandoned earlier on and started to strum.

They carried on the tune in their amateur fashion until the very end when they came to an abrupt halt and, as one, stared at Sam.

Tom looked at them through the glass, their grins wider than he had seen in a long time.

Then he turned to face Sam. 'Let's have a mess

around, shall we?' said their manager.

A few hours later, Tom was seriously impressed.

'Yeah,' said Tom, shooting a grin at the band. 'You lot can actually sing.'

'Age and experience, mate,' said Mick, raising a bottle of beer to him.

'So what are your plans?' asked Tom. 'A Christmas album?'

'Nah, Michael Bublé's been there, done that.'

'That's right,' said Sam. 'You guys have got to make it your own. But it's not a bad idea.'

'What about your own tunes, mate?' asked Mick.

Tom nodded. His own album was slowly coming together. He had given it the tentative title of *By The River At Dusk*. The title track had been penned over the previous few evenings. 'By the river where we fell in love, under the darkening skies,' it began.

He knew in his heart that he was writing a love letter to Eleanor.

He just hoped she would want to listen to it.

# Chapter 50

The day before the fete, Eleanor was busy in her workshop when her friends arrived.

'You okay?' asked Annie. 'You look a little flushed. Mind you, it's so warm in here.'

'That's nothing to do with the heatwave,' Megan told her. 'And everything to do with our singer.'

Eleanor broke into a sunny smile. 'You mean Mick? I hardly think so.'

'You seem very smiley today,' said Megan.

'I'm just happy that we're all together again,' declared Eleanor, grinning.

She couldn't stop smiling, she found. Tom and his kisses had knocked her world off its axis and she had never felt better.

Megan shot her a look. 'Did you open the gin already?' But her warm smile belied her bitchy tone.

'If there's any alcohol to be had, I'll be at the front of the queue,' said Annie. 'My to-do list is up to twelve pages long and the fete is tomorrow. You're ready though, aren't you?'

Eleanor looked around the workshop and nodded. 'I think so.'

The whole place was bursting at the seams, full with so many products that she was also using the next stable along to store them.

One of her favourite things was her soaps, which she had thought of naming after the people of Willow Tree Hall.

So Rose's soap had been decorated with edible gold dust for shimmer. Just like Rose. Annie's soap had daisies dotted across the top. Megan's was topped with a sprig of lavender. Arthur's soap was for men and made with sandalwood oil that she had bought. There was even a soap named Bert, which was carrot-flavoured.

The only person she hadn't been able to think of a soap flavour for was for Tom. To her, he was the river, the fields and the woods combined. Too many ingredients for to mix together.

So she had told herself that he would want to keep his privacy and probably wouldn't want to have a soap named for him anyway.

'So you're all ready. Great,' said Annie, ticking off something on her list. 'You can help me with setting up some shade for all the families to sit under.'

'Assuming the weather holds,' whispered Megan.

Annie looked frantic. 'Oh god! Do you think it will rain?'

Megan sighed. 'I was joking. Take a chill pill, yeah? It'll be fine.'

'But we'll need some chairs for some of the older

visitors,' carried on Annie, looking down her list.

'Why don't we put the word out for everyone to bring their own picnic rugs and chairs, if needed,' said Megan. 'Leave it to me.'

'So umbrellas and rugs,' said Annie, still reading from her list. 'Portaloos and wet wipes. Do you see where I'm going?'

'You mean, apart from insane?' said Megan, rolling her eyes. 'Quick, find her some lavender to sniff.'

Eleanor was still smiling as she grabbed her phone to read the text she'd just been sent. It was a photo of her mum standing in the changing room of a clothes shop, showing her a pair of shorts she wanted to buy.

They're great, she replied. Definitely buy them!

It was lovely to watch her mum getting her confidence back after so many years. But better still, after a few weeks of him asking, June had agreed to go away for a week's holiday with Ben, hence the last-minute clothes shop. They had both been beaming as they had told her all about their trip to Italy. They were so comfortable with each other after so many years of close friendship that their relationship was able to move along quite quickly now that there was romance involved.

Eleanor had already bought up all the cushions, tablecloths and pretty napkins that her mum had made out of material that she had found in the charity shops or been donated by friends.

If anything, it was Eleanor that was feeling the nerves about the fete. If the stall did well then her whole future could change. It could be a brand new start. A new business and career for her to try.

If anyone bought anything, that was. She still wasn't sure.

But she hid her nerves in front of Annie who was still stressing out on the morning of the fete.

'Brown grass wasn't quite the look I was going for,' said Annie, with a grimace as she stared out of her bedroom window.

'Personally, I think it's better that the ground is hard and dry,' said Eleanor, who was standing next to her. 'No mud.'

Annie nodded. 'Maybe you're right.'

'Of course she is,' said Megan. 'Don't fret.'

Annie turned away to glance at her scrawled notes. 'So do you think we're pretty much ready for everything?'

She gestured at the marquees and gazebos that had been erected to keep out any rain. Luckily the forecasters had pushed back the bad weather for another twenty-four hours or so and were predicting a warm and sunny day.

'If I forget to say later, thank you for all your help with today,' said Annie, drawing her friends into a group hug. 'I couldn't have done it without you both.'

'You jump, we jump,' said Megan.

‘Exactly. Let’s get this show on the road,’ said Eleanor.

‘Not so fast,’ said Rose, appearing at the doorway. ‘I have a little something to show you.’

As Rose led them into her bedroom, Annie glanced at her watch. ‘I really need to get going soon.’

Rose smiled at her. ‘This won’t take long. But it’s very important. It’s about your future.’ She walked over to the window seat and lifted the lid under the long cushion.

‘I didn’t know that was there,’ said Annie, walking across the room.

‘Another one of Alex’s secret cubbyholes,’ said Rose. ‘It’s just big enough if I need to hide a secret lover or two in there.’

They all giggled.

‘But, for now, it’s been keeping something else safe for me.’ Rose drew out a long, deep box whose pattern had faded over many years. ‘This is for you.’

As Annie took the box from her hands, she looked at Rose. ‘What is it?’

‘Something borrowed,’ said Rose, with an enigmatic smile.

Annie placed the box on the bed and lifted the lid. Beneath sheets of tissue paper, she finally drew out a long white delicate dress. It was dotted with pearls and subtle sequins that shone in the morning sun streaming through the window.

'It's beautiful,' said Annie, looking at the dress in wonder. 'It's light but so beautiful.'

'It was my mother's wedding dress,' said Rose, as Annie tried it on. 'From the 1920s, would you believe? Beatrice borrowed it when she married Arthur. And I wondered if perhaps it was just different enough for you to wear at yours.'

Annie stood in the middle of the room, staring in wonder at her reflection. The dress fitted her perfectly and glittered in the sunshine. As a tear rolled down her cheek, she stepped forward to give Rose a hug. 'I love it. Thank you. It's precious.'

'Just like you, darling.'

Annie looked across at her friends. 'What do you think?' she asked, beaming.

'It's beautiful. And I think that no dress you've ever tried on has made you look so happy,' Eleanor told her.

'You look absolutely stunning,' said Megan.

'And as a future countess, you'll certainly look the part on your wedding day,' added Rose. 'She held Annie at arm's length to look at her. 'And just remember, my dear. Whatever happens today, you have the love of a great man whom you adore and cherish in return. Everything else is just bunting.'

Then they were all hugging and crying before Rose declared they all needed a fortifying sip of champagne to overcome any last-minute nerves.

As they drank, Eleanor took pleasure in her best

friend's wedding plans coming together. But she then felt a pang, wondering when her own love life would be as blissfully happy.

# Chapter 51

Standing on the front doorstep, Annie glanced at her watch for the fifth time in as many minutes.

'It's two o'clock,' she said to Eleanor. 'What if nobody comes?'

Eleanor smiled and pointed at the long driveway. The villagers were beginning to walk or drive into the estate.

'They came!' said Annie, looking relieved.

'I don't think there was any ever doubt, was there?' said Eleanor, before heading off towards her stall.

And so it began. The huge front lawn filled with people from every walk of life in the village. They walked, they stood, they chattered and lounged on picnic rugs.

The children enjoyed the balloons, the face painting and the many stands of cakes. The cakes were also enjoyed by the grown-ups, as well as the drinks stands and old-fashioned games. The tug of war was won by a group of scouts, the croquet competition by the vicar.

The sweet stalls and raffles were particularly popular and sold out quickly. The beer tent, run by the local pub, also did a roaring trade. Stick candy floss rivalled the ice cream sales and, later in the afternoon, Tom was busy with the barbeque, cooking sausages for something more substantial to eat.

Eleanor's stalls turned out to be one of the most popular. In fact, she had to rope in Megan to help out.

She was grateful that the feedback from the customers was all positive.

'We want local,' said one woman. 'It's so important.'

'I'm sick of chemicals,' said another.

'Me too,' Eleanor told her, picking up a pot. 'My eczema was bad before I started using this cream.'

'And it's all handmade here at Willow Tree Hall,' added Megan.

Eleanor smiled. Her friend was a natural saleswoman.

'Do you do hand cream?' someone asked.

'This is a good all-round body cream,' Eleanor replied, handing over one of the tester tubs.

She glanced over at her mum's stall nearby and was pleased to see her surrounded by customers as well.

During a brief lull in the afternoon, when Annie was asking how it was going, Alex came to join them.

'You did good,' he said, giving Annie a nudge. 'It's... what's the word? Charming, that's it. It's charming and country.'

Eleanor looked at the colourful bunting and checked tablecloths, fluttering in a gentle breeze. 'Yes, it is.'

'I'm not saying there's not a few fashion disasters,' he carried on. 'I've lost count of the socks and sandal combinations. But, darling, you'll be a fabulous countess.'

Annie beamed at the praise. Eleanor knew that she was still reeling from the discovery of her perfect wedding dress. And that Rose's subtle timing had given Annie more confidence than ever before.

The dog show was a huge success. Arthur had a marvellous time judging the dogs, his pocket full of treats meaning he was the most popular person there, as far as the entrants were concerned. And most of the entrants received a prize. But the winner of the 'Dog I Most Want To Take Home' was, of course, Dylan.

'Because he already is,' Arthur told everyone, beaming with pride.

There was a teddy bears picnic storytelling in one corner. Mick was doing Jackanory which went down a storm.

'Although I'm pretty certain he's making up most of the stories,' said Sam, looking concerned.

'Just don't listen too closely,' Eleanor told him.

By late afternoon, both Eleanor and her mum's stalls were empty. They had completely sold out of every single item.

Eleanor knew then that this could work as a business. She was thrilled. But it would mean no more London. She waited for the pang of regret but it never came. She had made the right decision after all.

With the stall empty, it meant that she could wander

round and enjoy the fete as well.

Early in the evening, it appeared that nobody was making any moves to leave even though the fete was supposed to officially end at six o'clock.

So Arthur, in his laid-back attitude, let everyone stay on. 'Why not?' he said to Sam. 'After all, the idea is that everyone should enjoy themselves.'

As the sun began to set on the horizon, the tea lights and candles were lit. There were hundreds of them, in old jam jars and bottles placed on every table and stall. Sam switched on the fairy lights that were wrapped around the trees and strung from stall to stall. The estate began to twinkle and took on a softer, gentler feel in the dusk.

Annie stood on the stage, after all the prizes had been given out, and thanked everyone for coming. 'You've raised so much money today for the local hospital,' she told the audience, to a rousing cheer. 'The oncology unit will benefit hugely from today's event.'

Eleanor clapped and cheered along with everyone else. But she found she was also glancing around for Tom. She hadn't seen him for at least an hour and was beginning to wonder where he was.

'And now,' continued Annie, breaking into a wide smile. 'As a little extra treat for you all, I've persuaded some of our dearest friends to come up here and play some music on this lovely summer's evening. So first please give a huge welcome to Tommy King!'

Eleanor was amazed. She didn't even know that he had volunteered to play.

Tom stepped up to the stage, waving to the audience who had surged forward to see the global superstar. But once he had begun to sing in his soft voice, accompanied by only his guitar, they all settled down onto the grass to watch and listen.

Standing nearby, Eleanor was entranced and couldn't tear her eyes away from him. Nobody had ever kissed her like he had. Nobody had ever made her crave the next kiss as much as he did. She didn't need her armour of make-up and designer clothes around him. Nobody had ever helped her relax and be herself around them. She knew, right there in that moment, that she was desperately, hopelessly in love with Tom.

As they went into another song, Eleanor kept watching Tom. He was so different to the reserved, almost gruff man she had first met in the kitchen all those weeks ago. She had let her guard down towards him. He had seen her innermost thoughts and fears and still she felt as if she could trust him.

After about half an hour, Hazy Memory came onto the stage to join Tom and together they all sang some Frank Sinatra songs. Accompanied only by Tom's acoustic guitar, their strong voices held the notes well and they were given a rousing response by the crowd.

Then, with a soft smile, Tom announced the next song. 'This one is for someone special.' And they launched into an a cappella version of 'Elenore, Gee I think You're Swell'. Eleanor smiled but blushed like crazy, especially when both Annie and Megan looked over and grinned at her.

When they had finished, the band and Tom stepped down from the stage, leaving Sam and Annie to announce the end of a wonderful fete.

Tom wandered over to where she stood in the dark shadow of a tree.

'That was, unexpected,' she told him. 'But really good. I can't believe you sang that song.'

He stared down at her before reaching out to take her hand into his. All around them, people drifted past. Most had walked from the village or had parked in the lane so headed down the driveway and out the front gates. Their excited chatter and laughter filled the night air, confirming what a special day it had been. But Eleanor and Tom stayed silent, only their eyes telling each other what they needed to hear.

In unison, they both began to walk across the grass away from the crowd. Around them, everyone was making sure that all the candles had been extinguished. With the fairy lights also switched off, only Willow Tree Hall remained lit up from inside. Eleanor thought that she had never seen it more beautiful than at that moment.

They carried on walking hand in hand towards the stables. At first, Eleanor thought that was where they would stop, but Tom kept going. It was then that she realised where he was leading her to.

Finally, they were back at their favourite, magical spot in the woods by the river. Only the moonlight lit the rugs and cushions on the ground.

Eleanor stopped and turned to say something to him but the words died in her throat as she faced him.

Then, as one, they both stepped towards each other. With a groan, he pulled her against him and dropped his mouth onto hers. The kiss was one of the sweetest she had ever known.

She wasn't sure how long they stayed wrapped in their embrace. Minutes definitely. Hours possibly. The kiss had deepened and grown until she was sure she could never think about anything else.

'I did warn you that one day there wouldn't be an audience here to watch us,' Tom murmured, as he ran his lips along her jaw and down to her neck.

'So what happens next?' she asked, gasping at the feeling of his lips on her skin.

He drew his head up briefly. 'That's up to you,' he said, his voice unsteady.

Her mind was already made up. Had probably been made from the first time that he had kissed her all those weeks ago.

Eleanor took his hand in hers once more and drew him down to lie with her on the blanket.

# Chapter 52

Eleanor woke up to find herself in the woods, surrounded by soft cushions and birdsong but no Tom. She sighed to herself in the soft morning light. Was that true what she had felt last night? Did she love him? But as she stared up at the sky high above the trees, she realised she did.

She was totally and utterly in love with Tom. She had never felt like this before about anyone. Any past loves had been fleeting and slight. This was all-encompassing.

She found she couldn't stop smiling as she realised that Tom was now standing next to the blanket, facing the river.

'Good morning,' she said, her voice husky.

But when he spun round, he was holding his phone and staring at her with hard eyes, his face white with shock.

'What's the matter?' she gasped. 'What's happened?'

'Is this you?' he said. 'Is this really you?'

She finally registered that he was holding up the screen to that she could see it.

'I'm plastered all over the front page of *Hot Gossip!* Magazine,' he told her. 'That is the one you work for, isn't it? At least, that's what the story says.'

'No, I...' she began.

But he was too cross to listen. 'You lied to me. It says here that you're a journalist. And not for some money magazine.'

She groaned, shaking her head. 'No. I'm not,' she told him with a sigh. 'Well, yes, I was but I left a long time ago.'

But he wasn't listening. 'Is this what all this was about? Did you sleep with me just for the story?'

'No! Of course not!' she told him, desperate for him to believe her. 'I don't know anything about a story. I haven't written anything about you.'

'Is your real name Eleanor?' he asked.

He looked so furious, with eyes so full of hatred that she was shocked.

'Yes, of course it is,' she replied.

'And you never gave them a story about me?' He was looking at her as if she was the lowest possible lifeform.

She sat up, knowing that she had to tell him the truth. 'That was the idea at first,' she told him. 'But then you weren't what I expected at all. None of this was. And I stopped it, a long time ago because I fell in love with you....' She gulped. 'I love you.'

Finally, for the first time since her father had walked out, she was able to say it. She thought the words would be hard to say. But the fact that it felt so right meant that she believed every word. She truly loved Tom.

She wanted so much to hear him say that he loved her too. But instead, he snatched the phone from her.

'You're lying. It's all lies.'

'No! It's not,' she said, quickly getting up to grab hold of his arms. 'I really do. I love you, Tom. You have to believe me.'

'Of course I don't believe you!' he shouted at her. 'I should never have trusted you. Just go. Leave. Go on, get out of here.'

But she stood still. She couldn't leave him. Not like this. Not when she loved him so much. 'No, Tom, I...'

'Fine,' he finally snapped. 'If you won't leave then I will.'

He stormed off through the woods, marching away from her and taking her heart with him.

For a second, she just stood there, reeling from all that had happened.

And then she sank onto the ground, crying for the love that she had briefly shared and just lost.

*

Eleanor had only managed to get as far as her workshop by mid-morning. Weak from crying, she couldn't have moved much further anyway. She stayed huddled in a corner, trying to call Tom over and over on his mobile. But he had turned his phone off.

Sometime later, Annie and Megan appeared at the

door.

'Thank god you're here,' said Megan, sighing with relief. 'We've been looking for you everywhere.'

'Is he still in the house?' said Eleanor, looking up at Annie with pleading eyes.

Annie shook her head. 'He left about an hour ago. He's catching a last-minute flight to New York. Says he needs a change of scenery.'

Eleanor bit her lip as more tears spilled down her cheeks. 'It's all my fault.'

'You didn't really write that article, did you?' asked Annie, the tears glistening in her eyes.

'No, of course not,' said Eleanor, her voice breaking. 'It's that bitch editor of mine. She made the whole thing up. With Lucas' help, of course,' she added bitterly.

She had read the whole wretched story in horror and disbelief. Various quotes from 'a close friend' only confirmed what she had guessed. That her ex-boyfriend had spoken to Theresa. She hoped the VIP tickets he no doubt received in exchange would choke him.

Her friends were still looking at her with worried faces.

'Anyway, I wouldn't do that to you. To either of you. I promised,' Eleanor told them. 'Besides, I love you, you know that.'

Annie and Megan looked at each other in shock.

'You never say that,' said Annie, her eyes wide.

'Not after your dad left,' added Megan, equally

astonished.

'Well, I do. I really love you guys.' Eleanor began to sob again. 'And... and I love Tom. He's the love of my life and he hates me. I'm never going to love anyone ever again.'

'You love him?' asked Annie gently.

'I do! I really love Tom!' wailed Eleanor.

'We know,' said Megan, stepping forward to give her a hug. 'We just wanted to hear you say it out loud at last.'

'What do I do now?' asked Eleanor, frantic. 'He won't answer his phone to me.'

Her friends sat down on the floor next to her.

'I don't know,' said Megan, with a shrug of her shoulders. 'We'll just take it one day at a time, okay?' She paused for a second. 'You might not want to hear this right now, but there is some actually quite amazing news this morning.'

'What's that?' sniffed Eleanor, hardly caring.

'You won't believe it,' said Annie. 'Rackelle has gone into *Celebrity Big Brother*. Apparently she's been raving about your products and now Megan says the brand new internet site she's built for you has crashed!'

Eleanor was stunned. 'You're kidding,' she gasped.

'Nope,' said Megan. 'Isn't it great? Well, you know. Apart from losing the love of your life and all that, obviously.'

Eleanor began to cry again.

'I don't know what we can do about all this,' said Annie, drawing her into a hug.

'Nothing,' said Megan. 'Except be here for you.'

They all leaned forward into a group hug.

'You jump, we jump, okay?' said Annie.

And Eleanor nodded through her tears, pleased that their friendship was whole again despite her broken heart.

*

The fete was hailed as a huge success in the local newspaper later that week.

Annie took full credit as the future countess, which helped her self-esteem rocket. 'If I can do this, I can do anything,' she said, beaming. 'What about holding a Christmas fete?'

'Er, what about your wedding?' said Megan.

Annie shrugged her shoulders. 'I can do both!'

'Remember that I'll be busy with Eleanor's website,' said Megan, in a warning tone.

Ironically, although her personal life was in free fall, Eleanor's new career was on the rise. Thanks to Rackelle's television recommendation, she was inundated with orders for her products.

And she wasn't the only one who was doing well.

'Have you seen this?' said Sam, his eyes wide, as he crossed the main hall one day.

'What is it?' asked Eleanor, bracing herself for a photo of Tom.

'Somebody's put a clip on YouTube from the fete. You know, of the lads singing with Tom.'

Eleanor stared down at the screen, the pain hitting her hard as she stared down at Tom's face as he sang. She willed her eyes to tear themselves away from him, trying to focus on the numbers. 'How many hits does that say?'

'Twenty million and rising,' Sam told her, breaking into a grin. 'My phone's gone mental. The whole thing's gone viral. The buzz on Hazy Memory's new Rat Pack album is huge.'

'Wow,' said Eleanor, smiling for the first time in days as she looked down at the screen once more. 'Well, good for them.'

Another unexpected outcome of the fete was a phone call from scary Theresa, her ex-editor. 'If you want your job back, we could always offer you a column. You know, life of a pop star's girlfriend type of thing.'

It was the lifeline that Eleanor had dreamt about all those months ago. But now she wanted nothing to do with it.

'No, thank you,' she told Theresa and hung up.

Another unwelcome phone call had been from her dad. She knew he had only got in touch because she and Tom were splashed all over the gossip magazines again. But she let the call go to voicemail and then deleted the message. Once the media moved onto the next story then her dad would forget all about her once more.

In contrast, the text messages from her mum had brought her much joy. Various photos taken of her mum and Ben looking suntanned and happy on their holiday were the only good points in the worst week of her life.

Eleanor wandered along to her workshop, thinking how pleased she was that her mum had found happiness. But also how cruel love could be when it was taken away from you.

Outside, the long grass had fallen over under its own weight and was beginning to yellow and die. The air felt cooler. The horse chestnut tree leaves were turning yellow. The other trees would soon follow. Autumn was just around the corner.

Her friends were busy. The wedding for Annie and Sam would come round quickly. And Megan was cheerful, helping with the business as well as trying to keep up with her young family. They were trying to buoy Eleanor up each day and they needed her help too. Annie with becoming a countess. Megan trying to juggle having both a family and a life for herself as well. And Eleanor was determined to be there for both of them from now onwards. After all, what else were best friends for?

It was ironic, really, she thought. She finally had a job she loved and was proud of. Her skin was smooth and free of any flaky patches. She was full of ideas for the business. Someone had requested nail and cuticle oils and creams. She was also considering sourcing some goats' milk from a local farm. Then there was the possibility of using local beeswax. She also wanted to try out coloured soap. Her mind was racing with possibilities. It was a job she could shout to the rooftops about. But her heart was completely broken.

She hid away in her workshop, working day and night to fill the endless hours without Tom. It was so different, knowing he wasn't about to walk into small room. She felt empty all the time, especially in the evenings now that he wasn't around to share those precious moments at dusk with him.

Arthur popped in one day as passed by on his afternoon walk with Dylan. 'We should get you a wood-burning stove in here for when winter comes,' he told her. 'It'll be liable to get a bit chilly otherwise.'

'That might be an idea,' she told him, reaching down to stroke the dog's head. Dylan looked almost as miserable as she felt, both of them sensing that Tom had left forever. Once more, the guilt overcame her. Not only had she broken her own heart, she'd broken Dylan's too.

'You know, I think this could be the start of something new,' said Arthur, looking around at the other stables. 'A small business start-up place. Like a group of workshops. I shall put the word out and see if we get any other interest from my tenants. There must be some other creative people like yourself out there.' He ran his hand along the shutter. 'I must say, he was an awfully good carpenter.'

Eleanor just about managed to hold it together until Arthur left. And then she cried at the thought of winter without Tom. It would be a bleak one without him. Her heart didn't hammer from stress any more. It just hurt so much from being broken in two.

# Chapter 53

Tom stared out of the window at the skyline of New York as he talked on the phone to Sam. Manhattan didn't feel like home. He wasn't sure anywhere ever would again other than the tiny hamlet of Cranley.

'Have you changed your mind about converting the old barn in the grounds?' asked Sam.

Before he had left, Tom had mentioned the idea to Sam a fortnight or so previously. He had thought it would give him space to breathe but not so far from the family who had made him so welcome. He felt as if he belonged there.

There was just one thing missing from the picture. One person that he wasn't sure he could face ever again.

'I'm not sure,' he finally replied.

'It doesn't matter,' said Sam. 'It's yours if you want it.'

'Thanks.'

He thought briefly of his Gran's house. He had received an email the previous day, confirming that the sale had been completed. At least the last link with his father was broken. He would carry his Gran's love and wise words of advice with him for the rest of his life but he would have no further contact with his dad.

How different families could be, he thought. If any good could come out of the summer he had spent at Willow Tree Hall, it was to show him the happiness that kindness and love within a family could bring.

Sam sighed down the line. 'Talking of dilapidated buildings on the estate, it seems that my brother might need the gamekeeper's lodge to hide in, after all. Have you heard?'

Tom grimaced. 'I saw the headline somewhere.'

Apparently Will had become embroiled in a scandal involving a cabinet minister's wife. His playboy ways had finally caught up with him and it was splashed all over social media.

'I don't know what to do,' carried on Sam. 'It's such a mess. Ah well, that's for me to try and sort.' He paused. 'Dylan misses you. He's kept me up most nights whining for you.'

'Sorry,' said Tom, with a sigh. 'I'll probably take him with me back to London when I come back later this week.'

'Not sure how he'll cope in your apartment without the grounds here to dig up.'

Tom shrugged his shoulders. 'I can rent somewhere bigger.'

You know, you're welcome to stay at the hall when you come back to pick up the dog,' said Sam.

Tom closed his eyes. He didn't know where his future

lay any more.

Sam sighed into the silence. 'You know, if you were just a story, she would have published it a long time ago. And published many more details since. But she didn't.'

Tom stayed quiet.

'None of those words in that article made sense,' carried on Sam. 'Mainly because she didn't write them. She told Annie that it was her ex-boyfriend who did a number on her. She wouldn't lie to Annie. Not about that kind of stuff. Think about it,' said Sam as he hung up.

It was all Tom had thought about for the two weeks since he had last seen Eleanor.

He had always enjoyed New York before; the busy streets and skyscrapers had always welcomed him. But this time he didn't feel the peace that he had begun to feel all those weeks at Willow Tree Hall. He wasn't anything except numb.

Eleanor had told him that she loved him. And he hadn't said a word in reply. Instead, he had left, very angry with her.

He should never have made love to her but he hadn't been able to stop himself. He should never have trusted her not to hurt him. But he had let her into his heart.

Because deep down, he knew that he did love her. He loved her so much that he ached from it.

He also knew that perhaps Sam was right. That maybe the story had had nothing to do with her. But it was too late. He had pushed her away. Had probably hurt her as much as she had hurt him with her lies.

He kept telling himself that leaving Willow Tree Hall was for the best. For her and for him. So why did he feel so utterly miserable?

He looked out across the skyscrapers again. He needed to see Dylan. He missed the dog so much.

Maybe his heart wouldn't hurt so much if he was in the same village as Eleanor again.

At least, that was what he was hoping.

# Chapter 54

In the fortnight since Tom had left, Dylan had become Eleanor's constant companion at the workshop. It was as if he sensed that she was as depressed as he was and didn't want to stray too far from her.

Both joined in their misery of missing Tom, they spent each day together, before she left to go home each night.

The sky was turning black one night as she began to close up the workshop but she didn't realise it was a storm until the thunder rumbled overhead. Dylan shook in fear and cowered beneath the bench.

'It's okay,' she told him, crouching down. 'You're safe with me.'

But as the first crack of lightning appeared, she realised too late that the door to the workshop was still open and Dylan rushed out in a panic into the darkness.

She hurtled out after him but he was nowhere to be seen. Knowing how afraid he would be, she searched the woods first, the branches cutting into her bare arms, but she didn't care. She just needed to make sure that Dylan was safe.

It was so dark now that she needed to use the torch

on her phone, but still she couldn't see the dog anywhere. He wasn't by the river, nor near her and Tom's secret hideaway.

She turned away from their special place as the pain overcame her once more. Nothing was secret any more. And they would never be together again there or anywhere else.

Having searched the woods, Eleanor rushed towards the main house. Finding the family in the kitchen about to have their dinner, she told them what had happened. Immediately, everyone began to search the house from top to bottom but the dog wasn't there either.

Close to despair, she decided to search the grounds again.

'He won't have gone too far,' said Arthur, pulling on his coat. 'He'll probably have sought out his favourite spot.'

It was then that she remembered the large willow tree that Dylan had always enjoyed playing under. Was it possible that he had gone there?

She flung open the front door and began to run over to the tree, just as she saw the lights of a car heading down the driveway.

The grass soaked her jeans and legs as she ran, but she kept moving as another bolt of lightning lit up the grounds. Sweeping a large branch of the willow tree aside, she peered into the darkness and, to her relief, there was the big, grey shaggy dog. Crying with relief, she threw herself onto the ground and gathered the dog up close to her. Dylan was shivering, hunched up as close to the trunk of the tree as he could.

'I'm so sorry,' she told him, sobbing as she held him close. 'I shouldn't have left the door open. It's okay. You're safe now. I'm here.'

As the dog continued to tremble, she kept whispering into his fur. 'You don't care, do you? You don't care that I'm an idiot. It's all my fault, you know. I know you miss him. I miss him too. But I've messed up so badly.'

The dog looked up and began to lick the tears from her cheeks, which made her laugh a little. In response she received a little wag of his tail.

'I'm sorry I caused you more pain,' she told him, hugging him close once more. 'You don't deserve it. Because you're the best dog in the world, do you know that? The absolute best dog.'

'He'll get a big head if you keep telling him that.'

Eleanor gave a start and looked up to find Tom standing between the branches of the tree, watching them.

They gazed at each other, the only sound was Dylan's excited panting. She couldn't find any words to speak, her throat was suddenly so dry.

She gulped as she took in the sight of him after the longest fortnight of her life. He looked so devastatingly handsome in his T-shirt and jeans. Tired, yes. But it was Tom. Her Tom. The man she loved.

Of all the scenarios she had run through in her head about when or if she ever saw him again, sitting on the soaking wet ground in the pouring rain wasn't one she had thought about. She looked a mess. A wet mess. She wiped the mixture of tears and doggy saliva from her cheeks.

Dylan jumped up in his delight to see Tom, leaving her on the wet ground. He raced back and forth between them, eventually deciding that Eleanor required his help more and sat between her legs, wagging his tail.

She kept looking down to avoid seeing any more hate and disappointment in Tom's eyes.

'He's a clever dog, aren't you?' she heard Tom say before he paused. 'Dylan found his own way here. Like me. Eventually.'

She looked up as a tiny piece of hope fluttered deep inside. 'I'm so sorry,' she said, her breath catching on the words, but she was desperate to speak. 'I know I've broken your trust. I should have told you the truth about my past, but I was scared of what you would do. And then you left anyway. I had nothing to do with the article. I know you don't believe that. And I know you don't care about me the way I care about you. I know you don't love me.' Her voice cracked slightly but she was determined to carry on. 'But I just want to be with you. So if you want to be a friend, then I'll always be here for you.'

She gave him a small smile but he still hadn't said

anything. Instead he was just watching her.

'But, for the record, I've realised that I definitely, absolutely, love you and I think I always will.' She paused. 'I just wanted you to know that.'

The silence stretched out between them, so she slowly stood up, trying to regain some kind of dignity. She knew she had lost him for good. It was for the best that she left him now. Maybe she should leave Cranley altogether now that he was back. It wasn't fair on Tom. She'd caused him enough pain.

'Well, I'll leave Dylan with you,' she said and turned to go.

'It's true that I was angry with you,' said Tom, finally speaking. 'I did try to get you out of my head. I even went as far as New York to get away.'

She stopped walking, unable to move whilst he spoke.

'But everywhere I went,' he carried on. 'All I could smell were flowers.'

She slowly turned around, trying to take in what he was telling her.

He took a step forward. 'The apartment where I was staying had a roof terrace. Full of roses. There was always the smell of roses. I couldn't get you out of my mind.' He took his hand out of his pocket and a dozen rose petals fluttered down to the floor.

She caught one in her fingers and turned it over and over in her hand, suddenly filled with hope. She gasped as the realisation hit her. It was his message. He really did care about her.

He reached out and dragged her towards him, wrapping his arms around her.

'You're wrong,' he told her, almost crushing her with the intensity of his embrace. 'I most definitely care about you. In fact, I care so much that I love you.'

'You do?' she said, looking up at his face in wonder.

'I love you, Eleanor McCartney.'

She began to cry at the words she had so longed to hear him say.

He laughed, reaching out to wipe the tears from her cheek. 'That's a fine start to our relationship if you're going to cry every time I say that I love you.'

'We're going to have a relationship?' she asked, still stunned.

His eyes crinkled up at the edges as he smiled softly at her. 'I very much hope so.'

'And you forgive me?' she asked, desperately.

'There's nothing to forgive,' he told her.

'I know I let you down,' she said, looking up at him. 'And I know that you're someone special and I'm most definitely nobody.'

He reached out and drew her close to him so that their bodies were touching. 'I've thought for a long time that you're amazing. And you're definitely my someone special.'

He then leant forward to kiss her, gently at first

before it developed into a deeper embrace. When they finally drew apart, she wrapped her arms around his neck and pulled him close to her once more. She felt so safe in his strong arms. She felt as if she were home.

'By the way,' he said, when he finally drew away. 'I've got something for you. To help you believe me.'

She stroked his cheek. 'You don't think your kiss just did that?'

He smiled before pulling out a written list on a scrap of paper from his jeans pocket.

'What's that?' she asked.

'The play list for the new album.' He handed it over to her.

She ran through the song names. They were all connected with Willow Tree Hall. 'In The Meadow', read one. 'By The River' was the next.

And then she saw the last song.

'Eleanor, gee I think you're swell,' he sang softly, as he pulled her close to him once more.

She began to cry once more as she saw that he had spelt her name properly for the title, not as in the original song. This was his way of confirming that he really did love her.

Tom shook his head. 'No more tears,' he said. 'I'll spend the rest of my days making you happy. Trust me?'

She nodded. 'I do. Do you trust me?'

He smiled down at her. 'Always.'

Then he drew her into another kiss, his lips crushing

hers, and she knew that he meant it. That Tom loved her and knew that he was loved in return. That they were both truly home. Truly together. Forever.

As they carried on kissing and the storm moved away, Dylan settled down at the base of the old willow tree for a nap, feeling content that all three of them were finally going to get the happy future that they deserved.

# Acknowledgements

A huge thank you to my lovely editor Caroline Ridding for her patience and kindness whilst this book was being written. As always, it's been an absolute pleasure to work with you.

Thank you also to everyone at Aria and Head of Zeus for all their hard work on this book, especially Jade Craddock for her help with the edits.

Thank you to my agent Judith Murdoch for her support so far.

Some books need to be written even during the most turbulent of times, so special thanks to all my lovely friends for their endless encouragement and support, especially Jo Botelle, Kerry Fisher, Claire Dyer, Adrienne Dines, Kendra Smith and so many members of the magnificent RNA.

Grateful thanks also for my wonderful family for their continued support this past year, especially Gill, Simon, Louise, Lee and Sian.

A special thanks to Cara, with whom a chance conversation about sunburn and carrot cream gave me the idea for this book.

Finally, thanks and much love to my wonderful

husband Dave for listening, encouraging and helping so much with my imaginary book world problems. I will never moan about your lack of patience again!

# HELLO FROM ARIA

We hope you enjoyed this book! Let us know, we'd love to hear from you.

We are Aria, a dynamic digital-first fiction imprint from award-winning independent publishers Head of Zeus. At heart, we're avid readers committed to publishing exactly the kind of books we love to read — from romance and sagas to crime, thrillers and historical adventures. Visit us online and discover a community of like-minded fiction fans!

We're also on the look out for tomorrow's superstar authors. So, if you're a budding writer looking for a publisher, we'd love to hear from you. You can submit your book online at ariafiction.com/we-want-read-your-book

You can find us at:
Email: aria@headofzeus.com
Website: www.ariafiction.com
Submissions: www.ariafiction.com/we-want-read-your-book
Facebook: @ariafiction
Twitter: @Aria_Fiction
Instagram: @ariafiction

Printed in Great Britain
by Amazon

76202521R00261